COLONY'S FALL

BOOK TWO OF THE NEW EUROPA TRILOGY

N JOSEPH GLASS

MONOCLE BOOKS, N. JOSEPH GLASS

| AIMÉE |

Thick clouds of dark gray unfolded, spilling under the door's header, and crawled over the ceiling tiles like an upside-down nightmare. Aimée sat on her bum behind her desk in a dizzying mental fog, having been tossed from her chair. Red, she thought Red had been there. Gift, where could she be? How many were dead? Morbid thoughts plagued her mind as Aimée pulled herself from the floor.

Hands brushed dust and ash from her blouse as her eyes found Red, already on her feet with a blank look of shock pulled over her face like a mask. This had to be the endgame Gift warned them would come, Aimée knew it. Perhaps the end of the colony, of everything and everyone she knew. Take stock of the situation, assess, try to reach Gift. Her desktop terminal dead, she searched for her handheld in futility.

"What's happened?" Red moaned.

It took Aimée a moment to process the question, her ears ringing. "The endgame. Something exploded."

"What do we do?"

"Are you hurt?" Aimée asked Red.

"Don't think so."

After taking a second to consider if she had been injured herself, Aimée incautiously raced out the door, through the open Resident Services welcome lounge, and into the passageway. Red tailed closely behind. Bellowing in from the dome, the smoke floated higher above their heads, the ceiling an extra story tall in the spokes. Chaos surrounded them. Frantic people staggered through the turmoil in both directions, not seeming to know which way took them into danger, which led to safety. Unmoving bodies littered the floor—injured or dead, Aimée didn't know.

One wore a familiar face—if she wiped away the blood and fixed his hair. Colin, New Europa's news reporter. Up to that moment, he'd never had much to report. He twitched; he had a pulse. His camera operator didn't fare so well, his lifeless body still clutched the device sending images of horror to anyone who dared to glance at a screen. Desperately Aimée searched the two for a handheld, some way to check on Gift, make sure she hadn't been injured, or worse. She couldn't think of *worse*.

Red lifted the camera, switched it off. "Maybe, we should show the colony what's happening here." She hoisted the bread-loaf-sized thing onto her shoulder and aimed it at Aimée.

"Me? Show them what? They're all seeing it, living through it, or dying in it. We need to find Gift, the others. They may be in the middle of this... *merde.*"

"We can do more than show people what's happening, we can tell them why, what's really going on. Maybe we can stop some of this frenzy before we all kill each other without understanding why."

Although Red had a point, Aimée didn't want to agree, she wanted to run through the fire and rubble and find Gift at all costs. She struggled to subdue her impetuous nature, consider the situation, and let Red's words sink in. "I..." She needed more time to process.

A red light blinked on over the camera eye staring at her, its blackness beckoning her. Red pointed and mouth something that looked like *hair*. Did she want Aimée to fix her hair before starting? "You're on the air," she said. When Aimée stared blankly at her green eyes rather than the lifeless one of glass, Red said, "Go."

It wasn't stage fright—Aimée had never been shy or afraid of a camera. Her pause came with a single tear pulling itself over her eyelid, falling just on the cheekbone and lingering to give a moment to the scene. Then slowly, as if gravity had been assaulted and lost some of its strength, the drop crawled down that cheek to her jawline, hanging there, not wanting to let go and fall into the chaos below. Aimée stood silent, blankly staring into the camera, into nothing.

With the uncomfortably long wait, Red panned the camera to show the insurrection's remains scattered throughout the passageway. When the hollow eye with the red light returned, Aimée regained enough composure to relate the accounts of sabotage and expose the source of the violence, telling the colony for the first time what had really happened, what had been happening for weeks. Her first dispensation of truth to the colony, in full transparency. Would anyone have even seen it?

In the aftermath, her broadcast lit screens throughout the colony for weeks, ensuring everyone saw it. While it couldn't be called polished, or even dignified at some points, it led to Aimée being offered a new role as Public Relations Director of New Europa.

***

Seeing nothing, thinking less, Aimée soaked in peaceful relaxation through every pore. Slowly, thoughtfully, her eyelids separated to reveal the endless blue and, in that moment, she knew Gift had been correct all those years ago when they fought over that crayon. The sky had to be blue. The soft azure hue was just considering fading into twilight, the show queued. Shimmering sparkles of distant light would soon speckle her view. Gift shouting her name across the calm water told Aimée her evening would be far less magical.

"You know anyone can just walk up here, right?"

"Just proved that, eh, Love?" Aimée floated on her back a few meters from the shore.

"I mean, look at you? Why don't you wear a swimsuit, like everyone?"

"Not like everyone, me. I'm one with nature," Aimée said through a giggle. "It feels right like this. Try it, Love. Strip down and join me."

"*Aimée*. Someone could see you."

"Proved that one too. You're two for two."

Gift chuckled. "Also too, you're late. Again."

***

While Gift came to give Aimée the reminder, she didn't attend this meeting. Aimée would have preferred to stay on the float, coercing Gift to shed her inhibitions with her clothes and join her, but her role as the trusted face of the colony had expanded to include being the spokesperson for intercolonial relations. While she hadn't yet made live contact with United Africa, her messages, although unanswered, seemed to get through. Over the past few months, her only communication on behalf of New Europa with the outside world put her face to face with their Russian neighbors. The size of the R.F. colony amazed Aimée whenever she visited, much larger than New Europa and with about twice the population.

She hadn't met the tall tree trunk of a man waiting for her beside Miss Heller in the Boardroom. Frank eased himself into a seat beside Heller as she stood to welcome Aimée.

"Hi Maggie. Who's this hunky fellow with us today?"

Miss Heller smiled softly. "This is Sergey Lazarev."

The tree trunk stood and his giant paw swallowed Aimée's petite hand. "Pleasure, my dear Aimée." Close to Heller's years, he looked stronger than most young men Aimée knew.

"Pleasure is mine."

When they sat, Heller outlined the point of this meeting of so few. Rumors had been spreading about the Russians and a group many in New Europa had labeled the Others, while some whispered the name earth-dwellers. Of course, Aimée knew of recent attacks on the R.F. by this rogue group and the futility of those. The R.F. colony's outer wall seemed impenetrable. Of greater interest, at least according to Gift's excitement for the topic, those earth-dwellers had somehow survived outside any colony.

Sergey's words screamed like an insurrection day klaxon in Aimée's head. "We have reason to believe they are larger than we thought, spread throughout many old military bunkers. And we think they may try to attack you, and you have no wall." Scary words from such a powerful voice.

When Aimée insisted the residents of N.E. needed to be told, she learned the entire Board didn't know. How she hated secrets—such led to the conspiracies and sabotage that nearly destroyed their colony. She only agreed to her new position when promised she'd report the news with full transparency. Yet she understood the caution as Frank explained it. New Europa residents knew of the Others and their feeble attacks on the R.F. from Aimée reporting what she knew of them. As far as everyone was concerned, this small band lived somewhere near the Russian colony and posed little threat to anyone. No one wanted to cause a panic.

Still, Sergey's words haunted Aimée for days. What could it mean? What could they do about it? How she ached to tell Gift. Knowing how her best friend obsessed and worried, Aimée kept it from her. Hopefully, Aimée considered, this one additional secret wouldn't spark another insurrection.

1 | AFTER

Drawn to the water in shorts and a tee, Gift dared step farther into the unknown. Waist high, her feet were still visible. Her hair dripped from the splashes. Aimée had gone ahead of her, already submerged. Fearless. The splashes taunted Gift to go farther into the frigid lake. Too afraid for more, she fought off her carefree friend, determined to get her head underwater. Several days passed before that happened. Then Gift beheld an unbelievable sight, someone in the middle of the liquid expanse, meters of water beneath them.

Swimming—a new word to describe the activity that astonished her when looking out over the near-still waters of Colony Lake. Gift cared little for the name, it seemed a lack of creativity to name the lake beside the colony, Colony Lake. It didn't detract from its beauty or wonder. Four words had changed her life, again. "Let me teach you."

Tom knew how to swim. He had explained how a few guards had learned the skill in the hydroponic reclamation system drainage channel. At the time, he never thought they'd need the skill. Gift concluded the few who knew of outside, of the lake, must have figured it to be a matter of time before it would be useful.

As much as Gift loved being in the water with her feet on the lakebed, she panicked when the connection to something solid slipped away. It tested Tom's patience and Gift's determination, but three months later her confidence carried her to the center of the lake. Never alone, just in case. Swimming became her new love, go-to exercise, and the best part of her near-daily routine for the last five months.

Colony Lake quickly became a favorite spot for many, so Gift had amended the regulations published by the Board to include safety and use guidelines for the lake and a few other areas of the surrounding landscape she thought presented potential dangers. Her updates to the official New Europa Resident Code of Conduct had helped the colony in what she felt had been her first real contribution to the Board.

After her first days of swimming in shorts and a t-shirt, the shirt's tight thin fabric squeezing around her torso and the shorts pulling and riding up in obtrusive and indecent ways, Gift tried Aimée's solution of wearing only a bra and underwear. Aimée called the outfit a *bikini* and said it was standard swimwear from *before*. Too immodest for Gift, plus the cut and fabric of underwear made it uncomfortable for the movements of swimming.

Gift and Aimée had worked closely together on designs for new swimwear. As the new face of the colony, Aimée had taken the role upon herself to be the new look and style of N.E. Her first drawing presented so little fabric Gift said they may as well swim naked. Little could she have known—she knew as the words escaped—that the idea would take the woman to the lake that very day to test the theory. Aimée swam in her birthday suit ever since.

Eventually, Gift found a perfect compromise of freedom and her need for conservatism. A new synthetic fabric, which Ivy the dressmaker patterned for modesty, kept the material in place without that body-squeezing discomfort. It also helped lessen the bite of the frigid water. For ten rations they came in a choice of colors and sizes. Another update by Gift to the code of conduct made the new swimsuits mandatory for lake access. Gift never could bring herself to report her free-spirited friend for the violation, though, for all her contributions to the project, Aimée never wore the swimsuit.

***

Eight months in, and the wrongness of being on the Board persisted like the wet fabric bunching up, the shrinking fibers tightening on her skin. She missed her tasks. Being assigned to supervise Cultivation—Charlie's former assignment—was both a painful reminder of loss and an opportunity for Gift to be herself. Cultivation meant lots of equipment, equipment meant maintenance tasks, and she determined how best to assign those to the engineers, including herself. Gift most enjoyed being on the ever-expanding exterior farm.

She paused her work on a controller for the sprinkler system to take a cool drink. The heat of summer had Gift longing for her plus two degrees inside the colony. Glorious as its rays felt on her skin, the sun's heat was not always welcome.

As the water from her cup rose through the air, Gift shrieked. Arms jerked as she leapt from her feet, the water landing on her head and shoulder. It cooled and refreshed her, but she didn't consider that until the hysteria of her jump-scare settled. The sudden touch on both sides of her waist with the *boo* behind her ears came from nowhere, followed by the sound of gut laughter.

"*You*. You... little brat." From her slap to Matteo's chest, more playful than vindictive, he feigned pain while not breaking his joviality.

"Got you good."

"Brat. I never should have promoted you."

"Hey, you did it so we can work together. Much for you as me."

"And this is how you thank me?" She smiled through the complaint.

"I saw you take a break and figured I'd come say *ciao*. When you didn't seem to hear me, I just couldn't resist."

"Yeah, yeah. So whatcha need? Or did you just come to bug me?"

"Just bugging you... and to ask if you want to have a swim after shift."

"That sounds delightful, really, but I don't think I can. I have a meeting right after and I haven't even prepared for it. I should be doing that now, but some doofus keeps distracting me." Of course, she had prepared. Not enough for Gift. No amount of preparation quelled the uneasiness saturating her and pinching her stomach tight.

"Guess I'll have to get up early then. Okay... for you, I'll do it. Let's swim in the morning, first light as you like."

"Oh, that'd be fantastic. *But*... if we agree, you'd better show—I don't go out alone."

"Have I ever let you down?" Gift smirked. Matteo added, "*Today*?"

"Why do I love you, little brat? Just be there, lakeside by O-seven hundred."

They heard it before they could see it—they always did. The unmistakable sound of an air transport on approach from the Russian Federation. There had been many since their arrival on that still unimaginable day. They came then to offer support, assist with damage control and resupply. Now flyers from the R.F. visited for various reasons such as diplomatic meetings and trade of goods. Gift knew why this one approached and the special guest it carried.

2 | MONTH EIGHT

History taught that Russia had at times been considered an ally but more often an enemy. Its war with Ukraine being its last stand against what seemed the entire world ended badly for them. Those details were surely taught subjectively in the colony teaching them. What would those born and raised in the R.F. think of N.E.'s founding nations once being on the wrong side of a devastating global conflict three centuries prior. What they were at present mattered to Gift more than history.

To improve both colonies, they agreed on Mutual Intellectual Advantage, the sharing of information. Trickling at first, levels of trust required time to build, to overcome decades of whispered silence. One key piece of information shared by the R.F. roiled through Gift's mind in search of a resting place. People lived outside of the colonies for the entirety of the past two centuries. Yet the Earth outside couldn't fully sustain human life. Gift's concern about this exceeded the earth-dwellers. Could their two colonies—three if they establish communication with United Africa—work together to accelerate environmental studies and enhancement protocols to *live* in the open air?

Humans had changed and so had the planet, but not in harmony. They had evolved independent of each other, become out of sync. While the environment had healed of humankind's decades of ruination, it and its would-be killers were not compatible, not fully. Gift felt the effects less than most. Hours in the clean air outside, in its waters, eating its produce, took their toll on what the human form had become. From living in the near-ruined ecosphere for decades before the colonies project, to dependency on chemically enhanced nutrients, to generations living in a sealed microenvironment, they had changed in ways the healed Earth rejected.

Humans were a new virus in the organism of a new earthly environment. Only their bodies saw it the other way. The virus was everywhere, outside the colony, infecting *them*. For all its joyous wonder and majesty, the Earth outside became the contaminant. Limited exposure proved harmless, and weekly Medical Day visits checked that closely. Colony residents had prescribed limits of outdoor access well below their desire, based on a simple categorization system Sakura had developed.

Not an Environmental Scientist, nor a Medical Science expert, Gift had to push for this meeting. Only by stretching the definition of her role as Supervisor over Cultivation had she squeezed it through for approval. Raff chairing the Environmental Recovery committee helped. Gift needed to be on her game to prove she belonged with the bigwigs, the smart people, the ones in whose hands everyone placed their lives. Over the codes of conduct, distribution of exterior resources, adjustments in rationing, the exterior farm, and her swimsuit mandates, the issue of reaching the delicate balance between man and mother-earth was paramount.

Gift arrived early to ready everything for the meeting she'd host in the ground floor reception room. Not that she didn't trust the staff, she had to do it herself, set everything in place symmetrically.

In single file they entered, disciplined, as if everyone she saw from the Russian Federation had military training. Her first time in New Europa, Nadezhda Anoykina led the delegation and greeted Gift and Raff with a smile and firm handshakes. In the impressive woman's entourage, Gift knew Nailya Usanova and Valentin Galaktionova, while a fourth nameless Russian guardedly entered last. Miss Heller said she might join late.

"Thank you all for coming." After a calm start, Gift addressed the nameless one. "First, may I meet our distinguished guest unknown to us? I am Gift Ojo. I'm not sure if you know Raffaella Di Gaetano. May we know your name?"

"I am Vitaliy. Vitaliy Filatov. Pleasure to meet."

"The pleasure is ours. And good to see you again Miss Nadezhda, Miss Nailya and Mister Valentin, sir. Dobro pozhalovat." Gift practiced their names and the Russian word for *welcome* and hoped she had done them justice.

"Thank you, Gift. Your accent is improving."

A complement from Nadezhda settled Gift a little. To say the woman slightly intimidated her was to say the sky was slightly blue. Not only that the most important person in the R.F. came specifically for Gift's meeting, but she was also a formidable woman. Stern and proper. Not much taller than Gift, she towered over her in every metaphorical way possible. Her black formal suit hung crisp, appearing to have been pressed just before she entered, and she wore her *salt-and-pepper* hair with stately womanhood.

"Dears, is that lovely Aimée to join? I expected we would see her. She is your spokes piece, no?"

"She is our spokesperson, correct, Miss Nadezhda. But we're here to get down to business, so she won't be joining us."

"Good. You may begin getting down to the business, as you say."

Gift breathed deeply to calm herself. "Raff and I aren't scientists, not environmentalists. If I'm not wrong—done my homework—you, Miss Nailya, are on the environmental restoration team, correct?"

"Da. You are correct, my dear."

"And Mister Valentin? I know you are an accomplished soil nutritionist." He touched his earpiece as his device translated then nodded his confirmation and smiled in appreciation of the compliment.

"Mister Vitaliy sir, may I inquire as to your position?"

He replied with a wide smile under piercing blue eyes that sent a shiver down Gift's back. Inexplicably, she sat up straighter in her comfortable sofa chair, now less so. Gift thought the stubble of his buzzcut hair could prick skin. Before Nadezhda Anoykina spoke, Gift guessed his role.

"Is my personal escort." Carefully chosen words not to label him her bodyguard. The Russian Federation followed the same corporate structure as New Europa, or a semblance of it, but had a president. Gift couldn't shake the feeling the R.F. patterned itself after the former Russia's oligarchy leadership structure. Yet the most powerful person in the R.F. felt Gift and her meeting important enough to attend in person. Gift felt empowered. Her mind allowed a half-second's respite to picture Tom going everywhere she did, being important enough to have her own Vitaliy, or a Tom—she would happily settle for a Tom. She returned to the moment to appreciate Raff's filling the silence.

"We're honored to host you. We hope your accommodation and the refreshments were to your liking. Anything else you need, please don't hesitate."

"Is fine, dear. But next time, we host. And adorable Gift, you must visit us."

"Yeah. I'll try to come soon, never been. I could go for your go-lub-si fresh. Delicious." Gift hoped she pronounced that well.

"Golubtsi is my favorite." Vitaliy pronounced it the same way, at least to her ear. "My mother makes them so good. So good." His gruff voice had an overlaying softness. It reminded Gift of her first impressions of Tom. That comparison to the burly bodyguard was endearing, granting her shoulders permission to relax.

"Okay. We are here without our scientists because we want to discuss logistics and strategy. As you know, you have an enormous head-start in environmental studies. As I've learned recently, you didn't keep the charade going nearly as long, and you've been studying the environment since long before you breathed it." Nadezhda made an *Mm* noise. Unsure of its meaning, Gift paused. A hand gesturing in a loop told her to go on. "Right. What we would like to propose now is a closer... collaboration."

"We share already much data." Nailya's tone sounded defensive, but Gift had to remember she had little familiarity with their culture. The tone could have meant anything.

Raff had more experience in such situations. "And we appreciate that so much. You've given us much data, and we've shared what we have. What we propose now is not so much the sharing of collected data—I should say not solely that. To make advancement and get us to the point of being able to live, actually live outdoors, we must work together."

"Mm." Nadezhda pinched her chin, perhaps a good sign.

Gift had no read on her whatsoever. She hoped Raff picked up on the nuances of her body language better than she could. "Gift? Please outline your suggested action plan."

Valentin grinned at Raff and raised a finger. Through his translation device he said, "'Action plan.' You have the most exciting words for everything. I love it. Please tell us this... *action plan* of yours."

A drop of sweat fell on the small of Gift's back where her blouse draped off the skin. It caused a subtle squirm which raised Nadezhda's eyebrow. Her uneasiness exposed, Gift needed to recover. Deep breath in, hold, release...

"Okay. We propose to create mixed teams at each of our colonies. Scientists, nutritionists, soil and environmental specialists, the best of the best from New Europa and the Russian Federation. You have that huge lead in data and great scientists. What we bring is advanced cultivation techniques and technical expertise on data gathering, our monitoring stations and roller droids. But it's vital to use that data, parse it, process it. We have that skillset, to produce valuable conclusions from which we can draw reasonable hypotheses and create projects to help our environment to be more suitable to, well... us."

"Interesting, dear. Very interesting." Nadezhda leaned forward and took Gift's hand, pulling her gently toward her. The posture laid the blouse's material over the moistened skin of Gift's lower back. "But we don't have so great this problem you have, I don't think."

"Which problem is that?"

"Your people lasting few hours out of doors. Then must come in before to become sick. They vomit all over. *Disgusting*. In bed for days filled of chemicals. We are strong, our people out for days. No vomit. No sick. What do we get of this?"

Gift forced a swallow, heard by everyone. Not an abundance of saliva but that all-too-familiar lump in her throat she had rid herself of in the weeks after the violence. Her pause gave Raff a cue to interject. "Well, your own data shows that few of your people could sustain that type of exposure, staying days outside."

"Mm."

Gift thought Raff's answer may have been overly direct, too contradictory.

Nailya rebutted. "Is not over half your population has very limited time, few hours and not two days together."

"Yes, that *was* right. But we're improving that. And as Raff said, your people cannot live outdoors either. Even those you mentioned with days outside? Your medical records showed them needing extensive treatment before, during, and after. It seems clear we all benefit by working together and being able to make our homes outside of the colonies we've been in for so long. You like our words? We have exciting words for this, we call it a *win-win*."

After a short pause Valentin reacted with a laugh that sounded like deep whining breaths. "You see. I told you... they have the best words," the artificial voice from his device said.

Nadezhda looked Gift in the eye. "You said, my dear, you did homework. When we started, you said this. I see is true and you are smart girl. Nadezhda always likes you. And I mean when I say you must come to visit us. I think your name is good one. You are a gift... to this colony. Da... a gift."

"Um... thank you?" It seemed they respected her and Raff for taking a hard stand. "So, sorry, sometimes slow to get things, me. Does that mean we'll work together?"

"My lovely girl." Cradling Gift's jaw in her boney hand, she said, "Da, what you propose is good. Now we have details to discuss, yes? Much details to discuss."

"Let's do that over dinner." All effortlessly agreed with Raff's suggestion.

While a monumental success, getting the R.F. on board, moving forward in collaboration on environmental issues meant they had much more to do. The two new Board members knew well agreeing to do a thing was easy when compared to doing that thing.

'Much details to discuss,' she said. Oh mamma.

3

A wake in bed, Gift stared at the darkness replaying the meeting she had called and successfully held, and the dinner after, which continued the meeting over food and drink. She had little tolerance for alcohol, one beer being her limit on a full stomach, so vodka was never a good idea. Neither was refusing liquid hospitality from an inebriated Russian oligarch, especially when she needed said oligarch to endorse an agreement vital to the future of her colony.

Water and vodka were hard to differentiate by sight. Gift's first bout with the infamous elixir came when she assumed her guests had offered her water—a slap in the face as the first drop hit her tongue. Insistence by her new neighbors had put that vile liquid in her mouth, down her throat, and later into the toilet after passing through the same channel in less than pleasant fashion. Her memory of that evening wasn't the most reliable, but clear enough to withdraw all desire to repeat it.

What once tricked her she used in her favor. Gift kept two glasses, identical in every way but for one holding water, which she set between her thighs. Playing upon their generous nature, and considering herself clever for the plan, she held the bottle. She'd grab someone's glass to refill it, and then slide her full glass to them, keeping the empty glass and filling it for the next person but looking like she'd replenished hers. She occasionally sipped her water to maintain the charade. It worked. She stayed sober and her guests happily believed they shared their vodka, a generosity they loved to an extreme. Gift received the go-ahead from Nadezhda to create her environmental teams.

***

Dawn's retreating darkness slowly made way for light, making the grass under her feet a blue that seemed almost dense, its hidden green waiting for sunlight's touch to awaken it. The distant mountain always captured her eyes' attention at that hour. What appeared gray and blue and brown in full daylight was on fire, brilliant and glowing. The sun greeted it first, permitting the shaded valley the added time to start the morning. Gift loved to reach the lakeside just as the light took its first dip into the cool water and the shimmering dots of glistening diamonds danced over the ripples to dazzle her eyes.

Alone, Gift took her first steps into the water but no farther until the luminescence allowed her to see her feet through the crystal-clear water at waist deep. Only then could she give herself to the lake. With Matteo nowhere in sight, her feet needed the lakebed, the security of solid ground. Even though she could easily swim the distance of the entire lake, she never went past her waist without a swim partner.

The shrill scream met the water as it splashed up in her face. Her jump took her footing and she fell back, plunging her bum into the cool lake as her arms went back to steady her while her eyes found Matteo somehow in front of her.

"You *brat*."

"Morning Gift." The prankster cupped his hands and splashed her again. "Gotcha. Didn't see it coming, eh?" His extended hand aided her up.

"How'd you hide in the water so long? Can't hold my breath longer than, like, a minute."

"Swam under from there." He pointed to a bush dipping in the water like a bather afraid to get their feet wet.

"Why... Why must you? Every time."

"Hey, it's what little brothers do."

"*Ciao*. Not *all the time*. Give a girl a break. For that, I'm not going easy on you."

Her splash was subtle, then she moved swiftly into a stretch over the water, gingerly, with careful precision. Just as Tom had taught her, Gift set off arm over arm, gaining speed Matteo found hard to match. Nearing the lake's center she paused, turned onto her back, and eased into a float to watch the endless sky above. Truly at peace.

In Matteo's time in the water, he hadn't mastered buoyancy. His feet pulled his legs under. A few pointers from his *big sister* got him doing it. "You got it. Now... close your eyes. What do you feel?"

"Like I'm flying."

"Now slowly open your eyes."

"I'm in the sky."

"Yep. Can't you just stay here forever?"

"Amazing... I can't thank you enou—"

Water swallowed his last words as Gift's weight pushed him below, sinking them both. Large bubbles freed by her tickling rose quickly from his mouth to break on the surface. "Gotcha back." She pushed the words out with water and joy.

"Oh yeah? Now—"

Before he could grab her, Gift was off, swimming faster than he could lend chase. The human fish reached the shore well before him and laid on her back in full sunlight, arms stretched out above her head. "I wish we could stay here all day," she said when he finally lifted himself from the water and plopped beside her.

"Yeah. Maybe *you* could."

"No, I have work to do."

"I mean, you *could*. I'm pretty good, can stay for seven to eight hours a day. Good for working the farm."

"I haven't stayed over twelve hours, and only a couple times. But no, I never had any problems, never puked, medicals checked out."

"Anyone else like you?"

"No one's like me. Unique, one of a kind, me."

"You *know* what I mean."

"Yeah. But no, not that I know, but maybe. I've heard some Russians stay out for days."

"Oh, Russians. How'd your big meeting go?"

"Bene, dai. We got them to agree. We'll start making teams in the next days. Should help us make progress."

"Well done, sis. I'm proud of you." The sound of approaching feet swishing the grass drew Matteo's eyes. "Hey, look. You were right. Here come the morning swimmers, right on queue."

"You're surprised? That I'm right, I mean. Like I'm not always." Her giggle was genuine, and Matteo joined her in it. "*Ciao.* Let's get out of here."

"We need to do this more often."

"We do. And thanks for coming early. It's so much more peaceful when we have the lake to ourselves. Told you it's worth getting here early."

"I said you were right. What, you want honors now?" He smiled at her with soft, loving eyes gazing upon his *big sister* as they pulled themselves from the grassy shoreline.

"Hey, when I get to being your boss again... I'll need an update on the new seed germination progress. Part of what we'll share with the R.F."

"You got it, boss."

4

Changes aren't permanent, but change is. A line from one of Mike's songs. The singer's unusual voice never appealed to Gift but the music itself, its harmonics and raw power, resonated within her. One of the few bands from *before* in his repertoire she almost enjoyed. The lyrics characterized what life had become. Little things before the airlock brought subtle changes. Larger now, and more profound, they came more often since Earth revealed itself. Some brought new experiences, others gifted new friendships.

Colonial management's radical alterations in structure and form would, in lesser circumstances, have been the biggest and most awkward restructuring of their lives. In recent months, circumstances were far from lesser. New Europa evolved into a new colony, and Gift and Raff were part of the machine, greasing its gears.

"That's going to be so nice. Thanks for that." Gratitude for Raff swelled in Gift after learning of the honors to be given Aimée for her role as colony spokesperson—easier to say than the official title, Public Relations Director.

"Infatti. *Ma*... it wasn't me. It was Margaret's idea."

Consistently lost battles with feelings of inadequacy left Gift unable to call Miss Heller, Margaret.

"Wow. She wasn't so keen on her at first." Gift sipped her espresso. Raff had already finished hers.

"Even she agrees Aimée's been amazing. We couldn't have made the progress we have in so little time."

"Yeah. Still not crazy about everyone knowing who we are though."

"Cara, va bene. People love that they can talk to us. And if they see us act on what they've told us—a suggestion, opinion, or complaint—it makes this whole thing work so much better. *Vero*?"

"Well... of course you're right. I get that. I'd like it more from the other side. I don't think I'm cut out for this."

"If you had any reason to think that, and you didn't, you do great work on the Board, yesterday should have removed it. You not only got the President and Chairperson of the Board of Directors of the R.F. to come here, but you also talked her—the *mal'd* President—into working with us. No one else would have pulled that off."

"You really think so?"

"Didn't you notice how Margaret never showed?"

"Yeah. That was odd. I expected her to back us up."

"She trusts you. You've earned your place. And you're the one who pushed me to recommend Aimée. Dai, it was your idea to create the position for her, and you let me take the credit for it."

Uncomfortable with accolades, Gift changed the subject. "I guess you and I will be working more with the Russians now that they agreed to our proposal."

"We desperately need this partnership. You did well."

"Yeah. And we'll bring Mike and Tina in, too."

"Getting the band back together."

"Huh? What band?"

"A colloquialism from days before our time."

"Not real good at those. Mike said something about horses and a barn door the other day when we finally figured out how to prevent those auto-weeders from pulling the basil plants. Didn't get that one either."

"You're so cute."

Gift shook off the compliment. "Where the heck is she? She was supposed to be here like, ten minutes ago."

"And you expected her then?"

They shared a smile over what they each should have expected. Reliable as a circuit regulator for meetings and work assignments, Aimée was never on time for anything else. At 10:12, she strolled up with nonchalance adorning her steps.

"*Raffa*. You magnificent creature you. Come stai?" The enthusiasm in the greeting, her sheer joy of life, drained the upset away. Gift couldn't even try to be mad at her friend's tardiness.

"Molto bene. Et toi ma chérie?" Raff's French pushed its limit.

"Great. Marvelous... Gift, Love, seeing lots of you."

"Hey sweet girl. You know we can't get enough of you."

"It's why I've graced you with my presence."

The barista may have been called Kavith, but Gift lacked the certainty to call him that. A raised index finger signaled her order for an espresso, which he promptly prepared from fresh roasted beans. Gift spoke over the momentary loudness of the grinder.

"Anything, or just an espresso?"

"Just the caffeine, please. Gonna need it."

Aimée collapsed in a chair beside her friend, sprawled herself over the small seat, legs spread and extended, and flopped her arms. No lady in the like.

"Such melodrama," Gift said with a giggle.

"A queen, me."

Raff smiled at the banter. "Why the urgent need for a caffeine fix?"

After extending her bottom lip to direct a forced puff of air to slightly lift her bangs, Aimée sat up. "*Russians*. I'm meeting them right after this. Hoping an advance of coffee counters the vodka."

"They don't *always* drink vodka." Gift didn't appreciate the stereotype.

"Da. Is true." Aimée spoke with a poor attempt at a Russian accent.

"Stop that. If someone hears you. You, the voice of the colony. You have an image now."

"Love, if that were a concern, really? Would you two have vouched for me? Raffa, you were to be knowing exactly what to be getting, da?" The bad accent again. Gift hoped Aimée would keep it in check when needed. It seemed she always knew when to be her free-spirited self, when to rein it in.

Raff chuckled. "It's why you're perfect."

"You ain't so bad yourself, doll-face," Aimée replied whimsically with a slow wink. The meaning floated over Gift, assumed to be another colloquialism she didn't get.

Aimée and Gift took their last sips in sync, though Gift's had long since cooled.

"So, a meeting with the Russians?" Raff asked.

"The Queen herself. Maggie arranged it."

Gift squinted to the unrecognized name. "Maggie?"

"Margaret Heller. A nickname. Like Max for Massimo."

Aimée got an elbow jab on the callback to Max. "That's low, even for you." Gift hadn't thought of that name in ages. Happily, she hadn't crossed paths with him since Sara broke their promise of Union. Sara and Gift had been cordial, close to friendly since, but nothing beyond pleasant chats in the shower queue.

"*The two of you*. So, Margaret arranged an interview with Nadezhda?"

"Yep. I think they want some good P.R. Maggie told me of your success yesterday, way to go Gift. If they'll be working with us, we'll see more of them. Maybe they want us used to them before we're tripping over them in the corridors."

Gift's chin crinkled to the logic. "Makes sense. We barely know them, as a people. And I'm really hoping this new collaboration works out. We need this."

"Anything you want me to say or ask?"

Quickly Gift answered, "Nadezhda's a character... as you know. Once you get past the intimidation, not likely as hard for you, I'd show her as a real person. We need to see them as people, not as Russians. Not as foreigners but as friends."

"Comrades you mean, da?" The accent failed again. "Raffa?"

"Allora..." The stretch of the word gave her a moment to think, to collect her thoughts. It took Gift years to see it and copy the trick herself. "If both colonies see it, it could help establish unity between our peoples. Try to focus on the purpose, the need for collaboration. If people see its importance, they'll be more likely to support it."

"Transparency. You know that's the only reason you convinced me to take this assignment. When you first asked, I thought the Board wanted a pretty face as a mouthpiece, you know? I trusted you both, that I would be telling the truth, and that everything would be open and shared."

"We know," the two said in unison.

5

Their shared office never felt cramped and neither minded the closeness when they found themselves in it at the same time. On comfortable chairs of deep orange gel-foam with black trim, Gift and Raff turned from their terminal displays to fix their eyes on the newly installed holographic screen filling the wall opposite the window. The catchy opening jingle would revisit Gift many times throughout the day.

The show's logo faded into an outdoor vista. A wide shot of the lakeside showcased sparkling water glistening behind two tiny figures. Slowly the camera faded to center on Aimée perched on what she called a director's chair—a high stool of a synthetic wood frame folded open to support a tension-cloth seat and back with a built-in footrest. Crossed at the knee, her legs showed their slim, toned form. Golden sunlight shined brightly off her white blouse, eclipsed only by the smile exuding joyous confidence.

"She's elegantly beautiful," Gift said to the screen.

"*Infatti*. The voice, the face, and sitting like that? The *legs* of the colony."

"Shh. She's starting."

Far from normal, every display in the colony showed this midday live broadcast. All work assignments paused to watch. Never had such a high-ranking diplomat of the Russian Federation been in the Colony overnight. None ever interviewed. Only a handful of people in N.E. knew what the R.F. leader looked like, likely less could name her.

"Welcome to Your New Europa. Thank you for taking time from your day to tune in to see me." Her bright-eyed smirk to the camera was as adorable as it was meant to be. "And I suppose you may also want to meet my very special guest." The camera switched to show her and the special guest beside her. "It is a pleasure to be joined by none other than the President and Chairperson of the Board of Directors of the Russian Federation, Nadezhda Anoykina. Welcome Miss Anoykina."

Tailored so perfectly to her form, Nadezhda's dress seemed of the opinion only she could wear it. "Thank you. The privilege is mine." With the verdict on her humility's sincerity inconclusive, her stateliness couldn't be disputed.

"On that, we agree. We're hitting it off already." Her wink accompanied a pat on the formidable woman's knee. Aimée appeared so comfortable in a situation that would be anything but to anyone else.

"You are funny girl. Nadezhda likes you very much."

"How are you enjoying your stay? This is your first time here, and the longest visit we've had from any representative of the R.F."

"Da. All your people are very hospitable. Lovely rooms, and excellent food. I had tour this morning of your Farm Dome and your wonderful new out of door farm. Your colony is most lovely."

"We're happy to hear. And glad you're being treated well. We always receive such a warm welcome whenever a delegation of ours visits you. And you introduced us to vodka. For that you have my eternal gratitude." Aimée smiled mischievously. "I understand part of your visit, and one of the reasons for our lakeside chat today, is the environmental issues. But let's hold that for a moment as everyone watching is dying to know who this fabulous woman really is... *And* this mysterious person beside me, too... No, really. You, you magnificent creature. We want to know about you."

"You flatter Nadezhda. And yourself too." She laughed heartily at her own joke. As Aimée joined her in the joviality she had done it already, humanized the foreigner. The unusual woman of fierce power and presence now a normal human.

"So, what do you do for fun? You know, when you're not running half of what we know as the whole world."

"I am simple woman. I have family with one son, Yuri, he has about your age. Very handsome, has little crush on Aimée. I introduce you next time you come to Russian Federation. And I have daughter, sixteen. Driving me crazy, as you say."

"*Nadezhda.*" Aimée sold her expression of disbelief to the camera in believable fashion. "You do *not* have a son my age. Come on, *you* are barely my age."

"Is true. You flatter again, but is true. My Yuri is turned thirty last month."

"Thirty. Wait, are you trying to pass your partner off on me...? I take Yuri off your hands, and you snag yourself a younger man. Sly Nadezhda. I like that."

"You make laugh. But you will meet Yuri. I insist."

"Now I must, or I will never believe you're old enough to have a thirty-year-old son. Tell me about your daughter, sixteen you said?"

"Da. Never happy, my little one. We called her Oksana because she was such a beautiful baby. Not like my Yuri. Good-looking now, you will see, but such an ugly baby. She is still a beauty, my Oksana. But such a mouth she never closes. I can tell you each thing she do to me that gave me this gray hairs. For each gray I tell you story."

"Now her, I *have to* meet. Sounds like my kind of girl."

"I think you two get along like peas in pod. Is settled. You come, stay in my home with Yuri and Oksana."

"Deal." The oligarch grabbed Aimée's extended hand and gave a firm shake to seal the agreement. "So, the business end of your visit. I understand you are here at the invitation of Gift Ojo of our Board."

"Da. She is lovely girl too. Such lovely girls. Yuri should be so lucky to have either of you for mate."

Aimée offered her signature half-snort laugh. "You're so funny. So... your visit. What were you and Gift chatting about and why should we care."

"Why you should care? Indeed. We all should care. We are out of doors today at your beautiful lake to tell about the environment. Such joy to be able to go out from colonies. And we breathe. But we do not stay for too long out of doors. No one lives out of doors. Not yet. This is important topic. We had meeting but more is done at dinner than in meeting. All the afternoon and evening we talked of need to work together..."

"She's doing it. She's going to announce our collaboration on the project."

"Mi dispiace, Cara. I wanted Aimée to interview *you*. You should announce it. It was your idea, your work."

"No, *dai*. You know I hate being on that stupid camera."

"People love you, Gift. You're one of their heroes since Aimée's first broadcast told everyone what you had done. And your work on the Board is well known. They should see you, you do so much for us."

"It's better this way. I'm happy that Miss Anoykina is doing it. I think it's better for people to see, shows'em we really are cooperating. And look at what Aimée did in just a few minutes. She made that stern, harsh woman of stone into a soft, sweet, funny human. Relatable."

"Likable."

"*Right*? I think *I even* like her now. Oh, except one thing she said."

"What's that, Carina?"

"I've met Yuri. She had him on a vidChat once."

"And?"

Gift's shiver with a withdrawn face told the rest.

6

Nobody could forget their first time stepping outside. The wonder of what was lost expanded before eyes so wide and hyperactive they hurt, only in the best way it could hurt. The joyous abandon for the rediscovered Earth with all it offered. Nature reclaimed. The sickness it brought, unfamiliar to Gift, ranged from mild headache and nausea to violent abdominal contractions sure to empty the stomach.

When Shower Group Sara vomited in the queue after returning from a four-hour exterior excursion, Gift couldn't believe the volume she expelled. After the medics came to collect Sara, the shower took what splashed and splattered from Gift's legs. When she exited the shower, the cleaning crew had vanished the putrescence along with its stench, leaving the sparkling corridor in the fresh scent of cleaning compound.

Among the influx of urgent issues the newly restructured Board of Directors had to address after the airlock opened, colonist's tolerance for exposure to the environment took top priority. In those early weeks, Gift led a committee to study and classify fifty thousand people in mere days. She recruited a team of those with tolerance of seven hours, including Tom, Tina, and an older woman named Erikka, lab rats for Sakura to monitor and compare to others with lower tolerances.

As people stayed out too long, pushing their limits, Pronto Soccorso couldn't keep up. Nearly half of these were eventually classified as level two.

Policing external exposure came from biometric sensors Gift installed at the six egress points. Raff wrote a basic program to tag the time each resident exited and when they returned. With a large enough base to formulate a hypothesis, Sakura created a simple test for categorization using Gift as her control. Every resident received a classification, a simple labeling system based on the number of hours one could safely be outside.

The widowed medic and Gift had a lunch meeting, her favorite kind of meeting, to discuss the breakthrough. Sakura had said she classified Gift as twenty-four, to give it a number, but thought she could stay out much longer. Gift had asked for a breakdown. Several thousand had been classified as two. Over a thousand as one. The sweet spot for most landed on four and five. A few hundred got to six or seven and a handful to eight. That's when Gift learned the name Holly had given the condition. Soon, everyone started calling it earth sickness.

Desperate to no longer be 'special,' Gift had asked if anyone else had similar resilience to her. No one came close, with eight to nine being the highest she had found. Yet Sakura spoke confidently about increasing those levels, perhaps by one or two hours. She would never forget Sakura's reply. 'You are special in many ways. We already began using your DNA as a control for the E.CID patients, and that gave us a head start for the earth sickness. It is related, as your special condition makes you immune. We confirmed that hypothesis with Erikka. We gave her an eight, but I am certain she would last ten or more.'

That had gotten Gift's attention. She asked if Erikka, anyone, had the same condition, or similar. No, Gift held her unique status. Special. What made Erikka stand out, she did not have GM at thirty but claimed hers came as a teenager. Sakura explained it made her less affected by the chemicals and sterilization. That had taken Gift back to Aimée's teenage years and young adulthood, then dating at twenty-six. She wondered if her best friend had these similarities as well, and if she could last ten hours outside.

Then the conversation had shifted in an unexpected direction, Gift hadn't been prepared for it. Memories often revisited, clear as the day they happened.

When they had finished lunch and technical talk, the topic of all the committees Gift served on brought Sakura to say, "I am glad you accepted my Charlie's place on the Board." The widow's eyes filled instantly as the words exited her mouth.

Gift's tears had already been flowing. "How are you, really? I can't imagine."

"What are the words people say? Coping. Managing. Those fit. Finishing the work Charlie and I started with the E.CID patients really helps. You know?"

"Yeah, actually... I do. Everything I do...? It's *his* legacy. I guess that's how we honor him. Keep him with us."

"Such a beautiful thought. I will treasure that. Thank you." Sakura reached her hand to rest it on Gift's with a gentle squeeze. A shared moment in silence felt right for them both.

With the gracious time the passing months allowed, Sakura's team made progress. Most of the colonists advanced up two categories in their tolerance ratings, with hundreds more rated for up to nine or ten hours. No one could match Gift's resilience, not even close. Exterior farming teams were more productive, working longer shifts. Environmental science teams prepared for more outdoor activity, good news for Gift's new multi-colony partnership.

Soon after joining the Board, Gift had learned the seven day per week work shifts had been structured to keep everyone occupied. With so few options for anything to do and no outdoors to explore, it maintained order and likely kept people sane. Reduced shifts with a free day each week were a welcome change. That, plus increased outdoor allowance, improved the overall mood of every colonist.

While Raff had suggested shift reductions after a meeting with Sakura and Miss Heller, most residents gratefully ascribed the adjustment to Aimée—often bestowing gestures of appreciation upon her—as she was the one to break the joyous news. Life had changed on that insurrection day. The Board had yet to agree upon a better name for it, though Earth Day and Reunion Day were the favorites. Gift figured they had until its first anniversary to settle on one.

The passage of time seemed both to dawdle along and scamper by, reaching toward its ninth month. So much work had been done. So much more to do.

7 | DESCENT: DAY ONE

As the slider ascended, the rapid clicks of the zipper bounced off the thin fabric walls that hid the silent morning. The watertight material, of similar texture to coveralls, didn't induce a feeling of suffocation nor the panic of confinement. It was Gift's second morning after a night sleeping outside the colony. The control for Sakura's latest experiment.

The first pull on the zipper that had sealed her inside two nights prior came with a brief trepidation. To avoid tainting tests of her endurance, Gift could not enter the colony. Lack of shower access—which had been increased from two to three times per week with water closer to liquid than mist—wasn't an issue as she spent a good bit of her added outdoor hours in the lake.

During much of the daylight of her first two days she worked with Matteo on the farm, in her own skin doing her maintenance tasks. Tom spent the first evening with her, most of that in the frigid water of Colony Lake. Alone-time came only when her eyes closed to the escapism of her dreams. The second evening's meal and companionship had arrived with Raff and Aimée taking dinner out to the picnic area. Waking in her tent this second time, Gift began her third consecutive day outside the colony, something unimaginable less than a year earlier.

No illness, nausea, or headache. In fact, she felt great, amazing, as the first rays of sun peaked in through the growing separation of the tent's opening, gently caressing the skin of her face, which absorbed it like a sponge in water. Slow steady motion allowed her pupils the seconds they demanded to make their needed adjustments as she was welcomed to a new day not by her busy corridor but by Earth saying, "Buongiorno."

Foremost on the agenda: dispatching three new roller droids. That meant spending the whole day with Mike and Tina, and the thought drew a smile on Gift's face. These rollers were an improved version of the existing ones which had been roaming for months. When she assigned herself to help on the updated design, the opportunity to be an engineer overjoyed Gift. Such new equipment was vital for the newly forged partnership with the Russian Federation, one New Europa contribution being their technological expertise.

Data operators were a second value Gift's team brought, so Raff had tasked Red—Gift wasn't sure but thought she might be called Melanie or Melody—to recode the OS. The antiquated software of the two-hundred-dred-year-old models often lost input from its sensors. The critical fault, discovered long after they had been deployed, caused three units to 'take the plunge,' as Mike said, failing to turn or stop before rolling into bodies of water. A need emerged for the diminished force of aged rollers to be replaced. Rations had been wagered on which of the remaining rollers would go next, with odds on the Mediterranean over the smaller target of the Adriatic for the southbound units. Mike played the odds, despite Gift's objection.

The morning's swim partner, Marco, awaited Gift's return from the exterior farm toilet. "Ciao Gift. Lovely morning."

"Certo. Buongiorno."

"Saw you going…, so I waited here. I hope that's okay." The shyness her presence evoked always made Gift smile, she found it cute.

The back of her hand met his chest playfully. "Just need to slip back in and change. Pull the zipper down for me, would ya?" When she opened the tent in her red swimsuit, they strolled toward the lake.

"How's it feel sleeping out here in that?"

"The tent? It's fine. Last night there was such a pleasant breeze I laid on the grass for a while. The full effect of sleeping outside. I couldn't sleep for staring at the stars, so I went back in."

"I love the night sky. I see that first glimpse of it so clearly, from the secret farm ceiling."

"I'll never forget that first peek but look at us now. *Outside*. Swimming in a lake. Who could have imagined it?" Gift's pace quickened as the water neared. "Gonna do it this time." Her young neighbor had finally learned her ways, so didn't reply.

Halted abruptly with no trace of poise or panache, Gift stopped herself at the shoreline. One foot slipped into the water, but she kept her balance.

"What was that? You said you were gonna do it. Do what?"

"Run and plunge right in. I still can't. Much as I love this stupid lake, I have to go step by step. Such a baby." Her forced pout over an extended bottom lip fit the analogy.

"No worries."

Unexpectedly unbalanced, Gift's torso twisted, her feet trying to stay planted on the ground failed the attempt. After the loud clap of her splash all noise ceased and morphed into distant liquid echoes. When her head instinctively shook in its rise from the surface, the sounds returned to her ears carried Marco's laughter.

"*Brat*. Why...?" Wet giggles came from anger blended with joy.

"You did it. It won't be scary next time."

"Not the same. *I needed* to do it." An attempt to splash water on him fell short as he was still on the shore.

"Then come out here and do it."

"No, *dai*. Can we just swim already? *Brat*."

"Trust me, please. Come here." Marco quickly learned the mistake of extending his hand to aid her from the liquid folly as she tugged with all her weight, yanking him in and pushing herself under beside him. Their laughs were hearty as they broke the surface.

"Get up there and jump in. C'mon, you can do it."

"I just wanna swim. I can't go alone, so let's go."

"As soon as you dive in. We'll do it together, dive right into a swim."

Standing shoulder to shoulder, Marco had a look of confidence rare in her presence, mustering up her courage. It felt odd, but empowering, making her dauntless to the water before her. "*Go*." She dove in ahead of him, coming up into a full-stroke swim he had to work to catch. Angry when he had done it, Gift felt gratitude for Marco helping her overcome a fear and add a fun new aspect to her morning swim.

***

Dome Six, as each dome, had its pedestrian door for transitioning from colony to Earth and back again. It also held a cargo bulkhead. Standing outside, Gift gazed upon the massive dome stretching up and away, its curvature hiding its true height and making her small and insignificant yet significantly important. Her roller droids were the next phase of environmental recovery and marked the start of their collaboration with the R.F. on geological and atmospheric analyses. Naılya Usanova was there as the leading environmental scientist of the Russian Federation and soil nutritionist Valentin Galaktionova came to N.E. to meet with Matteo.

The massive doors split down the center, nubs of interlocking steel fingers separated, exposing the dense darkness they withheld. The contrast of the sunlit day to the artificial illumination in the colony demanded time for the eyes to adjust as the blackness eased into shadow, eased into silhouettes. Stepping into the dome's shade allowed Gift to see but she couldn't enter before her third day ended. Mike emerged as the first recognizable figure.

"Ciao Mike."

"Morning Gift. How are you? How was it being out here alone? Sleeping in the tent?"

"Slow down, sweetie. I'm good. Being out here is fine. And I'm only alone when I'm sleeping, like always. Oh, last night the moon was crazy bright. You gotta see it at that time, the way everything looks this... awesome steel blue. Trees, grass, the mountain... Everything a different color than now. It's like I could *feel* the quiet of it all."

"I'll take your word for it. But I think I'll just keep to my Box at night, safe and sound, thank you very much."

"You're welcome." The back of Gift's hand landed on his stomach. She learned to tease him for his quirky expressions. "Tina? My rollers?"

"On their way. But we need to talk... about a name."

"Name?"

"I get why the old ones were called that, big round metal balls that literally roll around. *Rollers*. But these new ones? Don't you think they need a new name?"

"Haven't thought about it. They're not balls that roll around, but they do kinda still roll, on wheels, no?"

"I was thinking something like Blade Droids or Tumblers."

"Blade Droids? What kinda name even is that?"

"You know, they have those cool blades, to cut through stuff. Droids with massive sharp blades. Blade Droids."

"O... *kay*. Ma, that's not what they *are*. And Tumblers? They never tumble. Shouldn't anyway, or I think they'd be in trouble. It'd be like calling the old ones sinkers because when they find water, they sink."

"No, no, you're not getting it. I'm talking Tumblers like acrobats or gymnasts, moving, twisting, tossing any way they need. These things sort of do that. Plus, it sounds so much cooler than roller droid." Mike moaned the words *roller droid* to make it sound lame.

"I don't see the need. They're still rollers, just improved versions. Two-point-O."

"Gift, take some pride in your work. And for once, take the credit. You led the team on the design and now you're leading the team using them. You should give'em a new name. How about Ojo-bots?" His snicker unveiled the joke in that suggestion.

Pensive, she paused for two breaths. "Rover."

"Rover? That's your cool new name? Rover?"

"Remember, so-called history buff? Early exploration of Mars, I mean, actual Mars. They had these things they called *Mars Rovers* that ran all over the land scanning and taking pictures and stuff." He nodded. "Well, we *thought* we were on Mars. Now we have these things to go out and explore as if we were, sorta, on a new planet. I mean, Earth is all new to us. So, we'll call these guys Rovers."

"Still lame, if you ask me."

"I didn't." She winked.

"But, like, jazz it up a bit. Rover-bots? Or Terra-rovers?"

"E.R. Rovers. That's what I'll call them. Environmental Recovery Rovers. We're working with the R.F. on this and we," a hand waved between them, "...are the equipment engineers, experts. Let's put on a professional appearance."

"Whatever. May as well keep *rollers* then. But hey, you're the boss... boss."

"Don't forget it."

After a teasing salute Mike said, "At least, if we go with your lame idea? I remember each Mars rover had a cool name. Let's at least give them each a name so we don't just call them by their asset numbers."

"Now that's a *good* idea."

Already on his handheld, Mike suggested, "Spirit, Sojourner, Opportunity, Curiosity, Perseverance. We have three so far."

"Let's go with Perseverance for the first. I like that name, fits us, persevering on Earth. Curiosity and Sojourner for the others."

"Perfect. Well, less lame anyway." Mike's reply got him another playful slap.

"Speaking of three new Rovers... where are they? And where's Tina?"

8

S trong yet feminine, Tina looked like an awesome warrior woman, the one in that show with the ugly spaceship with the bright yellow glow. Recently, Gift learned why the ship was called a *firefly,* noting its resemblance to the insect. More significant to Gift, Tina had strength of character, all hundred eighty-one centimeters of her. When the violence of insurrection came, Gift was happy to have Tina beside them in their righteous battle against terror. A battle that was, in any respect of analysis, lost miserably.

Yet in defeat came victory of sorts. That opened airlock exposed a world beyond the colony, a planet that now needed to be explored, studied, made subject once again to human domination—perhaps this time in a more symbiotic relationship. In this phase of that noble quest, Tina would be a key player.

"Hey Gift." The monotone didn't mean Tina wasn't happy to see her. Gift knew she was. "Brought you a gift, Gift."

"Ooo. Can't wait to see the final version." The words oozed giddy excitement. "Haven't even seen them yet."

Slicing the air with her hand Tina said, "Behold."

Hard rubber wheels pushed back the smooth concrete as the machines came forth, deafening squeaks escaping the open dome like screams from a giant's mouth. While their metal bodies were as round as their predecessors, they didn't roll the way the old ones did. These stood a meter from ground to top, less than that wide. As they neared, electric motors hummed a symphonic melody. Gift gasped at her first look at the finished product. Not entirely her design, she contributed much to engineering the machines which had yet to prove themselves. "Gorgeous. Absolutely gorgeous."

"Not sure I'd say that. I mean, they're cool, but at least the old ones were shiny. These are dull gray."

"Beautiful machines."

"Alright, let's get on with it." Curt yet jovial tones laced Mike's words. "The way you're drooling over these would make Tom jealous."

"Shut…" Gift offered the back of a hand to his stomach, a little harder this time. "Up." A laugh came from deep in Tina's belly. "I'm eager to see'em in action… Anyone seen Nailya? Don't want to launch without her."

Looking around, Tina said, "It's just a test, let's launch these beasties."

"No, we can't start without her. This is our first project as a united team with the R.F." Pulling her handheld from her pocket, Gift commanded it, "VidChat Raffaella Di Gaetano."

"Buongiorno, Carina. What can I do for you?"

"Looking for Nailya. Nailya Usanova. From the R.F."

"You know I know who Nailya is, *vero*?" Raff flashed her a playful smirk. "*Ma*, let me see… She had breakfast… from O-eight hundred to nine at Douceur De France in Dome Three. It's only five minutes past nine. Her agenda shows meeting you at Dome Six by the access hatch. Is that where you are?"

"Yeah, we're here. If she had breakfast on the other side of the colony, we'll just wait. Grazie."

"Niente. I don't know who made this agenda. Breakfast till nine in Three and then being at Six by nine."

"Bureaucracy," Mike bellowed. "Better with you two, sure, but still the same detachment from reality for the rest of 'em. That'll never change."

"True Mikey, so true." Tina turned to Gift. "Hey, let's let Mikey get these outside and ready for us. Make himself useful."

"Yeah, I'll get them prep'd. Seems like some girl talk's about to go down. I'll be glad to get far from that mess." He paused and smiled. "Unless you find yourselves in need of my expert advice."

Jovial as it was, Tina's punch to Mike's shoulder made a sharp pop and his face showed a hint of pain. With definition worthy of jealousy, Gift loved how toned Tina's biceps were. Tina regularly hit the gym, but Gift was too busy for that. No, too disinterested. Swimming had replaced her morning runs except in the coldest of months. She swam when her skin complained, only stopping when the bones objected to the icy chill. The new routine rewarded her own arms with improved definition and tone.

Watching Mike walk to the departure point with the rovers on his heels reminded Gift of a mother duck and ducklings waddling as she'd seen once in a vid.

The women sat at a picnic table of a sepia-brown composite material, soft to the touch and hard and solid at the same time. "What's up, sweetie? Nothing serious, I hope."

"Nah, relax. I know how anxious you get."

"How I get?" Gift chuckled. "I'm getting better."

"*Sure you are.* So, two things, I guess. It's been a while, but I remember a chat we had months ago, when I was still with that *turd*, Max."

"*Turd*?" Gift giggled. "I could do without hearing that name. *Ma*, I never asked, Sara said his nose was broken *before* the violence started. That was you, wasn't it?" Tina's broad smile provided the answer.

"I don't want to talk about him. Gift..." A long pause brought a flood of uneasiness. The anxiety was still there. Gift considered it getting better, but still there. "Tom." The name hit the table as a complete thought, an idea so powerful Gift understood the conversation and the concerns motivating it. "I want to ask you about Tom. If... I... If that's okay."

"I guess. Depends on what you want to ask."

"Are you guys *together*-together... or just together?"

"Whoa... That's, well... not what I expected. Also too... a bit personal. And you were so closed about... *the turd*."

"But I was already in GM. You're only twenty-seven. Twenty-seven, Gift. And... I think, maybe... it's my fault." The way Tina's head dropped was off-putting.

"Your fault? What are you on about?"

"That night. I guess you wanted to talk to Raff, but she wasn't there. You asked me about your feelings. You were starting, you know, boys. Men. I think maybe I... I may have given you some bad advice. Really *terrible* advice. Now with Tom, I wonder... if you're not ready. *And*? I should... should have helped you then. Why'd you even ask me, anyway? What do I know?"

"Oh... I see." Too many words bounced around Gift's head, making it hard to select the right ones from the clutter. "First, sweetie, if I asked you, it's because I trust you. I love you. That's why I asked you."

"Sure. Love-you-too, by the way." Tina's words were mumbled and hurried. "Even if I don't always show it. But I gave you crap advice. Didn't mean to. It's... I'm an idiot."

"Don't say that. I don't even remember what you said that could be so bad." Gift slid her hand across the composite table and rested it on Tina's.

"Go with it."

"*Huh*?"

"That's what I told you—at *twenty-six*. I told you not to over-analyze it. You. I told *you* that. But that's what I said, 'just go with it.' Awful advice."

"Oh no, Tina. I didn't think it was awful."

"But it was. You were too young... you *are* too young. I was in GM, and you saw what a mess I made. And look how long it took me to knock his lights out. Now you? Tom? You are too young Gift. And... it's my fault, all my fault."

"First of all, it can't be your fault. I'm a grown woman and make my own decisions. So, whatever it is, it's on me, not you. Sorry, but you don't have that much power over me." A smirk failed to soften the mood. "Also too, me and Tom? It's not like that. What did you say, *together*-together? We're just... together. Sort of."

"Be straight with me." She turned her hand to hold Gift's. "Are you sleeping with the guy? Having—"

"*Ciao*! Tina."

"C'mon, Gift. You knew that's what I meant by *together*-together."

"I... I thought you meant romantically. Like if we had feelings for each other. Not... *that*."

"So that's a no, then?"

"Yes. I mean, that's a no. We're not even close to ready for Union."

"And the romantic part? You're kidding yourself if you think it's not there. And what about him? Are you sure he's not into you like that?"

"*Into* me? No. Well, okay." Words coming to Gift's mind refused to form themselves into sentences. She saw them on the mental display between her and Tina, but the Sort button wasn't there. Deep breath. "Okay, let me try to explain. There could be romantic feelings there. I mean, there is, yeah, for both of us, I guess. It's not like Mike, or Matteo, or Marco. I know what those are. It doesn't feel *totally* different with Tom but it's... *different*. And for sure he feels it too. But he's like me. I mean, he's not had a relationship. We know to go slow."

"But remember, he's what, thirty-one?"

"Thirty. Well, he'll be thirty-one next month, yeah."

"So... he's in GM. You aren't."

Gift retrieved her tiny hand from Tina's—returned to its normal size out of the giant's paw—and raised both her arms, interlocking her fingers atop her head. "Thank you. You're a good friend, and your advice isn't crap. You're right, he's older, and it's me that's too young. But I promise, we're going slow. And..." A word indicating more to follow snuck out before Gift had made the choice to offer more.

"*And*?"

Gift paused, hoping the next decision would be clearer. It wasn't. Stretching the word, she started with, "Allora..." Nothing came in the time given for coherent thoughts to surface. Tina responded with a raised eyebrow. "This whole *the-only-one-not-getting-sick* thing? It's, well, sorta... related. I mean, the reason why I can stay outside and not get sick like the rest. It's related to my..."

"Your what?"

"My... condition. I have this thing about me. Sakura told me. I'm... not like everyone with the Gen Maturity. It's like I've... *reverted*, I guess. Never thought of it that way."

"Reverted? Condition? What are you on about?"

"My body... inside. It's more like ... like we were, *before*. I'm not as dependent on chemicals. I could have a baby."

"Have a baby? Most of us can."

"No, it's that I, I can have one... a baby... 'the *natural* way,' Sakura said." A squint expressed Tina's confusion. "You know, by being..." Making air quotes, Gift whispered, "*together*-together with someone."

"Oh. Now *that is* different... So... it's a good thing you and Tom ain't then, eh?" A shared laugh took the weight from the mood. Tina's was infectious.

"You said you had two things." Gift happily moved to a new topic.

"Oh, I did. *I did...?* Right. Seems silly, now that we did all that with you, your *condition*, you called it. Condition. But okay. There's this other guy."

"Oh mamma."

"Here's the deal. I'm hesitant, so, I want to do a little homework before I get my ticker involved."

"And what does that mean, exactly?"

"It means, my dear friend who just told me how much you love me, you and Raff are going to use some of your new powers to help me."

9

Original estimates came shockingly close. Told the terraforming project would take two hundred fifty years, they now knew it was the initial prediction for the earth reaching near sustainability. Gift herself the attestation. Earth *could* support human life again. It was the chemically and genetically mutated version of humankind holed up in colonies that weren't ready for *it*.

Believed to have been rolling along for two centuries, the Roller Droids had spent most of that time in storage. Raff had found archive records on a secure server and learned how every five years they rolled for thirty-two days. Comparing data from each run gave the environmental sciences team updates on the sustainability of life, from soil nutrients to insect and bacterial populations. Atmospheric readings included oxygen and carbon dioxide levels, moisture percentages, and light-dependent and light-independent reactions of photosynthesis. Radiation levels were precisely tracked. These data allowed updated projections on human livability, factoring the rate of genetic adaptation into the equation.

Rovers, while not as pretty, were far more advanced. Built on knowledge of the strengths and weaknesses of the earlier design, updated versions of the same motion and tracking sensors were produced. Gift's idea was to add the four rugged wheels with twenty-eight-centimeter ground clearance to provide greater dependability at the expense of its maneuverability—an advantage that didn't benefit the older rollers. Objections tossed were of tilting, tipping, or of something blocking the wheels, ending the journey. By Gift's proposal, arms for collecting samples, removing debris, and recovering from a fall made it into the final design.

The time had come for the field test before they'd set off into the unknown. To any who asked, Gift's confidence level hit a hundred percent—tucking away that one percent chance she gave her Rovers for failure. By 09:38, Mike had completed all his checks and preparations, so of course, Gift had to check them again. Not that she didn't trust Mike, he understood it well. With her approval, the three new Rovers were ready to rove. Except they weren't. One thing missing stalled the departure, a critical component without which the units could not deploy.

"Where the heck is she?" Not that the time mattered. The deadline Gift set for 10:00 could have been at any time. The test runs were set for a five-kilometer radius of the colony's perimeter, one being purposely sent toward the lake. Gift's team would monitor them throughout the day, then a night shift of two engineers. At the twenty-four-hour mark they would be evaluated. If all checks showed green, they would be dispatched.

"She's coming," a distant voice of Mike called.

As Nailya Usanova approached, Gift said to Tina from the corner of her mouth, "Not a word about her being late."

"Good morning, Gift. How are you, my dear?"

"Very well, thank you. And you? Have a good sleep?"

"Da, very nice bed. A little soft for Nailya, but nice."

"And your breakfast with Norman Peeters? Were you two able to discuss this launch?"

"Oh no Milashka. Breakfast is not for such talkings."

"Sorry, milashka?"

"Is you dear Gift. Milashka means... cutie." Gift blushed.

"Hello Nailya." Tina had enough of the chatter.

"Good day Tina." Turning to Gift, Nailya said, "Are we ready to begin?"

"Yes. Mike and I did all the system checks. We'll observe the rovers from here with tablets, and drones will follow them to confirm their course."

"Very thorough. Am impressed with this team."

On her raised handheld, Gift entered the command to deploy the rovers. A smile painted itself on her face when she noticed Mike had updated the tracking app with the names of each unit. The soft click of the drive followed subtle hums as the electric motors engaged gears to turn the wheels until the rovers were roving. Perseverance veered right and rounded the dome out of sight. Curiosity took off straight through the field ahead, adjusting its course slightly not to hit a bush. Raff and Red's navigation program looked to be working well. Sojourner roved left toward Colony Lake.

The team took position on a picnic table where tablets were waiting. Nailya's open hands floated in circles over the composite's texture. "Soft to touch. But is firm. Strong. We must learn this. At R.F. is no such picnic area. We do not use out of doors as you."

"Excuse me, Nailya," Mike said. "May I ask what you mean about not using the outdoors? Don't your residents enjoy going outside?"

"Enjoy? Of course. But we have colder climate, do not go in lake, even when lake is not ice. But I think maybe you know, we have neighbors. They do not like us." Gift nodded. She had heard the stories.

Mike's concern peaked. "Do you think they could attack us?"

"No." The force of Gift's reply may have been suppressed fear. "We're monitoring a wide perimeter. And they have no idea where we even are. They must be close to the R.F. and don't have any transports, so to walk here? No, it's highly unlikely."

"So was an insurrection in the colony." Mike's sarcasm-laced words had a point.

"And that we were on Earth this whole time," Tina added.

To change the subject, Gift asked, "Shall we check the progress of our rovers?"

All were quiet as eyes swept over their screens to find the units behaving as expected. Logs showed pinpoint accuracy in the object sensors with course adjustments from minute to full turns. Vectors were always maintained or quickly reestablished. *Nothing but green so far,* Gift thought to herself with pride and glee radiating through her smile.

"Curiosity's really moving." The excitement in Mike's pitch gave rise to Gift's suspicions.

"Tell me you didn't play odds like some sorta race." His shrug said, *you bet I did.* "*Mike.* You're too into that. *Ciao.* It's not good. I wish you'd cut it out."

Tina smirked. "What? I put my rations on Sojourner."

"Am chosen Perseverance," Nailya said.

"You too? How?"

"Is an app Mike showed to Nailya."

"I... I just don't believe you people. I heard people bet for euphoric drops, not just rations. Some stupid idiots used it to try to stay outside longer. Maybe died."

"No." Mike pulled his face from the tablet. "This app and the folks running it are on the up-and-up."

"Up-and-up? Whatever that means."

"Mikey's right. Win or lose, it's always fair and gives or takes exactly what it should. And only rations."

"Wait. If they're arranging the trade of rations... they'd need Admin authorization."

"No conspiracies here." *Interesting coming from Mike.* "Transfers happen person to person, just facilitated in the app."

"I don't like it."

"Milashka, is harmless fun. I bet for who gets next honors from your Board. I won when was you. Ten rations. I place large bet for Aimée next."

"Wait. How are *you* betting rations? You're not even a resident here."

"I have guest rations account. All on mixed teams do. How would we eat and drink?"

"I guess… I hadn't thought about it."

"Am scanned, and I get anything I want. I love it. We should use same system."

Gift just shook her head. Was it harmless fun or would Gift, a member of the Board of Directors, involve herself to put a stop to it? Musings on the dilemma were interrupted by Tina's shout. "No, no, no. What happened? Where's my Sojourner? I've lost it."

"Me too."

"I see only others," Nailya said. "Where is Sojourner?"

The dread that filled Gift felt familiar but had been dormant since the insurrection ended. "*What?* No. It's gotta be there." It wasn't.

Minutes became the past in quick succession as two engineers, a technician, and an environmental scientist stayed glued to their tablets, each as confused as the next. The data stopped, and the transmission ended. Gift found the last of the logs with the video feed attached. "Play last ten seconds." With Mike craned to see her tablet, the two observed in horror as the last recorded view filled the display. The shoreline of Colony Lake, static, nothing. "*No.*"

"Could they have messed up on the control code? Same as the old ones, took the plunge."

Gift snapped, "No. Red, Raff—they didn't mess that up."

"Hardware then." Tina's matter-of-fact reply pricked Gift's pride like a needle.

"It's not the hardware. The hardware's perfect."

"One thing child learns in Russian Federation: nothing is perfect."

"You know what I mean. They're good, great design. There's... something else. Has to be."

"Gift..." Her former bench-mate's tone was surprisingly soft. "I didn't want to tell you when we named these, but maybe... you cursed it. Sojourner, I mean. It's the Mars rover that failed, traveled like, just over a hundred meters or so and was lost."

"Lost?" Gift's eyes shifted from her imaginary display to the pane of glass in her hand. "Lost. Idiot." She meant herself. "The drone's live feed... *There*. There's Sojourner, going around the lake, it's there. Something must have jammed the signal. Sojourner is fine, perfect. Just a jammed sig—Wait... What could jam the signal?"

10

What could jam the signal? Gift held the full weight of the question. The Russian Federation was too far to interfere with comms. Minimal disruptions could occur when a transport approached or departed, lasting only a few seconds. Sojourner went dark for nearly three minutes before it reestablished its link. No other breaks in connectivity or disruptions. *Was it an anomaly?* Gift wondered. *Safe to ignore?*

To ignore a potential problem, no matter how improbable, was poor engineering. Permitted to run the full twenty-four hours, the test continued. When Mike and Tina insisted she stop her frantic search through the logs to eat, Gift refused. The passing hours brought no satisfactory answers but helped isolate the exact moment of the interruption. *Interference?* she speculated. *Not a system fault, nor an error in device or code. Something interfered, that's worse.* Finding a fault in a single unit Gift considered 'perfectly engineered' presented the easier task compared to checking every piece of equipment that could have interfered with it. A daunting task when Gift looked at it that way, and that became the only way to look at it. She ignored the rumbling pangs of hunger.

"Gift. I will make it an order if I must. Please, just come with me." Sakura had been trying to convince her to come for more than twenty minutes. The medic had to track her down when Gift failed to report to Pronto Soccorso for the all-important exam to evaluate her three days on the outside. As much as Gift hated to give in, Sakura had the authority to order her to comply.

"*Fine...* Sorry... I'm sorry. Yes, I'll come. I know your thing's important, *ma,* mine's too—super important."

"I understand, sweetie, but we need these results. Like your project, our medical research is for our future."

"Tina? Nailya?" Seeing only Mike, Gift noticed the others had left.

"Gone. Like an hour ago. Man, you can be stubborn."

"Stubborn? Yeah, I guess. Sorry if I snapped at you."

"You did. And at Tina, then poor Sakura."

"Nailya? Please tell me I wasn't rude to her."

"I don't think anyone is rude enough for her to notice. And she didn't give you time, wandered off a while ago. Had zero interest in watching you insulting your tablet."

"I was a bit... *off.* Sorry."

"Just go with Sakura. She's right, her thing's important too. You need to show us all how to be special, then *you* won't be any more. Win-win." His grin brought a much-needed smile to Gift's face.

***

The medical exam began with a sample of every fluid in Gift's body. *Why do they need so much blood?* Unpleasant yet necessary for helping the population progress, or regress, and adapt to the Earth's ideal of what humankind should be to live upon her. Everyone desperately wanted to know when that would be. "When will we know something?"

"It will take me a few days to gather and understand the results. Then likely weeks to determine if we can replicate the DNA markers in your genome that make you unique and compatible with the environment.

Doing something with that knowledge could take months." A shrug full of disappointment from Gift. "And Gift, sweetie... Please, you need to rest now. And eat. You have a project and I get it is important. You have a team monitoring it, so you need to let it go until tomorrow." Sakura placed her hands on Gift's shoulders and looked into her eyes. "Can you do that?"

"Not really."

"You said it will be tomorrow before you have the full dataset collected. If you do not rest, you will not be able to give it your best. Does this project not deserve your best effort and attention?"

"You sound like an engineer. You sound like me."

"I will take that as a compliment."

"Okay, I'll try. Really, I will."

"Good... Dinner plans?"

"Yep. Raff and Hans Fuchs... and Tom. Want to join?"

"Thank you, I have plans. Seeing my parents."

"Nice. Give them my best. Hey, we were talking about a group dinner soon. I was supposed to send a message to everyone—I'll do that later. We want you to join us."

"Sounds lovely. Tell me where and when and I will be there."

***

'Dinners must always be one part sustenance, two parts friendships, three parts fun.' Aimée's one-two-three dinner rule was the reason she found Board-sponsored dinners so agonizingly boring, as she told Gift emphatically whenever they made her attend one. Gift wanted to follow Sakura's advice. A nice evening with friends—likely to include counsel from Raff about her and Tom—filled with lighthearted conversation. Just the thing to bring her mind down from its turbocharged frenzy from the rover incident.

The suds splashed thick and lush, cascading over her flesh. Not to abuse her Admin building privileges, with access to the amazing showers, Gift took hers in her block's shower box. *Three days outside warrants a great shower and mine's not for two days.* Justification to keep from abusing her authority—she feared she might fall in love with power and privilege. Reality afforded little of either, the shower and those boring dinners the extent of such *privilege*. The full-flow water still towered above the increased mist of standard shower booths—exhilarating. Until she peeled off her coverall, Gift hadn't noticed her stink. Rationalization of going in the lake being a suitable substitute for a shower was squashed by the reality of her body's odor. The days washing off her, their sweat and grunge fleeing down the drain, she wished for her anxious concerns to go with them. Not even the blasts of hot air pulling the moisture from her skin could remove them. They were hers to be carried with her to the dinner table.

***

When her Box door opened, Tom stood there waiting for her—something he hadn't done since being her guard. In the same stern pose, meant as a joke, he greeted her with a smile. While their *relationship* began that way, Gift thought those early beginnings were best forgotten to new realities. He escorted her to Augustiner bräu. Memories she wished buried plagued her, a mental image of her hugging the toilet and Raff finding her on the floor proved hard to suppress. To focus on the positive, Gift would have an evening with Raff.

"Ah. Double date?" Hans Fuchs emoted in such subtle variations, Gift still couldn't discern his feelings. He'd grown on her, with residual resentment for the occupation of Raff's time and attention. She reckoned it would be the same for any man who stole a gram of her precious moments with Raff. Just a normal part of life, people eventually ending up in Union—of course, she wished Raff's sooner or later came a little later.

"*Hans.*" In playful anger Raff slapped his shoulder. "Just four friends having dinner."

"Buonasera, Bella." Gift's greeting lifted Raff from her seat for a two-cheek kiss.

"Cara, you look amazing. Bellissima."

"You like the dress? Can you believe it? I used to never wear'em and now I toss'em on all the time." With a half twirl Gift showed off the new dress, black lace over a thin silky underlayer that flared out just a touch from the hips.

"Veramente bella."

"You look lovely Gift. Good evening." *He had to do it. Hans Fuchs just had to be charming.* Deep down, Gift knew she could not have picked a better man for her dear friend.

"Thank you. Good evening."

Making his existence known, Tom said, "Good evening. Nice to see you both."

Although her previous retching had come from emotional overload, Gift decided to play it safe and ordered a small beer. Talk over food—around it when the men forgot their table manners for words too important to wait for the swallow—was light and casual. Hans Fuchs and Tom had spent little time together, so they devoted part of the evening to exchanging questions and stories. With laser-accurate focus, Raff studied Tom and how Gift looked at him. Overprotective sister mode fully engaged. Hans Fuchs had to ask the question... "So, what is this thing between you two?"

"Hans!" Zero playfulness in Raff's objection this time.

"Sorry, it's just, what is it? You two are spending a lot of time together, and Gift? You know how Raff worries."

"I do…, I do, Raff. But please, not tonight. I actually need to ask you something… about work. Sorry, it's, it's important. Maybe hugely."

"Va bene. *Ma*, promise we will talk soon." Gift nodded. "So, what is this maybe hugely important thing of yours?"

In exhaustive detail, Gift explained what happened to her rover, its communication interruption, and how she had pored over all the logs and checked several pieces of equipment in the surrounding network node… "There wasn't any signal, nanowave, radiation spike, or anything else that could possibly have caused the issue. Dark time on the rover was two minutes and thirty-eight seconds." An odd detail to Gift, the random duration *felt* specific. "I mean, two minutes thirty-eight seconds… Why two thirty-eight?"

"Because two thirty-eight. If it had been two forty or one fifty-six, you'd say why that. Seems a random number to me. I'm sure it'll make sense when you figure it out."

"I hope so. I've been running checks on systems all over the colony. I can show you the data on my handheld, you've got a much better eye for data streams." The men leaving the table went unnoticed until Gift reached for her bag and saw Tom's empty seat. "Where'd they go?"

"You're so cute when you're obsessing. They left ten minutes ago, uninterested in the shop talk. They're at the pool table."

"Oh." Confusion blanked Gift's face.

An open hand requested the device. Gift gazed upon the data stream reflected in the deep green of Raff's irises as she analyzed the information. As data compiled from over a hundred devices flowed, the data operator was in her zone, deep in a data stream. Within seconds Raff said, "Gift. You may have found something here. Maybe hugely important."

"I knew it. Didn't know what I knew, but I knew it."

"The same time the rover dropped connection, to the nanosecond, every device in a five-hundred-meter radius glitched. These sorts of things happen all the time on wide-band networked devices—never triggering an alert. But I've never seen it happen to *every* device in a clustered node."

"Could it be an issue with a central relay or router?"

"No, every *device*... blipped. The network was fine, no issues."

"So why did the rover do more than blip? I mean two minutes, thirty-eight? It wasn't random, was it?"

Eyes burning brightly, Raff scrolled. "I see it. You were right, again. How'd you know?"

"A hunch. Like my gut telling me something."

"Good hunch your gut had. There was a second blip at exactly two minutes thirty-eight seconds after the first."

"Good. I mean, not good. We're getting somewhere. Any idea what it was? What caused it? A malfunction in a transmission array? Mistimed packet burst?"

"Now you're guessing like a data operator. *Ma*, those would have been logged. It looks like... can't be."

"Can't be what?" Impatience bled into Gift's tone.

"To me... it looks like there was a targeted scan."

"Targeted? At the Sojourner?"

"Another good guess. Maybe. Only thing I can think of that would make it stay offline for the entire time."

"Who? I mean, who could? Who would... scan us?"

"You won't like my best guess."

"Russian Federation... Nailya Usanova."

"Gift, we don't know. Please, don't overreact and don't do anything yet. We need to tread lightly. You and I are on the Board, so we must consider diplomacy. If we accuse them of something, we'd better be sure or we risk this new partnership, which we desperately need."

11 | Day Two

Success is stumbling from failure to failure with no loss of enthusiasm. When her supervisory tutor in engineering design quoted a person of historical fame called Winston Churchill, he explained every good design was the culmination of many failures. At fifteen, Gift considered glorious success after glorious success a surefire way to maintain enthusiasm. By twenty-seven she had many successes. This success forgot to bring enthusiasm along.

At the twenty-four-hour mark, the rovers returned to their exact places of departure, navigation precise. Every system performed as good as Gift had hoped, and she hoped large. Although her design had proved flawless, failure may have been in the proposed alliance for environmental recovery. By bringing the Russians in, had she made a huge mistake? Lesson learned the hard way months earlier, *guilty until proven so* proved an ineffective approach, even if it proved true in Max's case. *Stupid Max!*

"Good morning, Milashka."

"Good morning, Nailya. Sleep well?"

"You always ask for my sleep. This is strange. Is sleeping well not common in your colony?"

Gift chuckled. "It's, sort of... it's a polite thing to ask, I guess. Like, *how are you?*"

"Am fine. That question makes sense. Use it instead of sleeping question. But I think we need to talk for more important things than my sleep. Unless perhaps you do not sleep well. We should talk about this?"

No, Gift hadn't slept well. Returned to the comfort of her Box, slumber should have been sound, but her mind had been in overdrive. "You're right. We do have more important things to discuss. Yeah."

"Your rovers worked, even the one that hid from you? I see it has come home, did not go for swim."

"Worked perfectly. Something in our communications equipment acted up. We've collected good data so you and Norman should have a good start."

"Wonderful. Well done, my new friend."

'My new friend.' The words bounced in Gift's head. The woman who came under the guise of friendship may have sabotaged the project. To what end? Were they advancing their own agenda, trying to keep New Europa from gaining an advantage? The *why* didn't come to her. Why would the R.F. do such a thing, and to what end? The pieces sought a place to fit but only gave Gift a headache. Lost in her thoughts, her silence must have been longer than she realized.

"Gift? Did you go somewhere without Nailya?"

"Huh...? Sorry. Get lost in my own mind sometimes."

"Welcome back. If all was perfect, as you say, what are Mike and Tina doing to your rovers? I ask you this already. You didn't heard me?"

"Sorry. Just detailed diagnostics. Part of the plan before we send them off. We need to be sure they'll do well out there, we have too much riding on this."

"Riding on it? Someone will ride these rovers?"

A chuckle may have been too much, making Nailya think Gift laughed at her. "Our words, like Valentin says. It means this is a very important project."

"He loves your words. They confuse Nailya."

"Me too sometimes. Mike uses these old expressions and I almost never get them. Come, I'll escort you to meet one of our data operators. She'll work with you to get this new sensor data into an app to make it more meaningful."

"Where is my Belgian?"

"Norman Peeters? Sleeping. He monitored the rovers all night. He's scheduled to meet you after lunch. We have you working with Red for the morning. She'll be at your disposal to get you what you need."

"My disposal? This means something very different in R.F. Do I understand this red person will do as I wish?"

"Yeah." Wild images of what *disposal* could have meant to Nailya flooded Gift's mind with recalled history lessons of the U.S.S.R. making the pictures unappealing. "She's a brilliant data operator and masterful app designer. She'll work the data for you in the app she's writing."

"This is good. Show Nailya the way."

***

Entering a memory, Gift escorted her guest into her former workspace. Miss Jane greeted them, arrayed in the friendliest face Gift had ever seen on her—her former supervisor usually wore a blank stare. Feasibly, she saw Gift as her boss. Being on the Board of Directors tended to have that impact, though Gift preferred no one to think of her that way.

Red worked at Raff's bench alone, no one had been assigned with her since Raff and Hans Fuchs moved on to other things. No longer Raff's bench, it would always be that to Gift. Two junior engineers were at her and Mike's old bench. *No Sky is My Sky*, Mike's favorite song, started playing in her head along with memories of him first joining her bench. She hated that song and now it would be stuck in her head all day.

"Ciao, Red."

"Hey Gift, great to see you. Is this my boss for the day?"

"No. Well, sort of, I guess, yeah. This is Nailya Usanova of the R.F., one of our new environmental restoration team scientists."

"Pleasure to meet," Nailya said, extending her hand. "Red? This is most unusual name. Are many of your people named for color of hair?"

With a chuckle Red replied, "I don't suppose so. Red's a nickname. I'm Melody McKinley, nice to meet you."

Melody. I was right. Well, half right. Fifty percent.

"I will not call you Red. Melody, I love this name."

"Thank you, me too. Gift and Raff are about the only ones to still call me Red. Goes back to a more... unpleasant time. Melody is just fine."

Noted, Gift thought. *Start calling her Melody and tell Raff to.*

"So, Melody," Gift said with a smile. "If there's anything you—" A chirp of her handheld snipped the thought. "Sorry, excuse me. Just let me know if you need anything. Ciao."

An incoming vidChat request from Fred, her onetime interrogator turned colleague on the Board and fellow committee member in Cultivation. "Accept."

"Gift, I need you here right away."

"On my way." Outlining his face, Gift saw the exterior farm. She had learned asking for details over vidChat was pointless with Fred.

The sight of Fred waiting for her behind Dome Four summoned memories of his dark, empty stare and stabbing questions. That was another lifetime, but the man still intimidated her. Gift feared he'd drop an unwelcome change Mike called a *curveball*—another one she didn't get. When she had told him, 'Balls by definition are spheres, therefore curved,' Mike bellowed hearty laughter.

"What's happened?"

"Your man." A stoic reply in his accusatory tone.

"Maybe... you give me a little more than that?"

"Matt. He was your recommendation. Your friend, or whatever he is."

Not going over her head as much as they used to, Gift didn't care for the innuendo. *Fred with his tactics,* she thought. "What about him?"

"You need to do something with him."

As Fred led her toward the farm and through rows of crop beds, the levels of anxiety rose as on the lift to the Boardroom. One, two, three... When the purposeful ding sounded, what would she find as the doors split open?

As they rounded the corner of what Gift assumed by the latticed vines were tomato plants, she heard grunting—assumed to be the noises of human exertion doing what bots couldn't. As Matteo came into view, something was most definitely off. Lying flat on his belly, his feet kicked rapidly. With hands frantically digging centimeters before his face, the face of a madman, the angry grunts weren't born of hard work.

Kneeling beside him, Gift raised her voice instinctively. "Matteo. Matteo." He didn't respond or acknowledge her existence. "What's wrong with him?"

"He's on the drops."

"*What*? No. What do you mean?"

"Euphoric drops. Your boy here is deliriously high."

Lucidity came to the wild man on the ground. "Oh. Hey Gift."

"Ciao, sweetie. Whatcha doing?"

"We need this hole."

"Okay... Why?"

"Water. We need to find water. The crops. They're all dying. *Look.* Would you look at them. They're dying."

They looked healthy and had plenty of water, drawn from wells. In the senseless ramblings Gift could see, anyone could, her little brother wasn't in his right mind. Frightened thoughts said, *Could it be the drops?*

"It's the drops. You need to handle this." Fred parted, leaving Gift without a clue what to do.

"Come with me, sweetie. Please." When Gift touched his hand, it stopped digging and he twisted his neck to face her. Clouded eyes trembled. Matteo wasn't the man looking at her from behind them.

"No."

"Yes. You need to come with me."

He refused, returning to his digging.

To get him up required more strength than Gift could offer, so she called Tom to be Tom the Guard and subdue the poor fool flailing on the ground. Her sweet little Matteo. Deep concern for him outweighed the anger.

Tom administered a mild sedative formulated to counteract the side effects of Euphoric Drops. Lifting Matteo and tossing his arm over his shoulder, Tom led him to Pronto Soccorso as Gift alerted Sakura they were coming. Knowing how important Matteo was to Gift, Tom offered to stay. As hard as it was, they had to leave him, trusting the excellent care Sakura would surely give.

12

Freewill. Its enticement had the power to spark the flames of revolution. No doubt in Gift's mind, it contributed to the insurrection that ravaged New Europa. Freedom of choice seemed hard-coded into the human spirit, an indisputable right—when it's yours, Gift considered. With someone else's freewill the lines blurred; those rights got as murky as the waters of Colony Lake after a storm.

If someone you loved used their freewill in a way that damaged themselves, how much of it must you respect? At what point did it become acceptable or righteous to impede it, to stifle the rights of someone else for their own good? Gift wrestled those questions considering her little Matteo's choice to take that hateful substance, those *mal'd* drops. His freewill. What should she do?

What *could* she do?

An inescapable thing about days, they continued despite challenges or circumstance, even in the wake of monumental revelations or devastating discoveries. Days just kept going. Gift's day had more to offer, demanding her time and attention. If the day carried on, so must she. With the rovers green-lit for immediate deployment, the second part of her day would take her away from the colony. Away from Matteo, though not from her anxious worry for him.

Remote monitoring stations needed upgrades to keep up with the data they'd soon relay from the rovers, massively greater datasets than they were designed to handle. The upgrade crew Gift led included Mike and Tina. N.E. had no ground transport to carry them farther than Gift had ever been from home.

If necessity was the mother of invention, its father was the next project. A memory from Gift's apprentice days. The project to upgrade the remote monitoring stations with additional parts and an improved OS created a necessity. Union of mother and father produced the invention needed to move equipment and people greater distances over outdoor terrain. Mike had the brilliant idea to convert an electric cart into an external transport.

With approval of the Board, two such dismantled carts progressed into proof of concept turned prototype turned production transport. Parts from one cart were stripped and reclaimed for the other. The rubber wheels perfect for in-colony carts, squeaky as they were, couldn't handle exterior terrain. *Don't invent the same thing twice.* Another principle of engineering Gift put to good use. With adjustments to the axles and wheel mounts to support greater weight, the wheels designed for the rovers were perfectly suited for the new ground transports.

Recalling how the vehicle struggled when asked to pull the weight of five people, Gift suggested using all four motors from the two carts to give it sufficient torque to pull three people with a full stock of supplies. A second battery would reduce space and add weight, so solar panels were affixed to the cart's roof, something never conceived for internal-use people movers. Mike insisted it be painted and happily took the job. Nothing glorious to look upon, it was functional, and the engineers found that most satisfying.

***

They set off on an adventure with Tina at the controls. Another lost expression, Mike called Gift's seat beside the driver, 'riding shotgun.' He sat behind Gift beside a modified storage crate in the space where half the rear bench had been cut away. The hum of hard rubber tires with the clacking of pebbles and twigs thrashing against the wheel wells made the soundtrack of the day until Mike unveiled another of his modifications.

The sudden smash of bass jumped Gift out of her skin and the vibration of the subwoofer tickled her back. *Tom Sawyer* blared as the first of many songs, one Mike knew Gift somewhat liked. The two lent their voices to the singer's as loud as they could in jovial accord. Arms raised and hands in fists, Gift shouted out her favorite line: "He knows changes aren't permanent... But change *is*." Merrily they rolled as the transport disappeared into the forest with its fresh coat of a mess of splotches in varying shades of green Mike called 'camouflage.'

Halfway through U2's *Beautiful Day*, which only Gift seemed to be enjoying, the blue dot met the red one on the nav screen. At 13:06, they had reached their first target as the abrupt stop thrust Gift forward. The sound of Mike's hand slapping the back of her seat popped in her ears.

"Smooth." Mike's tone was playfully sarcastic.

"We're here aren't we?"

In a gentle tone not to anger her large friend, Gift suggested, "Maybe... next time you could *ease* into the stop."

"Whatever. Can we just get started on this upgrade?"

Mike climbed out first. "Where is the stupid thing? All I see is bushes and trees."

Gift lent her eyes to the search. "Bushes and trees make sense, we're sorta in a forest."

After a mock chuckle, Mike said, "It's gotta be here," then announced he'd found a machete.

"Did someone say machete? I'll take that, Mikey."

The small monitor station hid behind a bush. Twigs and branches flew as Tina hacked away. Mike ducked something on course for his head and Tina ignored his complaint with gleeful grunts. A heavy thud of the blade as it struck metal reverberated like waves in the air swirling around them. An unimpressive small gray box stood naked, the branches and leaves stripped away.

"Smaller than I thought it'd be." Again, Mike pointed out the obvious.

"*Right*? I mean, it has so much inside, and batteries."

"C'mon, Mikey. Get to swapping out parts. Only reason you're along for the ride, so make yourself useful, eh?"

The Remote Monitoring Station, a fifty-centimeter-square polymer box, held onto a pole reaching toward the sky. Climbing eyes found its end above the tree line with a solar panel mounted on an angle. With three new sensors installed and a realignment of the crystal chips, the unit was ready for Gift and the new software package on her handheld. Connected to the control module's near-fi data port, a few swipes followed by behavioral biometric authentication started the OS installation.

"Hey Mikey, fetch my water bottle for me. Might as well do something while you're doing nothing."

A hard toss of the bottle conveyed his noticeable frustration.

"One down," Gift said pridefully, then remembered to verify its online status. "Let's keep moving, we're on a nine-hour limit for you guys, and we've got five more units."

Standing outside the transport, Tina objected. "Um... Aren't we forgetting something?"

"Don't think so. I tested it... Cover's back on."

"And it's nearly fourteen hundred... *Lunch*?"

After they consumed legume-based salads with protein crumbles, the second and third units went smoothly. The third being under heavy brush took Tina a while longer to clear. In short order they had half their units upgraded and online. No towering trees blocked their view of the solar panel at the fourth station. Gift saw the issue clear as day—an expression that made more sense since the airlock opened.

"Oh mamma. That's... not good."

First out of the transport, Mike said, "What're we looking at?"

"Damaged solar panel. No point upgrading it if we can't fix that." Deflated, Gift continued, "We can't skip it. It's a linked relay system. With one offline, the whole thing's dead, the project's scrapped."

"So, we fix it. You guys are engineers. Any bright ideas?"

Mike said, "Parts isn't the problem, we've got the parts for solar panel repair, expected we'd need them."

"So, what's the problem then, Mikey?"

"Getting up to it." Tilting his head summoned a whistle.

"So, we have a problem." Gift needed to take charge. "We have the parts to fix it. We just need a plan, a way to get up there. What are our options?"

Tina's eyes scaled the pole. "Climb."

"Right. Someone's gonna shimmy up the pole like a monkey? I don't suppose you're volunteering?"

"Shut it, Mikey. Got any better ideas?"

"Guys, please. Let's calmly look at the situation. We have no ladder or climbing equipment. How'd we take parts for these with no way to get up there? Anyway, we need to improvise. Think. What do we have? Mike, open that toolbox and tell me everything that's in there."

"Okay. We have the machete, clippers, and the power screwdriver. We have a small hammer, a hand shovel, rubber boots for some reason. There's some rope, couple wrenches, a tarp... Duct tape, of course, two rolls. Flares and a rain jacket. That's about it."

"So, let's think. Can we use any of that?"

"Not really." Tina's doubtful brow sapped Gift's hope.

Looking over the inventory, Mike said, "Maybe we could use the rope to fashion makeshift climbing gear. The rubber boots could be good for friction. I think so. Yeah, I think we can do something."

"Bravo, Mike."

"Yeah, well done, Mikey. But who's going up there?"

After a minute of silence, Gift said, "Me. I'm going up. My team, my job. Now how do we make climbing gear?"

The rubber boots being much too large for her feet, Mike wrapped the duct tape around the tops. He took the rope and formed a long piece into two loops he fitted on Gift's upper thighs then took the loose end to wrap around her waist, joining the harnesses to it for a secure hold. A knot made a loop in front, and he left the free end hanging. "There." He wore his *proud of himself* face.

When Gift stepped up to the pole, Mike gently nudged her forward until her nose nearly touched it. He took the rope and wrapped it once around the pole and pulled the end through the loop below Gift's navel, then once again through the same loop. A firm tug on the loose end pulled Gift into the pole, banging her nose on the hard metal. She checked it for damage—mild pain but not broken. She didn't think so, anyway.

"Sorry... Now lean back. Let your weight go." When she did, he pushed her farther back then pulled up and down on the rope. It resisted movement. "Perfect. That should work."

"Mike..." Gift's voice developed a nasal twang. "Sorry. What should work? I'm tied to the bottom of the pole."

"Right, I'll show you how to do it... So, here's how this works. Quickly lean in and flick the rope a little higher." When she did the rope fell limp. "No, be quick. Lean in and at the same time, flick the rope up a few centimeters, then quickly lean back."

"I think I get it."

"I don't like this. What if she falls? She's gonna fall."

Gift eyed Tina. "Let me try it. If it doesn't work, we'll have to come back. But that'll put us behind schedule, and we'll have to stop the rovers."

Lean in, flick up, lean back. The rope rose a few centimeters and held. Her feet were still on the ground. Setting the rope higher, Gift squeezed her feet tight on the sides of the pole and pushed upward. She rose a mere two centimeters, give or take. Hanging from the pole for the first time, feet off the ground, she tried again. The pain in her coccyx was sharp. Determined, her second try didn't bring her to her bum, but failed miserably. The rope loosened its slack and fell around the pole and Mike bent to reach for it.

"Stop." Tina's order had no authority other than her commanding voice. "You're gonna fall. And... if you somehow get *any* height, you'll fall and kill yourself. This isn't working. Don't make me drag your dead body all the way back to the colony."

"It'll work. She—" Mike stopped himself.

"No, it's not working. Gift, stop. This is crazy."

"A few more tries. I think I'm getting the hang of it."

"*Wait.* Just wait... What's this?"

13

The brain of an engineer didn't like to not be engineering. At least that was how Gift's brain worked. It yearned to design, build, and create. Two engineer brains amplified that exponentially. Mike had a solution to get Gift to the top—if only it worked. If only Gift could do it, had the upper body strength and balance to pull it off and make it work. She didn't. Good thing for her, she wouldn't need it.

"*Wait*. Just wait... What's this?" As Mike pushed the words out, pegs extended from the pole on both sides, alternately spaced to form ascension holds.

Shocked, Gift asked, "How? How'd you do that?"

"When I reached down for the rope, I saw this panel at the base, opened it, and found a lever... So, I pulled it."

"Twenty minutes ago would've been nice, Mikey."

"What stupid idiots, all of us. I mean, really. Help me get this contraption off. You could'a killed me with this thing."

"I wouldn't have let you climb if it wasn't working."

"Kidding sweetie. I know. And... I was all for it too. Like I said, stupid idiots, the three of us."

"Hey, I was against Mikey's dumb idea from the start."

"Only brain among us," Gift replied with a half-snort.

"Bout time you two realized it."

"Okay. Okay. So, it wasn't my *best* idea. But who found the secret lever? *Hmm*? That was also me."

"You're so cute Mike. We know, and we love you."

"Speak for yourself." Tina's tone brimmed with witty sarcasm.

It puzzled Gift when Mike removed the harness but kept the rope around her waist. "What's this for?"

"At the top, you'll need your hands. Wrap this around the pole and tie it."

"Good point. Thanks." As soon as Gift grabbed a peg, Tina's shout halted her ascent. "What's wrong now?"

"What, *exactly*, do you expect to do up there?"

"Check the solar array, remove the broken panels, and install new ones. Whatever needs doing to get it charging."

"*Right...?*" The word dragged itself into a question.

A puzzled glance at Mike got nothing from him. Like a smack to the forehead, Gift's mind caught up. "Mike, please get me the tools I need and three spare solar panels."

Placing everything in a satchel, he zipped it closed and adjusted the carrying strap. When he tilted his head to find the top of the pole, a quick whistle escaped his lips, pulling Gift's eyes upward. "Oh mamma. That's high."

"Fifteen meters, give or take."

"And you were about to climb up there with Mikey's death-trap in your crotch."

Undaunted, or pretending to be, Gift tossed the bag over her shoulder, its strap crossing her torso, ready for the climb. She pushed the first few pegs to the ground easily enough until an awareness of the height paused her ascent. At three meters up, trepidation vibrated through her bones. "It's a ladder, you got this," she said to encourage herself. *Raise the right hand, right leg. Left hand, left leg.* Fifteen meters. The top.

"Way to go Gift." A distant hollowness in Mike's voice was right beside her.

"Don't look down."

How Gift wished Tina hadn't said that. On the ground below, so distant, Tina's bulk lost its intimidation. "Shake it off Gift. Get this done." Her self-pep-talk worked.

Wrapping the rope while not letting go of the pegs with both hands took a few tries. Hesitation fought her leaning her weight back... she felt the rope hold. The screwdriver went to work removing the broken panels. Gingerly, Gift reached in, laying one beside the good ones in the bag. Broken glass on the panels made her movements slow, deliberate.

One damaged panel fumbled briefly when an edge caught the zipper. Her grip held until the prick of the shard entering her finger jerked her hand, releasing the panel. Its fall lingered, as if watching a vid at half-speed, while her finger found its way into her mouth. Watching in horror, Gift saw it crash on Mike's head, the blood visible even at her height. Then it wasn't. He had stepped out of its way. Faster than reality, her mind had visualized a fear that was thankfully unrealized.

Shaking it off, she attached the first and then the second good panel. The third. Rejoining the power cable to the array, she heard the satisfying click of the connection.

"See if it's charging now."

"We're good. Now climb down very carefully."

Happy to do as Mike suggested, descending proved more frightful than up had been. By the halfway point, the satchel full of tools and broken parts became too painful a weight for her shoulder to endure. To lift it over her head onto the other side meant her holding onto the pole with only one hand. When the strap slid off her clavicle, instinct reached her hand for it, unbalancing her at seven meters from the ground, slipping a foot from its peg. Deep and full of morbid fear, her scream roared as her body swung out from the pole, one hand trying to hold tighter than the white-knuckle grip it already had. One foot on a peg, the other dangling over nothing.

The clatter of the bag meeting the ground hit her ears *nearly* instantly, the delay stressing the still deadly height. Frantic words soared upward but Gift couldn't discern their meaning, only their fright. Stopping her outward swing, she tensed, becoming a flag extended from the pole. Deep breaths in, out, in, out. With one hand on the peg, her arm retracted, pulling her body to the pole. Gift's free hand and foot rejoined their holds. Pause, breathe. She descended very slowly.

"Sorry about almost splitting your head open with that panel. What was I thinking, climbing up there like that?"

"You always lead by doing. Makes you the best boss I've ever had."

"Mike... I'm the *only* boss you've ever had."

"Yeah. Guess that makes you the best... *and* worst."

Playfully, she slapped his stomach with the back of her hand. "You're funny. And a stupid jerk. Let's get going, got two more before we quit."

With the battery recharging, the team completed the upgrade, closed the panel, and loaded themselves back into the transport. Gift found a bandage and attached it to her bleeding fingertip. Off they went to the next one of the two remaining, hoping no other solar panel repairs would be needed. At Gift's request, Mike's tunes yielded to the motor's hum, rattle of the transport's metal chassis, creaking composite body, and the roar of the tires.

"Six hours out. We underestimated our timing. An hour for these, and nearly two hours to ride back, and that's pushing your nine. That solar panel killed our timing, now we gotta move fast to get you both back as close to the nine hours as possible."

"I can go longer, stretch it to ten. Maybe not little Mikey here."

"No, you've seen how sick people get. Nine's our limit."

Finding the fifth unit in an open field meant not having to hack their way to it. Small favors. They drove on, Gift asking Tina to push the speed to the full limit of the transport's electric motors. Smooth enough through the fields, it got rough as they entered a wooded stretch with more uneven ground below the cart. Generously outfitted with dips, fallen branches, and rocks, the trail was easily managed by the new wheels. The seats, however, had not been upgraded, and their backsides absorbed the full force of that neglected detail.

Mike leaned forward as the rumbling vehicle tossed its passengers up and down, its effects more noticeable on the women. His grinning face between them and the goofy way he said 'bouncy' annoyed Gift, but for some reason, Tina laughed. Gift palmed his forehead to push it away.

Full stop, they had arrived at the last of their six remote monitors for the day. The woodlands had cleared to a rock outcropping where they found their last unit mounted to a much shorter pole rising from the solid mass. Of course, its solar panels were fine, and Gift realized she had climbed one of the two highest poles they had seen. That figured.

As twilight settled over them, blanketing the landscape in shades of gray and blue, Gift knew they'd been out too long. "Tina. Fast as possible."

"Sounds like fun. Mikey, hang on and enjoy the bounce." Thunderous laughter roiled over her words. Happy they shared it; Gift could never quite get the connection Tina and Mike had in humor.

14 | Day Three

Until recently, Gift and fifty thousand plus residents of New Europa considered their planet lost. A world was more than a planet, even though the words were used interchangeably. Planet Earth, with truly remarkable restorative capabilities, was healing itself. What had caused its near ruination?

The world.

A world that once included the planet along with its dominant inhabitants and their social, governmental, and economic systems, their greed and selfishness, idealistic pride, nationalism, and racism—which ranged from where someone called home to full-blown xenophobia. Some people viewed their little slice of the world as the greatest for nothing more than having been born there. As a child, Gift saw the hubris in it as she read her history assignments.

Such ill-conceived ideologies littered the pages of her lesson material. Nearly every nation of Earth's past, no, *the world's* past, suffered a similar plague. Could the same be true of their new world? When acts of sabotage devastated their colony, why were people quick to assume blame on the New Republic of China?

With speculative rumor about the Russian Federation replaced by the presence of actual Russians, were N.E. colonists bound to repeat the mistakes of their ancestors? Gift saw it—friends, neighbors, and colleagues, speaking negatively about a people they hardly knew. And too often some-one suggested the superiority of New Europa. Conclusion reached in Gift's mind: humans may have changed chemically, genetically, and circumstantially, but they were very much the same.

These musings found their base in the latest rumor—someone sabotaged the rover. Quick to believe it, Gift may have been one of those who started it. Her first guess, her entire team's first guess, was the Russian Federation—easier to blame someone else. Could a form of colonial patriotism rear its ugly head? After everything that happened in their own colony, by the hands of their own people, why did it have to be the outsiders? With so much at stake in the fledgling alliance, Gift knew speculative rumor and prejudiced inclinations risked its destruction.

After three days, the upgrade team had thirty-two remote monitoring stations done. That these were performing beautifully was not the magical part, not the volatile bit of the plan. An alliance can survive failed equipment and faulty data. The remarkable part was in how Nailya Usanova and Norman Peeters worked together brilliantly on the data with support from Red—she's called Melody—on the app she created and tweaked daily to give them the exact data they needed in any format they desired.

Nailya's entire team at the Russian Federation collaborated with the Environmental Recovery Team in New Europa on those datasets. An unprecedented and vital partnership had begun. Had Gift or one of her team acted on presumption, the whole project could have fallen to pieces. A sad outcome to ponder, not for the alliance, but for the future of humankind. Gift had been wise to be cautious.

***

Soon the prerecorded weekly update and main newsfeed would begin. If something was important, Aimée covered it here. In the ground-level meeting room of the admin building, Gift sat with Tom, Mike, Tina, Raff, and Hans Fuchs. Marco said he would try to join them. Using her pull on the Board, Raff reserved the room each Wednesday to watch *N.E. This Week with Aimée Toussaint.*

"Any guess on the main topic?" Mike asked excitedly.

"You know we can't *guess*, right?"

"Hans means we already know," Raff clarified. "The Board approves the topics and one of its committees oversees it from concept to broadcast."

"Not everyone here's in Union with you. I like to be surprised."

"What he means is, he likes to wager on it."

Tom caught Gift's meaning. "Wager? As in gambling?"

"Relax yourself, Mister Guard. I use the *What's Your Wager* app. It's on the up-and-up."

Tina chimed in, "I bet on new water restrictions. Back to two showers, sure enough."

"Well, that app hasn't been stopped. Not yet." Tom looked to Gift. "Is the Board concerned about this?"

"Way more important things to worry about. I mean, I don't like it. I wish you'd stop it, guys, really. But with the environment, the new regulations for outdoors, the R.F. and U.A.? I don't think anyone's worried about that stupid gambling app."

Raff said, "Not yet. One of the issues we have, which will be discussed tonight, is stopping the manufacturing and use of those euphoric drops. That's a real problem."

"*Yes.*" Evidently Mike had odds on that topic.

"That poison almost killed Matteo. He's still in Pronto Soccorso."

"Cara... I'm so sorry."

"Yeah, me too. I like the kid," Tina said softly.

"Thanks... Now shut up, everyone." Gift barked the order to keep her tears at bay.

The updated New Europa logo had the red planet replaced with a circular graphic of blue and green in vague patterns—they had limited cartographic data on the lineation of ocean and land. The same circular pattern of stars held over from the former European Union outlined it. As it swirled on the screen, the opening jingle played.

Refusing proposals for a studio desk, Aimée opted for a director's chair, supposedly so she could have the same set in the studio or on location. Knowing her, Gift figured Aimée just wanted to be different—something Gift loved about her lifelong friend. The logo dissolved into Aimée sitting crossed-legged, always showing off her long, toned shanks. Likely the bigger reason she didn't want to hide behind a desk. A new emerald-green dress Gift hadn't seen looked to have grown over Aimée's flesh to become part of her. Longer than her usual, its high slit showed her thigh, which Aimée doubtless loved.

"Good evening. As always, it's nice to see me. Maybe... even *nicer* today." Standing from her tall chair, she bent her arms at the elbow, angling her hands away from her hips. Her pose to say, *look at me*—been doing that since she was five. "A gift from my friend Nadezhda Anoykina. After our lakeside chat, she said I had to have it, and sent her personal tailor here from the R.F. to fit me for it. My first bespoke outfit. The guy happily took his sweet time meticulously measuring every millimeter of my body... *twice*. Then he told me I could've kept my clothes on." Aimée's infectious laughing induced chuckles all around.

"*Lucky.*"

"Only in your dreams, eh Mikey?"

"Obviously, she's joking," Gift said, not a hundred percent sure.

Sitting back on the tall director's chair, Aimée crossed her legs at the knee. "Our top story, well, top two stories and one sub item, are about the

R.F. Of course, you've guessed I'm not starting with top stories. I know, *such a tease.* Let's start with a subject that has become of more pressing need."

A camera change showed her profile. Turning her head slowly she covered herself in a serious look.

"We need to talk about Euphoric Drops. Harmless fun? Some think so. Have I ever taken them? Well... a reporter must be thorough." Her wink came across with joyous abandon. "No. Seriously. We need to get serious about this. I want to show you the effects of these drops. The euphoria fleeting. Addiction, side effects, *horrifying.* I warn you the following interview may be disturbing."

A transition to the entrance to Pronto Soccorso faded into Aimée sitting on the edge of a patient's bed. Distant eyes lifelessly rolled upward, their lids splitting his irises. A line of drool traced from his lip to his chin. Taking a tissue, Aimée wiped his face, held his hand, and said in a soft voice, "Hi, sweetie, it's Aimée."

The name Matteo Leitner scrolled across the bottom of the screen as he barely said, "Hey." Twenty-three-year-old cultivation worker, the text added before it ran off the screen like it was embarrassed to be there.

"How are you feeling?"

"Kay."

"I understand you've been here for three days. I'm told your condition is improving. You got your appetite back."

"Yeah. Eating... a lot."

"That's good. If you can... I have a few questions." He nodded. "Thank you. Do you remember the first time you took the drops?"

"Yeah. After... got nine," he stammered.

"So, after they classified you level nine. And why, Matt? Why did you take them that first time?"

"To stay out longer. They said..."

The interview continued two more agonizing minutes before it switched to Sakura with Aimée asking pointed questions on the real effects and dangers of the drops. Then came the question the committee agreed should be the final thought on the matter to make the point clear.

"Sakura, do the drops allow people to stay outdoors any longer than someone could if not taking them?"

"No... If anything, the opposite. Matteo is not a unique case. He has been reduced from level nine to eight after a few days on the drops. Now he cannot go anywhere or do anything. Three days in urgent care and at least two more before he can go home. *No.* Drops *do not* allow you to stay outside any longer than you can without them."

"That's it right there. Thank you, Sakura."

A recorded message from Miss Heller played, imploring everyone not to take Euphoric Drops and encouraging anyone on them to talk to a friend and get help.

Logo swirl and back to Aimée in her tall chair. "Now, for the latest on our friends at the Russian Federation. We have excellent news on the new Environmental Recovery Team, the coalition of scientists and technicians from N.E. and the R.F. But first..."

She paused for a camera change to show her profile. Aimée placed her hand on the low arm of the chair, bent at the elbow and leaned forward as she twisted her torso to face the camera, crossing her legs at the knee—her *this is about to get serious* pose.

"Troubles persist with the earth-dwellers. The R.F. call them Philistines. Yesterday saw a second attack, invasion, strike, whatever you call it, against its perimeter. I've seen security vids I was unable to obtain permission to show. Thanks to persistent efforts—meaning I didn't take no for an answer—I got permission to recount the events I witnessed."

Camera change, frontal view. Aimée sat back straight switching her leg crossing and with one hand on her top knee she intersected her wrists, leaning into the camera. The pose made her appear connected to her audience on the other side of a screen.

"Philistines. Curious name. I'm no history buff, *boring*. So, I did what any good reporter would do—had someone else check it out for me. Seems a Philistine is a person who is hostile or indifferent to culture. The R.F. believes these attacks are the manifestation of a tribe of descendants of those who either didn't qualify or didn't want to join the colonization project. Who are they? What have they been doing for over two centuries? What are their intentions? The answers will have to wait. All we know from the R.F. is they must have survived in old military bunkers... originally designed to survive nuclear war.

"Are they uncivilized savages? Perhaps. By standards *we set*, based on *our* lives. I wonder what they must think of us... I saw them approach the outer perimeter and take position by a guard tower on the wall as a small band tried tossing a rope with a large hook over the top. Seven, eight times they missed until the hook finally latched onto something. The first Philistine started climbing the wall."

"Oh mamma." Knowing the story, Gift felt the anticipation.

"Time failed the would-be invaders as R.F. guards lined up atop the wall some six meters high. Then blasts of rapid gunfire... Screams silenced... They were all dead." The screen slowly diminished into black.

"How horrible," Raff said, soaking her words in sadness.

Gift sighed. "Those poor people."

"What poor people? *They* attacked the R.F. Didn't you hear what she said?"

Tina's comment silenced the group then the broadcast resumed with a set change to an espresso bar in Citadome One. Each holding an espresso cup, Aimée sat at a table with Nailya Usanova and Norman Peeters. They sipped in unison then placed their coffees on the table. Aimée crossed her legs and had more of a discussion than an interview. Asking the right questions, she hit each of Gift's main talking points to promote the project. The goal was to build enthusiasm for working with the R.F. and Gift thought she nailed it.

Marco never showed.

"I got nothing, Mikey. You?"

"Yep. Won on the euphoric drops but lost on the main topic. Also won on how many times Aimée crossed her legs. Lucky guess, that. Up five rations, not bad. At least I didn't lose any."

"You *two*. I think she did great, as usual. And our new environmental team, that was very positive."

Raff took Gift by the hand. "Matteo's part was filmed day before yesterday, *vero*? How's he doing?"

"Better. Talks like normal, coherent I mean. Sakura said one more night, his body almost rid itself of the craving. She needs to be sure he won't relapse. Physically, he's fine though. Thanks."

Drawing a wide smile, Mike asked, "So, dinner? All of us? Been a while."

15

Controversy, public opinion, far-left, far-right. Humans have always managed to find—or create when none were found—dividing lines. The United States failed to live up to its name with its two civil wars. Near constant tribal warfare had plagued Africa's history. Repeated conflicts sprouted throughout the nations of Europe, even in its supposed union, which Gift reckoned was more a logistics compromise than unity. History and reality ran rampant in Gift's mind, colliding, fusing, morphing.

Did this preoccupation with controversy allow disease, hunger, economic collapse, and environmental degradation to run rampant for decades until nearly ninety percent of the population was gone? Now there were others, outsiders, a new foreign state to oppose and criticize, to elevate oneself above. Antithetical factions found in New Europa had led to insurrection, violence, and death. What would come next?

Aliens. A word to describe someone of another nation became more widely thought of as visitors from other worlds. Perhaps the world of yesterday had become too small, its nations so common, people needed a new basis for fear, speciesism, controversy. Is there life out there? Among the theories floated around the events of sabotage in the colony was an attack by aliens, the most likely being Martians rising from the depths of the planet humans thought themselves inhabiting. And, of course, there were those diametrically opposed to such foolishness. Like weeds in the farm,

Gift reckoned this thirst for divisiveness—conceivably rooted in a more elemental construct of human nature, pride—had endured and began to sprout.

"Aliens?" Gift shouted at her handheld with Raff's face in a frozen pose of shock looking back at her from its glass panel. The readouts on her display couldn't be right. More communication blackouts throughout the colony, rovers lost, presumed destroyed. The farm dome had sustained heavy damage. Casualties rose by the minute, the death-toll unimaginable. "Who are they and where'd they come from?"

"Cara, how can we defend the colony?"

Unhappily, Gift accepted that weight. "I'm going to the Banzai. I'm gonna knock these *mal'd* aliens back to wherever they came from."

"Get'em Gift."

On the bridge, Gift commanded her crew with Tina at the helm operating controls like those on the land transport. From a tactical display panel, Mike blasted *Cygnus X-1* through the bridge of their *Rocinante*, called the Banzai. A song about a spaceship, Gift allowed it though she had to bark orders over its deafening racket.

"Fire. Fire. Fire."

At the weapons console, Marco shouted, "Aye Captain," as he hammered a fist onto the red football-sized button. "Torpedoes away, Captain."

Staring into the darkness, Gift soaked herself in sweat. It had been months since she had such vivid dreams. Those of late had been pleasant reenactments of happy memories or scenes of her and Aimée floating over Colony Lake. In one, Aimée convinced her to join the float *au naturel*, as she put it, evoking a feeling as invigorating as it was horribly embarrassing.

After a wipe down of herself and her bed cushion, Gift imagined drifting gradually back to sleep. Reality defeated imagination so she recounted the scenes from earlier that same evening, the first dinner in months with the whole gang. Sakura joined for the first time since Charlie. It was bitter-sweet. While the widow showed remarkable strength, Gift often became an emotional wreck at the mention of his name or anecdotes where he featured prominently.

When Tina and Mike had drifted from the group's conversation, Gift tried to listen but missed the words. Mike outgrew the need to sit next to her, which blended a hint of sadness with pride for him. A couple times Tina chuckled, roaring in laughter once and capturing everyone's attention from the talk about how Miss Heller had been placing increasingly greater responsibility on Raff. At a table full of her friends, Gift felt isolated. "Okay you two. You can't have a laugh like that and not share it. What's so funny?"

"Yeah, we could use a good laugh." Months ago, Tom had officially joined the group.

"You won't think it's funny," Tina said, still laughing. "I don't understand why you lot don't get Mikey's humor. He's hilarious."

Raff frowned. "More juvenile humor then?"

"Isn't it always." Hans Fuchs was right.

With little cajoling Mike retold the joke responsible for the jovial giant's outburst. Laying in the dark, eyes wide-open, Gift tried to remember. Something about a couple at the lake. Try as she did, the punchline wouldn't come. Just as well, it was childish humor and not funny, she remembered that much. Everyone chuckled more from a sense of courtesy than humor. Tina laughed from her belly the second time more so than the first. That's what brought Gift to laughter, making it the better part of the new memory, no need to recall the rest.

There was some serious conversation as well, Mike and his questions. "How are the E.CID folks doing?"

"No more in comas, all responded to the new treatments. Those medical studies... were crucial to moving our research ahead." Sakura masterfully avoided mention of Gift's DNA in the explanation, unsure who knew and who did not. Although grateful for the consideration, having told Tina, everyone knew.

Stalks so high they blocked the sun confused her as Gift tried to make her way out of the farm. Entrapped in a maze, lost, panicking, Gift cried, "Matteo... *Matteo*." No reply—only the sounds of relentless silence consuming her. Helplessness overwhelmed her, drenching Gift in her body's hot moisture. Instinct moved her legs, faster, faster. She ran. Where didn't matter, she needed to run, escape had to be possible.

"*Matteo*." Standing beside him, Gift heard laughter. "How can you be laughing?" Empty drops packets were strewn about. "You're high again." Vomit spattered from his face, covering her coverall. She saw the irony in that. The removed garment unhid her swimsuit, she expected underwear. Matteo floated beside her—*no, he's drowning*. "Help. Somebody... *help*." Noiseless air surrounded them as his flailing arms went limp. The lake's surface, smooth as glass, swallowed him. Gift plunged, but not into water. The fall roused her.

Staring at the darkness, Gift had trouble differentiating the currents of her dreams from memories flooding her semiconscious mind.

With beady eyes, Mike looked up from his dinner. "Tom, you were one of our keepers, when you guys took our freedom. What do you guards do now? Found anyone else to harass?" The lingering taste of resentment in the words dried Gift's mouth. Mike couldn't understand how she wasn't angry with them, how she'd always been polite. Often, he reminded her how she thanked Tom that first day. Now he had to accept a guard in the group, more so in Gift's life.

"Funny." Tom blew it off as humor. "They reassigned some to outside access doors. New posts have been set up around the perimeter and by the lake, and we keep an eye out for any residual antipathy from the insurrection."

"I feel safer already."

"He works at the admin building." Gift recalled patting Tom's arm. "Since it's open to the public... we have guards there all day."

Hans Fuchs said, "It's great things are more open now. The anonymity the Board had mostly worked, but I can't help thinking it also contributed to the conspiracy theories and distrust. What we have now is much better. I hear lots of words of appreciation toward Raff and Gift. People love having them on the Board."

"I feel better with them there." The hearty pat of Tina's paw on Mike's back popped. "Don't you, Mikey?"

"Yeah, it is. I trust *you two*. And I know both of you have the good of the colony foremost, especially you, Gift. More than anyone I've ever met."

"Wow. That's so sweet."

Something happened after that. What was...

Laying in the blue grass for Sakura's outdoors test, moonlight striking the meadow unhid the strangers surrounding her. When Gift noticed her nakedness, blades of grass tickling her skin left her shame in the soil below.

"Raff," Tina spoke... from a memory. "You've been in Union now, what, two months?"

"Just about."

"You all know about Max, even you I guess, Tom." He nodded. Tom knew the basics, though Gift omitted the bit about Max's confounding effect on her. "So, I messed that up, first relationship and all."

"Cara, you ended it. You did well."

"I guess. Should've clocked him sooner. So... I'm not going to be all private... I thought we could go for a coffee. I've asked this guy, Anderson, to meet us after dinner."

"Here we go again."

"*Mike*. She's asking for our help this time." Gift's words settled him.

"Yep. Not sure why, but I want you all to meet him."

"We'll be happy to."

"Thanks, Raff. I especially want your advice. You're the most mature friend I have, and you and Hans, you seem great together."

"We are." Hans Fuchs smiled and nodded agreement. He looked at Raff with such affection, it made Gift happy for them, although jealous for Raff's time and attention. Their roles on the Board putting them together helped offset the deficiency.

Leaving the dinner table, Gift noticed how quiet Sakura had become. She could hardly imagine the impact on her, discussing a new Union and budding romance when she lost her dear Charlie. "If you rather not go for coffee, meet this guy, we understand."

"Really, we do," Raff affirmed.

"It is fine. I am fine. I would like to meet him, be part of Tina's support. You know I wanted to be more involved with you all, before. And now I am happy to be part of the group. Happy you want me, not just tagging along as someone's partner."

"You were never a tag-along." A reassuring hug accompanied Gift's words.

Anderson seemed kind and funny. But how much could be judged over an espresso? Gift thought it best to leave the advice to those better able to offer it, certain it wasn't her. Happy to help Tina with her special request, Gift thought, *What's the harm in a little background checking on the guy?*

Deep sleep finally claimed dominance over Gift's memories.

16 | Day Four

To clear her schedule for an hour at lunchtime was a minor miracle and major hassle, but Gift had done it. She needed to take Matteo home from Pronto Soccorso. *Okay, so his mom will be there too.* As much as she would have preferred to do it without her, Gift couldn't fault the woman for it. She couldn't imagine her mother not being there if she were in Matteo's place. Neither his primary medic for addiction withdrawal nor on his medical team, Sakura looked after him and Gift was grateful.

Memories swept like a fog through Gift's mind. She had her fingers treated here and endured a horrific interview for Early Chemical Imbalance Disorder. Yet all she pictured standing in Sakura's office was Charlie looking at her from behind the desk when he answered a vidChat in a fleeting moment when he was a dishonest man whose Union was a sham. Before he was *Charlie* again. Before he died. *How does Sakura go on?* she wondered.

"Hello Gift." Sakura sat behind her desk and motioned to the seat. Gift sat unbothered by them being in the same places they assumed for that interrogation. At least that's what she tried to tell herself. It wasn't true. "I wanted to thank you again for last night."

"Thank me? For what?"

"Including me."

"No need. You're one of us. We were all so happy you joined. *Ma...* may I ask? Was it... difficult? I mean, for you to be there... without—" She couldn't say it.

"A little, yes. But it was more... nice. I see my parents often, some of my old friends, of course. But I really fell in love with you, all of you."

"I miss him," she said to his widow. *Stupid idiot, Gift.*

"Me too. You know... something you said, a few months back. I told you I would cherish it, and I think of it often."

"Something *I said*? I'm usually a mess with words."

"The work we do, you and I, you said it was his legacy. It is how we honor him. Keep him with us."

"A beautiful thought." Gift heard the words for the first time.

"Your words. Yes, beautiful... and I recall them often."

Thoughts unable to keep pace, Gift's mouth ran on its own. "Sometimes, I mean, when I think of... him, I just cry and become a mess. And, and other times, more now than at first... I smile. Is that weird?"

"Weird? No, that is lovely. Why would that be weird?"

"I mean... am I doing it wrong, or something?"

"Doing what wrong?"

"Thinking of him. I don't know... grieving. Shouldn't it still hurt? I mean, all the time? I feel guilty when I smile. Like I should be sad... and... and I'm not. Not all the time, but sometimes."

Leaning over her desk, Sakura stretched open palms toward Gift, taking her hands in them. The warmth, not from human flesh, brought a comfort Gift wanted to crawl inside of and stay in forever.

"You are doing it exactly right. We all grieve differently. But that you can have a memory or thought of Charlie and smile? That means you loved him, and you remember him for that, for who he was, for how he made you feel. That is more his legacy. That is how we keep him with us. Never feel bad about that."

Sniffles came with eyes turned red from trying to push out tears Gift was fighting to contain. A shared weeping was shrouded in grief yet full of joy—the joyous memory of Charlie shared between two people who loved him dearly.

"Let me take you to Matteo. My display says he has been discharged and is ready to go home."

***

The walk to Matteo's Box heard his mom nagging him to come to her home. 'Your father and I can take care of you,' she said at least three times. Much of what the woman said was on repeat loop. Gift could see frustration building in Matteo's eyes and marveled at how mothers can reset the years, reverting you into a child, submissive and dependent. Lots of '*Yes ma'am*'s were tossed her way but no action with it. They arrived at his Box.

Inside, more lectures came regarding drops and every poor choice he ever made. Mixed in were the, '*you can always come to us,*' and, '*we're here for you,*' loops. It felt like hours before he convinced her he needed to rest. Finally, Gift was alone with Matteo—*she was alone with Matteo*. She had no idea what to say or do once Marie left. Not that Gift would ever call her Marie. Matteo only said it when talking about her, never in her presence.

Was a hard stance the right one? Should a friend come down hard on the dangers of drops and how he'd better never touch them again? Or should a friend be supportive, sympathetic? Gift hated the word association, more the word within a word. Those often drove her crazy. *Why was most of the word sympathetic the word pathetic? Its meaning related to pity, but people often misused it. Why must stupid humans use it as an insult? If someone is pathetic, they deserve sympathy*, she concluded.

Sitting beside him, Gift chose supportive. "Sweetie, tell me, honestly, how are you?"

"I'm fine, really. Better now Marie's gone."

"She's just worried for you."

"I know. And I hate it that I did this to her." The sadness emoted in his lowered head pulled Gift's arm around him.

"Don't think like that. I mean, yeah, don't ever do this again. Maybe think about how you scared us all. *Ma*, no. What I mean... Right now, you need to focus on you and why you started on those *mal'd* drops."

"*Gift*. Language."

"Well, they are. They're crap, look how sick you got. I was so worried for you, you stupid little brat." A tearful hug followed a playful slap on the chest.

"Don't worry, I won't ever do it again."

"We'll make sure of that, be checking on you often."

"I don't think that's necessary."

"It is for me."

"Fair enough."

***

Not just another boring dinner, this one would be special. The long over-due honors were to be given to Aimée. Like a curtain about to unleash a magical performance, the lift doors pulled apart to the Boardroom. Gift pushed through and dashed to the honey where she found Raff in a stunning new dress. Aimée's suggestion to blow off the dinner and hit *La Musica* might have been tempting if Gift weren't, well, Gift. She feared Aimée saw her wink at Raff. Would her friend be more likely to leave if she knew, or stay for the attention? Gift settled on the latter. Aimée's speech was as expected—short, funny, and full of self-praise. So unalike, the two, yet the best of friends.

The cauliflower was delicious, its outer crunch encasing a surprisingly creamy interior. Gift always looked forward to what new delicacy would enthrall her tastebuds at each of these dinners. She had yet to be disappointed. They always had honey. Another good thing about the dinners—besides the delightful food—they were not long-drawn-out affairs. Aimée dragged Gift to the lift before the rush of departing guests overran it.

Pulling her away from the exit, Aimée led Gift by the arm. Laughter filled the corridor along with Gift's feigned protests—she knew where Aimée was leading her. Unwilling to join, never wanting to abuse her privileges—except she did when she showered after her three-day outing, but it was justified—she'd planned to wait for her jovial friend to shower and walk home together. It surprised Gift as much as Aimée when Gift entered the next shower booth, and the suds enveloped her in warm, foamy luxury. A wonderful indulgence she would not have taken if not for Aimée. It was also terrifying. Gift couldn't shake the dread of being caught, getting in trouble. Still, it was exhilarating.

17 | DAY FIVE

Being on the Board and multiple committees meant too many meetings. Gift failed to cancel even one. Try as she did to send a memo that covered a simple point and negated the need for an hour-long meeting, it would be another hour-long meeting. Work got done around what Gift deemed time wasters and she finished her day with engineering tasks... until Miss Heller called. A last-minute after-hours meeting brought a familiar yet unwelcome trepidation.

"Good, we are all here. Most of you had plenty of meetings and the last thing any of you wanted was another one at the end of the day. As you no doubt surmised, an issue of the utmost importance has presented itself. I apologize for the lack of an agenda, things are happening at too fast a pace, but we need everyone in this room to be at the same level of knowledge."

Everyone in this room? Gift wondered what they had in common. Raff, Boss, Sakura, Aimée, Tom, Nailya Usanova, a nameless man from the R.F. *What's this about?* rattled impatiently around the synapses of her mind.

"Rather than trying to repeat what I only just learned, I think it would be better to listen to our guest from the Russian Federation, the highly decorated commander of the Rosgvardiya. Mister Sergey Lazarev, please."

Miss Heller took a seat as the man stood in her place. They oriented the boardroom reception sofa chairs to face one direction. In the space

Miss Heller had occupied, he was a giant, so wide and impossibly tall. His gray-blond, crop-cut hair stood at attention.

"Thank you, Miss Heller. I too wish to thank you all for coming. This group is perhaps not a team or committee, so you likely wonder, why all of you? Let me explain the situation and then we can talk about your roles."

"His English is the best I've heard from anyone in the R.F.," Gift whispered. Aimée nodded in agreement.

"We are talking today about the Philistine problem. I think you call these... *people*, earth-dwellers. In time, of course, we all hope to be dwelling on Earth. Miss Nailya and the environmental recovery team will see to that, we are sure. So, what is this problem? More than you know. You know they have attacked our colony. Tried. The small force was no problem for us. Unlike this colony, Russian Federation has the big wall, all around. This makes an attack from them unlikely for success. Miss Aimée has seen the video. They were no match for our weapons, our guards. And from the top of the wall, is no problem stopping them."

"Sorry," Boss said. "We know this. These people are no real threat."

"Da, Mister Frank. From what you were told, and I just summarized for you, is true. This is what I am to explain. What we share today is that we learned much more about these Philistines. We do not know their exact location, but we found old maps showing military bunkers in Russia territory. From these, we identified ones to support them for first years when they had to be protected of the environment. No one was able to survive unless they were sealed. We now work to update these maps based on our land explorations. The locations of these bunkers are close to discovered. We will find them."

"That sounds promising. You made it seem so ominous. Sounds like you've got the situation in hand." Boss' words calmed Gift's anxiety, but Mister Lazarev had more.

"Problem is two-folded. First, the bunkers were heavily stocked with food and medical supplies that kept these people alive. They had weapons more powerful than they brought to attack. We believe they tested our response, and they are planning to full assault on us."

"Oh." Boss' crinkled his brow heightened Gift's fear.

"For this point number one, we are asking for help to New Europa. Help designing new weapons. Miss Nailya tells us you are right when you claimed technology advantage to offer our science teams. She is very impressed with your equipment, especially your new moving robots."

"Rovers. We call them E.R. Rovers."

Smiling at Gift, the burly man continued, "This is why you are here, my dear. You are head of engineer team that designed and built these rovers. We wish your help and anyone you need, Russian, or New Europian."

New Europian? Gift mouthed to Aimée. They had never called themselves that, but with other colonies in contact, a name could be useful, and that fit well enough.

"Is there a problem, Miss Gift?"

"Problem? Well... not sure. I mean, about weapons. I've never done that. I'm... not sure I'm... comfortable, with doing that."

"Nailya tells you are brilliant girl." *Girl?* she mouthed. "Miss Heller the same. We are sure you can do this. Is electronic engineering. You are an excellent engineer. This is why we have chosen you."

"No... I mean, thank you, I guess. But I'm not so keen on creating *weapons*."

Miss Heller said, "Gift, we'll talk about it. We may have no choice but to fight. For now, we need to move on and perhaps, when we hear the rest, it will become clearer."

"Thank you," Mister Lazarev said. "We need weapons for defense. If you are thinking to our history, we assure you, we intend no strike against these Philistines. This is why Miss Aimée is here. We wish to speak to these people. We hope to reach a peaceful outcome. Doctor Sakura, we hope to examine them, offer medical help. Maybe learn from them how to be living in the environment. We know little about them besides they survived outside of a colony, are having weapons, and attacked us several times."

"*Several* times?" Aimée was clearly agitated.

"This is for another time. We wish to talk to them but must be ready to defend. Our weapons are old, and our ammunition is not many. If they have the weapons we think, we need something to defend ourselves... and you."

The last thought brought Tom to his feet. "What do you mean us? We were told these people have no transports and we are too far to be concerned about them."

"Da. This is true from what we know. But if they are using all of bunkers? We think they may be moving one to another. While we are happy to be working together, the air transports maybe are what caused our problem.

"What problem?"

"From the ground, they maybe can see them. They must know we are going somewhere and may have assumed the general direction of another colony. If they are using multiple bunkers? From the last one to the west, they are days walking to here. Could be twelve or fourteen days."

"*What?*"

"Seriously?"

"This is why we need to cooperate. And New Europa has no wall, no outer defense. You will need defensive weapons more than us."

From a fiery face, Aimée said, "This is way more than you told me. I was assured I had the complete picture. I told our colony. Now this? We need to warn people."

"Wait a moment," Miss Heller cautioned. "Let's get all the details, discuss how to handle this. Then the Broadcast Committee will meet to determine how best to inform the colony."

Aimée didn't reply but put on a dissatisfied face.

"Miss Heller is smart woman. Causing panic does one thing only… causes panic. Makes difficult even to prepare, to do what must be done."

"Making weapons?" Gift asked rhetorically. "Sounds to me like we need to prepare for war. Do we have any idea how many… of these people?"

"No. We think hundreds but not likely more than a thousand."

"And you said they have advanced weapons. What kind of weapons?"

Lazarev straightened his crimson uniform jacket though it didn't need to be. "We think larger guns. Much ammunition for them. Bombs, rocket-propelled grenades. With these they can breach the wall. If they do, even with greater numbers, we cannot defend their weapons."

"How well-trained are your guards?" Tom asked.

"Very well. But not experienced in combat. We wish to know what you learned from your insurrection. How you fought a battle inside your colony. If they breach wall, we will be facing the same."

"Worse. Our rebels had tools, clubs, and fists."

"This is why we need new weapons. And this is why we asked your help, Miss Gift."

"I see." Though she didn't like it, Gift saw the logic.

On her mental display, she placed the new information and cross-referenced events of recent days. Was there a connection coming into focus? The potential closeness of the earth-dwellers, they may have had at least a general idea of where New Europa was located.

"The two minutes thirty-eight seconds," Gift blurted.

A collective, "What?" came from several voices.

"An interruption of our communication with the rover. We think… something scanned us. Could it be them? Oh mamma. It could be them."

"Milashka, what is this scan you say, this two minutes and those seconds?"

Gift eyed Nailya as if she had just appeared in the room, a ghost from a spooky vid. "When we lost the Sojourner. Only we didn't… lose it I mean. It was fine, still going, actually. Sorry. The issue was a comms blackout. We lost contact with the Sojourner for nearly three minutes. Other devices in the area blipped too, but only for a moment. It seemed like—Raff thinks so—maybe it was some kinda scan or something. At first, we thought…" Fortunately Gift had enough mental clarity not to say they suspected Nailya and the R.F.

"Thought what?" Lazarev asked.

Raff jumped in to save Gift's slip of tongue before it caused a fire. "That it was a misread. As Gift said, we'd never seen anything like it. So, we dismissed it as a fluke."

"What is fluke?"

"Another of our words, Nailya. Means a weird anomaly. Glitch in the network's matrix. Since it hasn't happened since, we… like Raff said, we dismissed it."

"And now the wheels turning as you say. Now you think to consider perhaps this was our Philistines?"

"Maybe. I… who else could it be? If they suspected a second colony—the project had at least five, right? Likely, that knowledge got passed down. These earth—I mean Philistines? They must know there are other colonies."

"And that scan could have been them trying to pinpoint our location?" Miss Heller reminded Gift she was there.

"Who knew about this?" Tom showed an intensely hard face to Gift. "Why didn't you tell me? Does anyone know about this?"

Gift's shrug said volumes. *I'm sorry I didn't tell you as Tom my special friend. I should have told Tom the Guard. The Board should have been informed; the guards alerted.* If the shrug hadn't conveyed it, the thoughts were there.

Again, Raff came to Gift's rescue. "We only made the connection now. Before, there was nothing to tell. As we said, a glitch. A one-off. If we reported every system alert or data stream blip, you'd have nothing to do all day but read our logs and reports."

Tom's blank look was less than convincing.

"We need to act on this, Margaret," Boss growled. "We cannot defend even an attack like the one reported by Aimée. And if these people possess more weapons, our colony will fall."

"Do you have any suggestions?"

"We need to outline objectives, how to reach them, and who best to do each."

Frank Bauer—Gift still called him Boss, and he seemed to like it—related the objectives, starting with the weapons. He indeed tasked Gift with leading a team of engineers to explore creating defensive weapons. While unhappy about that part, she saw the need. Once again, Gift found herself becoming something out of necessity she couldn't enjoy becoming. She was back in Charlie and Sakura's Box bugging the place.

Objective two would be the delegation to sue for peace with Aimée suggested to lead it. The majority agreed it should be Miss Heller in charge with Aimée taking point in the initial attempts at opening a dialog. With much insistence, Gift finagled getting herself on that team, but only after a claim that seeing the enemy would help her on objective one. She didn't see how, but they bought it. Tom the Guard would also go. Assuming a second delegation, Sakura and Nailya would meet the Philistines next. Mister Lazarev would assign one of his guards to join each group of envoys.

After they had laid out all their objectives, Gift raised her hand. "Going back... I mean, back to objective one? I think we need to fortify a security perimeter." She turned raised eyebrows to Raff. "You and Hans Fuchs can modify the software for the sensors in the remote monitors. And... we could even repurpose the last good roller droid. I mean, to sorta... patrol the border."

"Brava Gift. Yes, we'll need advance warning if they do make a move. Hans and I can work on that."

With a plan in place, objectives laid out, all was symmetrical and orderly, yet it didn't feel fine. In a place familiar yet distant, the dull pain became a hammer in Gift's head. She wanted the conflict and its dread to be far away, yet it drew ever closer until its steps snuck up from behind like Matteo's jump-scare.

<h1 style="text-align:center">18</h1>

History repeats itself. The notion seemed basic enough when Gift learned it from her tutor, Mister Josef. The more fundamental idea was 'people are people.' Change the circumstance, venue, era, or environment, and people were the same. Humans had been finding reasons to fight and kill each other throughout history and it was about to be repeated. 'No choice but to fight,' Miss Heller had said.

Gift couldn't help thinking they were too shortsighted. New people, a potential threat, and the first reaction was to make weapons, to fight. Satisfying an itch, that deep inner craving for savage outlet humankind had tried to bury in themselves for ages. If the threat were real—all indications suggested it was—then protecting themselves was the smart move. Their lives were threatened to a greater degree than the uprising of a few hundred disgruntled colony residents.

Difficulty bounced between Gift's thoughts as she lined them up on her mind's display. Multiple attacks against the R.F. by people with superior weapons—though not used. Did it cement the conclusion they posed a serious threat, and not only to the Russian colony? New Europa was a target of the group's hostility—based on speculations from the Russians and data from a scan on their systems they couldn't begin to identify or confirm.

Choiceless situations were nothing new to Gift. Officers of the colony had interrogated her repeatedly without just cause. She surrendered her dignity multiple times. Then Gift watched herself die in a narrow metal coffin beside an airlock. Not having choices made sense, the freedom she relinquished her own. To what would she subject her colony by putting weapons in the hands of an otherwise peaceful people. Would that be embracing their freedom... or removing it?

"Or is there a choice?" The workday had ended without them and left Gift and Raff in their shared office.

Scrunching her face, Raff asked, "What do you mean?"

"Miss Heller said, 'No choice but to fight,' right? I mean... *no choice*? What if... what if we *did* have a choice?"

"We are going to try to talk first. *Vero*?"

"Yeah. And that's the whole... that's why I even agreed to it. I mean, the weapons part. Still not crazy about doing that. *Ma*... I mean, I see the need. But do we know for certain these people mean us harm?"

"We should assume so. They attacked the R.F."

"I hate that I think this..., do we trust the R.F.?" Raff shrugged. "I guess... we carry on as we agreed. Primary focus on establishing a dialogue. We need to get Aimée to talk with them. I just—" A long pause stalled the thought. Gift thought her brain had more, its coming delayed.

"You just what?"

"I just... don't know."

Raff took her hand. "I know. The R.F. said they wanted to talk. What Aimée saw and reported was them shooting in response to an attack and the new weapons they want are for defense. That seems reasonable, no?"

"Yeah." Gift's reply didn't overflow with conviction. "If we do this? I mean... if I lead a team making weapons? We need something that won't kill these people. We know nothing about them. How they survived. What they want. We can't kill them just because we're projecting *our fears* on them."

"All the R.F. has are guns. Guns with bullets. Bullets kill. I remember something about a type of bullet from *before* they called less lethal."

"*Less* lethal? That's, oxymoronic. What does that even mean? How can something be *less* lethal? I mean, sounds to me like it's still lethal. Kills you, but not kill you *as much*? That makes no sense."

"We can't invent fictional weapons like laser guns with stun settings on that vidShow you watch. That's science-fiction. What do you have in mind?"

"I've got some ideas pulled up from the archive. We've only got stunners. Our guards, I mean, not us." Raff smiled; no clarification needed. "They're close-contact, short-range. The ones Tom has, I think it's less than three meters, or *up to* three meters. Anyway, short. What if we can make them go longer? Could work. Also too, I read of success with stunners using sound waves. Says here, 'sonic weapons can incapacitate both humans and robotics.' Something like that may work. I mean, we can't... *kill* anyone."

"Brava. If you're going to help make weapons, that's the way to go. I found something too: incapacitating agents. You might get Sakura to investigate this, could be an option. I'm sure we could easily make dispensers for a gas agent."

"Send that to me please."

As ideas flowed over her troubling thoughts, Gift's mood elevated marginally. If they could find humane ways to address the perceived threat, they could leave room for diplomacy after a defensive. A call to arms enacted in such a way made it a bearable option. A choice. If they had no choice but to fight, their choice was in *how* to fight.

Gift spent the evening in the shared office in the admin building. No actual work would start until tomorrow, but messages needed to be sent, research done, plans laid out. If Sakura, still busy on the earth sickness issue, could glance over the incapacitating agents Raff found, maybe she could start on a safe means of knocking people out. Gift filed that one slightly above wishful thinking.

She needed a team. Who'd be best to work on her ideas? Mike's engineering skill and love of music made him the top pick for sonic defenses. Love of music may have been a stretch in his qualifications. That Russian engineer would be a good second for him, show cooperation too. *What was his name?* Gift wondered as the smell of salame picante drifted in to tickle her nose. She hadn't noticed Raff leave until she returned with two pizzas. *Anton something?*

Between slices, they considered options. Raff agreed on Mike and Anton for sonic weapon research and offered to add Red to the team in case they needed a data operator. A logical assumption. Gift would lead the team on taser or stun gun enhancements. She preferred saying stun gun, it sounded more like something out of Banzai. But she also needed to be on that first diplomacy team—not that she was a diplomat by any means or stretched imagination—to protect Aimée, even if she had no clue how.

Tom politely declined to join Gift's stun gun team. His obligations were bound to the services of the diplomatic expedition and to protecting Aimée... and the others. Second to himself, he volunteered Sara as an expert on the tasers. A bit of a tech geek, too. Gift considered it an amazing idea.

As she planned to be on that delegation, Gift needed a talented engineer on the stun gun team. Like a slap to the face, it hit her, overlooked because of his senior transition to vocational tutor. If she learned all she knew from her trainer in her apprentice days, who would know more than Karl Fischer? A quick vidChat got his agreement to join the team, after a few minutes of catch-up chat with Gift, of course—it had been years.

Well into the evening, work hadn't finished. Miss Heller arranged an after-dinner group vidChat to plan the first diplomatic delegation. Assembled were Miss Heller, Aimée, Tom, and Gift. Lazarev hadn't yet assigned one of his guards to join the delegation.

"Sorry for the late hour. Thank you all for joining. I have received and read your update, Gift. Very thorough. Thank you for getting on it so quickly. We'll all sleep better once we have defenses in place. Now, on to the hopeful course of action, opening a peaceful dialogue with the Philistines. Our first delegation will be limited, and hopefully we add medical and sciences to a second one."

Gift raised her hand and waited for the nod. "Sorry, do you think, maybe, we could *not* call them Philistines?"

"It's the Russian's term for them. Some of us called them earth-dwellers. Do you prefer that?"

"Well, as we said, we all hope to be Earth dwellers one day. And I guess, we are. I mean the colony, it's here on Earth—Sorry. Maybe something that doesn't distance them so. We don't know these people and well... I mean, putting labels on them... it sorta alienates them. Makes them *not* us, not like us. I think... it's just, it doesn't help us trying to understand them, make friends with them. If possible."

"Hundred percent, Love. She's right. Does us no good to put them in a category. And I'm sure the Russians use the word Philistines in a derogatory way. We need to think of them as potential friends."

Gift's smile to Aimée's flattened face on the screen was wide and warm, overflowing with gratitude.

"Okay. So, what do we call them?"

Tom said, "All the terms I've heard are negative. From Philistines to outsiders to others, they all distance them. Come to think of it, 'earth-dwellers' is the only one that doesn't. But I don't like that either. To me, they're like settlers. Or... we could even think of them as pioneers."

"*Yeah*. I like pioneers," Gift enthusiastically agreed. "They are settlers on the frontier in what is now an undiscovered country. It has a positivity to it."

"Settled. That was not one of my bullet points for this meeting, but fine. It is good we have a more positive way to refer to them. Aimée, sweetheart, would you start using that in your broadcasts?" A nod. "So back on point. I would like to leave as soon as possible to reach out to these, Pioneers, and try to make contact."

"Miss Heller?" Gift asked politely, hating to interrupt. "We expect it'll take some time searching for them. And, well... besides me, none of you can stay out very long."

"True. Therefore, we are not leaving tomorrow."

"Oh, good."

"We leave the day after tomorrow."

"What?" Tom and Aimée said in unison.

"Let me explain. Tomorrow, Gift, you and Raff will work on trying every form of communication to reach them. If you are correct, and they did scan us, they possess working technology. If we can transmit a signal and get a response, we will save valuable time."

"I see... But one day for that, then we go out searching. Can we even get close in eight hours?"

"I can do twelve," Aimée boasted. "Or longer."

"That's not enough. We're gonna need days, not hours."

"There is something I haven't shared with the R.F. Of course, once we learn their guard assignment, we'll make them aware. Sakura has had a breakthrough in recent days. No one outside of her, one assistant, and the four of us knows, or can know. Not yet."

Gift's face soured. "We said no more secrets."

Aimée emphatically nodded.

"This is not like that. And it's not a cure, not even close. Sakura is confident her new treatment can prepare us to withstand four or even five days outside. We don't need people knowing this until we have something that benefits everyone."

"Wait." Tom rarely questioned authority. "Is it safe?"

"Sakura feels confident. Gift, your three days, the data she collected, was a tremendous aid. Aimée and Erikka's bloodwork also helped. She was close before and now has made tremendous progress. We'll have three treatments tomorrow and bring three injections each for each day we are out. I'm told three days would be best, but we should be able to push to five, even six if we must."

"Should?" Aimée questioned.

"And…?" Gift paused but Heller didn't reply. "What are the side effects?"

"Should be minor. Relatively."

"Now you sound like a bureaucrat." Gift knew Aimée didn't mean that as a compliment.

"I'm taking it as well. It's the only way we do this, and it must be done. I trust Sakura. Gift, I'm sure you do too."

"Yeah, but *she* doesn't need it." Tom had a point.

"I'm saying we all trust her. Please report to her office at O-nine hundred tomorrow for your first treatments."

"And then? Just a normal workday? I think we need to prepare. What will I say? How will we open the dialogue? What are our objectives? What will I wear?"

"You truly were an excellent choice." Gift inferred Miss Heller meant more than Aimée's role on this delegation, but her position as Public Relations Director. "That's what our day will be tomorrow, my dear. And Tom? We hope to have our Russian by morning. You two will coordinate the security detail. You will be given a drone to configure and prepare for the journey as well as maps and the possible locations of the closest bunker. I believe that data to be an approximation at best. You will be our driver as well."

Gift saw a problem in the plan. "Even if we take out the storage box, our transport won't do so well with five. And we won't have room for any of our gear."

"Leave that to our friends at the R.F."

19

Outsiders. Earth-dwellers. Foreigners. If this plan went sideways, 'enemy' would be a fitting word to describe their new neighbors. Gift hoped the designation 'Pioneers' would become a word to accurately describe who they found.

To get an early start, she and Aimée cut their swim, more of a float, short. With Aimée, Gift always cut it short—get her out of the water and dressed before others made their way lakeside. The day had to start early, so Gift hastily swallowed a muffin and sipped an espresso. She needed to split her time between starting the stun gun project and searching the communications arrays with trying to get a message to the Pioneers. Since Raff could handle the messaging, she left Gift free to be the engineer she loved being.

"Ciao, Sara. Buongiorno."

Much had changed since they were Guard and Subject. A friendship sprouted thanks to Gift's persistent efforts to check on her condition. Sara's burns had completely healed. The only trace of the swollen blistery mess her face had been hid shyly in the less-than-a-centimeter scar at the hairline when she pulled it tight back into a bun. She didn't do that often any longer, and Gift found her so much prettier with her hair down.

"Hi. How cool we get to work together."

"Yeah. But I'll be dividing my time. Also too, be going out for a few days starting tomorrow."

"If you're not here, I won't be able to do much. I can help, sure, tinker. But I'm no engineer."

"Got it covered."

In came Professor Karl Fischer. Working from a small bench in the lower level of the admin building to keep the project under wraps, they had little elbowroom. The stately gentleman's presence filled the room in more ways than one as Gift's respect for her former trainer occupied the entirety of the space.

"Gift, lovely to see you. How's my favorite apprentice?"

The hug from the slim man barely taller than Gift was warm and lovely.

"Buongiorno, Mister Karl. Great to see you. This is Sara."

"Pleased to meet you, sir."

"Pleasure, Sara. But please, young ladies, call me Karl. We are teammates, no longer teacher and pupil. Come to think of it, I guess I am working for you now."

"Let's just say we are working together." Gift hated to correct him, but the idea of being his boss was as bad a fit for her as Matteo's t-shirt had been.

Pleasantries done, Gift shared her preliminary research and straight away Sara and Karl agreed they needed a new model for perimeter defense. The existing ones relied on coiled wires connecting the handgun to the projectile providing electric shock. Sara proposed a self-contained projectile that could deliver enough shock to immobilize a target and free the gun for the next round. Karl expressed his approval of the idea and thought it possible, and Gift was beyond pleased at the project's start.

"Ciao, Sakura." Gift opened a vidChat to see if she had time to begin the research into a chemical agent to be weaponized into a defensive option for the colony.

"Hi Gift. I hear you are getting ready for a trip?"

"Yes. And will my travel companions be ready for it?"

"Looks good, yes."

"And what about that data I sent over? Will you have any time to look into that? We want to consider all options for defending the colony. I mean, we hope not to need it. But maybe..."

"Understood. However, I must focus on preparing the treatments for your team. The two more I will give them today and more to take with them. Another medic will look over the data and isolate possible agents or compounds, and tomorrow we will work on it together."

"Perfect. Thanks so much."

***

As suspected, Raff had communications well in hand. They worked together through lunch anyway. Raff had sent open broadcast messages on every known channel and frequency and got static in return. A data capture ran over every network node, searching for traces of communications blips they assumed to be a foreign scan. It had not occurred again since that day with the Sojourner. Making herself useful to the endeavor, Gift shared a notion.

"The Pioneers were in a bunker or something, right?"

"Um, *pioneers*?"

"What we decided to call them. Aimée will use it from now on. The other names were too... negative. We need to look at these people optimistically."

"*Infatti*. Well done."

"Yeah, what I mean, we all have two-hundred-year-old stuff, right? But *we* planned for growth, I mean, technically. Not that we *technically planned* it, I mean, we planned for the technology to grow." Raff's smirk said she needed no clarification. Gift's excitement for her idea rambled her words. "We had teachers, engineers, and such. And we've upgraded most of our stuff over the decades. *Ma*, the Pioneers? I doubt they had engineers, maybe not the tools. They must be using tech from before the project."

As if Raff's eyes glowed a deeper shade of green, she was onboard what Gift called her thought train. "I need to try old frequencies and broadcast channels. Brava."

Tedium monopolized the early afternoon as the pair heard nothing in reply to the *hello* ping going out on every channel and frequency known to the old world. Gift said she needed to check on her teams, but the boredom more than anything pulled her away.

***

Joining a brainstorming session, Gift immediately became impressed with Sara's mind for the technology, wondering for a moment if they had evaluated her incorrectly for guard duty. No, Gift trusted that system. Sara and Karl bounced ideas off each other like ping-pong balls in a friendly game. Gift took the liberty to begin rough sketches of their ideas on a tablet, both for an automated gun with free-flying projectiles and an improved version of the handheld models. They had a way to go, but the journey was underway and off to a great start.

Nearing 18:00, Mike's team showed no signs of quitting, taking her back to the twelve-hour shifts he pulled with Tina for their counter-terrorism duties. It didn't take long for Gift to pick up on what could be a hinderance to their progress, so she pulled Mike aside.

"Sweetie, how are you and Anton getting on? I sense a little tension here."

"No, it's okay. I mean, he's a bit of a jerk, that's all."

"How do you mean?"

"He pushes his ideas, like they're better than mine."

"Then you push back, because your ideas are better than his."

"Exactly. Wait, what? No, it's not like that."

Over interlocked arms, Gift smiled warmly. "I know. When two brilliant minds work together, one tries to dominate. That whole alpha male thing, you know?"

"You make it sound... primal."

"Well... it is, in a way. Normal, I mean. I think? If you show him respect, tell him you like an idea of his, even ask his opinion? He'll act the same way towards you. You'll see."

"You really think so?"

"Know so." A wide smile drew itself on Gift's lips. "Worked with you, didn't it?"

Back at the bench, Red's glow said she had none of Mike's trouble getting along with Anton.

"Anton, thanks for your help on this. Mike tells me you're already offering excellent ideas and he's sure you'll work well together."

"Really? This is very good. Mike is excellent engineer. And Melody here is master data operator. When we have physical design, she will make us beautiful code to run it. Beautiful code."

Melody blushed—Gift had never seen that on her. Freckles dotted her face with greater intensity. Now *Red* described her cheeks as much as her hair.

***

A brief update. The Broadcasting Committee wanted to let the colonists know about the expedition, limiting the doom and gloom parts. Aimée looked as lovely as ever as Gift and Raff watched from their office, monitoring the comms array for a reply from the Pioneers. With Gift still bored as a child in her mom's Box with nothing to do, the update was the toy that stayed the dullness.

Aimée explained the expedition as the logical follow-up to Gift's three days in the environment and would include a resident of the highest outdoor classification. That part could be considered true enough, even if weeks ahead of schedule. Aimée withheld identifying herself as the one going. Although Gift agreed with Aimée about transparency, they understood the need. Next week's broadcast would provide full disclosure.

Static. Nothing but static. No reply.

20 | Week Two

The R.F. visitors landed at 08:30 behind Dome Six in what they called a heavy transport. Anticipation slowed the cargo door's descent until it became a ramp. The silver beast birthed from the belly of the flyer, massive compared to the makeshift land transport, looked formidable. All-glass doors and front cabin, the roof had high-capacity solar panels covering it like a blanket. More than a little impressed, Gift wondered why the R.F. needed *their* help.

"Good morning, Mister Lazarev." Gift contemplated his stature.

"Lovely to see you, dear Gift. Now where is Tom? I must show him to drive the Zil. Is easy for him, we need only a few minutes. Is everyone on your team able to make three to five days, at least?"

"At least? Well... yeah. They're ready. Just got a final treatment now. And what about you?"

"Don't worry for Sergey. I will be fine."

As Tom and Lazarev drove around in circles, Miss Heller and Aimée walked up behind Gift. Heller looked a tad green in the face. It was the first time Gift had seen her in casual clothes.

"Miss Heller... are you okay?"

"Fine," she pushed out in a breath.

Aimée frowned. "She's not. Told her to sit it out."

"I'm fine. Sakura believes it will pass."

"Everyone got what they need?" Gift hoisted her tote. "Clean undies, tooth sticks, body wipes?"

"Love, that transport got a shower? We may have to learn to love each other's stink. You packed enough food and water, right?"

"Plenty. Just tell me you brought more than shorts and a tee. If we make contact, you'll be the one they talk to."

"Have I ever let you down?"

"No. Embarrassed me plenty. But you never let me down."

Miss Heller stayed quiet as the two chortled. Her face appeared to be trying hard not to puke. Getting in a bouncing vehicle for hours on end didn't seem the best idea for her.

"Maggie, please, if you hurl in that thing, aim at Gift. As she said, *I'm* the one everyone will be looking at." Aimée giggled at her own witty humor.

Suppressing a chuckle, Gift said, "Miss Heller, I think if you take the front seat, it's better. And keep your eyes straight ahead. If you need to stop, just say." The normally stately woman didn't look good.

They boarded the transport the Russian called the Zil. Soon Gift would be the farthest she had ever been from the colony, from home. Excitement for the adventure lacked the intensity to ward off the overshadowing gloom of the fear of the unknown. On top of that, apprehension sat deep in her gut that their new neighbors may be just what the R.F. feared them to be.

The ride had plenty of bounce, the uneven ground not groomed to accommodate travel by electric vehicles, even ones with wheels up to Gift's navel. Quality engineering smoothed the journey as Gift and Sergey discussed the suspension system on the newly refitted Zil, the most advanced generation of the impressive vehicle since the prototype.

"Besides the frame, whole thing is new. Nothing here over twenty years old."

"Very smooth. I mean, considering."

"Has everything we need. Even drinking water. And the back makes into bed. We could live inside."

"Got a toilet?" the low voice of a groggy Aimée asked.

"Need one already? Worse than even me."

"Nah, just asking. How about Maggie? She blowing chunks yet?"

"She's asleep."

One knee raised, Aimée laid herself out over the seats behind Heller, gazing out the window as the world went by. Arranged back-to-back, three per side, the rear seats faced the side windows. A hand rested on Aimée's knee; Gift looked down at her every few minutes. Her own view of the gorgeous scenery of the wondrous outside became repetitive. After an hour in the forest, all the trees looked the same. Surprisingly, Gift missed Mike's music on the road trip. Her hand occupied itself tasseling her friend's short black hair and her hazel irises soaked in the smile drawn on her friend's heart-shaped face.

Aimée yawned. "What's it been, bout four, five hours?"

"More like three." Gift patted her weary friend's knee.

"Sheesh. This is going to be a long trip. Any tunes?"

First Gift raised her shoulders in an apologetic shrug, then she jumped out of her skin. Thoughtfully, Mike had set Tom up with some music and Sergey showed him how to load it into the vehicle's immersive audio system. The noise jolted Miss Heller to life with eyes glossy and wide to the disturbance, only to resume their closure.

"*Now* it's a road trip. Sing with me, Love."

The two best friends sang with all their hearts to Raff's cover of a classic song from *before*, one of their favorites. "Don't stop... believin'. Hold on to that fee-e-e-ee-lin'. Streetlights, peop-o-o-o-ole."

***

"How long's it been now? Gotta be at least eight hours since we stopped last."

"Tom?" Gift asked more than his name. *How long until we reach a good rest point? When will this mal'd vehicle stop?* It had been dark for some time, and they hadn't stopped for dinner, everyone having eaten less-than-tasty dried meals from emergency rations as they drove—the only time Miss Heller was awake. She looked ill before they left, and the journey wasn't kind to her. At the twelve-hour mark, Tom and Aimée seemed fine. The next hours would test Sakura's treatment.

"The navigator data from the scout drone shows what looks like a suitable spot, thirty more minutes or so."

"I'll give you a hundred rations if you stop this thing right now." Aimée piled on the drama.

"Thirty minutes isn't bad, sweetie. You know this is the shortest run, having a late start and all. Tomorrow will be more like sixteen hours."

"*Kill* me now."

Sergey raised an eyebrow. "You wish this?"

A shared look between the women said, *He* is *kidding, right?* with a hint of doubt, which the man's sinister laughter didn't fully remove. It woke Miss Heller, who whimpered as if drained of strength, "How much longer?"

Not an improvement per se, the sleep removed the green and took all the color from her cheeks. No one knew to blame the treatments, motion sickness, earth sickness, or the flu. That she puked four more times gave Gift pause.

Pushing through that final half hour, Gift reverted to a child waiting for her term-completion present. She'd worked for months, studied, worried, studied more. Waiting for Mom to come home with her celebratory gift made that last hour excruciating. This was worse. At least then she didn't have to hear anyone else complaining.

With Aimée already reaching for the door latch, the vehicle came to a stop. The travelers stepped out into a night of steel blue under a speckled black sky full of stars with a cloud-like division splitting the expanse vertically. A magical spectacle, unlike any cloud formation. Sergey said they were looking out at the galaxy, seeing the Milky Way. The group gave the sight the minutes it deserved, and Gift placed *milky way* in her bin of expressions from the world of *before* she didn't get. It didn't rob the moment of its magnificence. Tom had ended their torturous trek in a small clearing, about a dozen meters around.

Sergey broke the majestic silence. "We can do which way you prefer. Two tents, not so big. We can sleep grownups in one and children in the other."

Assuming Sergey meant he and Miss Heller in one, she, Tom and Aimée in the other, Gift objected. "Um, I don't think so. Nice try though." A wink softened the objection, as if she believed he was joking. She didn't. With no read on the guy, he could have been equally serious about this as he may have been about killing Aimée earlier—if she wished it.

Tom leaned around the rear of the vehicle. "Sergey, didn't you say the back of the Zil can be a sleeper?"

"Da. It does this. For more than two is not so comfortable."

"I'm thinking of one. Miss Heller, would you be more comfortable in the transport than in a tent?"

"That is thoughtful, Tom. Thank you. Maybe I would be best in there. Sergey, would you show me how it converts."

In no time he had it configured for sleeping and Sergey settled her in the vehicle. The windows switched to privacy mode, for which Miss Heller was grateful. She likely fell asleep by the time the door closed. The men started on the tents and Gift helped with the one she claimed as 'the girls' tent.' When Tom moved beside Gift to help plant a tent support, he seemed to want to say something to only her.

"I have a surprise for you."

"A surprise? I'm intrigued. What is it?"

"I know you'll have us leave right on time, bright and early at O-seven hundred. But if you get up early, just over there past the tree line..." His hand raised slightly, like he didn't want anyone else to see him pointing. "There's a small lake. I know how you love a morning swim."

"Really?" Giddy shoulders retracted as if she finally got that special present. A problem. She slapped his chest playfully, but firmly. "You should've told me. I didn't bring a swimsuit. I mean, why would I?"

"It only showed on the navigator a while back, why I chose this spot. I'll keep Sergey here. We'll break down the camp and prepare breakfast. You and Aimée go have a swim, use your bikini like you used to. We won't leave the campsite, promise."

After a quick peck on the cheek, she said, "Thank you. We'll go at dawn, should be about six. We're in the Zil and out of here by O-seven hundred. Sharp."

"Yes, ma'am," he replied with a goofy salute.

Inside the tent, Gift's mind raced. "I don't like being cut off. I need to know how my teams are doing. Part of me thinks I should've stayed."

"Then I'd be here with poor sick Maggie and those two... guys. You couldn't do that to me, Love."

"No, I guess not. But really, my excuse to come?"

"Was weak, I know. Worked though."

"I guess it did. It's... not that I just wanted to come with you. I mean, I did. But also too, I couldn't let you go alone. I mean, you wouldn't have been *alone*..."

"I'm tickled you came. I'd hate it without you."

"Oh, Tom gave me a surprise."

"Promise of Union?"

"No. *What...?* No." The second 'no' came with a slap on the arm. "We need to get up at dawn, there's a lake here. We'll have a swim while the guys break down camp."

"No problem for *me*. But Love, you have a swimsuit?"

"I'll do what you called a bikini. Like we used to."

"Or..." Aimée dragged the word, leading to its obvious implication. The very thought of it colored Gift's cheeks while Aimée giggled at the same.

***

They found the lake right where Tom said, glistening as the new morning sunlight met it with a gentle kiss. With cautious eyes, Gift confirmed privacy from the campsite as Aimée stood beside her in her swim attire, her usual nothing. Still in her nightshirt, Gift showed Aimée a wide smile connecting ruby-red cheeks.

"In that stupid Zil all day in soaking wet underwear? That'd be too annoying."

When the nightshirt lifted off, Gift had no bikini under it. Unhindered, she dove in ahead of Aimée, who gave the situation whopping laughter. Seconds distanced Gift from Aimée—not as strong a swimmer—in the glorified puddle compared to Colony Lake. From the other side, she swam back to the middle and treaded water next to Aimée, who laid on her back over the calm water to enjoy the float.

"You made it this far, Love. Float. No one's here."

Eyes walking the shoreline, Gift hesitated. With privacy confirmed and courage gathered, she got into a float and laid there beside her friend, staring at the infinite sky.

"What'd I tell you?"

"I guess... yeah. You were right, *it's amazing*."

The two splashed and played, taking turns dunking one another. Gift gave Aimée some pointers to improve her stroke and they swam three laps, ending in another float before returning to shore. Aimée laid out on the grass in full sunlight and patted the ground beside her. "Come. Let the sun dry you before you get dressed. We have time."

Or maybe they didn't.

Rustling leaves sent gentle sound waves to the sunbathers. With Aimée unaffected, Gift craned her neck in panic, the girl crying over the crayon while her friend laughed. One of the guys? Terrified, Gift pulled herself up, wore her hands as clothes, and started toward her nightshirt but froze after a half-step.

The sight overwhelmed her. A creature the size of a recycler pump with pure white feathers. Duck? Penguin? She always got the two confused. Its S-shaped neck looked longer than Gift expected, and it wore a black mask over its eyes. A long orange nose reminded Gift of synthetic composite. On a bird, duck, whatever, it's not called a nose. The word hung on the edge of memory, refusing to come forward. The young ladies stared in amazement as it gracefully entered the water and raised its wings like the doors of the Zil opening. Gift knelt beside Aimée, who propped herself up on her elbows, to watch the thing glide away over the glassy liquid with effortless grace and beauty.

As they stood to dress, another sound reached their ears, similar, but in sporadic shuffles. Gift's shame didn't revisit as she expected another wonder of nature. From the still, tall grass blades it leapt toward them, centimeters off the ground, and plopped at Gift's feet. After the white duck-penguin-bird-thing, this appeared hideously ugly yet held the full beauty of a newly rediscovered creature of their mysterious Earth home.

Brownish green was how Gift described the color of the low, wide, whatever-it-was before her. Its front legs were short and thin while its thick hind ones were long and reached behind it like muscular arms bent at the elbows. As Gift's head lowered toward it, the thing turned and hopped from where it came, disappeared by the brush.

***

The rest of the day slowly etched away and would have been maddening if not for the changes in scenery. Leaving behind the one distant mountain by the colony, the landscape morphed into mountain ranges rising heavenward on both sides. Some were blanketed in evergreens while others wore the brown of solid rock like a protective shell.

Miss Heller's skin had regained some color, not enough to look healthy, and Gift saw a ghost of the woman haunting the place Heller had occupied. Her team had been taking their injections, three a day like clockwork, Gift making sure. Sakura had shown her how to check for earth sickness and potential reactions to the treatment. Although Heller rode the dangerous side of okay, she insisted they press on. Against Gift's better judgment, she didn't try to protest, it wouldn't have accomplished anything.

Stopping only for necessary natural functions—and by mutiny, a thirty-minute lunch out of the *mal'd* Zil—they were making good time. Not that anyone expected them, quite the opposite, they had to imagine. With no idea when the Pioneers might attack the R.F. or when they may head Southwest toward New Europa, they raced against the clock of pure speculation, and time was running out.

They expected to be in the vicinity of the closest bunker by late afternoon the next day, and Gift became uneasy at pushing Sakura's estimation. For her team, her friends, to stay outdoors for the maximum six days—the return trek demanding as many as the outbound journey—unsettled her to the core.

Miss Heller may not make it that long.

21

Dinner nourished the five bodies crammed into the confined space for a second day. While the food couldn't be called good by anyone with functioning taste buds, the experience of sharing the meal led to the telling of stories and exchanging of jokes, creating a social occasion that happened to be traversing the surrounding unknown.

More animated than she'd been thus far, Miss Heller shared an anecdote. When she joined the Board of Directors of New Europa, she had to tell someone, violating the anonymity rule. Her best friend and coworker in Oversight for Resident Services noticed she'd started disappearing from work with no plausible reason given. "It took little pressing," Heller confessed. She swore her friend to secrecy, who in turn swore her own friend to the same. "Quickly brought that to an end. I told them I'd cut their rations if anyone else found out. Of course, I couldn't do it, but they didn't know that." The group graciously joined her in a chuckle. "Never abused my position like that again."

As always, the last bit of the wait proved the hardest. Fifteen hours of travel and stir-crazy boredom outdone by that last hour of pent-up frustration ticking the degrees up to its boiling point. Aimée crawled over from her side, pushing herself between Sergey and Gift, and threw herself over the burly Russian to grab the top of Tom's seat with two hands and shook it violently. "Stop this *mal'd* thing."

Tom swatted at her while Sergey took matters into his own hands by grabbing the frantic drama queen and setting her down beside himself.

"Got you all," she said in a burst of laughter.

The drone flying scout identified a suitable campsite close enough to the sixteen-hours, if not stretching it a hair. Tom transformed from evil villain trotting his captives to hero of the hour simply by bringing the rolling jail cell to a stop. At just past twenty-three hundred, they needed to set up camp. Experience from the previous night quickened the activity.

As she crossed her arms to rub them, Gift shivered. "A lot colder here."

A *brr* vibrated through Aimée's lips. "I'm freezing. These tents warm enough or will we wake up frozen to death?"

Gift giggled. "Wake up dead?"

Sergey emerged from the tree line hugging several large pieces of wood. "You will be fine with survival blankets and heaters in tents. We will make fire, warm up. A little vodka and you will feel perfect then. Perfect." After dropping the logs, he handed them each a small package that looked too slim to hold a warm blanket.

When Aimée and Gift exited the tent wrapped in thin yet ample coverings, they stepped into the glow of the roaring fire. On one of three logs providing seating, Sergey sat up tight against Heller, wrapping her in a thin blanket. A shadow in the darkness became Tom carrying a stack of wood pieces. Aimée and Gift snuggled beside each other, Tom on the last log. Through the flames, a silhouette of Sergey poured Miss Heller what Gift assumed was vodka. The object on a stick leaning over the orange-red heat caught Gift's eye.

"You lovely ladies need vodka. Warms you inside. Please..."

Joyously, Aimée hopped to her feet and strode toward the generous and perhaps slightly inebriated fellow and retrieved two glasses he'd poured for them. "Spasibo."

"Ne za chto." Like the moon on a dark night, a crescent smile cut Sergey's shadow.

"None for me, I can't handle that... stuff." Gift waved off the clear liquid that once lied to her about being water.

"Guess I'll have to drink them both," Aimée said happily.

"This girl is Russian at heart. I like this one so much."

To remind the friendly foreigner the women weren't the only ones in his company, Tom cleared his throat. Sergey responded by handing him a glass overflowing with the vile drink.

"Did you turn on the heater in your tent? Takes a while to get going but should keep it toasty warm for the night."

"Yeah, it's on." Pushing through a stretched-jaw yawn, Gift added, "Thanks, Tom."

Pulling the stick with the mystery object from the fire Sergey announced, "Before sleep, you must try this. Ration dinners gave us nutrients, but they gave no joy. You all must try this. Is delicious."

"What is it?" An outline of a fat creature the size of two of Sergey's fists danced in the flame's flickering light as Aimée asked. Gift didn't know its name, but she had seen something like it.

"Bullfrog."

The large, happy fellow removed it from the pointed stick and dropped it onto a plate, shook his hand rapidly, then cut into the carcass with a knife pulled from his belt. Miss Heller accepted a piece of the leg, which Sergey said was the best part. Tom reached for and was given his taste. Noises of delight came from Heller and Tom as they chewed. When Aimée reached for hers, the connection Gift's thoughts formed left her aghast.

"Where... um, where did you... where did you... get that?" Shame cracked her voice.

"Was by little lake near the last camp. He hopped by as we broke down tents and Sergey chased after him. Quick little guy."

Imagining the man at the lake that morning, his voyeuristic eyes upon her, Gift tucked her head behind Aimée's shoulder. Realization of the horror she'd up to then kept herself from by adamant refusal to join her free-spirited friend in tossing care to the wind and clothes to the side flooded into her as horror.

"What's wrong, Love?" The astute friend correctly interpreted the silent reply. "It doesn't mean he saw us. We scared the thing off and it leapt away from us. Remember?"

The gentle whisper failed in its quest to keep the words secret to Gift's ears. Or simply by coincidence, Sergey said, "Such a lovely morning. And such beauty these tired eyes found at the lake. Two angels laying on the water. Such lovely creatures. Lovely."

"It's okay, Love. It's a compliment. There's no need to be embarrassed by this."

Oblivious to the spectacle, Miss Heller said goodnight and Sergey graciously offered to escort her to the vehicle-become-night's-shelter.

Tom knelt before Gift. "Gift, I'm sorry. He was with me breaking down the camp and stepped away to pee. I didn't realize where he'd gone."

A slap removed the hand Tom laid upon Gift's shoulder and she ran to the security of her tent where she heard Aimée tell Tom, "She'll be fine. I'll talk to her."

When she entered the tent, Aimée had no words powerful enough to bring Gift's mind down, not from this. She was mortified. Nothing her friend could say would make that man's eyes *not* have seen her. No way to remove the image from his mind, wipe the memory, undo the irrefutable damage. Internally, Gift blamed herself, but the mouth didn't sync with the mind, siding instead with her emotional chaos.

"How could you?"

"Me? You know how I swim. Really, it doesn't bother me at all. *So what* if he saw us. We gave the old fart the treat of his life. He'll not forget this little adventure of ours any time soon."

"That's you. I'm not you. How could you do this to me?"

"Do what? You said you'd swim in your bikini. I teased, knowing you'd never. Then you did. *You* did, Love. And there's nothing to be ashamed of. You're a beautiful woman, now someone else saw that, that's all."

"Just... *stop*. Stop it. I'm going to sleep. Don't talk to me."

***

Only Miss Heller offered a morning greeting to Gift, to which she uncharacteristically mumbled *'giorno*. Tension ran high through breakfast as Gift ate steps away from the group and didn't speak. The conversation orbiting the small fire wasn't all about her. Her, a child who'd misbehaved when her mom had friends over and spent the rest of the evening in the corner being ignored. Last night's shame made room for anger, and for reasons she didn't fully understand, Gift focused it on everyone.

"What's wrong with her?" Heller asked, out of the loop.

Tom said, "She's embarrassed that Sergey saw them swimming in the lake yesterday morning. That's all."

"Lake?"

"Near our last camp. I sent Gift and Aimée to swim, told her Sergey and I would stay at the camp. He wandered off and saw them."

Heller's face crinkled. "Why is that a problem?"

"Is no problem. So beautiful." Sergey's words twisted like knives in Gift's side.

"We were skinny-dipping," Aimée said.

"Sorry?" Tom joined Heller's lack of understanding. Gift didn't know the term either.

"We were naked."

"*Oh.*" Heller's face blanked while Tom offered an O-shaped mouth without noise.

Gift angrily threw her tote in the Zil. "We need to go."

The mighty vehicle swallowed its cargo and passengers in silence, a silence that accompanied the uneasy travelers for the first half of the morning. No talking worked for Gift, thinking she'd never be ready to talk about this. Her consuming anger latched onto everyone, even poor Miss Heller, who did nothing but say goodnight and good morning to her.

When Tom motioned Sergey forward, Gift *knew* they shared a whisper about her. *Tom probably sneaked a peek too,* she thought. *Jerk.* Even the wonder of being surrounded by snow couldn't stop her piling up the anger. As her mind replayed the nightmarish event, it shifted to contemplating if the person most deserving of her wrath was her. Less appealing, it settled closest to logical, so her head kept it on rotation for a while.

The rumble stopped and momentum ceased—too early for lunch and no one called for a potty break. Gift finally noticed snow of such pure white it made the surroundings shine. A new wondrous sight generously offered by the Earth, almost enough to free her mind of resentment and shame. They fought to keep their place. The words *tree* and *can we get by it* turned her head forward to see what stopped the great Zil. The last to exit, Gift took a place between the other women where her attempted whistle hissed like an air hose.

"Must be two meters high. I mean... wide, I guess. But now its wide is its high." Shivers rattled Gift's words.

"Can we move it with the winch?" Heller asked.

"No, Madam. Look, the base where roots came out is several meters that way. The top we cannot see. No way my Zil can move this. No way around it."

Aimée's piercing whistle ripped through the wintery air. "Can we cut our way through?"

"We have nothing to cut through *that*," Tom said. "We need another way. I've rerouted the drone."

"Also too, don't know about anyone else, I'm freezing." Tiny bumps speckled Gift's skin.

Pointing a wobbly finger at Gift's breath Aimée said, "Hey, I see smoke."

"Russian Zil has warm clothes for you ladies." Sergey stepped to the rear of the rolling habitat Box, nearly as long as Gift's home. The rude man who looked upon her shamefulness returned a kind, tender soul offering each of the women a thin jacket as impressively warm as the blankets for their lack of bulk.

"Now what?" Aimée looked like a bored child driven mad waiting for something to do.

"While we wait for the drone, we may as well all use the break to relieve ourselves. Guys to the left, ladies can go there." Tom pointed to thick brush that invited privacy for necessary bodily functions.

Silence surrounding her squat *felt* unlike any she'd experienced. A crispness in the noiseless serenity gleamed from what was neither water nor ice, but somewhere in between, something magical. Gift tried to act natural when she rejoined the group, none of whom needed the time she did for what Mike called 'doing her business.'

Cold, wet sensations came only after the shock wore off. A face full of soft snow. No surprise to find Aimée deep in roaring laughter. Gift reached the ground and came up with a fist full of powder and packed it together between her palms as they turned red from the bite of frost. Her aim left much to be desired when the snowball splattered against the Zil over a half-meter from where her friend stood. Surrendering to the moment, Gift immersed herself in the uninhibited folly, laughing and throwing snowball after snowball. Miss Heller even joined, then the boys.

All guffawing ceased when a beep told the frolicking bunch the drone had found something. Eager eyes looked to Tom holding the navigator tablet close to his face. He wiped the snow from it when Gift finally landed one last toss to hit her target. A stern look, she thought he was mad at her until his lips separated and he spat the icy-wet powder from between them in unbridled laughter.

"*Now* you finally hit me? Wait, let me guess, you aimed at Aimée?"

"Ha ha, hilarious. But... *yeah*, I did." Gift wore a huge grin. The anger retreated.

"Looks like we got something but I'm not sure about it. We'll go check it out. Everyone back onboard. Let's roll."

22

"You gotta be kidding me." Dreadful disbelief spewed from Gift's lips. "We're not seriously considering this, *right*?" The glint in Tom's eye worried Gift as she could see him thinking about it. Just looking at it brought butterflies to her stomach, and not the good kind. Contemplating the height brought a sensation eerily similar to being on the cusp of peeing herself. An experience she unfortunately couldn't forget.

"It's the only way forward. It's this or we turn back to New Europa." The matter-of-factness of Tom's statement annoyed Gift, she wanted to find another way.

In full view of the bridge that didn't appear suited to the vehicle in which they were considering traversing it, Heller said, "It barely looks wide enough."

"And how old even is it?" Gift asked.

"Much older than colonies. But look to those tracks. Is strong Russian bridge built for freight train. My little Zil is nothing for this bridge. Nothing."

"But can we even fit on it? And... I mean, if we did? Even if we did... a little veer and we're..." Gift couldn't verbalize the fall into what she estimated to be well over fifty meters.

"Let's see." Tom crept them forward in what became an enormous vehicle in Gift's mind. Too big for the bridge for sure. A few meters from the ravine's edge the five promptly exited for a close inspection, bringing Gift to the immediate and adamant conclusion they couldn't cross. Level-headed Tom turned everyone's attention to the steel rails extending across the bridge from under the Zil.

"As huge as this thing is, check out its wheel track. The tires go just outside the rails and there's a good overhang on the bridge. We'll make it... and the tracks will ensure we don't veer. We've got this."

"Are we sure it's sound? Not only is it old, but it hasn't been used or maintained in centuries." Gift fully supported Heller's argument.

"Is sturdy bridge." Sergey nodded over thick folded arms. "Will be here *long after* we are dead."

"Yeah, 'cause that'll be *today* if we actually try to cross this thing." Gift's comeback summoned a throaty laugh that wheezed out of the Russian guard like coarse breaths on the verge of a deep cough.

"The drone's been checking the structural support. It's solid." Tom's gesture to assure Gift failed its intent.

"I got a bad feeling... I don't like this."

"Well, Love, I guess you can stay here while we cross, then. You can have my blanket." The fresh yet playful tone meant Aimée knew Gift had to come, and Gift knew she knew.

With all five climbed back into the Zil, Tom gingerly nudged it forward, not pausing when the wheels left the ground for the lateral planks of the centuries-old bridge. As when her feet left the lakebed, Gift swore she felt the change from the solidity of the ground to nothing below. Tom being right irritated her as she wanted—no, needed—everyone to side with her, find another way.

There was no other way. In her head Gift knew, but months ago she learned the logical part of her mind didn't always have control. In this moment, she didn't wish it to. An audible gasp accompanied the view when Gift allowed her eyes to look out the side window. It showed her nothing but the valley. No Zil, no bridge, just a too-many-meters drop to her death. Fear robbed her of the beauty of the vista, which Sergey and Aimée soaked in greedily.

"Halfway now."

If Tom thought that would calm Gift, he was wrong. Her optimism didn't span the dreadful crossing, and them not having died yet brought no assurances. Ahead, she estimated seventy meters to safety, to solid earth. As Gift stared with laser-focus on the approaching land, Sergey climbed over to Aimée's side to see something of interest Gift couldn't care less to note.

Lurched forward, Gift steadied herself on the console between Heller and Tom. Her ribs ached from the impact. "*We're falling.*" No. Tom's arms turned to stone with a fixed grip on the steering wheel, the Zil stopped moving, the planks of the bridge closer.

"Ow-*whuh*." When Gift turned toward the exaggerated cry, Aimée had vanished. She'd fallen to the floor between her seats and the door and Sergey was removing himself from her. "Watch the knee vodka breath... that's my stomach."

"Am sorry my dear." The big bloke lifted himself onto the seat and assisted Aimée to do the same.

"Everyone alright?" Tom asked.

"Think so," Gift said, shaky. Blood reddened Miss Heller's lips and chin. "Are you okay? Your nose."

"I think it may be broken. But I'll be fine." She spoke from a voice nasal and muddy.

"What happened? Are we gonna fall?" The chill nipped Gift's neck as a *whoosh* reached her panicked ears. Sergey had the side door open, Aimée seated by it. "Are you crazy?"

With a grip on a handhold, Sergey leaned out. "Two planks broken. Front wheels fell, got lodged under the forward plank. We must reverse." The closed door settled Gift.

The driver reversed but the spinning rear wheels didn't reach the ground. No amount of torque dislodged the front tires from the plank for the weight of the tilted vehicle. Sergey opened the rear hatch, hopped out, and pulled the hook and cable from the rear winch.

"What the heck's he doing?" Aimée shrieked.

"Brilliant. He's gonna use it to pull us back. I'll reverse, get the front free."

"Then what? We just go back home?" Refusal to quit drove Aimée—one of the few character traits she and Gift had in common.

An alert flashed on Gift's mental display. "He *needs* a tether. He could fall." Hurried hands grabbed the nylon rope from the gear duffle and, laying on the floor stretching over the open hatch, Gift attached one end to the anchor on the rear bumper. After joining the winch hook to a plank three meters back, Sergey approached. It took some convincing, but Gift secured the line around his waist.

"Tom, start the winch. I will stay here to shout if anything goes not right." The industrious guard put himself half-way between the Zil and the plank where he attached the hook and showed Tom a raised thumb.

The whine suggested strenuous effort of the electric motor trying to pull the full weight of the massive vehicle to yank the front wheels from their trap. Slight movement, almost imperceptible, it began to lower.

The echo of a violent pop roiling in from the valley instinctively pulled Gift's arms over her head, her face down. Another deafening pop came a split-second after the first. On the floor, her panicked eyes saw the hook centimeters from her head, below a large crack in the side panel of the inner storage compartment. *Sergey.* The empty bridge showed only the gap of a torn-away plank.

"*Sergey*! He's gone."

"*What?*" Aimée shouted, followed by Tom and Heller.

"*The tether*. I tied it."

Tom hurried around her onto the bridge and hesitated to peer over the side.

"*It held him*. It held him. I think he's unconscious."

Bracing his feet on the steel rail of the track, Tom began pulling the line. Veins tensed into twined ropes over his biceps for the weight of the large Russian. Without pause for thought, the young ladies leapt out, Gift lending her arms to the pull while Aimée held her at the midriff. Heaving the limp body over the edge and onto the bridge proved the hardest part, but they'd done it. Tom dragged the burly man by the underarms to the bumper and the three heaved the hundred-plus-kilo soldier into the raised back of the vehicle. At once, Aimée attended to the gash on his forehead as Heller crawled up with the first aid kit.

To assess the scene, Tom stood outside, untethered. After acquiescing to Gift's shout to tie it on, he returned to the lost plank pulling the hook along.

Climbing into the Zil, he said, "Gonna Plan B it," and clambered around Gift.

"And what's Plan *B*?"

"I've fastened the hook. With the plank gone, I latched it to the support base of the track. Not gonna break that." Taking a crowbar from the tool case, he crept his way to the front window. "And I'll take off that plank holding the front wheels."

Only as he edged through, did Gift discover the front windscreen opened. She examined the connection on his tether. A sharp crack of the composite plank pinched her ears. Tom reclaimed the driver's seat. "Get ready, we're doing this. Gift, watch out the back and yell if we're anything but straight."

"On it."

The complaints from the electric motor loudened into a steady whine. Centimeter by centimeter, the back end of the vehicle lowered, creeping backward. A brief bounce jarred them as the rear wheels reunited with the bridge. Full stop. Tom killed the winch and stomped the brakes. They'd done it, freed the mechanical beast of its trap. Still on a now questionably sound bridge, but free.

Now what? Gift wondered. *Press on forward or go back defeated by a fallen tree and an old bridge?*

"We press on, but we need to repair that gap."

"I don't know about this. I'm starting to think this bridge wasn't the best idea."

"*Starting to*? I've been saying that this whole time." The *I-told-you-so* tone Gift threw at Miss Heller tasted bitter on her tongue.

"No choice. I need to fill the gap, or we'll fall into it again." Crowbar in hand, Tom hoisted open the windscreen. "The tires can cross a missing plank. Not two, definitely not three. I'll move the ones ahead and behind the gap and secure them in the middle. We'll get across and be able to get back as well."

Pride flooded into Gift as she watched Tom carefully loosen the planks without breaking them and struggle to get them aligned in the opening, lessening the three-plank gap. With each gap shortened to one plank's width, Gift worked hard to convince herself of Tom's assessment, they'd make it across.

Miss Heller insisted on staying in the storage space with Sergey, still unconscious but on the journey back. With Gift taking her place beside Tom, Aimée leaned into the space between them. All gazed forward as Tom engaged the motors and crept the Zil until they were back on solid ground, putting all conscious passengers at ease.

"*Stop.*" The joyous smile on Aimée elevated the mood in the cramped cabin. "You guys need to see what Sergey and I were looking at before he summersaulted off the bridge."

The sight took the breaths from the spectators. Nature kept surprising and rewarding the band of travelers. The unimaginable volume of Gift's lake faded at seeing the *Colony-Lake's-worth* of water falling minute by minute. A couple of hundred meters away they heard the roar of its fifty-meter drop as thousands of admin building showers on full-flow water cycle. Everyone readily agreed when Gift suggested they take lunch there.

Thankfully, the afternoon's journey proved uneventful, bringing a boredom to please even the ever-antsy Aimée. Sergey rejoined them with a bandaged forehead and bruised ego. Oddly, it gave Gift a twinge of pleasure that wore on her like an itchy garment she couldn't remove, a morose satisfaction for justice after the *he-saw-me-at-the-lake* incident. Shame still outshined the other emotions and wasn't likely to let go of its captive any time soon. At least the bitter anger had subsided, mostly.

23

Perseverance. Gift had chosen the name for one of the E.R. Rovers because it embodied the human spirit, surviving—she'd say thriving—despite impossible odds. Even though they caused the very conditions to threaten their lives, humans persevered. While injecting medications via hypo-stick, Gift wondered how much more her friends could persevere outdoors. Endurance may have been the better word for what they needed. With the colony fifty-four hours to their backs, they had not yet found the Pioneers. The idea of pushing to the full six days was discomforting. Miss Heller still didn't look right.

Sergey handled it best, but he wasn't under Gift's care, and she had no idea how he did it. Of her team, Aimée had the least trouble, vomiting once in two and a half days compared to Tom's two times a day and Miss Heller's four or five, her skin painted an ashy gray.

Sergey pointed to his tablet. "We are nearing to closest bunker to New Europa."

"Let me have a look." Gift pulled the drone control tablet from Sergey's hand, and Aimée sat up from her sprawled out position. She claimed three seats as her daybed for the entirety of the voyage. "Get the drone in closer."

"*No.*"

"Maggie? Didn't even think you were awake. Why can't we take a closer look like Gift said, to see what we're heading in to?"

"We can't risk spooking them or showing any hint of aggression. Pull it back Sergey. Tom, stop us a distance from them, please."

"I found a suitable spot about three hundred meters from the bunker. We'll be there at... seventeen twenty-three. Twenty minutes, give or take."

"Oh mamma, we're gonna meet these people. Aimée? Are you ready for this, sweetie?"

"She is well prepared," Miss Heller replied.

Aimée slinked to the rear and hunched over her duffle. "I'll have them eating out of my hand in no time." After Gift handed the tablet back to Sergey, she turned, opened her mouth to speak, and let it hang there when her eyes fell upon her friend rummaging through the bag in her underwear.

"*Aimée.*"

"Love?"

"What... what are you doing?"

"Preparing. As *you* said, I can't greet these people in a t-shirt, can I?"

"Well... hurry up." Using her body as a shield, Gift covered *her* shame as Aimée had none. Sergey laughed deeply. To Gift's surprise, he respectfully looked forward.

"How do I look?" The black trousers and white blouse somehow looked crisp and pristine.

Miss Heller craned her neck. "Perfect. Very professional."

"You are lovely dear. Who would not listen to you? Lovely."

"Thank you, Sergey." A devilish grin glowed on her face.

Tom kept his eyes on the path and the drive steady. "So, what's the play? Do we just walk up to the bunker, knock, and say hi?"

"We must appear friendly, but also trusting. Weapons in hand or a show of force is not something I wish them to see. Sergey will accompany me and Aimée, no one else."

"Expecting trouble? I mean, maybe it's safer with Sergey and Tom. You stay in the Zil with Gift."

"Our hope is they see us as a diplomatic envoy, a first contact to extend the hand of friendship. You, me, and Sergey would be our best chance for that. Besides, I'll feel better knowing Tom is here with the motors on, ready if we need him."

"I don't know about this." The shakiness in Gift's voice didn't come from the vehicle's movement. "The closer we get, the more nervous I get. All we know about them is they attacked the R.F. What if they're not friendly toward us? And you want to walk up to them with a *Russian*?"

"Exactly," Margaret Heller said. "I want to show them we are cooperating with the R.F."

"Show our strength. They dare not challenge us. Da, is smart."

"No, Sergey. We want to show them we can get along with *them* too. A show of unity, not strength."

"Well said, Maggie. I'm good with the plan. You, me, and the big guy. If you're sure you're okay to make it."

Heller nodded.

The vehicle eased into a smooth stop, barely felt by the passengers. Tom had taken to the controls, learning not to jerk everyone as he did on his first few braking maneuvers. They exited the Zil and waited for someone to make the first move they'd come all this way to make.

"We should all wear these." Sergey pulled three thick heavy-looking vests from what Gift hadn't realized was yet another storage compartment in the rear of the wondrous Zil. "We know they have bullets, and they had no problem shooting them at us at the R.F."

Before he finished speaking Heller's palm rose. "Wearing those says we're expecting a fight, assuming them hostile. Not the first impression we need to make."

"Look at me you sweet brute. No one would shoot at this." Palms out at her sides, Aimée did a half twirl.

"Sergey would not. Not sure about these Philistines."

That name soiled Gift's ears. "We call them Pioneers."

"Okay. We've got a decent bit of light left, won't be dark for hours." When Tom pointed at the sky his nose quickly gauged his armpit after three shower-less days. "I'll keep the drone out of sight, but on you. When you make contact, give us a signal."

"Good." Miss Heller put on a confidence that somehow made her appear nearly healthy. "Aimée, Sergey, let's go meet our neighbors."

Unable to shake the fear, Gift hoped the confidence hadn't been misplaced. Her thoughts created dread for Aimée, manifested as a massive knot twisting in her stomach. On the trek to 'protect' her, Gift had no practical way to do that. At least now she'd have her eyes glued to the drone's camera—not much, but it was something.

A few steps into the trees and they were gone.

"Back in, we need to be ready." Unable to peel her eyes from the display, Gift whacked her head as she fumbled into the front seat. "Motors on, ready to go as soon as they need us?"

"Yes, Gift. I'm ready if, *if...* they need us. We're hoping for the best, aren't we? Where's that wonderful optimism I love about you?"

Love about me? Gift's mind raced over question after question, pondering the meaning of those words. *Later. Stay focused, protect Aimée.* "I lost them in the trees." Panic-stricken, she shook the tablet to force the drone's camera to penetrate the tree canopy, locate Aimée. It didn't work.

A distant pop rushed in from all around her, followed by another and another. Then what sounded akin to the planks that broke on the bridge. Pop. Another plank. More echoes of pops, shattered planks. Her head pushed into the headrest when the Zil jumped forward. Trepidation filled Gift's muscles, heating the blood in her veins.

"Why are we stopping? Get them. *Go get them.*"

"Far as we can go in this." The words curved around his head as Tom jumped from his open door then he disappeared into the trees.

An agonizing second ticked the clock as an hour. She needed to do something, and with no clue what, she trailed Tom without understanding what was happening. The popping continued as she ran headlong toward the source of its echoes. A figure emerged from the trees.

Running toward her, Tom pushed Aimée along with one hand, the other ducking her head. They had nothing above them, why were they ducking? Like watching an intense action vid at half-speed, Gift witnessed the commotion as Sergey and Margaret appeared. Something had gone terribly wrong. The massive guard had her draped across his arms, limp. Earth sickness? Shattered tree splinters chased them, falling to the ground behind their backs.

Someone said, "Get in the truck. Open the back."

In the front passenger seat Gift found a button to open the rear hatch and Tom appeared beside her and slammed his door shut. She hadn't seen him enter. When she followed his eyes, hers found Sergey and Aimée hefting Miss Heller into the Zil.

"Go-Go-Go," Sergey screamed before he'd even closed the door.

Somehow Gift had the mental clarity to hit the button, pulling the two doors together to seal the rear hatch. The pops that followed squealed a distinct pitch and tone, like metallic water drops. Tom's driving lost its smoothness, became jerky, frantic, fast. A hard bank left pressed Gift against the glass door as they fled the bunker with her only imagining what may have happened, anxious fear pounding in her chest.

Distraught, panic-stricken voices were trapped in the back of the Zil, wheels roaring from speed unlike any Gift had felt prior. Aimée came off the floor, tossed about by each bump, yet fought to keep her place. Concern overlayed Sergey's face where previously its variations were stern or jovial, nothing in between. When the movement halted abruptly, the vehicle sliding into full stop, Gift had no clue how much time or distance elapsed.

As Tom leapt from his seat and made his way to the back, Gift's eyes went with him. "What's happened?" No one answered, their focus glued to the intensity of the moment. When Gift climbed over Aimée's seats to look over Tom's shoulder, she saw what her brain failed to register earlier, Miss Heller's white blouse blotted with crimson. A vision of Charlie covered in blood, dying. Miss Heller was dying; she was sure of it.

"What's happened?"

"Before we got close, they opened fire." The tremble replacing her friend's typically jovial tone piled dread on Gift's already mountainous fear.

"*Fire*?"

"*Shooting*. Guns. Bullets."

"But why? You didn't see them? Get to say anything?"

"Nope, just bullets. One hit Maggie. Sergey grabbed her before she hit the ground. This looks bad. She's losing a lot of blood."

"Russian Federation," Sergey said as a statement they all should have understood.

"*What*?" Tom growled.

"From here is closer. We must take her there, excellent doctors there. We are too far from New Europa. Too far. She will not make it."

Gift objected, "No. She needs Sakura. We've got to get her to N.E."

"How far?" Tom kept pressure on the wound as Marco had done for Charlie. Charlie still died. "To each. How far to each colony?"

"Gift, help me. Grab the first-aid kit. Let the guys figure out the route." Taking over for Tom so he could drive, Aimée had Raff's calm under pressure.

Pushing the tablet into Sergey's gut, Gift went for the first-aid bag. Sergey tapped at the device like an animal—*a bear*?—banging it with his thick paws. "Thirty-five hours to N.E. at best speed... To Russian Federation is... fourteen or fifteen."

"R.F. She won't make thirty-five. Gift, we need to stitch her."

"*What*? We... we can't. You have any idea what you're even doing?"

"No clue. But I know she's gonna bleed out if we don't do something."

"Must remove bullet before you stitch," Sergey said.

"Oh mamma."

"We can do this Gift. Open that kit... What's in there?"

Gift cringed while Aimée used what resembled narrow-end pliers from her bench's toolset to dig into the open wound for the tiny projectile. It reminded her of removing crystal diodes from a module board—if that board were made of flesh and oozing blood. Beyond the sight, it was the squishing noises that crawled over Gift's skin until Aimée declared victory.

"*Gotcha.*"

The extent of Gift's assistance was handing her friend-turned-medic the synth-skin suture. Not an option, she had to turn away as Aimée pinched the ripped flesh of the wound with one hand and ran the medical device over it. What may have been the worst patch job in the history of New Europa was done. They hoped it would be enough for Miss Heller to cling to life.

On word of Heller being stable, the vehicle launched forward and sped off toward the R.F. Gift's first visit to the colony. She would have preferred the excitement to come from a far different source.

The women turned medic and nurse stayed in the rear as the Zil rolled along. When Gift began changing Miss Heller's bloody shirt, torn nearly off her in the frenzy to treat her wound, Aimée said the medics at the R.F. would cut it off. They wrapped her in a blanket when she began to shiver. Tom kept driving through the night with only a quick pee break permitted at first light.

***

Rays of morning sunshine cast the west side of the R.F. in shadow. So unlike her colony—domes peering over the reenforced concrete perimeter wall, its stature impenetrable—Gift wondered what weapons they feared the Pioneers having to threaten them. If they could breach that wall, how could N.E. survive an assault? A new dread flowed over her from scalp to toes.

Sergey directed Tom along the south wall until they reached a massive solid metal double-door, which opened for them. The hurried journey ended as they entered a large access hatch and the great vehicle stopped. Gift shuttered seeing remnants of Miss Heller's life fluid on her's and Aimée's hands and shirts. As two guards approached, Sergey gingerly lifted her from the Zil, then halted suddenly and went blank-faced, stopping Tom dead in his tracks.

"Problem?" Tom asked.

"These guards are not known to me."

24

Did Sergey say he didn't know the guards? The old dread withdrew, frightened by newer foreboding that overtook Gift and froze her muscles. Among a growing pile of everything going terribly wrong, Miss Heller needed immediate medical attention. Tom's hand hovered over the taser a second longer than it took Gift to see tips of the weapons across the guards' chests pursue his direction. An insignificant amount of fear left her when she saw his hands rise. Still highly probable they'd shoot them all dead, now anyone could be the first. If not her, who would Gift watch die before a bullet ended the story of Gift Ojo?

"Please surrender any weapons you have." The guards' two-meter distance called Gift's 'babysitters' from a memory, their two meters rich in discomfort, but without the fright these two meters brought. *Did he say please?* In full compliance, Tom dropped his taser on the ground then Sergey stepped forward, Heller in his arms.

"I have no weapon. She needs medical attention, *now.*"

Guard One stepped back another meter and raised a hand to his shoulder and spoke to it. Strained as much as possible, Gift's ears couldn't collect the words. He stepped forward to consider the woman in Sergey's arms then warily examined his face. Gift wondered if they knew the prize they captured. It brought an odd excitement to consider their first glimpse of the Philistines—her mind had reverted to the term, seeing them now as the Russians did.

"Anyone else have weapons? Tools on their person?" In unison they shook their heads. "We need to be sure."

The second guard stepped up to Tom and, with both hands, patted his arms, underarms, the sides of his torso, hips, and legs down to his feet. He stepped to Sergey and did the same, then studied the body in his arms. Gift half-stepped back when the guard approached and received a hard glare that said, *We're doing this*. After Aimée got her pat-down the guards appeared satisfied.

"Are you from the bunkers? We're hoping for a dialog, to discuss cooperation among our peoples." Getting silence in reply, Aimée shot Gift an *I've got no idea* shrug.

The open space had a high, flat ceiling, ample lighting, and room enough for the Zil and a half-dozen more like it. It held the transport they arrived in, themselves, and the guards. Entering through an open double door breaking the wall opposite the hatch they had driven through, two people in white coats pushed a gurney. They stopped before Sergey and placed the body—no, Miss Heller—on it. Whatever would happen, whoever these people were, it seemed she would get the care she desperately needed.

"She is my partner. I must go with her. And her." Sergey pointed at Gift. "She is our nurse."

Gift couldn't formulate a guess for the alter egos but liked the idea of Miss Heller not being hauled away alone. The dying woman's *partner* and *nurse* followed the gurney out of the space into the hallway. Stepping over the threshold, Gift cast a gaze at Aimée in anxious concern for the *what ifs* for her and Tom. The confidence she saw in her friend's stature with her look of solidarity instilled an unexpected and welcome calm in Gift.

Two guards joined their rear as they walked. Sergey's head shake may have meant he didn't know those guards either. The corridor resembled

New Europa's design with significant differences. The soft off-white color, not being gray, pleased her. They trailed through a narrow hallway just wide enough for the medics to walk alongside the rolling bed. Reaching a medical facility without entering a dome spoke to a vastly different colony architecture.

The double-Box-sized room had white walls with large green horizontal stripes filling the middle third on all sides. A massive fixture of six hexagonal lights suspended from the ceiling's center threw enough illumination to drench a small farm in artificial sunlight. Once the gurney halted and they locked its wheels, the first thing the medics did was cut off Miss Heller's shirt. Aimée had been correct not to put a new one on her. One medic, a middle-aged man with dark hair beyond brown, lifted Heller's shoulder, looked at her back, laid her down, and looked deeply into Gift's eyes.

"You close her?" He said in English.

"Da."

It was good Sergey replied, as Gift was about to explain how Aimée had done it, forgetting that quickly how Sergey had identified her as the nurse.

"Not bad for nurse." Medic One's compliment sounded derogatory.

The two guards stepped out of the square room. Gift observed them speak into each other's ears through the circular windows in the green double doors. One walked away, one stayed—a sentry at the gate. In a whisper Gift could barely hear, Sergey spoke to Medic Two in Russian. That his inflection was a question was all she understood.

Medic One spoke for a while in Russian, pointing to Heller and the blipping graphs on the medical monitor. If he meant Gift to understand, she didn't. Medic Two and Sergey exchanged dialog and Medic One attended to Miss Heller's wound and administered an injection. "An anesthetic."

"Will she... be okay?"

Through a translator he said, "Good you got her here when you did. The scan found hemoperitoneum, so we must perform urgent laparotomy to identify and control the source of internal bleeding."

"Oh my. Sounds serious. What exactly are you—" Gift's face turned green as the medic inserted a thin tube with a sharp metal tip into Heller's abdomen. Light-headedness nearing faint claimed the space her brain occupied.

"You are no nurse." Her queasiness exposed Sergey's lie yet the medic continued working.

Sergey started in Russian then said, "They are with us. Doctor Petrov is good doctor, will care for Margaret. This is Nikolay, one of mine."

"I'm lost. What's going on here?"

"Small incursion of Philistines. They've taken our Dome One, seat of government. They took Nadezhda and her family hostage, and most of the board members. Bulkheads sealed the rest of colony from them."

"What do they hope to accomplish?"

"This we do not know. They have most of the guards in custody. I must contact my men outside Dome One and mount an offensive to take it back."

"Oh mamma. How'd this happen?"

"We told you they had more weapons, better weapons. Two days ago, they breached wall behind Dome One, then an airlock. First wave we handled, then they tossed gas canisters to debilitate my guards. The few that retreated sealed the dome."

"What can they do from there? I mean the Philistines."

"They have not much control other than holding of hostages. Gift, stay with Margaret, see she is okay. Assist Doctor Petrov as needed."

"Wait, you're leaving me here? Where... *what?*"

"I must get my remaining guards, make plan and handle this situation. You must stay here."

"And Tom and Aimée? What's happened to them?"

"This I do not know. I assume to be interrogated, is what I would do. I fear it will become obvious they are not from the R.F."

"The Philistines would know that? Are they Russian?"

"Some. Descendants from two centuries ago. We think they most are from European Union nations."

"*Wait*. Aimée."

"I told you, dear. She is being inter—"

"She's supposed to talk to these people. I get things changed. I mean, all of this... stuff. Them being here and all. But can't we try to talk before you go in there shooting?"

"Of my men few remain, no idea what I am up against. If I try for your friends, it takes time and resources I cannot afford. This is our colony. We will handle this."

To start his '*We will handle this*,' Sergey walked to the door and gently knocked. The guard responded by pushing the door open and seemed genuinely surprised by the fist that knocked his head back. In half a second Sergey had the unsuspecting guy's enormous gun in hand and with it, waved him into the room and onto the floor. Medic Two, the alter ego of Nikolay the guard, tied the man's hands and feet then wrapped a cloth over his mouth, limiting him to muffled mumblings. Sergey and Nikolay vanished. Left in anxious suspense, Gift once again found herself in a conflict to take over a colony. The colony and players differed, the trepidation did not.

"Hold this."

"*Huh?*"

"Hold this, *nurse*." Medic One—Doctor Petrov—held a second tube. "Keep it slightly elevated." When Gift took hold of it, Petrov reached for a third tube, thin with a metallic weave where the others were clear synthetic.

"I found bleeding and am going to cauterize it. Please keep that tube exactly as you have it."

What Gift compared to gurgles of slurping soup combined with the coppery odor of burned flesh and dried blood brought her to the verge of emesis. The gagging started, a bitter taste at the back of her mouth, the tightening in her esophagus. Minutes passed too slowly and Gift began the calculations for a discrete way to vomit while maintaining her hold on the tube, half in her hand and half inside a human body.

"That's it. Done."

Gift released the tube, took half a step to let it flow. The mind's occupation while cleaning the mess of her sick provided a distraction exceedingly more pleasant than the sour stench of her stomach's fermentation. She tossed the last towel in the bin. "So, she's okay?"

"She should not be moved, but yes, I think so."

"Good, 'cause I gotta go."

"Not a good idea." The monotone translator lacked the bravado of the doctor's voice. "We are not knowing how things will be, and I do not recommend going anywhere near Sergey, his men, or Dome One."

"I need to find my friends. Try to talk to these people."

Emphatic mumblings from the bound, gagged Philistine on the floor met Gift's words. His *mm's* reached a higher intensity of volume. Without a proper thought process to reach the decision, Gift pulled the cloth from his mouth.

"Please... we don't want violence. Let me help. We only want to talk, don't want to hurt anyone." His words rang sincere if a little pathetic. Gift remembered pathetic people needed sympathy but struggled to find it for the guy. Doctor Petrov's skepticism didn't help.

"Not want to hurt anyone? You should have thought about that before attacking us. Killing many."

"*No*, we killed no one. Each time we shot no one, not a single bullet. Even now, we used gas to incapacitate your guards—not kill them, not even hurt them."

"Why? Why are you doing this? What do you hope to accomplish?"

"Dialog, Miss, like you said. We fought only to defend ourselves and our resources from you people. We've tried to contact you, to talk."

"*What*? We saw the vid. You shot at these people, tried to scale the wall. Your people were attacking them."

"*Them*? Hold on... You're not from this colony? There's another one near by?"

They hadn't known about her little colony, hidden in a secrecy now exposed by Gift's careless tongue. Immense guilt made its way through the fright and took root. With no idea how to walk it back, she ignored the question.

"Just... wait. Let me get this straight. You're saying *we* have been attacking you? Your resources? But *our* colony has much more than yours, so how does that even make sense?" Gift doubted her use of *we* and *our* convinced him, but it was worth a shot.

"No idea... but it's true. They're looking for weapons."

The doctor waved his hands. "Enough. We can't trust these people. He will say anything to save skin. They have been attacking us. They penetrated the colony and have hostages. This is what we know."

To control her tongue, Gift paused to think. "One thing I learned is what we don't know is much more than what we do. And too often a situation is far different from what we originally thought. So, we need to act wisely. Maybe... stop people getting hurt or killed."

"*Yes*," the man said from the floor. "Let me come with you and we'll do that."

"First of all, may I have your name?"

"Geoffrey."

"That's better. I'm Gift and you are going to help me, Geoffrey. But you'll stay here and tell me what I need to know. Who's in charge, the one we should try to talk to?"

Doctor Petrov remained silent while Gift continued the question-and-answer session. It turned out Geoffrey was most accommodating and cooperative. Unless, of course, he had handed Gift a bunch of lies and misdirects. Ever the optimist, she decided to accept his statements as sincere, yet resolved to be cautious about how far she would trust them. Not seeing a choice, she would test his information by finding and freeing Aimée and Tom—with no idea how she'd do that.

25

A naïve assumption led Gift to think all colonies were the same, built from the same plans. The Russian Federation's colony had more dissimilarities than the massive wall. Even with the rough map Doctor Petrov scribbled on the palm of her hand, navigating the corridors proved difficult.

The white medic coat she borrowed would have its usefulness tested in the first verification of the intel Geoffrey volunteered. 'They will let medical staff pass in this corridor,' he told her. 'Once you reach the service passageway, you should remove it.' To her dismay, his only advice from that point was, 'don't let anyone see you.'

Doing her best to avoid eye contact and present a face devoid of expression—hiding the intense fear mounting behind her eyes—Gift hastened along as two guards approached. *Purposeful walking*, she said to herself. *Look like you belong, Gift, like you know where you're going. And stop using the third person.* After the patrol passed, her lungs took what they needed to settle her nerves.

When the door that resembled the splotch in the line on her palm didn't open, Gift tried the next. In the small office, she found Tom's confiscated taser where Geoffrey said it would be. Two points so far on the trust meter. Here Gift shed the lab coat as a medic in the passageway would raise suspicions. The Philistines—if her new friend was right, Pioneers—were likely to spot her in the blood-stained shirt if she failed the 'don't let anyone see you' directive. Pressing her luck, she rummaged through the place, opening cabinets and bins hoping for a shirt, jacket, something. She found scissors.

Right where the line on her palm indicated, Gift found the T-junction—not drawn to scale, the map required estimations. The passage to the left was where Geoffrey believed they took Aimée and Tom. When a door groaned to warn of approaching humans, Gift ducked back into the office so cramped it could have been a closet. Muffled voices passed the door. The word *prisoners* reached Gift's ear and one said, 'she's cute, too.' In her cut-off shirt and armed with a taser and a pair of scissors, it was up to her to free her friends.

Breathe Gift. You can do this. I *can do this.*

If she dared call it a plan, it was a simple one. No one knew what she looked like, small, and unthreatening. The shirt cut above the navel brilliantly converted her exposed midriff into an asset. If needed, perhaps she'd use her femininity as a distraction—that always worked in poorly written action vids she enjoyed watching, where female protagonists captured dull-minded men in their sensual charms to get the drop on them. A confirmation the taser stayed tucked in her waistband behind her back, a deep breath, she flung the door open to find no one.

Having psyched herself up in the small office, Gift found herself ready for action in an empty corridor. Another silent pep-talk and two deep breaths opened the door the guards had exited. No womanly wiles needed, the taser kept its place. She found the prisoners she had come to liberate zip-tied to chairs back-to-back in the small yellow room.

"Nice shirt." Aimée spoke as if they had routinely passed in the hall.

"*Huh*? Oh, right. To get rid of the blood. I'm here to rescue you."

Tom jumped his chair, increasing the space between him and Aimée. "Can you get these ties off?" Bruised wrists outlining his restraints said he had evidently been trying to free himself without success.

"There's no release." After she pulled and twisted the zip-ties her open palm smacked her forehead. Gift had another asset besides her exposed abdomen. The scissors made quick work cutting loose four wrists and four ankles. Before her mind called up the third asset, Tom pulled it from her back, checked if it was charged and ready, and threw her a smile.

"You had it on safety lock."

From between lifted shoulders Gift said, "It's my first stun-gun."

"I'll hold it from now on, let's go."

"Go where? And Love, how's Maggie?"

"Follow me, then I'll tell you what's going on. Yeah, that'd be good. I mean—*Basta*, let's go."

When Gift led them into the small office Tom protested, rightly pointing out that when the guards returned to find empty chairs and cut restraints, they would search for them. Convinced they'd not look in the room just across the corridor, Gift held her ground.

"Okay, what do you know? How'd you get free? How'd you find us?" The speed of Tom's questions rattled Gift. Not knowing which to answer first, she borrowed one of Raff's tricks.

"Allora..." Stretching the O helped gather her thoughts. "A band of Pioneers managed to breach the wall and took Dome One, but the Russians sealed it. They have hostages, and most of Sergey's guards, but he's free and gathering what troops he has left to storm the dome and take it back... he said."

"Maggie? How's Maggie?"

"Fine. She's going to be fine. Doctor Petrov fixed her up, stopped the internal bleeding. Said your patch job wasn't bad. Oh, and it's good we got here when we did. She'd not've made—"

Tom's sharp tongue cut her words. "We need a plan. I should help Sergey. Where is he?"

"No, Aimée needs to talk to these people. Something's not right with this situation."

"Tell me about it. A lot's not right. Why I need to help Sergey round up these Philistines."

"*No.*" Surprised by her own forcefulness, Gift asserted, "Listen to me, I spoke to one of them. Things are... not as they seem, not as we've been told..."

After relating Geoffrey's information dump, Gift insisted a dialog could prevent needless bloodshed, one war inside a colony being enough for her lifetime. Silence absorbed their voices when guards returned, barked unpleasantries at the empty holding room, and raced away. Gift's smug *I-told-you-so* smile flattened when she realized it would be more difficult to sneak around with everyone looking for the escapees. They needed a plan.

Tom protested Gift's idea, wouldn't even call it a plan. Aimée hesitated but trusted her friend's judgment. When he exhausted all possibilities and admitted not knowing the layout gave them a tremendous disadvantage, Tom agreed. They would surrender. Door lever in hand, Tom paused to vibrations of thunderous footfalls trampling the concrete floor. The three froze until the commotion retreated.

Emboldened by the guards' preoccupation, Gift, Tom, and Aimée stepped out and trailed the clatter of boots toward Dome One. Echoes of violence filled the corridor before they reached the small archway as a newly recognizable sound bounced over Gift's ears, the pop of gunfire and the snap of bullets piercing the air. They were too late. After stepping through for a peek in the dome, Tom jerked himself back from the archway.

"There's not many of them, Sergey's men. They ducked behind some maintenance carts, but the others have the better position and a larger force. A dozen, maybe more. All well-armed."

Eyebrows raised, Gift asked, "You saw all that in a half-second...? What can we do? How can we stop this? We need to stop this."

"I'll go out there. Neutral party. Tell them who I am and that we came to talk. I'll offer to mediate."

"*No.*" To forbid her friend from going, Gift pushed all the authority her vocal cords could muster around the trepidation. "You'll get shot. No."

"She's right, it could work. Listen…"

It took a second for Gift to realize Tom didn't mean, *listen to me,* but listen to the silence seeping in from the dome. "They've stopped?"

Tom's head leaned out to verify. "Seems so. Hold on, I think something's happening… I see Nadezhda Anoykina, this guy with her and a young woman, teenager. Two men with guns on them. They're standing in front of, I guess, their admin building… facing Sergey's team."

Squeeks and clanks lifted from the fidgeting of Sergey's men in the dome and carried themselves like a breeze into the corridor. Words stirred in their wake, amplified as if from a radio with its volume cranked up the way Mike played his terrible music.

"We came to end this conflict and you greeted us with violence." A digitized voice filled the pauses with the translation. "We have hurt no one, yet you shoot us down like animals. If that is what you think of us, that is how we must be. We have your President and her children. Surrender or we will shoot one of them."

The maddening silence of the dome's reply lingered like too many minutes in the toilet box line. The approaching violence fidgeted Gift, teeth clenched, and her anxiety moistened the small of her back.

"You have five seconds." The voice loudened.

Stealing another look, Tom reported, "He's got a gun to the girl's head. My goodness, they're gonna shoot that poor girl."

"*Oksana,*" Aimée blurted. "Nadezhda's daughter."

"They're gonna kill her daughter right in front of her?" Gift's expressed disbelief expected no answer.

Sergey's robust voice needed no amplification. "*Stop*. Do not harm the girl."

"Wait," Aimée yelled. Where was she? Gift hadn't noticed her step into the dome. "Everyone, please wait. I came here to talk. I'm a representative of the New Europa colony. Please, we all need to talk. If I can get these men to lay down their weapons and I come forward to talk, will you promise not to harm that girl?"

Looking in for the first time, Gift saw Aimée creeping away, closer to Sergey, closer to the Philistines, closer to the violence. Frightfully watching her friend step into the line of fire, hands above her head, helplessness engulfed Gift, familiar and unwelcome.

The amplified voice said, "We need to see their weapons on the ground, guards standing with hands on heads."

Aimée faced the head of the Rosgvardiya. "Sergey?"

Compliance heard in the clattering of guns hitting the concrete preceded Sergey and his men rising in careful motion and placing their hands atop their heads. The handgun lost its interest in the girl's head, permitting her to her feet. Trembling, she fell into the arms of the President—reduced by the moment to nothing more important than her daughter's mother.

In slow time, Gift watched her best friend place herself in the hands of the enemy, if they were the enemy. It was impossible to untangle the sides of the conflict, the right and wrong. Perhaps truth fell somewhere in-between.

Minutes refused to pass at a tolerable pace when Aimée, Nadezhda, and the person Gift assumed to be the leader of the marauder band disappeared into the building behind the young lives of Yuri and Oksana, still with armed guards at their backs. A subset of the remaining intruders zip-tied Sergey and his men, who surprisingly offered no resistance. Although the right move, Gift found that curious. Her mind switched back to anxious dread.

"How long has it been? What are they doing? What's happening?"

"Try to relax." Before Gift could offer a biting response, Tom raised his hands in surrender. "I'm sorry, that was a stupid thing to say. I'm worried for her too. But this is what she came here for, right? Not quite like this, but still, if anyone can talk them to a resolution, it's her."

In a memory, Tom's arms wrapped tightly around her, his calming voice telling her it was okay, Matteo wasn't being burned alive in the fire. In *that* moment he was right, Matteo was fine. But his reassurance did nothing for Charlie. Charlie died. She found his words in *this* moment less comforting than he likely intended them to be. Aimée could die, and no words had the power to prevent it.

Movement, a break in the agonizing nothingness. A guard from the invaders came forward to summon Sergey, who followed him into the building. When the door opened to let them in, Aimée stepped out, lifting Gift's heart to the top of her chest. Aimée leaned into Yuri's ear and escorted the son of the President of the Russian Federation into that heinous building that kept her captive to whatever transpired behind its doors. Not knowing was torture.

26

To take the son of the Russian leader, a nobody—far less handsome than his mother claimed and nowhere near good enough for Aimée—to join the talks made no sense to Gift. She understood so little about their government but had learned that Nadezhda's children inherited no position in it.

"They're treating Sergey's men rather well."

That organic thought, or Tom might have broken the silence intentionally, intrigued Gift, adding weight to the already credible words of Geoffrey the Pioneer. Could it be they'd gotten it wrong? How quickly she blamed and distrusted the R.F. again disturbed her.

"Geoffrey told me they were peaceful."

"They were firing blanks, *nonlethal* force, trying not to kill anyone. Sergey's men? Live ammo, real bullets."

"*Non*-lethal. Thank you. Raff said *less* lethal the other day, and that made no sense. But these people... using nonlethal force? I think we got some of this very wrong."

"But don't forget, they opened fire on us at their bunker, unprovoked. Those were real bullets."

"How could I forget? I was so scared. And poor Miss Heller. I should check on her, but... I can't, not until I know Aimée's safe."

"I'd go, but I've got no idea how to find her."

Gift considered her palm map, now sweaty blotches of ink in shades of black and gray. One of them resembled that bullfrog, which brought unhappy memories into the chaos swirling through Gift's head. She suppressed it and wondered how often thoughts of her indecent exposure would return. Her mind preferred their absence. Tom may have said something she didn't catch.

"*Aimée.*"

A queen to address her subjects, Nadezhda emerged from the administration building and stood before those who'd gathered minutes after the shooting stopped. Aimée came out and stood beside her, followed by the nameless man Gift assumed the curious new people's leader.

"Shh." No one around Gift had spoken.

Perched atop a bench to see—or be seen by—the crowd, Aimée held a hand to her chin. "People of the Russian Federation…" Something amplified her voice and parroted her words in Russian. "And people of the bunkers. Terrible misunderstandings exist between your people, and terrible actions *independent* of both. I am Aimée Toussaint of New Europa. In cooperation with the leadership of the R.F., we came on a diplomatic mission to open a dialog with the ones who, for two centuries, have been peaceful survivors. We call them Pioneers."

Where Gift would be a nervous wreck, Aimée exuded steady confidence.

"What we learned today by calm and open talk, is that a faction within *your* federation operating independent of its leadership was the aggressor in the conflicts with the Pioneers. Even after being attacked and having their vital resources plundered, they have come here peacefully."

Shouts of protest hovered over the swelling crowd like a storm cloud about to unleash its fury. A formidable presence, President Anoykina barked *something* in a commanding tone, hushing the frenzied horde.

"The Pioneers used teargas and nonlethal ammunition against your guards. Their threat to Oksana was a bluff to end the violence, with no bullet in the gun. Their leader, Mister Dmytro Melnyk, informed us that in one of their bunkers, rogue forces from the R.F. overran their homes. It is why they came, to sue for peace. With such requests denied, they were fired-upon without provocation. Miss Anoykina affirms this, and Mister Lazarev has verified it by reviewing the security footage.

"We identified the leader of this movement and agreed to hold a tribunal to bring the matter to justice, to move forward in peaceful relations between our three peoples."

"Povesit' yego... Povesit' yego..."

A host of voices merged into a chant, repeating on a loop what Gift assumed by the accompanying gestures meant *hang'em.*

"Enough." Nadezhda held her fist to her chin and oddly spoke in English, the translation a macabre echo. "We won't have mob justice, but we will have justice. It pains me much to say, but it must be. Justice does not hide behind bureaucracy, or family. This is not the old Russia or the old ways. My Yuri will face tribunal, will face justice."

With the crowd settled, perhaps shocked, Gift pushed through to reach Aimée, with Tom trailing close behind.

"Love, we should've switched shirts. They'd've listened to me without needing the fear of Nadezhda put in'em."

"*That's* what you say? After all... *this*?"

"It's crazy. Yuri was as into me as Nadezhda said. Even tried flirting with me despite everything. I used it to get him talking, he's not the brightest."

"What's he done?"

"Recruited a bunch of guards, been doing it for several months. Organized raids, taking resources these Pioneers desperately need. The ones that fired on us, shot Maggie? Yuri's guys. Nadezhda thinks he was playing for a takeover here too."

"What the heck is with people? Our insurrection? Now this? Her own son."

"Human nature. As much as the world's changed, all we should've learned. In the end we're animals that can talk. But now talk is getting us someplace. Love, we can make some genuine progress here if we handle it right."

"*Wait*." Tom put a serious face over the already intense scowl. "Of all the bunkers they inhabit, Yuri's people took the one closest to *us*. Was *he* the threat against us the whole time?"

Aimée hoisted her eyebrows. "I think you may be onto something. Our colony is much easier for him to take than this one. They didn't plan this uprising. This was the Pioneers doing."

"Oh mamma. They're still there, and they know where we are." Turning to Tom, Gift's face paled. "We gotta get back. Gotta warn them."

"The air transport?"

A glimmer of hope brightened Gift's eyes. "They've got a communication array here. I can get Raff."

"Love? I think you and I should talk with Yuri. But first, you've gotta meet Dmytro."

"*Me*? Why would he want to meet me?"

"First, look at you, rocking that midriff." A slap on the arm repaid Aimée's smirk. "You're the only N.E. board member here. I mean, the only one conscious."

Tom said, "She's got a point. You need to speak for us."

***

"Gift Ojo of the Board of Directors of New Europa, meet Mister Dmytro Melnyk, speaking for the Pioneers."

"Miss Ojo, it is my pleasure."

"Very nice to meet you, sir. We came a long way and hoped to meet under very different circumstances."

"Frankly, we had no idea colonies existed. Imagine our shock to find this one. You see, we'd been taught from birth about how you all abandoned us, left us to die when you headed for your new colonies on Mars."

"Did Aimée tell you? We thought we were on Mars the whole time. We were just as shocked to learn the truth."

Aimée said, "Too much has happened because of lies. Our history is full of it. Now *we* need to stop it."

"Not only history. Secrets and lies are our now."

"True, Mister Melnyk. But we can change that. Aimée and I have so many questions, but we'll have time, later, I mean... For now, we need to proceed shrewdly."

"Miss Ojo, I'm glad you're here. Aimée assures me you're the right person for the job."

"Job? What job? Also too, please, no one calls me Miss Ojo. I'm Gift. Now, what's this about a job?"

"The tribunal, Love. Obviously, this is the first time for such a thing. Dmytro and Nadezhda agreed upon a fair, unbiased process with you, Dmytro, and Sergey as the tribunal. One from each people ensures fairness."

"Um... *what*? I can't judge anyone. You and Tom are from N.E. Or... we can transport Raff here."

"That's why you're perfect. Come, we need to speak to Yuri then go prepare. The tribunal is this afternoon."

"This afternoon. Are you crazy?"

"Sure, but you knew that. We need to move quickly, before the crowd decides mob justice is swifter. Come on, let's go see Yuri."

Reluctant, Gift couldn't argue and followed Aimée to find Yuri sitting under guard with a scarlet-faced teenager seething over him, her violent shouts bludgeoning her brother. The seating area resembled their meeting room, down to the single sofa chairs, reminding Gift how long she'd been on her feet. The thought ached her arches and curled her toes inside her shoes.

"Oksana, sweetheart. Please leave us to talk."

The blonde girl who looked a bit over sixteen glared at Aimée as if to melt her face. Unlike Yuri, she was as beautiful as her mother described. A powerful rage filled her aqua-blue eyes as she yelled an explosion of hatred at her brother and stormed off in a feral march.

"Well, to what do I owe the pleasure of two such lovely ladies here with me?" Yuri was Luca and Max in one, only worse. Somehow, much worse. "I love the shirt. You wear this for Yuri?"

Beady eyes walked all over her, then Gift mustered the courage to ask, "What was your plan? What about New Europa?"

"So... my tribunal starts in secret?"

"Gift, I hate to say, he's right. We cannot interrogate him, not like this."

"Then why are we even in here with this creep?"

"Creep? No, no creeping. Just me to tell what you must know. We make deal. You help Yuri, Yuri helps you. Is good deal for Yuri and for you, my pretty Gift."

"What are you on about? If you have something to say, say it." Gift became impatient and wanted nothing more than to leave the man's sight.

"Yuri knows things. About New Europa. About Russian Federation. United Africa. Informations to keep your colony safe."

"*Safe?*"

"Da. Threat is not Philistines, as you now see. Is not my people either."

Begging for satiation, Gift's stomach complained noisily about the meager breakfast they had racing toward the colony hours ago. Thoughtlessly her head tilted to find Yuri's eyes on her exposed abdomen.

"You are hungry for Yuri, my Gift."

"Listen, *creep*, if you don't stop playing games, we're outta here and the next you'll see is the tribunal."

"Playing games? Such wonderful expressions. We play no games in R.F. I have much to say, important things. But to learn, you must help me."

Aimée took some heat off Gift. "Out with it, then. What do you want for this information of yours?"

"I give what you need, informations to save your little colony, and Yuri goes free. Simple."

"Free? *Free*. Of all... I mean... *what*?"

"Yes, my Gift. Yuri goes free and you come with me. Is good deal." The smirk no one could mistake for a smile might have hinted at a joke. It angered Gift the same.

"Listen you—"

"Gift and I can't promise a deal. I need to run it by the tribunal. And your mother. Of course, we must evaluate your information. For all we know, you could be blowing sunshine up our butts."

Even now that she'd seen sunshine, Gift couldn't find context for that last comment.

"Yeah, she's right. You gotta at least give us an idea of what's so valuable. You say the safety of our colony, but what does that even mean?"

"I tell nothing before deal."

Aimée raised a hand to settle Gift. "Tell you what... I'll see if we can structure a deal that offers you amnesty, with banishment, based on the value of your information. Only if it's what you say, you walk. But if you're full of crap, you get nothing, just whatever the tribunal decides."

"If you get this in writing... *and* my mother signs, we have deal."

27

A face equally concerned and confused, Raff hadn't expected to hear from Gift for another day or two when they'd return from meeting the Pioneers. 'They shot at us,' as a vidChat opener did nothing to allay fear, reenforcing a lesson Gift had learned the hard way: words couldn't be taken back, their influence never undone.

"No, it's not like that. I mean, I guess... maybe it is... a little. But we're okay, really. We're guests of the R.F."

"Margaret's been shot, the Pioneers attacked you, you walked into a war... And you tell me everything's alright?"

"Well, when you put it *that* way..." a cracked smile didn't soften Raff a bit. "Miss Heller will be fine. The Russian doc took real good care of her. And the Pioneers didn't attack us, that's what I'm trying to tell you. It was some independent Russians. Yuri's got rogue guards, *they* fired on us, shot Miss Heller."

"Now you and Aimée are on a tribunal to judge Yuri?"

"I am. Aimée will be the chair, not a judge."

"Cara, are you okay with that? Doesn't seem something you'd be comfortable doing."

"*Right*? That's what I said. Said we should get you here on a transport."

"Gee, thanks."

"But I understand, I mean, it's the best way forward to have one from each people. Oh, time, I should be preparing. We need to talk about the threat to N.E. Yuri... he says he has some information, about our safety."

"He may just be trying to save his own skin."

"Yeah, I said that too. *Ma*, the threat may be real. That bunker, the one closest to us? I mean to you, not me... while I'm here. You know what I mean." Raff's smile said she did. "The threat there... it's trained Russian guards, not the Pioneers. And they know where we are. How are the alerts coming, and the weapons? Can you send me an update on those?"

"Of course. The perimeter alert went live yesterday. If they're on foot, we'll have early warning."

"Oh Raff, that's wonderful news. Grazie. My mind can come down a little. The weapons? We need them ready sooner than later."

"I'll follow up and get you the most recent updates."

"Grazie. Gotta go. Don't want to but gotta be ready to play judge. Oh, I don't like how that sounds..."

Gift finished the homemade *Golubtsi* Vitaliy Filatov, Nadezhda Anoykina's personal bodyguard, had brought her when he learned she was there. They cooled while she had her vidChat. It was fine. It delighted her to be right about fresh-made being kilometer's better than packed and shipped, and his mother's were delicious.

The judges and chairperson discussed the underlying guidelines and legal principles they'd use as a basis for the proceedings. Agreement reached meant a procedure to follow and they could begin. One last thing, they needed to settle Yuri's deal and evaluate his intel. When Sergey left to fetch Nadezhda to approve and sign the agreement, Aimée took fashion advice from Gift—that was a first.

"Sweetie, *really*?"

"Your idea, and I kinda love it. My blouse had Maggie's blood on it too, and we're representing our colony in this tribunal."

"It had a few drops of blood on the bottom, and you cut it almost in half."

"Couldn't have your midriff getting all the attention. Besides, you see how distracted Yuri gets. We could use it in our favor."

"True. If he saw your *swimsuit*," she put the word in air quotes, "he'd tell us everything, even without a deal."

"I can try that if you want," Aimée said with a mischievous smile.

When Sergey returned alone, a puzzled Gift asked, "Where is she?"

"She said no deal. Yuri gets what he gets. It cannot seem Miss Nadezhda is protecting her son."

"Well Love, I may need to try your swimsuit idea." Despite the playful wink, Gift knew her bold friend would do it.

***

A blank-faced Yuri ambled into the square in the center of Dome One and his gaze swept over the hundred plus spectators and the makeshift stage. Aimée sat on a tall podium chair beside the tribunal members with her midriff on display, holding Yuri's lustful eyes in captivity. They lacked the uneasiness Gift expected with his tribunal beginning without his deal.

"People of the Russian Federation..." Aimée's thirst for the spotlight soaked up the attention. "We are here for this tribunal to assess the actions of Yuri Anoykina..."

As the summary speech continued, the pauses between sentences for the translation let Gift speculate on hearing Yuri's surname. Union partners in N.E. held their birth names and children took their father's surname. With no identified father, Gift bore her mother's name. Doubtful she and Yuri shared this in common, a connection flashed on her mental display: Nadezhda never mentioned a partner.

"...and we are here to determine these facts. We will begin by inviting the accused to make a statement."

This time Gift needed to listen to the pauses as Yuri spoke in Russian. "Two centuries may have passed, but we are Russians. This never changes. The mightiest superpower—respected the world over. Our culture is rich. So rich. This does not die. This *must* not die. When the little colony of New Europa asked for help, we sent supplies. For nine months, my mother led us down the path of compromise. Cowering more and more to these people, like they are better than us. *Us. Russians.*"

Supportive grunts came from the crowd, a few pumped their fists, which Gift assumed meant agreement. The translator lacked the grammatical mistakes of Yuri's English.

"How do we handle these Philistines? These savages living in bunkers, in holes? No government. No education. They come here and threaten us, and we do *nothing*. This Russian Federation is weak. We want a strong colony, like the proud Russia from before we hid under these domes. It is time for Russians to be *Russians*."

The audience intensified, emboldened by the homely man's ramblings. What he lacked in looks he made up for in charisma, or at least in riling a crowd.

"Is this an admission of guilt, Mister Anoykina?"

"No," he replied in English, not waiting for the translator. "Is admission of pride. Nothing more."

"Then let's hear statements from the tribunal before the witnesses are called. First, mister Sergey Lazarev."

The imposing guard stood to face the observers. "We are Russians. We are proud. But we are humans first. We have an opportunity to make a new Earth for all humans." He sat. The power expressed in his few words amazed Gift and her respect for the man grew.

When Gift stood, tugs couldn't make the shirt longer, restore the cut-away fabric. "I'm here as a neutral party, an outsider to these events. But I guess that's not entirely true, is it? I'm *actually* here because our senior Board member is recovering from a gunshot wound, the injury we blamed on the Pioneers. We now know a rogue faction of the R.F. had taken control of a bunker and are the ones who shot at us. We will uncover the truth about this."

After saying nothing she had prepared and unsure what she ended up saying, Gift sat and handed the little black box she spoke through to the next judge.

"Mister Dmytro Melnyk, of the Pioneers, please address the tribunal."

"Hello. We came here to talk. It took some time, and some unfortunate events to get us here, but we started talking." When he forgot to pause the blaring translation startled him. "This tribunal could aid us in furthering these talks in cooperation. It is about justice. We move forward in the path of justice. Thank you."

"As our first witness, we call Oksana Anoykina."

Aimée is doing so well.

Oksana wore an elegant dress of red with speckles of gold laced over the sheer fabric. She looked ready for an elaborate ball, yet her fiery eyes held a dark fierceness.

"My brother's an idealistic fool. He always resented our mother, never satisfied he wasn't a prince in line for the throne. *Idiot*." Turning away from the translator to face Yuri she shouted, "*Zhopa*," then continued. "And those guards he recruited are his friends. I know them all—jerks, all of them. He had meetings at our home when he didn't know I was listening. He's an idiot. I gave the tribunal a list of everyone in his room planning to take over the bunker. He is guilty and deserves no mercy." Dropping the device, she faced the crowd and yelled, "*Povesit' yego.*"

As much as she wanted to be anywhere else and leave the judging to anyone else, Gift needed to weigh the facts. Yet she couldn't stop her mind pondering the relationship of brother and sister. Her own made-up sibling connection with Matteo created a relatable bond, but even in her ugliest anger at him over the drops, she couldn't imagine a basis for such raw, passionate hatred. Something she wanted to file for later.

Other witnesses testified, offering less than favorable comments about Yuri. One stood apart, pretending to be neutral and offering praise for what a great guy Yuri was, how he cared about people. Repeatedly contradicting himself, he lost any credibility Yuri may have hoped him to have. Oksana yelling to the judges in English, 'He was in the room, planning with Yuri,' made him an unreliable witness.

The video evidence proved the most damning. Closer inspection of enhancement-zoomed frames of the guards firing on the Pioneers showed all friends of Yuri, the same ones Oksana had named. Sergey confirmed these were not in any regiment he sent to defend the wall, and he had not ordered his guards to shoot. The replay confirmed no Russians were injured. A close-up of the lead Pioneer saw him speaking, neck folded to see the guards on the wall. He shot only words and received a barrage of bullets in return.

"All evidence has been presented and all witnesses and interested parties have spoken. The tribunal will recess for deliberation and return a verdict." Aimée had no gavel or other signal, so she clapped her hands in one deliberately booming thump that must've stung her palms. She led the tribunal of three into the admin building where Nadezhda Anoykina waited for them.

"Nadezhda, you shouldn't be here," Aimée protested.

"Nothing dear, is to say to all that you are to render judgment as you see fit. And the punishment. Do not regard that he is my son. He is a fool. Gift, Aimée, I promise we will learn what informations he teased you. No deal needed, we will learn this and share with you. I think is nothing, he knows nothing. But if he does, we will know, and you will know." She nodded and left.

Gift recalled what Nailya said days ago. *At her disposal* meant something very different in the R.F. Shivers shook her shoulders but passed quickly.

Sergey spoke first, declaring Yuri guilty, and Dmytro readily agreed.

"Of course, yeah, he is. I mean, he conspired, he knew the rogue guards. But have we proven that he sent them?"

"Da, he is guilty. All evidence is clear."

"Aimée, what do you think?"

"You know I can't answer, Love. I'm here to observe and to be sure you stick to the guidelines. Nothing more."

"Right, sorry. So, guilty. Now what's the sentence?"

"Under Russian law, he is detained and interrogated. Locked in tiny cell for the rest of his life."

"Mister Melnyk, do your people have a system of justice for anything like this?"

"Some of my people would say death. In one bunker they executed a criminal, eye for eye. This Yuri, he may not have pulled a trigger, but he has blood and death on his hands the same."

"*Wait.* Are you saying we should order his execution? I can't do that."

"I answered your question. I agree with Sergey, as a Russian criminal, apply Russian punishment."

"Okay, I think I can live with that. Aimée, we're ready."

***

In single file they marched onto the stage. Nadezhda and Oksana sat in front of the crowd. Aimée stepped forward. "The tribunal has reached a verdict." Facing a verdict and sentencing, Yuri focused on her midriff.

"This tribunal has found you guilty of treason, conspiracy to commit espionage against a foreign state, and collusion to commit murder. The sentence imposed upon you shall be life imprisonment under articles of law of the Russian Federation. Do you have any questions?"

"Just one. Will you come visit Yuri?" His lips formed a vile and devious smile, but not for his rude remarks alone. Gift saw a man unaffected by what transpired, apathetic to the prospect of life in Russian detention, the interrogation he must expect. His odd and unsettling reaction robbed the moment of the finality she expected.

28

"**S**tockholm syndrome?" Miss Anoykina questioned. "What is this and why do you say this about my Oksana? She is good girl, young. She was scared, so scared from being made hostage. But she is strong girl. She is fine. Fine."

The woman was clearly upset about the topic, the most vulnerable Gift had seen the leader of her colony. That included seeing her as a hostage with a gun on her daughter's head. This weakness didn't fit the woman, her only non-bespoke outfit.

"It happens sometimes. Ask Gift about Tom, her former guard." Aimée's wink to Gift met a hard, unappreciative gaze. "It's when someone develops an attachment to their captor. Like a coping mechanism. She feels sympathetic affection for her abuser. How she is with Brian, even after he held that gun to her head."

"No. Now we are having good relations with these... what do you call Philistine people now?"

"Pioneers," Gift said.

"Da, good relations. Is this, no syndrome."

"With all due respect..." As Gift's mouth moved, her mind considered how every time—whether in a vid or real life—she ever heard the phrase, *with all due respect*, a less than respectful comment followed. "Your good relations have been less than a day. She was captive to them, Brian, for days. To develop feelings for someone that held a gun to your head and threatened to kill you? That's... it's not healthy."

"Sweet Gift, dear Aimée, you are good girls. Your help yesterday is much appreciated. Today you helped start real talks with Pioneers. Wonderful. And you are brave for saying this to me. In this I see you care for my Oksana. This does not keep me from becoming angry, and I am not so nice a person when I am angry. So is better for you to not say these things to me, and your stay here is nice one. I so wanted you both to stay at my home. Let us not ruin with such talkings. Come. We eat and drink and have a nice evening before you leave us in the morning. Come. Oksana will join us for dinner."

Dinner dazzled the guests. Nadezhda—her servants—really knew how to throw down. They served a hearty, delicious *Borscht* loaded with meat and sautéed vegetables. Pelmeni came as a new and unexpected treat and Gift's tastebuds rejoiced when the flavor combined with the broth. While Gift cleverly avoided the vodka, Nadezhda appeared to have breached her tolerable limit. She fell fast asleep soon after they retired to the sofas. Gift marveled at how Oksana tossed back a full shot-glass of the hateful clear liquid as if it were water—after her mother was out cold.

"Oksana, did you see my interview with your mom? From what she told me about you, I couldn't wait to meet you. But sweetheart, I need to ask you about Brian."

"No. Actually... you don't. Not your business."

Taking her hand Gift said, "Sweetie, we're concerned you may not understand some feelings you have. He held you captive, put a gun to your head, and you spent almost the whole day trailing him, talking, doing things for him. We're afraid you may be... *confused*, and the heightened emotions of the ordeal are shifting into *other* feelings."

"So, you guys are shrinks now?"

Gift lost the reference, but Aimée got it. "No, Oksana. We just care about you is all. At sixteen these are all new feelings, and you've been through a horrible ordeal."

"Yeah, we just want to help."

"Oh, *now* I need help? Now that *I'm choosing* who to spend time with? Where were *you* the last four years?" The mumbled last bit trailed off, but Gift believed she'd gotten it.

"Last four years? Sweetie, what do you mean? What's happened?" Gift turned to Aimée to find a face carved from concern.

"Nothing."

Withdrawn into herself on the sofa with her knees to her chin, Oksana clearly fought tears. Aimée knelt before the girl, hands on her knees.

"If something happened to you, it's okay to tell us. We want to help."

"I don't even know you. And you don't know me. Know nothing about me. Just... *go away.*"

"Did Yuri do something to you?" When Gift asked, a look of shock descended upon Aimée. "He's a bit older, and he's a creepy jerk. What did he do to you?"

The rest of the evening had Oksana expounding the nightmare her life had been for close to the last four years. The caring young women were ill-equipped to handle the delicate situation, often unable to find the words. Their caring ears seemed to be a welcome release for the girl if nothing else. They extended reassurance she'd done nothing wrong, had been a victim, and that it was over. She absorbed compassion like a sponge. Gift felt they had only started. Necessary and beneficial, it was undoubtedly the first time Oksana poured herself out to anyone about this. To them, complete strangers, not to her mother.

"Mom? She's okay. I mean, she's not around much. She has no clue, really. I guess running the known world does that. No time for a wild daughter like me that only causes problems. And now the world is bigger than we thought, and she'll be even more distracted. You can't tell her this. You have to promise me... none of this."

"Sweetie, it's not our place. But I believe *you* should tell her... when you're ready. Yuri is gone and he won't hurt you anymore. But your mother can help. She can get you the help you need."

Aimée nodded. "She told me about you. She loves you dearly. You should try to talk to her."

Sniffles and a half-nod came as the only answer the somber teenager offered. Oksana likely hadn't expected what the evening had become. She readily accepted Gift's offer to visit N.E., and they promised to arrange it sooner than later. The young woman excused herself to her bedroom.

The dumbfounded young ladies spent hours trying to imagine what the girl had gone through and admiring her strength. She'd taken a huge first step toward emotional recovery but had a long way to go. If the R.F. didn't have the professional help she needed, perhaps they'd find it in New Europa.

Nadezhda sounded warning of her return to consciousness with a deep snort. "Where's my Oksana?" she groggily asked before her eyelids separated.

"She's gone to bed. She was real tired."

"You were right Nadezhda, she's a handful, and I love her."

Almost talking over Aimée, Gift said, "I offered her to come visit me, and stay a few days in N.E. I hope that was okay. I'd have asked, but you were... well... not with us."

"Is wonderful. She needs such a role model. Few friends here, and these are not good for her. Thank you, my dear. A visit with you is good for her. We make this happen soon."

"Nadezhda, may I ask you something about Yuri...?"

Aimée cringed. Gift saw it and understood why, but she wouldn't betray Oksana's trust. As much as her mother needed to know, Gift kept her place. A slightly raised hand settled Aimée.

"What's really going to happen to him?"

"As I told, we will get his informations. He will spend the rest of his days in tiny cell. Bad food. No visitors."

"He didn't look bothered yesterday by the outcome. It seemed to me like he expected he'd get out or something. I'd imagine someone about to be tort—*interrogated* and tossed in jail would be less, I don't know... jovial."

"My Yuri is not much of a Russian, but is stronger than he looks, trust me. Is what makes him hate me. Hate he does not become President when I am dead. Only reason he doesn't killed me, I am sure." She laughed deeply, like she believed her words. "I know morning transport takes you lovely girls from me, but come to my office before. Leave time for talking, we discuss much before you go. Breakfast will be here, then come to my office."

The guest bedroom had its own full bathroom and an amazing ensuite shower, even better than their admin building ones. A full bathroom in each bedroom, Nadezhda told them—the concept blew Gift's mind. With no time limit and full hot water flow, Aimée had to pull Gift from it to take her shower before going to bed.

***

After a lovely breakfast of fresh fruits and muffins with decent espresso, though not as good as the coffee back home, they joined Nadezhda in her office as requested. Off his normal, Tom looked tired, almost ill, and Gift feared earth sickness had caught up with him. The icy tip of Aimée's nose touched Gift's ear. "An evening with Sergey? He's got a hangover."

"Good morning my lovelies… and Tom. Thank you for coming. I told you when we know you know. And we know something. We will learn more, I assure you."

"That was super-fast. What did he tell you? Is it about New Europa?"

"Slow Gift, I am telling. Taking of bunker was preparing to attack you, not us. His people will move soon, headed to your colony. They are aware you have no defense, no wall. They suppose it to be easy. Once they take your colony, plan was to capture me, put Yuri in charge. No matter now. Sergey is preparing to work with you, Tom. These people are Russians. Rogue, but Russians. We will help you handle them."

"Most kind." The green painting Tom's cheeks warned of vomit.

Please, not in the office of the mal'd President.

"Is more, but we have not yet the details. Soon. The threat he spoke is not only this one."

"How do you mean?" Gift's high pitch neared a fearful crackle.

"Not only from bunker. He talked of Africa colony, the Chinese. No threat from Africa—barely a colony. We know little of China Republic, but we know they are largest, likely strongest colony."

"I thought the United Republic of Mars was the largest, most powerful, with the old United States and United Kingdom from *before*. I mean, The Founders were from there." Correct about the history, Gift missed a vital point. The U.R.M. lived up to its name, at least the *M*, as the only colony built off-world and located on Mars. Her mind caught up. "Oh, duh. Sorry."

Nadezhda offered a genuine chuckle. "You are cute, a real gift, as I said. We think China may be what he is talking. How he knows anything, we do not know. *Yet.*"

Lifting her heels, Aimée's face brightened. "Wasn't one rumor of our sabotage the New Republic of China? So quick to blame them."

"Yeah. That was a popular theory. Right up there with Martians woke by the terraforming."

In a breath of laughter, Tom said, "Hadn't heard that one." Cradling the back of his head, he looked as if he wished he hadn't spoken.

Checking the time Gift said, "Almost O-nine hundred. We gotta catch the transport before it leaves."

"My dear, transport does not leave without you. If Nadezhda keeps you until tomorrow, it waits for you."

***

To their surprise, Oksana and her large totes, three of them, sat waiting for them in the transport. Apparently, her visit would happen much sooner than later. It pleased Gift, though she knew she would be quite distracted when they got home. External threats to her colony tended to occupy her time.

"Maggie?"

"Went home on yesterday's transport."

With that, Tom said his farewells and closed the hatch. Duty called him to stay behind with Sergey to coordinate a response to the new threat.

29

Wonder dripped from Oksana's expression as she gazed out the window of the flying transport. "First time out of the colony?" Gift asked to allay her own fear—her first time in a flyer, so far from the ground. At least on that dreadful overpass she had the solidity of the bridge under the vehicle, though it hadn't convinced her she wouldn't plummet to her death. Her engineer brain worked to convince her of the safety of her predicament while a loop played in her head: *Is this thing safe?*

"Technically, no... I've been outside lots of times, but Mom doesn't allow me beyond the wall."

"Any idea how many hours you can stay?"

"Not sure I'm supposed to say."

"We have medical data from the R.F. and they've got ours. I don't think it's any secret."

"Well... it may be. See, my jerk brother, he was sort of the guinea pig of the *royal family*." Even the girl's air quotes had a sarcastic tone. "He was first to take the new medications. I thought it'd kill him, but unfortunately, he made it. Turned out the near-death phase is the key. If someone survives that, they pass the threshold."

"What threshold is that?"

It intrigued Gift but also made her more than a little upset with her friends at the R.F. for keeping secrets. The insurrection in New Europa resulted from such. *What else are they hiding?*

"Three days at least. Supposedly a few of the guards made it nearly a week before getting sick. I've not stayed more than a few hours. There's not much to do between the colony and the wall."

"Ever swim?"

"You mean, in water? No. Where would I?"

"It's tons of fun. I'll teach you."

***

After a quick lunch, Aimée took Oksana to show her the studio and likely put her to work researching things Aimée had no interest in doing herself. Besides, she'd be busy preparing the evening's update broadcast. With a clearly defined threat and looming dread of an imminent attack, Gift needed the afternoon to check on the progress of the defenses. On her way to the admin building, Gift lent a few precious seconds to her concern for Tom joining Sergey's raiding party.

"Good to see you too, Mike." Gift struggled to speak from within his tight hug. "Anton, hi. How's things going?"

"Quite well. We even made a prototype," Mike joyfully related.

"The range is not so good. Needs to be one meter or less or is just noise. Only noise."

"At least you've made something that works. I mean, it *does* work?"

"*Yes*. Melody has put me and Anton out cold a few times."

"That's great news you guys, excellent work. *Ma*, how are you going to increase the range? This would be great as a perimeter defense, but not at one meter."

"Da, Miss Gift, is our focus. Mike has good ideas for this, and we soon have something to test. I will work on increased power, and he is increasing range."

"Amplifying the signal, actually."

"Thank you, both of you. Please keep me updated on your progress. Is there anything I can do to help?"

"Please, you get for us Melody tomorrow in morning. We need for updating of the softwares running targeting and modulation."

"Also, he thinks she's cute," Mike said with a smile.

It pleased Gift how, in a few days, the two had put aside their issues and learned to work together, approaching what might even be termed friends. *Funny how sharing a bench tends to do that,* she thought.

"I will have her here, no worries."

"Hey, how's Miss Heller? I just heard this morning."

"I think she's good. Gonna go see her next."

"And you? Been through quite a lot. You okay?"

"Yeah. You know... same old and all."

"Well, you need to catch me up. Dinner?"

"Sure. Tacos? Been a minute. Oh, I'll be bringing a guest, too. And Aimée's broadcasting live later, so we should eat early. Anyway, let me go check the other team, hopefully they've made progress too. Great work you two."

A body vibrating in that way reminded Gift of being in the winter air of the mountains in a t-shirt, shivering uncontrollably. This was different. Sara scrunched her face in pain yet smiled through it, violently jerking shoulders, and all. Assuming a seizure, Gift ran to her.

"Sara. *Sara.*"

"She's fine."

As the words *she's fine* ended, so did the seizure, falling Sara to the floor. "Mister Fischer?" He stepped through the open door. "Where were you? What's happened to her?"

"We've greatly improved the range. And please, Karl, remember? She'll be fine. Fourth time I've stunned her today. We've got a working model of Sara's self-contained projectile stunner. She's working on a name."

"How long will she be out?"

"A few minutes. Then dizzy for a while after that. The enemy will be out cold then be in no condition to fight or do much of anything except vomit. Sara's done it twice, we'll see what happens this time. I told her to have a light lunch, just in case."

"So, a name? Why does everything need a name?"

"Sara says it's cooler that way. We thought of SWAC: Stun Without Actual Contact, but haven't settled on it."

"*Hm...* Maybe, more like... SWEEP: Stun With Electric Energy Projectile."

Sara's laughter sounded jovial and strange, like Aimée after a few shots of vodka. "That'th pitty awfffle Girf," she nearly said.

"Don't worry, it's normal. Her muscles all went numb, including her tongue."

"Are you okay?" As she helped the woman stagger to her feet, Gift turned to Karl. "Isn't there a better way to test it without doing this to her?"

"I'n fine, reary."

As Sara returned to herself, she and Karl gave Gift the thrilling update on their projectile stunner. They'd gotten it to shoot with accuracy and incapacitate Sara from nearly ten meters and were confident they'd increase it. That they'd soon have two nonlethal defense options delighted Gift. If Tom and Sergey were unsuccessful or were too late, they'd have a means to defend the colony.

"What about working autonomously? I mean, from a mounted position... for the perimeter defense. Without a guard holding and shooting. Could we make that work?"

Paused in thought, Karl studied the ceiling. "It may be more realistic to get them to be remote operated. If guards used handhelds to aim and shoot, that'd get you what you need. But I'd need you assisting on that. Sara has been great, but this will take some engineering. And a data operator."

"Yeah, you're right Mist—Karl. Let me see if I can make time tomorrow. Sara, are you good at keeping at expanding the range and accuracy of the targeting?"

"Yeth. Thath more my thpeed."

"Good. Melody is with Mike's team in the morning. I'll have her come here in the afternoon."

***

Sakura said the doctor at the R.F. had done excellent work and took good care of Miss Heller. She expected a full recovery. More good news on the day settled Gift's mind until she didn't find Raff in their shared little office. The powerful disappointment fled when Gift's shoulders tightened, and she realized Raff had come from behind to squeeze her in a warm, firm embrace.

"Where'd you come from?"

"Came up the corridor just behind you. How are you, Cara? I was so worried. What an adventure you had."

"Tell me about it. First long trip and figures that's how it'd go for me... Anything on the perimeter sensors?"

"Niente. At least we'll get advance notice. You're sure they have no transports at that bunker? And do we know how many of those rogue guards we should expect?"

"Mostly. And no idea." As her words finished, an alert flashed on her screen.

Message from Thomas Mills

"Play."

"Frank, Gift. I wasn't sure who to send this to. Got some more out of Yuri, rogue guards will move soon, could be as early as tomorrow. I'll be joining Sergey's team, the quickest we can go, late morning. It'll be before dawn for you. We believe we'll be the superior force, better trained than Yuri's goons. The bunker's not heavily armed and we expect about two dozen or so. I hoped we'd be able to wait to see how your weapons project was coming, but we've run out of time. I'll update when it's done. Out."

The complexion left Gift's face, leaving it pale and blank. *Why more fighting? Why the violence?* The weight of the message pulled Raff's arm across Gift's back.

"Always violence. When will we learn? I worry..."

"Me too, Cara. But Tom will be fine. He'll be careful."

"I know. I mean, I hope so. *Ma*, I worry about us, as people. Stupid humans. We just find out where we are, we have neighbors, Russians, then Pioneers. And what do we do? Fight. We meet new neighbors with violence. I just worry... we're repeating all our mistakes. If we don't kill each other, will we ruin the planet again too? Is this just who we are?"

***

After a brief *I'm back, I'm fine* visit to her mother, Gift went to collect Oksana. Aimée would finalize preparations for the live evening update and skip dinner. Gift and her new young Russian friend strolled together to meet Mike at the taco stand.

"Ever had tacos?"

"Not even sure what that is."

"You'll love'em. One of my favorites. You like spicy?" The girl's head nodded, and her face smiled. "Then trust me, order what I do."

The dinner crew shared greetings. Mike, Raff, and Hans Fuchs. Tina when she arrived last, as expected. They sat six at a round table with six chairs, appeasing Gift's ever-present need for symmetry. The conversation flowed, light and wonderful. Gift's head fought to bury every potential outcome for Tom, an invasion on the colony, the worse threat teased by Yuri. They cut dinner conversation short so they could watch Aimée's broadcast—Oksana with Gift in her Box after a hurried pace to get there on time.

Showing no signs of the harrowing experience lingering upon her, Aimée gave her update in a straightforward and honest report. Gift picked up her *tell* that all wasn't as good as it seemed: her lower-than-normal level of humor and self-praise. Gift may have been the only one who knew how much her friend had been shaken by the events she so casually reported.

The self-praise came as Aimée related her role in quelling the violence, running a tribunal, and starting open talks between their three peoples. It surprised Gift how she played down the danger but accepted it as for the good of the colony. Likely that danger would be over by the time Gift took her morning espresso.

Once the broadcast concluded, Gift walked Oksana to Dome Six to her hospitality flat, her three large totes waiting there. Identical to the flat Gift entered and bugged months prior except for an elevation in the decor. Closer to the gaudy interior design of Oksana's family home, it had an old-European style. Logic assumed it aimed to make guests from the R.F. comfortable, but Gift contemplated if its present guest would find it anything but, having come to free herself of her home and all that it had been.

"So, here you are. Should have everything you need, your own toilet and shower. I guess I'll head home myself. I'm beat."

"*What*? Someone beat you?"

Gift grinned. "You're like me with expressions. It means I'm tired."

"Why not just say that, then?"

"Because... well... No, you're right. I don't know." They shared a chuckle. Oksana's quickly faded. Fearing the prior evening's topic, Gift's silence stemmed from not knowing to say something or leave. Neither was right.

"Gift? Do... I'd... Do you think... you could stay?"

"Sure, we have time before Lights-Out. Is everything okay, sweetie?"

"No. I mean, could you *stay* here... with me?"

"Overnight?" The girl nodded sheepishly. "I suppose. I mean, I didn't bring my stuff, but that's okay. Have you ever been alone for the night?"

Under a lowered brow, Oksana's lips pushed into one cheek. "Lots of times. Well, a few, alone. Just, this is all new, this place and everything."

"I understand. This was just my first time in another colony, and I had Aimée. Get changed and come join me on the sofa. Maybe, bring me a t-shirt if you have one."

With her smile returned, the young lady skipped off to the bedroom with all the care of a five-year-old who'd been told she could stay up past bedtime.

The conversation took whatever course Oksana directed. Occasional questions about her, what it was like being the daughter of such a powerful woman, why at sixteen she hadn't been given a work assignment. Oksana chatted openly. They were two girlfriends having a heart-to-heart. Big sister

Gift mode engaged but felt out of sorts from the other side. They had a shared love of engineering, but Miss Nadezhda deemed it menial work.

"Work with the hands? Not my daughter. You wait to choosing what to do at twenty years." Oksana did a decent impression of her mother's voice.

Yuri entered the conversation and Gift stayed on her toes, doing her best to dance around the more delicate conversation points Oksana didn't choreograph. At thirty, he lived at home because no other residences were as nice or had private showers and personal chefs. Sensitively, Oksana implied herself as a reason for his not moving out, but her words instantly twirled and began a different step.

He didn't have a work assignment but held a position in the guard, which he resented as Sergey and others outranked him. Oksana believed he used the assignment to recruit his friends and get them on the medication, then on teams that took the bunker, fought the Pioneers, and stifled their communication with the R.F. Pieces came together to form a picture in Gift's mind.

Tom will be fine. It'll be over by the time I take my morning espresso, Gift repeated on a loop. The thoughts failed to calm her mind while she settled onto the sofa for the night after Oksana retreated to the bedroom. Purposely left open, the bedroom door was a conduit between them, exposing the young woman's soul. She was uneasy, but not about being away from home for the first time. That part was likely as thrilling as it was liberating. She was obviously uneasy about life, about herself. Scared of both.

30

More severe fighting than they anticipated, the R.F. strike force had been killed in the attack. Tom had gone with them. Gift's spirit drained and she tried to understand her feelings. *He loved me. Well, he said, 'Where's that wonderful optimism I love about you?' Not the same.* This felt different. Its impact numbed her, but not like Charlie's.

Was it relief?

A snort escaped as Gift twisted on the sofa—far less comfortable as a bed. The commotion changed the scene. She and Tom sipped espresso and read Sergey's report. They easily defeated the rogue Russians. Yuri appeared beside them; his eyes led Gift's to her exposed midriff. The evil creature posing as a man said, "That was not the threat, my beautiful Gift." He laughed ominously, vulgar, then he disappeared in a puff of purple smoke. His mother vanished him with the snap of her fingers.

"*Wait.* It was you. You're some kind of freak alien," Gift shouted at Nadezhda.

"Silly girl. No such things as *Asians.* Oh sorry, I meant to say *aliens.*" Her laugh shrieked, sinister and vile.

A shot in the chest from Tom's taser dissolved the woman into purple dust. Gift thought she should feel bad but didn't. A weight floated off her and she hovered above the ground to see the emptiness of the desert below, lifeless sand dunes, until she fell from the sky, fell from slumber.

"*Gift?*" Oksana's voice pushed concern and anxiety. The disturbance roused her and brought her from her bed to find Gift on the floor.

"*Huh?*" Consciousness slowly spilled into her. "Oh... Had a bad dream. I think I was falling. Guess I fell for real. Sorry if I startled you."

"No, so long as you're okay. Actually... you pulled me from a dreadful nightmare." Pain cried out from the girl's glossy eyes and her skin glistened in the nightlight's meager glow. Fear or hate, Gift didn't know.

"Sweetie, are you okay?"

"Just a bad dream. But... you must be uncomfortable, and... and... it's my fault, making you sleep on the sofa 'cause I didn't want to be alone. That bed is enormous, more than enough to share."

The sofa was fine, her dreams would occur wherever she lay. Doubt ran through Gift's mind if she should be getting so attached to the confused and hurting girl so quickly. But she was a confused and hurting girl. After Gift accepted the invitation, Oksana slept soundly through the night. Gift, not so much.

***

As promised, the morning brought Oksana's first swimming lesson. Unlike Gift, the fearless girl went in deep over her head the first day. Closeness and bonding brought warm familiarity akin to being with her little Matteo yet not quite the same. The differences in having a *kid sister* compared to having a bratty *little brother* fascinated her. Navigating the new sensations made a delightful preoccupation.

In contrast to Gift, Oksana's ferocious morning appetite consumed enough food for a week's worth of breakfast. Her muffin didn't stand a chance and disappeared before Gift had bitten into her brioche a second time or taken her first sip of espresso. A brioche for Oksana, then fresh fruit, and finally another muffin. Thankfully the Board had given the girl a guest rations account or Gift would have gone broke feeding the ravenous young lady.

Oksana wasn't overly talkative and refused to divulge the nature of her nightmare even after Gift recounted her own dreams. Just as well, as the handheld, which lived up to its name by avoiding her pocket, stole her attention. She needed the update so much it hurt. They had left the R.F. hours ago, before Gift and her new kid sister ventured out to the lake. Was a drawn-out battle still raging? Had it ended in a standoff, defeat, or victory? Shaking the device didn't summon an update.

"Stupid thing."

Oksana's face scrunched. "Sorry, what?"

"*Huh*? Oh, nothing... Yeah, talk to myself sometimes."

"No way. I do it all the time too. Drives Mom crazy. So, you know, that part's cool."

The corner of Gift's lip joyfully rose into a playful smirk, but then it came. The familiar chirp of a new message. Not a vidChat request, but a recorded message. Desperate to play it, she was too frightened to play it. Not even to look at the message text on the tiny display.

"Aren't you gonna watch it? You've been staring at the thing all morning, and now you're not playing it?"

The girl had a point. Trembling with trepidation, the device slowly rose with Gift's hand.

Message from Thomas Mills

"Play."

"Gift, hey. Wanted to message you first, I know how you worry. It's cute." *He's okay. They haven't shot him. He said I'm cute.* "It happened quickly. Turned out Yuri's men were no match for Sergey's. Sorry to say, we only had guns. Two of them died, but they surrendered quickly. The place was a mess, the bunker I mean. Food all but gone, not much of a weapons cache. Then we found something... *interesting*, but I'll let Sergey explain it in his report and debrief. Not sure I see any need for it anyway, but the way things go, who knows.

"Oh, this was odd. When we entered the bunker, we saw areas outfitted as places people stayed. Whole families lived there and... I think they may have killed them all. Men, women, children. These *animals* will face justice, we can be sure of that. We'll be here for a while, then back to the R.F. I'm not sure when I'll be home. Miss you. Out."

Miss me? Adding to the jumble of twisted feelings and still uncomfortable emotions, missing Tom felt vastly different from how she missed Mom, Mike, Tina, or Raff. She summoned Tina's words from the archive: *Twenty-seven is too young*. Perhaps the chaos within Gift proved that right. Or maybe the tossed salad of emotions in her gut indicated the exact opposite. Losing her weekly James Müller one-way chat suddenly hit her, as emotions got heavier to carry, harder to navigate.

"That's great." Oksana's words passed through a wide smile. "My idiot brother's plans all failed. *He* failed like the pathetic loser he is."

Afraid to speak, Gift nodded. Everything she thought to say was wrong. Happily, Mike's expression about a horse and a barn door came to occupy her mind. While she didn't get it, Gift knew it applied to their perimeter defenses—*nearly* certain. Neutralization of the enemy notwithstanding, her day needed to focus on beefing up their defensive posture for a now non-existent threat. At least that took some of the pressure off.

***

The first stop, Oksana in tow, verified that Red—Gift remembered to call her Melody—started with Mike and Anton. Present threat removed, Gift's concern about stupid humans and their inevitable return to violence stood on her nose and said, 'get those defenses ready.' She normally obeyed the voices from mental images projected onto the tip of her nose—they always served her right.

Ever the one to lead by example—she found delegating difficult—Gift insisted on being sonically stunned herself. It must have looked like fun because when she came to, she found Oksana out cold beside her. Proud of herself for trusting them, Gift left it to Mike, Anton, and Melody. Leaving them was easier than she let on because she'd get to be an engineer, working beside her former master.

"So, you wish to be an engineer, young lady?" Excitement twinkled in Karl's eye; the hands-on teacher missed working with apprentices.

"Been studying lots, tinkering a bit. My mom won't let me take a work assignment even though I'm getting close to seventeen. Says to wait until I'm twenty. Sucks."

"Indeed. Tell me my dear, does everyone in your colony normally start work at sixteen as we do?"

"Well, not everyone. See, lots of things are different there. If a job needs filling, someone can start earlier. One of my friends has been working since just after fourteen. Well, she *was* my friend. It's kinda hard to keep friends when your mother runs the place. Also, when they go off to work and see me waiting, living in luxury. Girls can be so jealous... and mean. Really... *I'm* the one jealous of *them*, you know?"

"I get it, sweetie. How about today—we won't tell your mother—today you get to be an engineer. Wanna help me and Mister Karl with this problem of ours?"

By the lunch break, which they took at the bench, they had made substantial progress. Oksana had a knack for the work. Gift supposed she'd have been assessed as an engineer in N.E. Thoughts wafted into her consciousness picturing the very different life the girl would live if she had been born in their colony. Then the sweet aroma of Pad Thai floated in and wiped her mind of all thoughts but one: *Did they remember the hot sauce?*

Working with Red brought back memories. While they were from a nightmare-come-true part of Gift's life, good ones sprinkled in, such as new friendships. Having worked closely with Raff and being a natural coder, Melody had become a master data operator in the passing months. Raff expected she would surpass her one day and felt confident leaving her post to another set of deep-green eyes watching over the data stream. In a few hours they had hardware specs, a 3D-printed prototype, and the code to make it work.

Gift and Sara volunteered as test subjects. Guinea pigs, Oksana called them—another lost reference. Gift learned they were animals with no relation to what she thought of as pigs. For their remote-control field test, the projectiles came from a mounted rifle, its control tablet in Oksana's eager hands. The device shot accurately and hit Gift at eleven meters, reloaded, and hit Sara at twelve while running, flooding the young shooter with giddy laughter. Red's adaptive targeting program worked beautifully, and Gift approved the order to print thirty units for immediate deployment.

With Mike's update that they'd increased their device's range to almost four meters, they would soon have what they needed to defend themselves. Everything but an enemy, and Gift had no complaints on that front.

Satisfied in her teams' accomplishments, Gift began her ritual of cleaning, straightening, and putting things away on the bench. Oksana joined her without being asked, but Gift's smile wasn't for the help. Seeing someone share even one of her idiosyncrasies made Gift feel a little more normal—a comfort which fit like a comfy nightshirt.

31

The new siren rang loud and shrill, not like the klaxons of the insurrection. Gift recognized it from when Raff had programmed and tested it. Perimeter breach.

"Tom's report said they'd handled Yuri's guys." Gift's words didn't expect or wait for any logical answer. How could she or those around her know anything about this situation beyond the siren's blaring? She looked at her handheld for answers. "vidChat Raffaella Di Gaetano... *Raff*. What the heck?"

"Checking... This was the first alert. Tells us something's coming. Nothing yet in camera view. We have the guards gearing up to head out for a perimeter sweep."

"All they have are hand tasers—short range, close contact. We spent the day testing new defenses, but they're not ready yet. How soon before we can see the... *enemy*? Who could they be? Maybe Yuri had more men, sent them before Tom and Sergey took the bunker. I mean... *Focus*... When can we see their numbers, weapons?"

"Depends how fast they're moving. We're sending a drone, hopefully get a look before they get close."

"Good Raff, that's good. We don't have much, but we'll take what improved stunners we've printed and meet the guards. Maybe it'll give them a little better chance, anyway."

"Careful Gift, please. Meet them at the Dome Two exit and give them the stun guns. But you stay inside. Leave this to the guards."

Counting the initial prototype, they had four new long-range stunners and a dozen projectiles—the new sonic defenses weren't online. Not enough to fend off an army or even a large marauder band, and Gift had no idea what was coming.

"Yuri's threat, or something he said was worse?"

"What's that?" Sara asked.

"Sorry, talking to myself." They stuffed the projectiles in their pockets and hugged the stunners. "But Yuri, Miss Anoykina's son, he said there's another threat, maybe a worse one. We need to move."

"*No.* You stay here. Don't leave this building."

Before Gift could fight off the notion and insist she was going, Oksana hissed, "*No.* I'm not a child, I can help. I'm coming."

"She's right, sweetheart. We don't know what this is and we're only giving the guards these weapons, nothing more." Gift suspected that wasn't true, but as no decision had yet been reached, no guilt came. She hastily tossed the new weapons and ammunition in a tote. "They'll lock the colony down and we'll be right back, so don't worry. But you stay put... I mean it."

How much that sounded like her mother irritated Gift, but she understood it now in ways she couldn't before and knew Oksana wouldn't either. Melody's hand on her shoulder provided all the restraint needed to keep the excited teenager at bay. Gift thanked her with her eyes and raced out behind Sara, guard-turned-friend, once again into danger.

Caught up to the line of guards in a military-style jog out of Citadome Two, Gift and Sara stopped the last pair. They hesitated until Sara explained the contents of the tote and the advantage it would give them. As Gift reached for one to teach them how to operate the unfamiliar devices Sara pushed her hand down, falling the weapon into the bag, and reached for its handles.

"I'll show them how to use them. I'll be on the line with the guards."

"Sara, no."

"I'm a trained guard, my place is with them. And I know how to use these. You stay here."

Empty handed and less than full of mental clarity, Gift followed Sara. When the guards reached a clearing, they stopped just inside the tree line and went belly to the ground. The thick canopy turned the late afternoon into a ghostly evening. Gift joined Sara, who'd held the commander back to explain the new projectile stun-gun to him and another nameless guard.

"Surprise may be on our side," he said as they each took a weapon and crept on all-fours to frontline posts. Leaves and twigs crunched beneath them like rolling thunder. The three laid ready for the intruders to expose themselves in the narrow open field. The only other person who knew how to use it, Gift took the fourth stun rifle.

Crackling noises from rustling underbrush crossed the five meters of open space from the opposing tree line sheltering their attackers. Wind or hostiles? The unmistakable sound of a twig broken underfoot. Who were these people coming to kill her? Gift put herself in a gun fight and brought a projectile stunner. Maybe it would be enough—she had to believe that, so she did.

"Hold." The commander raised a fist above his head.

Hours laying in the leaves wondering why he commanded them not to act were seconds in real-time. Gift ignored the chirping of the device pushing into her upper thigh from her pocket—the tree line ahead demanded her full attention. The chirping stopped, replaced by a single beep. Whoever had tried to reach her terminated their request and sent a message. *Good, I'll get it later*, she thought and then immediately forgot about it.

Propped on elbows—barrel of the projectile launcher extended low to the ground in front of her, finger on the trigger—she waited. A glance at Sara confirmed the position, ready but holding. Now Sara's command to stay back seemed sound as lack of guard training outweighed Gift's familiarity with the stun-gun. Silent, shadowy figures emerged across the twilight blanketed over the narrow clearing between her and them.

Someone fired.

It didn't pop or echo. If it was a gun, it sounded unlike the ones she'd heard shooting at Aimée, Sergey and Miss Heller. Not the ear-piercing ones in the R.F. firefight. A snap followed by a stretched *theew* of something slicing through the air—a projectile. *No.*

No expected pops or broken planks came in return. Her eyes searched for shadows now retreated to the safety of the trees across the way. She found that odd. One stun projectile, even if it hit someone, would hardly scare off an invasion force. Sara must have called her more than once.

"Why'd you fire?"

"*Me?* I..." In panic, thinking her nerves might have curled her finger around the trigger and squeezed, Gift raised the gun to examine its ammo loader. Three. "It wasn't me, still got all mine."

Sara made the same face as when Gift answered a rhetorical question. "*Julio.* What the heck?" Sara had been yelling at a guard. But he hadn't started a war. No shots, no fighting. Beyond Sara's voice they heard only silence. The eeriness brought tingles in anticipation of violence. No one flinched or spoke as all eyes impatiently gazed across the opening, seeing only the stillness of evening trees.

The message. Gift played the vid message, lowering the volume after the shout of Raff's voice brought an evil eye and a shush gesture from Sara.

"They're women and children, a few men. We think they're unarmed. Do *not* engage, they're not hostile. Gift, tell the guards, I can't reach Commander Tucker. Do not engage."

End of Message

"Sara, you get that?"

After a nod, Sara crawled away toward Commander Tucker and the two stood slowly, dropped their weapons, and raised their hands above their heads. Carefully, they stepped from the safety of the tree trunks' protective care into the open field. If those people had guns, nothing prevented them from blowing away Gift's new friend and the head of the New Europa Guard.

"It's okay." Sara spoke, not Tucker. "We're sorry for the misfire, it was a mistake. No one will harm you and we have laid down our weapons. Please, let's talk about why you traveled all this way."

A middle-aged man and woman emerged. Gift could see that much for the onset of evening that painted them a purplish-blue hue. A tiny figure pushed through to show herself. A small girl, a child.

The woman said, "We are mostly women and children, a few of our men made it. We are here in peace, seeking aid. Please, we've lost our home, our possessions. We've walked the last two days with no food and little water. We have children. *Please.*" The last words pushed through her sobbing. The peculiar strangers' faces became clearer as Gift neared, showing her palms.

"No one will hurt you. We were defending what we thought was a threat. You are safe here." Sara's soft kindness settled the trembling woman. The little girl examined the grass swallowing her shoes.

"My name is Gift. I am on the Board of New Europa." The response in the couple's empty eyes said they had no idea what 'board' meant beyond a plank of wood or composite material. "I'm with the ones in charge of our colony. I speak for them, for us."

Something in her voice raised the girl's chin and folded her neck to see Gift. Gift knelt before the tiny one. She looked no more than five or six. A dirty little round face held bright wide eyes that pushed traces of desperation blending with hope.

"Hey sweetie. It's okay, you're safe here. We'll help you."

"Oh, bless you. Bless you all." As the woman spoke, the dirty-faced girl wrapped her arms around Gift's neck and Gift embraced her.

The man looked down into Gift's eyes. "We are from a bunker that was overrun. They tried to kill us all, shot most of our men. One of them convinced the rest to let us take provisions and go, telling us they'd shoot us on the spot if we ever returned. We've been walking nearly three weeks."

"We know about the bunker. The R.F. just took it back and rounded up those jerks." When Gift rose to her feet, the child dangling from her neck refused to let go, so she supported her with crossed arms under her bottom.

"You knew about this? What they did to us?"

"No, not exactly. Well... let me say we only just found out. We went to find you a few days ago... in the bunker. They shot at us... Must have thought we were you coming back. Those men who raided your camp were from the Russian Federation, another colony. Oh... but they were an independent group. The R.F. didn't do this to you. They are the ones that got'em this morning, actually."

Distrusting eyes bounced to process the information as the man stood in silence.

"Please, come to the colony. We'll get you food and water... then we can talk, understand each other better, see where we go from here."

The couple nodded, but not at Gift. Others stepped out from the heavy shadows into the steely moonlight mixing with the last of the twilight as it chased the withdrawn sun.

***

Given food and much needed water, the group showed signs they were beginning to trust they were not in danger. Sakura sent a medic along with Holly and all guests checked out fine. Nothing worse than a hint of malnutrition and mild dehydration. The logistics created an issue for Gift and the Board. They hadn't guest lodging enough for thirty-one people. (In total they were six men, sixteen women, and nine children.) *Where could we put these refugees?* Gift pondered it for a minute before her own word provided the answer.

Charlie's E.CID refugee shelter hadn't been dismantled in the passing months. With the expansion to the exterior farm the priority, the secret farm warehouse was low on the list of to-dos, and storage space no longer came at a premium. Along with Sara, Oksana, Mike, Tina, and a crew of cleaning personnel, they made the place ready—well, ready enough—for the guests to pass the night.

It pleased Gift deeply how another of Charlie's legacies lived on in the repurposing of his refugee space. Following Sakura's loving advice, Gift allowed herself the happiness of the thought, with wonderful memories of Charlie no longer allowed to burden her with a guilty conscience. She felt nothing but joy for her dear friend living on in such meaningful ways.

Gift left the matter to Board members less pressed for urgent tasks than herself. It wasn't truly delegation, as this was never her responsibility. She happened to be there, lying on the ground about to be shot to death by a marauder band that never was. As peaceful as these intruders-turned-guests had been, the need for those defenses remained a priority and Gift's team would spend the following day completing the installations outside the colony. Oksana was excited to help.

32 | WEEK THREE

Sui juris is what the Board of Directors officially called it. Raff used the word emancipation. It meant Oksana was free. Well, Gift didn't care for that word, it sounded as if she had been a slave, property for the first sixteen years of her life. Maybe she was, her life having been dictated to her, controlled by her mother and colony alike. And she had endured Yuri.

During the Board meeting, the topic of that one sixteen-year-old wanting to be out from under her mother's wing proved more than it appeared on the surface. New Europa considered residents sui juris at sixteen. Gift, like everyone, had full rights to her life on her sixteenth birthday. Of course, she didn't have to leave her colony to obtain it, where Oksana put everything behind, walking away from all she knew. From her mother.

"We're risking a major incident with the R.F." Mister Jonson repeated the basic thought for the third time, making only slight adjustments in wording—a failed attempt to appear to offer something new.

Jean said, "The girl is in distress and requesting asylum. No, that's not the right word. Are we considering her a political refugee? How do we define her request?"

"She has requested residency, to receive a work assignment, a habitat allocation, and a resident rations account," Heller clarified. "She is sixteen, and by our policy she is free to do so. However, her colony has a slightly... *different* structure and her mother is at the top of the pyramid."

"Exactly. This may cause a major rift with the R.F." 'Rift' was Mister Jonson's clever way to say the same thing again.

"We must tread lightly, true. But we cannot ignore the girl's request. The young Miss Anoykina deserves our consideration."

Gift admired Miss Heller's way of not being dogmatic or putting others down when she didn't agree, no matter how stupid Gift assessed their point.

"She is the daughter of the President and Chair of the Board of the R.F. but has no life there, as we understand. They hold off her work assignment, she has no friends, no social life, and spends most of her days alone as her brother is in custody and her mother is busy running their colony."

"Yes, thank you. That's what I've been saying. We just need to let her stay. We can do that without an incident, no accusations against Miss Anoykina or the R.F." Satisfied with her summary statement being concise and logical, Gift assumed them ready for a vote. She was wrong.

Fred looked at Gift and trapped her once again in his expressionless gaze. They were equals now, Gift no longer a suspect or person of interest being interrogated, yet she couldn't shake it. When he captured her eyes as he did, she froze inside and couldn't quell her shivers.

"I agree with Jonson. We've had great dealings with the R.F. ever since they came to help us that first day. But I'm sorry, Gift, let's be realistic here. Most of it has *not* been with Nadezhda Anoykina. The few times she's been involved we always, *always* end up compromising. Now we're talking about taking her daughter?"

"*No.*" Perhaps Gift gave that a bit too much bluster. "First of all, I mean, yeah sure... she's a hard woman, been difficult, but she's super cooperative on the environmental joint task force, even doing that interview. She's no evil queen we have to cower to. Also too, we're not *taking* her daughter. The reality... it's... I mean, she's here most of the time already."

"Gift is right," Raff said. "I say we grant the girl's petition. Gift and Aimée can speak to Nadezhda."

A few nods and a yes came across the boardroom table. *Take the vote*, Gift thought, hoping to will Miss Heller into complying. *We have a majority, just take the* mal'd *vote*.

Heller ignored the prodding of Gift's mind. "Perhaps we're getting ahead of ourselves. We've spent the better part of an hour on this one agenda point without a decision. And what have we been discussing the entire time? Speculations. How we *assume* Nadezhda Anoykina will react. One thing I've learned about that woman, no one can predict what she'll do, not even with her family. It was she who insisted on the tribunal for Yuri, her own son. She is the one who sanctioned his interrogations—and let's be honest, we all know that meant torture."

Nods came with mumbles of agreement.

"I have a proposal for a course of action we may take. Let us take part of Miss Di Gaetano's suggestion and have Miss Ojo and Miss Toussaint speak to Miss Anoykina. Not to inform her of a decision, but to present Oksana's wishes. They don't have to say anything about it being permanent."

Getting a touch bolder, surer of herself, Gift didn't raise her hand or ask to speak. "Yeah, we could even present it as a suggestion. Better still, like we're asking her advice on what to do with her daughter. Seeing how the woman's been happy to have Oksana with us, she may even suggest she stay. Then it'll be like it was her idea."

With Miss Heller's steering and Gift's words, the Board agreed on a way to help the young lady without angering the unpredictable mountain of formidable character that was the Russian President. Nadezhda still intimidated Gift worse than her meanest tutor when she was six.

***

Pushing in through the glass and polymer composite of the Zil's cage, the roaring slammed intense and powerful on the eardrums. They couldn't see it at first as the trees caved them in with smatterings of blue between foliage so thick, even the sun struggled to pierce it with the thinnest rays like thread through a needle's eye—something Gift knew from her swimsuit design days. As they stopped, Oksana ordered the driver to remain with the vehicle and he responded, "Yes, ma'am," as if the command had come directly from Nadezhda Anoykina herself.

Oksana took the lead as they exited the land transport and headed into the bush, trekking over its moss-covered ground with the crunch of slender twigs cracking under their shoes. Like an open yawn, the girl's giddy chuckles spread to Aimée then to Gift. Oksana's voice drowned in an increasing noise saturation Gift recognized from her last outing in the Zil.

When they stepped around the rock outcropping, their eyes marveled at the first glimpse of what caused Gift to gasp. Well-deserved awe over the volume of falling water matching its thunderous roar became secondary to what captivated Gift's full attention.

"I mean, I see it there. But it looks like it's not there."

As her brain worked overtime to keep up with the flood of optical signals, Gift listed the colors. Initially she saw red, green, violet-blue—translucent, each. They arched up from the shower-steam-thick mist over the water but didn't touch it. More colors distinguished themselves. A yellow stripe filled a gap between green and red, then orange and violet appeared. The magnificent curiosity evolved before her eyes.

"Breathtaking. It's called a rainbow. I saw it in a picture," Aimée said.

"It's amazing. Come on, let's get closer."

The energetic teenager traversed the terrain on the downward slope over rock, moss, and grass, like she was born to it. Aimée trailed close behind at a slightly reduced pace while Gift descended with enough caution for them all. She caught up when they stopped to admire shifting views of the waterfall. Wider than the one by the scary-high bridge, the wall of water gushed in a constant vertical descent. Gift wondered when the water at the top would eventually run dry.

Oksana climbed to a flattening beyond a massive rock outcropping. It resembled the shoreline of Colony Lake in miniature, with calm water at their feet hidden from the violence of the crashing fury around the bend. What dripped into the natural pool didn't form a water wall but appeared as strands of clear, twisting wire draped over a rock ledge five meters above. Its sparkles danced and shined over hundreds of points of light hitting the spiraling liquid and playfully splashing below.

In a blink, the young woman had stripped down to her swimsuit and plunged into water so transparent that, when the surrounding ripples faded, Oksana appeared to be floating on air, defying gravity. With words chipped for the shivering of her bottom lip, Oksana said, "It's grrrreat. Come in ya-you guys."

In consideration of the blue-lipped young lady, Aimée wore her swimsuit. Or it may have been Gift's deliberate nagging that kept her decent. Her headfirst dive ended in a head shake flicking drops in all directions. Gift hesitated her jump, contemplating the bumps riddled over Aimée's skin from the frigid water rattling her to the bone. *It's why Vitaliy said to wear our swimsuits under our clothes. This is why we're here. Don't chicken out Gift.*

Thousands of needles pricked the flesh of her thighs. With knees tucked to her chest and wrapped in her arms, Gift sank until her toes gently touched the bottom and she released her legs into a push straight to the surface. She felt herself rapidly vibrating as her chin trembled uncontrollably. In all her winter swims in Colony Lake, Gift had never experienced the biting pain brought by this icy water.

"Come on, gotta move or we'll freeze to death." With that, Aimée was off to the trickling waterfall's end with Oksana closely trailing her.

The best swimmer of the three, Gift easily caught them, and they climbed in unison to stand under the shower of gelid liquid. In a shallow pool they stood knee-deep under the numbing strings splashing on their heads, bouncing off shoulders, and snaking over goosebumps. Bone-chillingly magnificent. Laughter and playful screams competed with the roaring torrent around the bend.

With purple lips and unstoppable shivers, they stood by their clothes trying to dry themselves without the towels they'd forgotten. Late hour sunshine lacked the intensity to do more than gently illuminate the valley. Hands did their best to rub warmth into upper arms slightly raising their body temperatures. When dry enough, not dripping wet at least, they dressed and made their way to the Zil. The poor driver, he may have been called Lev, sweated profusely on the journey back as the women needed the heat cranked to sauna level.

***

"I have never seen my Oksana so happy." Nadezhda led them from the dinner table to the impossibly comfortable sofas. "I am so glad for you girls to be here, but especially for time spending with my darling daughter. She loves you both so much. So much. I never see her so happy."

Exactly the opening Gift could use. "And we love her, really. Aimée and I were talking, trying to see how we can continue spending time with Oksana. What do you think, Miss Nadezhda?"

"Da, much time together is good. And what I say before is still true, no, is more true. You two are always welcome here, in Russian Federation and in Anoykina home."

"Most kind Nadezhda. Gift and I always appreciate your generosity. But we keep very busy. We may not be able to visit so often. And Oksana seems to love being with us at New Europa, don't you agree?"

"All she talks about when she visits me. She loves it so much... I am thinking..." Nadezhda paused. Raising a hand, she placed her chin between her thumb and index finger, squinted one eye, and raised an eyebrow. "Am thinking perhaps she likes to stay more with you then. This is good for my Oksana. So alone here, too much alone. Is good for her to be more time with you lovely girls... Will this be problem? I do not wish to make problems for this."

Gift paused to consider *Nadezhda's idea*. "Well... she's been in guest quarters, but if she'll spend more time with us... I'm sure we can work it out. It won't be a problem."

"Could we get her a rations account? Like we have for all the R.F. folks working joint teams?" Aimée played along with the ruse masterfully.

"I'm sure we can work something out."

"Is settled. If my Oksana wishes this, she spends more time with you dear girls."

"*Oh yes*. I'd love it. Thank you, mommy. Thank you. I love you." The girl leapt into her mother's arms like a five-year-old. A sharp contrast to the callousness and sarcasm she typically directed toward her mother.

"I know my darling, I know."

The woman of stone patted her daughter's head with little visible emotion. Gift hoped for an '*I love you too*' to reassure the girl, but realized that, besides anger and what looked like contempt for Yuri, Miss Anoykina expressed the most emotion she'd seen from her.

Success. They were free to grant the young lady's petition for residency without angering the beast inside the powerful ruler of their much-needed ally and trade partner.

33

The United Republic of Mars was the largest of the colonies and built off-world, the only one on Mars. Some debate persisted about the New Republic of China being larger, having kept so many secrets during the colonies project. In over two centuries, no word or even a single character of text from the N.R.C. reached other colonies of Earth.

Communication had been sparse before the airlock opened, with environmental updates every few years between the R.F. and New Europa after the old rollers completed their runs. Information about United Africa was scarce. Since the airlock, they responded twice in brief vidChats. Aimée spoke to a woman of robust character she said oozed the same power-persona as Nadezhda, but in a less menacing way. Gift didn't know how to take that, so held off assessing the lady based on Aimée's perception.

Were the people unfriendly? Untrusting? Resentment from decades of colonizers contaminating rich African cultures and plundering resources? That world died. Unity within N.E. transcended racist notions left to die in the past, making people just people, with cultural variation adding to the beauty of the community.

"Could it be they need something?" Gift asked when they received a message from U.A.

"The timing's interesting." Raff paused. "Maybe it's about the updates we've sent them."

"So, they know about the Pioneers? Sakura's work with them? She's made great progress since they've been here. I think we're headed toward livability out there.... Hey, why aren't you playing it?"

"Not for me or the Board. They addressed it specifically to Aimée. Is she in her office?"

"*Boh*." Gift offered her *I have no idea* shoulder shrug. "She's always got her handheld. Well... most always."

"It's addressed to her, so I won't view it myself. But... if we're there when she plays it..."

"I love how your mind works, Raff. Let's find her and let *her* watch it."

All they found at Aimée's desk was a mess of papers strewn about. Gift straightened a few things up before Raff dragged her out. No answer on the vidChat, nothing to do but wait. What Mike called *a lightbulb moment*—a phrase Gift understood—popped to remind her about Aimée's favorite places to think, to prepare for her broadcasts, to get away. Her new job didn't exactly hold her to her office—a facet of it Aimée absolutely loved.

"Oksana's been spending lots of time with her," Gift said as they scurried to the first stop.

"Cara, are you okay with that? I see how you've taken to her."

"*Va bene*. I'm happy for it. So often I've got no idea what to say. She stays with me when I have engineering tasks, Aimée when I've got boring work. It's good for her to have friends."

"And Nadezhda's okay with her staying this long?"

"She's good with it, yeah. Actually... to me, she likes it. Remember when she joked about her on the interview, said the girl drove her crazy, gave her the gray hairs. With Yuri gone too, it may be the first time in three decades she's had some alone time."

"Do you think she'll go back?"

"Oksana? To the R.F.? I think she's working up the nerve to tell her mom she's staying indefinitely."

Aimée wasn't at her Box or at the little patch of grass in Citadome Three. Her favorite coffee bar had only two men of senior years sipping an aperitivo and playing a card game Gift could never understand or get the hang of, no matter how many times Raff tried to teach her. The cards for Briscola had ugly characters and, while the rules made sense, Gift couldn't track the cards for the unusual Italian suits. Walking toward the last of Aimée's spots filled Gift with anxious concern.

Relief settled the stir in Gift's veins when she saw Aimée in a swimsuit on the lake for the first time since her improvised bikini. Gift's insistence on swimwear for their day trip in Russia may have helped, or perhaps Aimée again knew when to rein it in. Not the best swimmer herself, Aimée focused on helping improve Oksana's float and she got the hang of it in no time.

***

With Oksana gone for a shower, Raff and Gift joined Aimée in her office to *happen* to find themselves on hand when she played the message from United Africa.

"Play it, *dai*. I'm dying here."

"Just a minute, Love. We're waiting for Maggie."

"You called Miss Heller?"

"I'm good with you two looking over my shoulder, but I figured if this is important—and since they messaged me out of the blue, I figure it must be—she should be here."

"*Infatti*," Raff agreed.

Greetings from Miss Heller didn't hold to the pattern of previous encounters. When she offered Gift and Raff their places on the Board she had softened, using their first names, and she'd been friendly since. For the first time, she leaned in for a hug. Near-death experiences tended to alter people in interesting or unexpected ways. With everyone present and beyond ready to watch the message, Aimée told her screen to play.

"Ello my sista. How you dey, Amy my dear? *Long* time. I hope you are fine. We have seen reports of your recent dealing with the R.F. people and the other new neighbors you found. I am *so* grateful you are okay. And Miss Heller, is she fine? When I heard they shot her I *worry-Oh*. But your new neighbors is why I'm reaching out to you. Please, we have a *big problem* here, *much wahala*. You know our colony is small-small. We are afraid it cannot sustain us very much longer without help. The situation is very, very *dire*."

The weight of desperation in the woman's voice crushed Gift.

"We also have outsiders that have survived on *this very* Earth like the ones you call Pioneer. They *no be* so peaceful, not like yours. More like the ones that took over that place from the Pioneer people. When we try to go near, they shoot *for us*. We believe they have food, things wey they grow for *medicine*. It takes long time for us to reach them by leg, then *they shoot*, and we return."

Hearing Nonna's expression for walking drew a smile on Gift's face. When a distant stern voice barked at the woman that smile fled.

"Please, *abeg*, we need help to try to *reach* these people. Hopefully talk, *just* to talk. We wish no fight *with them*. Please, will you help us? You can reach with transport, we *do not* have these things *here*. I wait your reply."

End of Message

"Sounds like those poor people really need help. Miss Heller, what do you think we should do?"

"Of course, we will help. I will convene the Board as it must decide the best course of action."

"Good, Margaret. I'm glad you, Gift, and I were here to see this. *Ciao*. With what they're asking, I'm not sure why it was addressed to Aimée. The Board needs to see this."

"They see my face and hear my voice weekly. All those updates she mentioned, that's me. I've explained my role, but you know how people are, equating the messenger with the message."

Gift nodded. "People even thanked *you* for the reduction in work shift hours and the weekly free day because you reported it."

"Yep. When you made me the face of the colony, you made me the face of the colony. Not saying it was a bad choice, people love me. But I get why they get confused. I mean, Blessing knows me, sees my face, and gets all her information from me. So, when she needed to reach out, she sent the message to me."

***

In the rare times her humility allowed a bit of realistic and deserved pride, Gift would say her work on the Board had been good for the colony. Raff reinforced that idea often enough it tried to stick. Still, at Board meetings Gift felt most out of her element—a sixteen-year-old copying Raff by wearing a dress to dinner. Told enough times how good it looked and how perfect the fit was, she wanted nothing more than to revert to her shorts and t-shirt.

Rewatching the vid message from Blessing brought a fresh tear to Gift's eye. Knowing they were desperate and in dire need of help made the choice obvious to her. Once again, she learned not everyone saw things as she did. While she had mustered enough boldness to speak to the Board, Gift never pushed, never insisted. Until now.

"You've gotta be *kidding* me. Did you not see the same message? I mean, we all did. Those people need help."

"But we're still recovering from our own internal issues and now have the added burden of all these refugees." Fred still intimidated Gift.

"He's right," Mister Lester said. "It's not like we don't have our own problems. Look what happened when we got ourselves involved in the issues with the Russians and those Philistines—"

"*Pioneers.*"

"—and they nearly killed Margaret. Sometimes other people's business should be other people's business."

Three heads nodded agreement with Mister Lester and Fred—five of twelve against helping. 'Of course, we'll help,' Heller had said. Why was she so quiet now?

"I agree we should help. We need to consider all colonies as one, unite ourselves or we risk falling back into the same divisive patterns that got us here." Raff spoke in a straight-forward, logical manner. It wasn't enough.

Miss Ashton grimaced. "What a surprise, *you* supporting Gift."

Boss, Mister Bauer, spoke from a sour face. "Let's not reduce ourselves to this. We have an issue and need to act unitedly to decide how to handle it. Everyone's opinion is valuable and considered equally."

Rumblings and mumbles halted as Miss Heller stood. "We have heard everyone's comments and counter points and have become repetitive. I believe all that *can* be said *has* been said. Now we need to vote. It's clear we won't be unanimous and, at this point, I'm not sure where the majority will land."

After straightening her already straight suit jacket, Heller continued, "Let me say one thing before we determine whether to offer humanitarian aid to our neighbors. Do we imagine such conversations having taken place at the Russian Federation when we called them and asked their help? Yet there was *barely* a delay. They loaded up a transport and were here in a few hours. We are in their position now."

Immense gratitude for the support filled Gift, lifting her spirits. Ready to go the distance, she would have rebutted, volume increasing each time she repeated herself. Calm and logical reasoning by Miss Heller settled the matter better than Gift's persistence could have. The vote was unanimous. Given Gift's passion, they put her in charge of the mission with security and tactical oversight given to Boss.

***

Boss would select the team of guards and Gift selected, of course, Aimée. She pondered the rest of her choices. Would she pick her friends based on nothing more than being the ones she wanted with her? No. She considered Sakura for medical issues, Matteo for helping with food production, Mike and Tina in case any equipment needed repair—all logical selections.

Oksana brought her to sense. Gift hadn't realized she'd been thinking out loud the entire time they sat on the sofa in the young lady's flat.

"You're thinking ahead and that's... great. I mean, how you want to help and all. But you said they need help with hostile neighbors, and your boss said this needs to be mostly a military-style operation, most of the delegation being guards, *right*?"

"Yeah. Oh, and he's not my boss. Mister Bauer, I mean. I just call him that, like a nickname. He's over the guards on the team, but *I'm* leading the mission."

"Gift, I love you. You're... you're great, and a wonderful friend. But you're being stupid. This boss of yours, on this type of mission? You're kidding yourself if you think *you* are actually in charge."

"This is *not* the R.F."

"And am I glad for that. I love it here. But going into a situation with hostiles? Military *always* takes charge. He'll say it's for everyone's safety, or that in security matters his authority supersedes yours. You watch."

"Whatever. *Ma*, that's not what you were saying." A sly smirk replaced Gift's frown. "Get back to the part about me being wonderful."

"I was saying you should consider this a first wave. I mean, you go to talk, use force if necessary. Take a small crew for the talking part, you and Aimée. Maybe identify the most immediate need and take someone for that. Anything else you want to do... that will be in the second and third waves and so on."

"How on Earth did you get so smart?"

34 | Week Four

Old Hindu ideals of humanitarianism intrigued Gift. Her favorite definition being: *'Marked by humanistic values and devotion to human welfare.'* The decision of the Board, thanks to Miss Heller's appeal to their humanistic values, made the people of New Europa more… human.

Only the fourth time in a flyer, Gift's nerves refused to be at ease in a two-centuries-old machine hovering more than a hundred meters above solid Earth. Four massive turbines provided lift with thrust pressure from forward momentum as Gift had never experienced. In a giant-sized drone called a heavy, nothing but air separated her from the ground. The fear factor increased when that land turned blue. So much water. Eyes saw what the mind couldn't have imagined, a sea between what was France and the African continent.

Light brown waves, larger than the blue ones had been, seemed to be moving. It took all Gift's mental cognition to force the logical mind to believe the flyer's movement, with its angular views, distance, and refracted sunlight, caused the optical illusion. She thought of the spice from that book she started reading but never finished. Something valuable came from the sand and giant worms guarded it. Looking over the vast wasteland, Gift wondered what value hid beneath its arid surface.

"It wasn't us," Boss said in a dull yell over the rumbling of the turbines and the wailing of an atmosphere being ripped by a blunt object.

"Huh? What are you saying?"

"That desert. Wasn't us, environmental ruin, pollution. Nope, this desert's been there for thousands of years."

"So, for *us* not to ruin something, it had to be ruined already?" Gift added, "That's not so reassuring."

"Just saying not everything is our fault. I think that's a little reassuring."

Aimée leaned over. "I think he means that if we fail, and he needs to order an assault... not our fault."

Boss pulled his cheek with his thumb, exposing the bottom of his eye. An awful gesture, Gift hated the way it made his eye so gross. Its meaning eluded her. Sometimes it meant *watch out*, or could imply *I'm watching you*. Once, it meant he agreed. Who knew what he meant by it in this setting.

Matteo stared out the window in silent wonder with guards sitting stiff but for the rocking—not authorized to enjoy the view, ever in guard-mode, even Sara and Tom.

"Now, *we* need to go in first."

Gift understood Boss to mean the guards but was confused as to why.

"Because of the recent takeover?" Aimée asked.

"Yes, my dear. It's a new government. Frequent coups, revolutions, and régime seizures are part of the continent's history. This is at least the third one in two years and if things are as they said? Likely someone's ready for another one. We go in first."

"You mean Blessing? She took over the government?"

"No, Love. She's their me, sort of. I think her father's in control."

"Welcome home."

A pleasant distraction, Matteo's words confused Gift. "*Huh*?"

"I did some research. I'm pretty sure we just came over Nigeria. So... Welcome home."

"Shiny. At lease there's green now. Um... also too, you know we flew over Italy, right?" She gave him an arm slap and a smile.

As the colony came into view—thanks to the pilot's sweeping approach—Gift could see rumors of it not being much of a colony appeared based on some fact. Obviously smaller than New Europa, it looked much older. Exposed supports on the main dome showed rusted metal eaten away by time. A key difference shone from the sunlight's reflection off frosted glass panels on the larger dome.

When the door let down, the dust swirled in little tornadoes though the turbines had halted. Ominously poised amidst a brown cloud, the greeting of armed guards unsettled Gift. Had there been another takeover in the time between their distress call and help's arrival?

"Blessing, hello," Aimée said once she cleared the craft and her throat.

"You are welcome. Thank you for coming."

No other introductions or pleasantries beyond that, just a hand wave to move them toward the U.A. colony. Boss remained with the transport while Commander Tucker led three guards ahead of Gift, Aimée and Matteo.

A corridor beyond the hatch—oddly not an airlock—showed signs of neglect and disrepair in peeling paint and cracks in the concrete. Several lights had died out or were flickering, putting Gift into a scene from a horror vid, wondering what awful creature lurked in the shadows. Commander Tucker held the procession before entering the open dome and turned to Blessing.

"Ma'am, what's the situation with the government? Who's in charge?"

"Richard is my father by name. He is in charge. We had a bad coup last week's time. Killed my father's lieutenant, but the leader was shot and the rest subdued."

"Where are these people now?"

"Banished, like all criminals. No wahala. It's *safe-Oh*."

Gift became curious. "We're told your people can't live very long outside." Blessing nodded. "So, isn't banishment like... a death sentence?"

"My sista, we are... *Wait*. You dey Naijá?"

"Nigerian on my grandma's side, yeah." That got Gift a tight hug.

"Things here no be easy *at'all*. We are barely surviving. Always it's been like this. Not enough food or water. Too many pikin born. Come, you need to speak to my father."

The dome, smaller than in other colonies, spread over one circular building rising in the center. The lack of the colony's ability to impress continued in with them. Dreary. As she walked, Gift saw unfinished concrete, everything dull and gray and vined with cracks. Comfort and visually appealing clearly didn't make the builders' mandate. Reaching a small office, the guards remained in the corridor and Tucker stepped in with Gift and Aimée. The presence of Richard filled the space—instantly more intimidating than Miss Anoykina—a man to be taken seriously. He said nothing at first, looking over his guests, leaving his eyes a bit longer over the women.

"Welcome to United Africa. Which is Amy?"

"Hello sir. I am Aimée. Thank you for having us."

"And I'm Gift. I represent the Board of Directors of New Europa. It is a pleasure to meet you, Mister Richard."

"The pleasure is mine, to meet both of you."

"Sir, my name is Tucker. My men and I are here at your request to assist with your neighbors. Shall I coordinate with your head of security on how we will proceed?"

"*I'm* head of security. We have a small government. Disloyalty spreads among our people like a virus, and they killed my lieutenant in the last coup. And, Mister Tucker, there's nothing to discuss. Your men will accompany mine and take the cave where these people hoard their resources. We will bring back what we can today and take over operations of their facilities."

"Sorry sir, but that's not why we're here." Hoping the exterior portrayed confidence, Gift trembled inside. "We talk first. It's why Aimée's here. We know nothing about these people, their... cave, you said. For all we know, they may cooperate."

"Dear girl..." Richard's tone made the term derogatory and rude. "When that fails, the guards will take the cave. Look around. This is not a colony. I rule this empire of dirt, and we keep fighting each other for it. This place? An early prototype built for the colony project and never meant to be occupied. But as with so many times in our past, the Europeans got what they needed, plundered our resources, and left us to die." He leaned into Gift's face with a deadly scowl. "Before you go on your fool's journey, let my daughter give you a tour. See our lives, our diminished resources, our failing systems. Look at our farm and water supply. Then go have your talks."

Depressing scenes saddened their eyes at every turn. Boxes smaller than Gift's slept four while others lived in areas separated by thin cloth walls in a space Gift wouldn't have put their refugees for one night. More children than Gift had ever seen ran around them. One boy of about six latched onto Blessing's hand while she scooped up a tiny girl of maybe three.

"Who do we have here?" Gift asked, holding the girl's hand, making circles. She leaned herself into Gift's arms.

"Rebecca. And this guy is Samuel."

The tour had to pause a few minutes for Aimée and Gift to play with Blessing's adorable children. Their bright, round eyes looked over button noses underlined by wide smiles. The boy with a missing front tooth refused to be detached from his mom no matter how much Aimée cajoled him. The joyful mom joined the ensuing tickling match while Tucker and his man watched with straight faces that wanted to move along.

"Blessing? So many children here. Do you, I mean, can your people have children, *naturally*? Or do you need in vitro, like other colonies?" Gift asked, desperate not to be unique, special.

"No. We have *limited* medical, but they *left* a prototype of the genetics lab for our *eggs and sperm*. Many fail, we lose so many. But as you see, our in vitro works *good-Oh*. And we have plenty-plenty pikin here."

Back on tour, Blessing's kids in tow, poor lighting cast shadows in every corner. Riddled with bullet holes, walls were scribbled with cracks like a connect-the-dots children's game. None of the domes had shops or food stands, only work areas, including a single large kitchen in each where cooks prepared food to feed the colony. The unmistakable aroma of Egusi soup saturated Gift's nostrils and wet her palate. One of the cooks with a face eerily similar to Gift's Nonna scooped a taste into bowls for each of them. Gift and Aimée joyously ate theirs while the guards' faces tried their best not to insult the generosity of their hosts.

A hulk of a man called Bright collected Blessing's kids before she escorted the visitors to the farm. Her brother had been helping her with them since her partner, her father's lieutenant, was killed. Learning those precious little ones lost their father tore Gift's heart, broken pieces lodged in her throat as a lump. She wondered in amazement at how the woman carried on.

Finding Matteo and the other two guards in the farm ended the tour. Barely the size of the ancillary farm in New Europa, the crops didn't appear healthy. Matteo explained how three-layered rice fields produced the staple food, often eaten doused in broths with sparse vegetables. They added proteins three times each week.

"Why don't they have an exterior farm? I mean, they know where they are, been going outside. They could have a nice farm out there." Gift pointed at a wall. "Miss Blessing, how long can your people stay out?"

"No medicines, only our natural strength. We are used to *harsh* weather for *millennia*. Some of us can stay out the whole day, talk-less those who made it *nearly three* days. Some of them will meet you by the cave."

"Wow." The nameless N.E. guard, category ten, hadn't had the new treatment yet to extend his hours into days. Funny Gift knew those details, but not the man's name.

Aimée turned to Blessing. "I think we've seen enough. We need to try to talk to these cave people."

35

What-ifs bounced like ping-pong balls in Gift's mind as the flyer pulled itself from an Earth that didn't want her to go, pressing her into the seat. The unpleasantness swirling in her stomach came from how readily assumptions led to conflict, fighting, shooting, war. Could their new humanity crest the summit to create a new default behavior? She had to hope.

"We must expect resistance..." Commander Tucker spoke in intense monotone. Slightly darker than most Europeans, Gift's speculated roots in Africa. "...seems King Richard's forces plan to take this cave by force, skipping any negotiations."

"That's your job." Aimée spoke with authority. "You keep them from starting a war while we try to talk."

Lifting his head, Boss said, "My dear, you see what we're up against here. Security is our top priority, making this a matter of administrative control. Commander Tucker and I will do as we see fit to address the situation, *whatever* it presents."

Slowly building the nerve to counter, Gift riled her inner self. "Oh no, we *are not* doing this. This is my mission. These guards..." A hand waved at the dozen men and women swaying in the transport. "...answer to me. Commander Tucker, you will take no action without my authorization. Is that clear?"

Which had greater insincerity, Tucker's *Yes ma'am* or Boss' head nod, Gift couldn't determine. A power struggle loomed and Gift and Aimée stood little chance to come out the victors.

"We're all just animals, aren't we?" Aimée spat.

Grabbing a handhold to steady himself, Boss stood. "Listen up, people. We have one clear objective here: unite the resources of this cave to the dying colony. We will try to do that with words. Whe—*if... that fails*, it is up to us to take this facility. Mister Tucker is correct to assume the U.A. will have our option two as their option one. Our initial position is to hold them off and give the talks a chance." Turning to Gift, he said, "My dear, if you plan to be with Aimée, you will not be able to make the immediate call to action. So, I'm placing that on Tucker, trusting his training and reasonableness. He will be under orders to give you every possible minute, assuming you get in there. Unless you stay with the guards, it must be this way."

An ultimatum cleverly presented as a choice suggested Boss submitted the mission to Gift's authority. He didn't. He also wasn't wrong. He knew Gift wouldn't send Aimée in there without her. Calling up her mental display, she listed the pros and cons in columns and found a compromise.

"Let's do this... Mister Tucker leads his team. You, me, and Sara join Aimée. You and I are here representing our colony, which is in full cooperation with U.A. We go in, no show of force, hoping for a peaceful resolution, and Tom monitors the situation with a live link to my handheld. Does that work for everyone?"

"My dear, you've grown into your role." Boss winked at Gift. "Everyone, we follow Gift's lead. Tucker, make sure all the guards are clear, no one acts prematurely, no escalating this needlessly."

With that settled, Gift moved on. "Got some talking points in mind?"

"You know me, Love. I'll make it up as I go along."

"It's... here we are again. And that last time... you didn't even get a word out and they shot at you, shot Heller."

"Far as we know, these folks are doing well, better than our Pioneers, supposedly with abundant resources. But there must be things they lack. That's where I plan to go. I mean, negotiations need something to offer on both sides, right?"

"What does U.A. even have to offer them? I mean, you saw the place. The colony's dying, barely able to feed themselves, and their tech is old and crappy. How do you negotiate with that?"

"Love? Just why are *we* here?"

"To help. Oh... *duh*. I just can't think straight, you know? Of course, what New Europa offers, we offer to a union of United Africa and... and what the heck are we even calling these people?"

"What did they say back in U.A.?"

"Please, I don't think *cavepeople* will work. Already got Pioneers taken for ours. I know you hate research and all, but didn't you find anything useful in your prep?"

"Actually... and of course you're right, you know me and research don't get along. Since I've got Oksana as my assistant, she found a few options we could use."

"Your assistant? *Ciao*. You're supposed to be a friend, a mentor."

"Sure. But she'd have been bored to death watching me work. Besides, she enjoyed helping and had a great suggestion. We can call them *Ubuntu*."

"Ubuntu? What does that mean?"

"In many African cultures, it embodies values and practices considered to make people authentic human beings. It's about community and cooperation."

"That *is* better than cavepeople."

"And this guy, famous for trying to unite Africa—Neldella or something—said a traveler going into a village didn't have to ask for food or water. People cared for and helped each other. I think that's the spirit we're going for, right?"

"Wow. Just... well done. It's perfect."

"If the people accept it. What if they have a name for themselves? Anyway, I think... having the U.A. see these people as Ubuntu helps them accept them as friends and put down their weapons. Then—*oh*, this is good. *Then* they will truly become *United Africa*. I mean so far, they haven't lived up to the name. Fighting among themselves—I know, we're ones to talk. Love, we can help them make a *real* United Africa and a thriving colony."

"Brava, really. And how do we announce ourselves. I mean, they'll assume we're from U.A. They've not been the best of neighbors, and if we go walking up, they'll just shoot us dead."

"You've got a point. Whatcha got in mind?"

"Boss? Do we have anything to amplify our voices?"

From Oksana's research, Aimée shared details of the survival colony burrowed deep into Ogbunike Cave in South Nigeria. Originally two hundred kilometers from the recessed shoreline, the navigator now put the ocean not fifty from their landing site. Gift yearned to stand on that shore and look over the vastness of a watery deep she couldn't get her mind to conceptualize. Some things must be seen for the brain to figure them out. That would be later, after they'd brokered peace, a peace Gift deeply hoped they'd be able to establish.

A band of warriors crested a grassy dune when the turbines moaned to a stop. Eight men and one frail-looking woman made their entire compliment. Sagged shoulders and ashy skin withered by dehydration accentuated their boney features. After introductions, Gift learned the team had trekked on foot, or by leg, for five days with no tents, sadly low provisions, and suffering the effects of earth sickness. At once, she supplied them with water. As a force, their intimidation paled in comparison to the image Gift's anxious pondering had conjured up of the U.A. soldiers. In their pitiful physical state, she doubted they'd put up much of a fight.

Cautiously nearing the entrance of the cave with Boss, Sara, and Aimée, Gift hoped not to be welcomed by bullets. The remaining N.E. guards held back with the group from U.A. and Gift kept an open connection to Tom on her handheld, just in case.

"We see the entrance. It's... not like a colony at all. It actually *is* a cave, just a big opening in the rock. I've got my earpiece, but radio silence unless absolutely necessary."

"Copy, Gift. Please be careful. First sign of anything off, call out to me and run. You hear me?"

"Sure. I mean, copy. What a stupid word for okay."

Through a fist-sized black square, Aimée said, "People of Ogbunike. We are visitors from the colony of New Europa and have traveled a great distance to meet you and wish to talk. We are in four and wish to approach. Please respond."

Like a hundred spiders, the silence of anxious suspense crawled up Gift's skin.

36

After Aimée repeated her message a third time, a figure emerged from the opening in the rock. Arrayed in vibrant colors flowing over a wide upper garment, it made the man appear to be a green, yellow, and red mushroom on the stem of his baggy green trousers. What remained of his white hair didn't flinch in the stiff breeze thanks to its close-cropped tight curls. The smoothness of skin lacking wrinkles of the years he presented led Gift to put him anywhere from sixty to eighty—she often missed by kilometers when she guessed age.

Waving as to a close friend he said, "Welcome. You are welcome here."

The four toddled to close the gap and Gift noted the lack of guards.

"You are very welcome." He extended his hand to Boss. "Please, where is this place you come from? You are not from United Africa; this I see beyond your words—a woman's words. One of you spoke then?" His hand waved over Gift, Aimée, and Sara.

"Hello sir. I'm Aimée Toussaint, those were my words. We are from New Europa in what used to be called Europe."

"And what brings you all this way? Not just to say hello, I am sure."

"Correct, sir. United Africa contacted us and—"

"No, no. Those people have no place here. If you are with them, you are not welcome here. Not welcome."

"Sir, if you will permit me... They contacted us, that's true. But we are *not* here representing U.A. In recent months we've had peaceful relations and trade with the Russian Federation. We recently met others who, like you, have been outside of the colonies for over two centuries and survived. Strong people, such as yours must..."

She's doing great, so diplomatic. How she's complimenting his people, being respectful. This could work.

"...are hoping to facilitate such a peaceful relationship between ourselves and your people. It is for the good of all our peoples to move forward in this way."

"My dear, I see why you speak for your people. There is indeed much—"

A yap from Gift cut the conversation. '*Gift. Gift.*' A piercing shout in her earpiece. "What is it?" She removed the small plug from her ear for all to hear.

"They're coming. Take cover now. They're *coming*."

"What? Who? Who's coming?"

"Those people of the U.A. They ambushed us... More numbers than we thought. Get inside if you can, shut yourselves in." Static. The panic rose to eleven, a setting Gift added to her scale when ten seemed inadequate for life-threatening situations.

"Come, this way. Come, quickly."

They hadn't even gotten the name of the guy in the colorful mushroom shirt they hurriedly followed into the cave. Eyes trying to adjust, Gift saw only ghosts of the others. Pressing onward, a soft yellow light glowed in their eyes and definition returned to their sight. The rock walls of the cave vanished; they stood in a metal room two meters square like an oversized lift. A *walls-closing-in* anxiety pressed in on Gift with a theoretical pressure that made her bones ache.

Light flooded in when one wall pleated, squinting eyes unable to discern what lay beyond. Gift trailed Aimée, who followed the friendly man, with

Sara clasping Gift's shoulder from behind, and Boss assumed to be at the rear. A metal antechamber presented yet another door in the labyrinth, a solid-looking hatch not unlike the airlocks in N.E. His turn to them unhid eyes brimming with a sorrow Gift didn't understand, a pain uttered in the arch of his eyelids from a source she couldn't suppose.

"Before we enter... I need to know what happened."

Aimée took a deep breath. "Sir, we spoke the truth earlier. We brought guards, but they held back. You saw that we came in peace. U.A. sent people here, and ours were holding them back. We wanted to talk, only to talk. What it seems happened back there... the U.A. tired of waiting and tried to get through our guards to attack you."

"Yeah. That voice you heard from my pocket? He's one of ours, Tom. He said they attacked them. We were trying to keep them away from you. They must be fighting them right now."

"I am Kofi, village elder. For now, I am choosing to believe you. We have lookouts, well hidden, and soon we will know all. Please, you three follow me, this way."

"*Three*? Where's Boss?" Gift asked Sara.

"He wasn't behind me when we entered the cave."

"Was he hurt? Shot?"

"Don't think so. He ran off to check the situation."

"Oh mamma, I hope he's alright. And, and Tom... and the others."

The opened hatch assaulted their eyes with an intensity of light which dissolved into a magnificent dome carved in rock by nature, not engineers. On walls arching upward, Gift traced sandy brown streaks marbled with darker browns and veins closer to red. Smaller than any Citadome in N.E., with no buildings, it fooled the eyes into seeing a dome of colossal size. The crop beds were small but flourishing. Gift estimated a couple dozen people working the farm space, no one else in sight.

"Excuse me, Kofi, sir." Gift waited for his eyes to say go ahead. "May I ask, how many are you?"

"We will hold your questions until we can confirm your account of what's happened. Then we may solidify our trust. Let us start with your names. I have only properly met Emmy."

"I'm Gift, this is Sara."

"Pleasure to meet you all. Now, come, let us sit and talk." He motioned to the ground.

Sara didn't sit. "Sir, I assume there is secure access in and out. Our guards are out there, fighting to defend you. Do you have guards or soldiers, anyone who can help our people?"

"We never had the need. When we see U.A. approaching, we lock ourselves in. That is the extent of our defense. We have no weapons, soldiers, or guards."

Sara's wide-eyed look to Gift said, '*May I go join them? You're safe and they may need me. I can save Tom.*' Gift may have put that last thought into Sara's expression. As the word *yes* crawled over Gift's tongue, eager to tell Sara to save Tom—*them*, she'd say them—a protocol reminder popped onto her mental display. The guard couldn't leave Gift and Aimée in unfamiliar territory with an unknown people.

Kofi's questions probed deep, and Aimée tossed Gift a look through the slant of her eyelids each time to verify permission to divulge information. While Gift appreciated the gesture, she had become so fed up with secrets she wished nothing held back, letting the N.E. spokesperson speak with full transparency.

"...what we offer is mutually beneficial cooperation. Regular visits and trade, an exchange of information and goods, such as medicines, and assistance with caring for your crops, growing food." Aimée had brilliantly summed up all the goals of the proposed peace agreement.

"You spoke of medicines. Please tell me what medicines you offer."

Gift answered, "New Europa has top-notch medical people. We have virtually no serious illness and people can live to well over a hundred, we think one-thirty." Agnes was among the few who had passed ninety-eight since N.E. discontinued compulsory departure. "And we're even making considerable progress in overcoming the earth sickness."

"Earth sickness?"

"Our name for it. Do your people get sick staying outside?"

"Some do, after a few days. Many of us can stay longer with no problem. The more robust of ours do not return for several days from lookout patrols."

"Wow. The Pioneers... the ones by us that were in those bunkers, have similar endurance."

The dialog moved in a good direction, trust building—one way at first. Hopes were high the other direction would germinate from this seed as soon as they had settled the issue outside. Worry for Tom and the others engulfed her, robbing Gift's mouth of words. Sitting cross-legged on a carpet of moss, she withdrew from the conversation, silently pondering their demise. Relief entered with Boss, looking a little worse for wear but okay.

"It's over. They came at our people from all sides, had many more than they let on, at least two dozen to our one. Fortunately, only a few had proper weapons. Tragically, we lost two guards, but managed to subdue the enemy with our projectile stun guns. Great work on that Gift, they saved us."

"Which two?" Gift squeaked.

"Harold and Maryann."

Subconsciously Gift knew Harold—the least likable of her former keepers—had been in the detachment. Hearing his name brought his face clearly to her mind, seeing him on the transport, head bobbing. He had greeted her when they boarded. A battle between relief and sadness warred in her gut and she wanted the sadness to win. It felt wrong when relief for Tom was the victor.

Once reports came from the refuge lookouts verifying the accounts and the veracity of Aimée and Gift's words, Kofi opened the vault that had held his confidences. They learned the cave housed the descendants of two former villages, one from Nigeria, the other from Ghana. Kofi had served as village elder for the better part of three decades and it astonished Gift to learn of his eighty-four years. He and his people descended from a small group of survivors who found the cave-turned-bunker two centuries prior with natural sources of fresh water and disused but workable farms. Their group numbered just over two thousand and had everything they needed to live in the cave indefinitely. Almost.

They lacked medicines, in truth, any type of health care. They also had no technical knowledge or engineering skills of any kind. Whenever something went wrong on the farm and endangered a crop, they lacked the agricultural know-how to save it. Aimée found the points to negotiate, to present her mutual aid argument, and Kofi was favorable.

Once the guards joined them in the cave, all graciously accepted an eye-dazzling tour of the place. Stunning caves, tunnels, and hollows resulted from the combination of nature and engineering. The subterranean complex, a pre-colonies solution for human survival, had been abandoned due to the last religious conflict between factions from Ghana and Nigeria.

That a tribe from each side joined unitedly to make the cave a refuge, to work peacefully together and help each other, epitomized the word Ubuntu. Kofi agreed to the term being applied to them as—not to cause any division among their two tribes—in two hundred years, they never named themselves.

While the success elated Gift, she wondered if Richard and the people of United Africa would welcome their new Ubuntu neighbors.

37

Colony Lake blew Gift's mind as a wonder to behold in a panorama beyond what any dream state or fired imagination could conceive. Irresistibly drawn to it, she stood ankle-deep in its liquid, marveling at the volume it contained. It soon became a significant and joyous means of recreation and relaxation. Perhaps those were equally important to life as potable water.

Until visiting Nigeria, that had been the largest body of water she'd ever seen. The small puddle of a lake she and Aimée bathed in on their road trip was unimpressive at best by comparison to her lake, but had its own charm, its water just as crystal-clear and inviting. Ice-cold—Gift called it super-freezing—entry into the invisible pool under the waterfall assaulted her flesh as it went from normal human body temperature to something close to hypothermia. Each thrilling encounter made her believe she understood water.

High above what they called the Mediterranean Sea, a vision staggered the mind. To the left of the flyer, Gift saw the remnants of one of her ancestral homelands, not exactly resembling the boot shape history said it had before the seas rose. To her right, deep blue water led to more water, and then more water. Colony Lake became a drop in a bucket. The agitation atop the sea, water churning over itself, fascinated Gift. White ripples highlighted the tops of waves with an unseen force constantly pushing the turquoise liquid, yet it never emptied. In relentless motion, yet unchanging. She thought it a fitting metaphor for life, except of course, when life became unrecognizable in the wake of its waves.

None of her prior aquatic adventures prepared her for such a mind-blowing experience as this. Synapses exploded and tears flowed as she stood in awestruck wonder before it. A more powerful cocktail of positive energies streamed through her veins than an entire week's worth of double espressos. Gift could climb a mountain, break down and rebuild a water recycler in under two minutes, or swim the length of the sea. What was the length of it?

It had no end.

Standing ankle-deep she saw its end, but the recesses of her mind understood she wasn't seeing its termination. Bewildered eyes told her brain the distant horizontal line, where the deepest blue she had ever seen met a haze of diffused cerulean at the sky's dissolution, was the end of the ocean. Her brain argued a logical rebuttal it couldn't grasp yet knew to be true. The delineation in the extreme distance of the farthest horizon she had ever seen was no more the end of the ocean than the end of the sky. Both continued farther than her eyes could see, so she let her mind drift into imagining both sky and ocean extending on, blue over blue, forever.

Mike had to be Mike and told her she wasn't technically in the ocean. "It's the Gulf of Guinea," he said more than once, this time pointing to his tablet.

"Sure, your map says that, but look." Tapping emphatically, she said, "The seawater comes *here*. They just call where it meets the land a gulf, but tap it and it says it's 'an inlet of the sea.' *Sea*, as in ocean. It's part of the Atlantic Ocean, says it right there in the description. I'm in the ocean. I'm in the real live ocean. Isn't it amazing?"

"Pretty mind blowing. I mean, look at how far it goes. Just keeps going and going. You know they used to have massive transports that floated over the water full of people and goods? Called them ships."

"Yeah, I know. I'm not *that* bad at history." Her elbow jabbed his side. "*Ma*, why didn't they just fly over it?"

"Some ships were gigantic, transferring huge cargo. No way a flyer, they called them planes back then, airplanes, could carry it all."

"Why'd they have so much stuff to move?"

"Trade. Like we do with the R.F. Wanna hear something cool? Way down underneath the water, there are still all these sunken ships with all their cargo. Amazing treasures even. Lost to the sea centuries ago."

"Not sure how that's cool. I mean, people must've died. Anyway, shut up. I wanna enjoy this."

Silently they stood as Gift shifted her vision back and forth from the distant horizon to the waves breaking on her shins. Her feet stayed visible when the liquid's stir didn't disturb the sand, but it had nowhere near the clarity of Colony Lake. Somehow the rolling water hid her feet in the sand.

"You gotta do it, Gift. You'll regret it if you don't."

"I know... It's real scary, so shut up."

"Because it's not crystal clear and goes on forever and you're afraid you may get swept away, taken out to sea and lost in all... that."

"*Right*?"

"It's your chance to swim in the ocean. Don't be scared, I'm right here."

"Yeah, but you can't swim for crap."

"Gift? Why would anyone swim for crap?" Yet another elbow jab, which his lousy sense of humor deserved.

"I mean, if I needed help... what would you even be able to do?"

"Tell you what. Let's go deeper, but where I can stand. You swim parallel to the shore a bit and turn back."

It sounded reasonable. Mike often did. He'd call her back from a situation in which she took an extreme stance and help her see the middle, the merit of an opposing viewpoint or her own previously spoken words, or options her mental display hadn't shown her. This trait allowed Gift to merrily overlook the annoying ones—most of the time. Though the gulf verses ocean thing pushed his leeway.

Hand-in-hand they stepped into the sea, pushing against waves that wanted them to move back to shore. A shout escaped Gift's lips, pushing through the splash chilling her face when a wave popped on her chest. Once she was up to her neck with her chin raised, she stopped, Mike's visible shoulders her safety buoy.

"I'm gonna do it," she told the water. She didn't do it.

"You got this. I'm right here."

She did it. Gift swam in the ocean as much as through her own disbelief in her newfound courage to do so. Unlike in the serene lake, her actions weren't the only thing moving her body. Her left side rose, then the right. Her left side tilted down, then her right. The rocking unsettled her, but she maintained even strokes until she decided she'd gone far enough and turned around.

Raw panic crawled up from her stretched toes when they didn't connect to the land below the water, and she forgot to tread. The sea she ingested when her legs pulled her below the surface tasted salty and felt thicker than the lake. Not as much as the clean liquid compound of the fire suppression system, but thicker than other waters she knew, and she was drowning in it.

Her throat burned. Through a gap in her spasmatic coughing, Gift's name pushed through the accumulated liquid muffling her eardrums. When her chin lifted from the thick salty water, she managed to inhale a desperate gasp of oxygen.

She went under again.

Between distortions of light piercing the deep, surrounded by booming echoes, her elbows bent, and flattened palms pushed water down her thighs. Thoughtlessly she kicked. Her head shook as it broke the surface and muscle memory must have taken control over her arms and legs as she hadn't remembered how to tread water but found herself doing it. She could get her bearings.

The shoreline appeared farther than she thought a safe distance and the sea removed the ground from below her. Desperate eyes didn't find Mike where he should have been. He had drifted too far over, closer to the security of land. No. The idea of being farther out to sea intensified the panic lacing through the realization of her mortality. *Focus Gift. Don't panic. You know how to swim, that's all this is, so swim.* She failed to convince herself.

Mike pointed at something. A signal—of what? His waving hand said she should swim to shore, not to him. Once again that was reasonable, and in that moment of *I'm-going-out-to-sea* fright, it helped her mind come down. Arm over arm, legs kicking rhythmically, she made her way to shore and crawled out of the shallow water's edge with waves breaking on her backside and down her thighs, gently nudging her forward.

In one swift movement, her body rotated and collapsed, plopping herself flat on her back with arms out to the sides shaping her into a lowercase *t*. The foam of waves stretching toward her and retreating tickled the soles of her feet as she pushed away the fear and anxiety of nearly drowning with laughter from deep in her diaphragm.

When Mike rushed to her side, he tried to reassure her. "*Gift*. Thank goodness you're okay. It's okay... you're okay... Oh, wait... are you *laughing*?"

"I did it Mike. I swam in the ocean. I *really* did it."

"Yes. Yes Gift, you did."

Mike sprawled out beside her, and they stared into the endless sky. Claps of waves smacking the beach followed by the dull roar of retreating water created a surprisingly soothing ambience. Gift wrestled with thoughts of how waves that pushed water to the shore had the opposite effect on her, taking her out farther. Mike may have been joking, but her fear had almost materialized, she had nearly been carried out to sea, lost with those ancient ships, a forgotten speck in the vast deep blue.

That didn't happen. I'm okay. I swam in the ocean, that *happened.*

When they rose to prepare to return to U.A., they didn't care if they'd be late for their expected return from the Ubuntu caves. They would send a message as soon as they were close enough to the colony's communications array. No one expected them at a specified time as Gift set her own schedule.

For the entirety of the drive back, her thoughts were on returning to the ocean with Aimée and Oksana. She missed Aimée terribly.

38 | Month Three

Things change, Gift understood that. The way they changed unsettled her. One year had flipped her life upside-down and turned it around in ways the twenty-six before couldn't have imagined. Changes of a personal nature were part of life. Throughout her life, Gift observed her character shape itself into the woman she would become. Tutors had changed every two years, then her work assignment, Box allocation, new friends, new social habits.

Life itself; when that changed, she was ill-prepared.

Who wasn't?

While she liked to think of herself as that same person who strolled the corridors of New Europa without a care in the world, she'd changed. Not into a different person, Gift had grown into someone more mature, something born of necessity. That may have been true, or, as Aimée would say, she could have been blowing sunshine up her own butt.

Six weeks had passed since she watched Aimée broker peace between the U.A. and Ubuntu peoples. N.E. stood right in the middle of it, being involved in active trade. Going one way at first—described by New Europa's Board as humanitarian aid—eventually trade flowed in the other direction with colorful clothing and handmade jewelry. It was a start, and many of the items from the Ubuntu were gorgeous. Oksana wore her Ghanaian earrings just about every day since Gift gave them to her.

Now a full member of New Europa, her mother feigned some resistance for appearances, according to Oksana. Tasked together on two engineering projects for U.A., Gift and Oksana had spent most of the last three weeks there working, bonding. Mike and Tina came to help rebuild the technical infrastructure of the dilapidated U.A. colony. A first major initiative, they salvaged spare parts to build a ground transport to ferry people and supplies between U.A. and the Ubuntu village. Gift accepted village as the better term over refuge. The way Gift figured it, that transport helped transform the African people into something that lived up to the name *United* Africa.

Gift and Oksana strolled out to the new exterior farm to check on Matteo's progress with the soil enhancers sent from New Europa.

"Ciao Matteo."

"Hey Matt," Oksana said. Her cheery tone caught Gift's ear.

"Hey Gift, Oksana."

"How's the soil taking to the new treatments?"

"Slow, but progressing. Now that we've prep'd this plot of land, enriched the soil, I think this farm will do well."

"Shiny. Great job."

"Great work, Matt."

As Oksana spoke over Gift, Matteo smiled warily. With reasonable certainty, Gift figured Matteo saw her as a child, so many years younger than himself. Reluctant to tag anything at a hundred percent after her own relentless optimism had disappointed her too often recently, she learned to be more realistic. Ninety-nine became her compromise.

The afternoon left Gift and Oksana on the farm as they had automation tools to repair and cultivation droids to upgrade for advanced techniques developed for the U.A. Gift marveled at the girl's proficiency as she worked her way to becoming an outstanding engineer. And she loved the work. Other than being in Matteo's presence, Gift never found wider smiles on Oksana's face than when she was elbows into a challenging engineering task. Her idea to add a flow-control modulator to the auto-trimmer to prevent it from removing good berries with dead growth would have saved many basil plants on the N.E. exterior farm.

"Hey, Aimée's coming tomorrow. Did she tell you?" Gift asked her young apprentice and new friend.

"Yeah, I'm so excited. Haven't seen her in two weeks. Except on vid-Chats, of course."

"Me too. Being here is fine, we're really helping. Also too, relations between all colonies are great now. But I miss people when we stay this long. Mom, Raff, Aimée. I hate not being with them."

"Yeah." Oksana's reply carried a sadness she tried to suppress. Gift saw through the mask, having learned her ways over the weeks they had been palling around close as sisters.

"Sweetie, is something wrong? You must miss your mom... and your friends at the R.F."

"Not really. Mom some, sure. But I've been back a couple times to see her, and she visited me once. Well, she came for a meeting. And... I didn't *really* have any friends."

"Something else then? I mean, if, if you want... you know you can talk to me. Or Aimée if you prefer."

"I know. And that's the problem."

"How do you mean? Have I done or said someth—"

"No... That's just it."

"Sorry sweetheart, I'm not following."

"I'm waiting for it, you know? One day, could be soon... maybe in a month or year. But I know it's... coming."

The girl's fight not to weep unhid itself. As Gift had done it herself many times, she recognized the emotional torrent behind her eyes—trying to be strong, forbid the tears. Options raced onto Gift's screen, *wrong, delete, next*. What could she be afraid was coming? A conclusion calculated, was it correct? Gift's mouth went with it ahead of the brain.

"Do you mean… losing me and Aimée?" Silence as Oksana examined her boots meant Gift had guessed correctly. Taking the girl's hands in hers Gift said, "I'm not going anywhere. And Aimée adores you too."

"But…" Apprehension cracked her voice, she paused to sniffle. "You guys are so much older. And… and… you've got Tom. You both have so many friends, adults. I'm just an annoying kid following you both around like a pathetic child."

"Oh no, sweetie, not at all. We love you, me and Aimée both. We don't keep you around out of pity. We love having you, honest. And we don't think of you as a child. In New Europa, adult life begins at sixteen, and you're nearly seventeen now. Besides, you know my friend Marco, from the Box next to mine? He's your age, and we're friends."

Oksana's head raise and return to her tasks may not have been total confirmation, but Gift believed her words reassured the young lady—a ninety-nine percent chance, anyway. The workday ended early to give them a treat for dinner they had been looking forward to all week.

***

Piled into the land transport, Mike, Tina, Matteo, Oksana, and Gift headed off for the Ubuntu village. With Tina driving and Mike beside her, Gift put herself between the teenager and her crush, to be safe. The ride offered plenty of bumps, but Mike's new suspension upgrade and gel foam cushions did a decent job smoothing it out. Thoughtfully Tina had made the back seat a little wider to fit most of the three bums onboard. Five and a half hours later they arrived at the village in time for dinner.

After a quick wash-up, they sat at a table on a natural rock ledge beside a miniature lake of *invisible* water fed by the constant flow of a natural underground spring. An entire panorama inside a cave was a thing of unspeakable beauty that reinforced the idea to Gift the engineer that nature's designs far outweighed anything made by human minds and hands.

Kofi's entire family joined, including his Union partner Paulina, whom he called a *wife*, and their three children. The eldest being Julianna of forty-two with Husband, she called him. It took Gift a while to realize that wasn't his name, he was called Jonah. Solomon, thirty-nine, came alone. The youngest, a seventeen-year-old called Gloria, instantly got along with Oksana. After a pre-dinner cocktail—of which Gift only sipped and stopped Oksana from partaking—Paulina and Kofi served the meal. Not Gift's first time having Ghanaian food, Kofi promised it would be something special, a delicacy.

It didn't look all that appetizing. Not that it resembled Sergey's bullfrog, but it reminded her of it. A dead carcass of some sort with a near black char covering the exterior, hinting it spent too much time in the fire. An elongated oval, the larger side had a face. Gift hoped the cringe she felt held itself inside and hadn't pulled the skin over her cheeks taut. Tina drooled with excitement for an adventure in new flavors.

The diced onion and pepper piled atop looked delicious, but Gift had no guess what the airy white balls beside the burned dead body could be. The room-filling fragrance from the carafe of sauce tickled Gift's nostrils and flooded her mouth with saliva. Maybe she could eat a bit and fake her way through the rest without insult, as she'd done with the vodka.

"One of the most amazing meals I've ever had, really. *Fantastic*." Taste buds rejoicing, Gift said the words in full sincerity.

The edible white balls called banku were a mixture of corn and cassava dough. Once Kofi showed everyone how to cut into the carcass, the flavor exploded in Gift's mouth. Wishing to add this fish called tilapia to her diet,

Gift committed its name to memory. Combined with the banku and the spicy sauce, they enjoyed an outstanding meal.

After a sweet dessert, they retired to Kofi's home. Not as impressive as the glorious dining location, the modest and tasteful home appeared half carved from stone, half constructed. After being granted permission, Gift ambled through the room to admire the African artwork, wood carvings, and several models made from stiff metal wire.

"The children made those when they were small. Your ancestors would have done the same," Paulina explained. "In the villages there were no toy stores, and most families had no money to spend on such things for their children. You read about the financial collapse? We had nothing to collapse." Raising an odd model—a toy as Gift learned—it had the shape of a lower-case *t*. "That one's an airplane. Like your flyer transport, but from the world *before*. It only goes forward, but they flew well-well."

"I'm not seeing that. I mean, it's hollow. Just an outline."

"It's just how the children made them. Real ones had engines and were solid. These arms were called wings and gave the plane lift. It was a real marvel of engineering."

"I'll have to look them up when I get home."

"Take it, please. Keep it."

"Oh no, I couldn't. Your children made it."

"Look around dear, we have so many. And the children have others in their homes. Please, take this one. I insist."

"Thank you. I have just the place to put this in my Box." When Paulina's face soured, Gift explained, "No, I don't mean *a box*. It's what we call our homes... because they're basically big boxes. I'm going to put this on the shelf next to my Nonna's carved giraffe."

"That sounds lovely."

Lodgings at U.A. were modest at best. On the first night, Oksana and Gift shared a Box less than half the size of her own. It barely had space for the stacked bunks. Lack of comfort didn't justify risking insult, but Gift found an excuse when she learned the occupants were made to sleep in the curtained-off quarters on the dome floor to offer the room. The next transport delivered a package Gift requested and she and Oksana shared a tent outside the colony ever since. Mike, Matteo, and Tina kept their modest accommodations. While Sakura's improved medications had increased exposure tolerance from hours to days, she strongly advised against anyone but Gift sleeping outdoors. Oksana had no issues, having whatever the Russian medics had given her. Gift learned the R.F. had since abandoned the treatment for its high mortality rate.

The modest room they gave them at the Ubuntu village was kilometers ahead of what the U.A. could offer. Sharing one small room, Gift, Tina, Oksana, Mike, and Matteo, each slept on a bed cushion on the floor. Tina snored.

A lovely breakfast combined tombrown with croissants, pancakes, and potatoes. Thinner and lighter, the pancakes were unlike Matteo's, who said his were American style. The ample breakfast bloated Gift's stomach, being much more than she usually would eat for her first meal. Having a voracious morning appetite, Oksana ate as much as Tina and even finished Gift's pancakes.

"How are you so thin?"

A smile was the only answer Gift received.

They'd head back after spending a good part of the day working on tasks for the village. Matteo worked in the hydroponics garden, Mike and Tina handled refitting the large harvester for the new exterior farm, and Gift and Oksana installed upgrades to the air recyclers. The ideal of Ubuntu became a reality and lifted Gift with optimism that humanity may develop the new default behavior she knew they could.

The alert on Gift's handheld crushed her spirit.

<h1 style="text-align:center">39</h1>

Aimée had been traveling back and forth more than anyone. In the critical first weeks, communications were the lifeblood of cooperation for the known world. It comprised three colonies and two remote civilizations. The level of collaboration and unity—a few exceptions and occasional hiccups—rivaled the colonization project itself. This new version of humanity had no neglected minorities, none excluded from the good of the whole.

Blessing took over administration, having deposed her father's government. Little of it had remained after the last coup and having most of his loyalists in custody after the ambush at the cave. A natural leader, she had appointed her brother Bright as her lieutenant. Added to her strength of character, Blessing had a kind and gracious demeanor. In her first four weeks, she had improved living conditions and had amicably mediated trade with N.E. and the Ubuntu people. It was a new United Africa and Gift's dear friend had been instrumental in shaping it. Gift couldn't have been prouder.

It had been nearly two weeks since Aimée went home—days dragged or flew by depending on the current mood. When thoughts came to seeing Aimée, they lingered intolerably, days taking weeks to pass. It was plainly evident Gift held this in common with Oksana. Knocking out the last few tasks for the Ubuntu village would have them loaded onto the transport at 14:00 to head back to U.A., to see Aimée.

At 13:37, the alert on Gift's handheld crushed her spirit. It played the code they established for critical alerts; Gift recognized the tone. In a shaking hand, Gift held the device slipped out from her pocket, hesitantly raising it.

Critical Alert from United Africa

"vidChat Blessing Omoruyi."

"Gift, Gift, it's gone down. It's gone down."

"What's gone down? What is it? Slowly, tell me what's happened."

"Your transport... the flyer. It's gone missing. We think it went down."

"*Aimée*," Oksana shrieked in Gift's ear.

"No. *No.*" Gift barked the words as if she could *will* it not to be true. "When you say it's gone, what does that mean?"

"It was on approach, it cleared the desert over Bukuru, *minutes* away. When it didn't show, we try well-well on all communication frequencies... but no *reply.*"

Gift's deep breaths searched for calm. "Okay. Okay. They didn't arrive on time, and you weren't able to reach them. Doesn't mean they've gone down, so many things could—"

"Gift, they are in *flyer*. Minutes away-*Oh*. We should have almost seen them in the sky for *naked eye*. What else could it be?"

"*Wait*. On approach you should have had them on your monitor, the system we installed two weeks ago. Have you checked it?"

"No one here knows how."

"Raff. I'll get Raff. Wait, Blessing... you need to send out a search party."

"Already did, but if the flyer didn't pass Bukuru, they won't reach for almost two *days*."

"Okay, but if they made it closer, your party might find them. Send as many as you can. I'll get Raff to check your monitor from her side... End."

"vidChat Raffaella Di Gaetano."

> Unable to establish vidChat remotely

"Stupid thing. Open comms relay. Request remote chat Raffaella Di Gaetano."

> Working...

"*Raff. Raff.* I need you. The transport, it's—"

Open relay vidChat had a two second delay.

"*Gift.* The transport went missing. I'm on it, almost into the system at U.A." As panic-stricken as Gift felt, seeing it on Raff raised her anxiety level to eleven.

That *mal'd* delay.

"She's not dead. She's not. She's okay." Did Gift's words have the power to make that true?

"I'm sure she's okay. We have to believe that." Oksana had such maturity, not losing it. Gift marveled at the young lady's strength and wished she had the same.

Raff found something. "Got it. We lost the transport—No, no, I mean... we lost *contact* at thirteen twenty-nine just after their last check-in with U.A."

"Did they make it past the desert line? Past Bukuru?"

"We lost their transponder signal... let me check... I'd say they may have made it halfway from there, maybe less."

"Okay, okay... Let's—"

Raff had more to say over the two second delay. "I asked the R.F. to send their other transport, but it's down for repairs."

"*Crap*. Okay, hang on... that's about... eighty to maybe a hundred km from U.A. We can get there by ground transport before the search party. We're going now. Raff, keep on it, please. *We need to find her*."

"Of course. I'm trying to see if I can get you a general location, at least narrow the area for you."

"*Please*, let me know *the minute* you find anything. I'm leaving now... End."

Mike became the designated driver when they scaled down their rescue team to him and Gift, with Tina, Oksana and Matteo remaining with the Ubuntu. The speed payoff would be substantial, plus they'd have room for carrying back Aimée and any other survivors. Kofi provided water and basic rations, blankets, and torch lights. They raced off at top speed with no regard for a smooth ride. Air pushing around the windscreen pulled the tears from Gift's eyes, stringing spaghetti strands of wet hair over her ears.

At six hours away, the pain intensified to anguish, its torture stemming from Gift's overactive brain. Try as she did to suppress it, images of the various ways Aimée had died looped on shuffle in her mind, tormenting her. If this were it, and she couldn't mentally verbalize what she knew she meant by *it*, it would be worse than Charlie. Not only for what Aimée meant—*no, what she means*—to Gift, but for the hours of agony. As intensely difficult as it had been watching his life flutter away, it was immediate, and she was there for Charlie. Who was there for her best friend?

"Can't this *mal'd* thing go any faster?"

Since his earlier, '*She'll be fine, we'll find her*,' hadn't been well-received by a frantically heated Gift, Mike had gone quiet.

"I'm pushing it, Gift. We're moving significantly faster than yesterday. We're under five hours out... depending."

"*Depending*. What do you mean? Depending on if she's already dead?"

"I mean depending on the location. Hopefully Raff gets us closer. I'm headed to the point between their last known position and U.A., going in a straight line, which is how it'd be flying, right?"

"Just get us there, Mike, fast as you can. *Faster.*"

Through the open plains between the Ubuntu and U.A., comms went dark. Repeaters and communication relays hadn't yet been installed on the path, so their devices were incapable of external communication. Gift would not learn if Raff had found something until they were nearer to United Africa, and she began losing lucidity.

"Raff," Gift screamed, but not into her device, not at Mike. She yelled wildly into the air, "Where is she?"

"Gift? You know we can't reach Raff until we're in range of U.A. We'll be there soon. Drink some water, you need water."

"Don't tell me what I need. You need to drive faster or move over and let me do it."

"You don't know how. We're going as fast as we can. Please, take some water, you're dehydrated. It's hot out here and we've been going for hours non-stop."

"Shut up. I told you."

The vehicle slowed ever-so-slightly, and Gift turned a fiery face to Mike.

"I'll stop this right now if you don't drink some water."

Reluctantly, she sipped at her water bottle as the jerky movements of the transport sent a trickle over her lip and onto her coverall. An additional reason for anger flared, burning like flames in her bones. It infuriated her that Mike was right, and she guzzled down the water. Shortly after quenching her thirst, her silent anger's heat dissipated.

"I'm sorry, I wasn't myself. I... I don't know what came over me."

"It's okay, I get it. Worry, dehydration, the heat, being on this bouncing transport for hours on end. I'm worried too. I know you didn't mean it."

"No, I didn't. And... I'm sorry."

"Was incredibly mean, though. I'd say you owe me big time now."

"Thanks, Mike." She gave him a slap on the arm and felt herself smile until the guilt of it pulled it back.

"I think we're coming in range of U.A. Try Raff on remote relay."

Raff had narrowed the search location to a reasonable area, but the good news came with some bad. If her data correctly isolated the spot, the flyer may have been in a range of rocky hills and outcroppings. Low elevations, but that would add delay and move them to searching on foot. If Gift's heart were a balloon, it would have filled with air until it popped. Her chest felt as if it had.

The vehicle finally came to a stop at the base of a rock outcropping after managing the first few inclines. Raff sent Gift's handheld a locator and, as they drew closer, Aimée blipped on the poorly detailed map as a blue dot. It indicated the flyer's beacon, but to Gift it was Aimée.

They began climbing the rocky slope. Mike had to push to catch up when he stopped to ease nature, as their new Ubuntu friends called it. With ferocious determination, Gift wouldn't let anything slow her, not even her own unstoppable need to urinate. The wiggling went on with Gift clenching every muscle she could while trekking over inclines and climbing an occasional rock. Defeat came a nanosecond before she wet herself, easing her own nature just before reliving the experience of soiling her coverall.

The hour of scampering toward the blip was the longest of her life, and Gift felt herself aging on the trek. Of course, it might have been sheer fatigue, physical and emotional. When she couldn't go straight, she screamed to no one before going around an insurmountable stone projection twenty meters wide. Long before Gift got close enough to the blip, she yelled Aimée's name every few seconds.

"We need to move... Come on. Gotta find her before dark."

"We're close Gift, we'll make it."

There it sat, in a subtle valley with a doable slope just minutes ahead. They'd found her, or it. Gift looked down at the transport. It appeared to be in decent shape if she ignored the gaping hole in the rear left part of the roof and the missing turbine that looked like a gigantic monster had bitten it off as in an old vid Gift watched. Other than that, it looked survivable.

Running down the slope proved a less-than-brilliant idea only after Gift took her first few steps despite Mike's warning. She slid and rolled the rest of the way, grateful for tall grass with scarce rocks to batter her flesh. As Mike skidded toward Gift on his backside, she heard vibrating vocal cords push out his words. "As... you... *wiiiiish*." The reach for humor, quoting a line from one of Gift's favorite vids from *before*, only aggravated her—not the time for that sort of thing. Moderately bruised and on their feet, they ran the last several meters to the flyer.

"You've gotta be *kidding* me."

After a look through the interior, Mike said, "No one's in there. I mean, besides the pilot. Didn't know him."

"I met him once. I don't remember his name, poor guy. *Ma*, what *gives*? Where is she?"

"Maybe they walked off toward the colony. I mean, they knew they were close, right? I'd start walking to the colony if I survived this."

"Stop with the *ifs*. The pilot's dead, the others aren't here. She's not here. That means they got out. Maybe you're right, they headed to the colony. Which way's the colony?"

In Mike's finger Gift found a new panic welling up in her. "Would she know which way to go? I mean, what if she went another way and now, she's lost out here? We gotta find her. Aimée... Aimée... *Aiméeee*."

"Look. The flyer looks like it landed pretty much intact. I mean, I think it—"

"*Intact*? A quarter of the thing is missing."

"Well, it has a hole, but... I mean to me... it almost looks more *landed* than crashed. Hard landed, sure, with three turbines, but landed."

"Do you have some sorta point?"

"They landed here, headed toward the colony..." Mike stood at the nose of the flyer and bent his arm at the elbow and slowly lowered it to point straight. "They'd go that way."

"Yes. Yes Mike. You're a genius. Let's go that way."

Mike exhaled deliberately. "Gift, wait. That's... basically the way we came."

"*What*? You idiot. Why'd you say all that?"

"I'm sorry. I'm trying to find her, them."

"Them? Do we know who was on it? The, the flyer, I mean. I hope she's not on her own out there. Someone was with her, right...? Must have been. Don't you think...? Aimée... *Aiméeee*."

40

Darkness had made the search nearly impossible, even with the torches they had from Kofi. They covered the small hilly outcrop around the transport's crash site well past Gift's voice going sore from the repeated shouting of her lost friend's name. Mike trekked alongside her after having split off to widen their search footprint. It had been more than seven hours and the U.A. search party had a day's walk to reach them. But if Aimée headed off to the colony she'd come upon them, she'd be safe. Nothing to do but hop back into the vehicle and close the gap.

"There, torches."

The searchers, not Aimée. When Mike stopped the transport near them, Gift asked if they'd seen her, anyone. Their answer punched her in the gut, and a sour taste climbed up to the back of her mouth. Her vomit wasn't abundant as she had barely eaten since the hearty breakfast and it was just after 03:00—late enough to almost be early, depending on how she looked at it. The thought of it being another day drowned her in dread, so she considered it late into the same day. The search party had camped for the night, set to resume at first light.

A choice split Gift in two, half wanting to stay in the search, half wanting to get to U.A. and finish repairing the drone so she could send it looking for Aimée. Once again, Mike proposed words of reason. Having the drone would increase their chances more than adding two more bodies to the sizable search party.

Gift hadn't slept.

Her eyes closed a few times as she rewired the drone's controller, and she pushed the guilt away. A battle raged between her spinning mind and weary eyes over how many crystal diodes she saw on the auxiliary board for the stabilizer. The brain insisted it counted five, while her optic chiasma interpreted an image of eight or ten. Uncertainty increased when two of the crystals hovered over the next set and fused into a single pair, yet her blurred sight was the only thing that had touched them.

The espresso in U.A. never tasted good, being a tad on the bitter side for Gift. This moment didn't demand flavor, only caffeine—a desperate hope for her eyes to regain the trust she'd lost in them. The coffee blended with her undying resolve into an energy-infused cocktail like adrenaline, and she readied the drone for flight.

Morning's first light had melded into full morning sun, providing excellent visibility. Since he took a nap, Mike insisted on taking the controls. His eyes would surely be much sharper and more trustworthy to show him what Gift's might miss. At least that's the argument that got her to give up the drone's control tablet. Gift drifted and struggled against dozing's formidable pull and jerked her head up every few seconds when exhaustion rested her chin on the breastbone.

"I'm fine," she said to no one.

A trip to the toilet reignited the flames of Gift's dread. "Anything?"

"Not yet, but we're covering good ground. You were right to come get the drone going. We've extended the search range a good measure."

Mike tried his best to be kind. *He* had insisted on coming for the drone. Throughout the ordeal, he'd been trying every trick in the book to make Gift feel better. As much as she appreciated the attempt, it wouldn't be enough, nothing could be, not until they found Aimée.

"It hasn't been long." Gift tried to convince herself she had a solid basis for optimism. It failed.

"Been almost three hours now. I mean... we're covering ground. She's out there, we'll find her."

"Wait, *three* hours?"

"You fell asleep for a while. Nothing you could do, and you needed it, so I left you."

A hard slap bounced off Mike's arm. "*Jerk*. How could... I needed to... you... you dumb jerk." The words nearly choked her on the way out. They were hurtful and left a bitter taste on her tongue worse than that poor excuse for coffee she'd been chugging. "Sorry, I... Sorry." As apologies went, not a great one.

"I understand. And I want to find her too. Promise, I've not taken my eyes off the screen. We'll find her."

Once again, words meant to comfort were offered as fact. 'We'll find her.' Could Mike know that? As much as Gift knew it, believed it with all her heart, she didn't *know* they would. Hope lacked the surety of Mike's words, being nothing more than wishful thinking. If the next words needed would be of consolation, would that make those words of comfort a lie?

***

The search had been officially called off after two days, yet Gift continued circling the drone. "One more time," she said before each of the eight *one more times*. Dozens of searchers had scoured the area and the only other air transport, a larger heavy flyer just returned to service from maintenance, hauled the broken one back to the R.F. for repairs. Both belonged to the Russians and the damaged one had been on loan as a contribution to the stabilization of U.A. and the Ubuntu people.

Like a loyal sidekick, Oksana stayed glued to Gift's side since she returned from the Ubuntu caves, each taking turns napping uncomfortably on the non-reclining chair in the operations room. Gift only became aware of her own body's stink when Oksana's assaulted her nostrils, and Gift realized she had been in the same clothes and unbathed a day longer than her malodorous young friend. Mike and Tina worked with the Ubuntu, upgrading their grossly outdated farm automation systems. If not for Matteo and Blessing bringing food, Gift wouldn't have eaten in days.

Which hurt worse, the initial report of the downed flyer, not finding Aimée when they reached the crashed air transport, or the devastation of having to stop the search for her? Each summoned different levels of pain. Some had potential attached, unrelenting optimism. What Gift had to do now stabbed at her heart like a thousand knives.

"Recall the drone."

Words devoid of hope.

Drained of all energy, malnourished, and likely a bit dehydrated, Gift lacked the vigor to put anything besides monotone words into her expression. Slowly dying on the inside, she went for a shower. Oksana followed and took the booth beside hers. Standing in the suds under the full-flow hot water, Gift thought it odd such an underdeveloped little colony had better showers than her housing block. It gave her something to ponder that wasn't Aimée and all the potential outcomes of her fate. In clean coveralls and eating the first proper meal in days, Gift sat in silence with her new teenage friend.

"She's not dead." Oksana spoke with an authority well beyond her years. Gift mistook it for naïve optimism, the sort she used to have.

"We... don't know. We, we just, don't know."

As her shoulders slouched, Gift's head dipped, letting her eyes find a bowl of pounded yam and leafy vegetable stew Blessing called Efo riro. Oksana's face showed a hint of joy at eating the dish the traditional way, with her hands. Gift's stare into her food wasn't into her food, the dish happened to be where her sight landed. The ball of sticky yam dough looked as if someone had ripped half of it off. When she checked why her fingers were so weird, she found her thumb and three fingers dripping a brownish-green combination with what resembled specks of wilted spinach leaves. She allowed it to fully occupy her mind.

"No, we do know." Oksana spoke and Gift wondered if they had been talking, because it sounded like a continuation of a thought. "Aimée wasn't on the transport. Wasn't on the surrounding ground... or anywhere. That we *didn't* find her... it's... a *good* thing. She didn't die in that crash. I just know it."

A particular logic in the girl's words resonated with Gift because she was right. They didn't find Aimée alive and well but hadn't found her dead carcass either. Only the idea didn't settle Gift's mind, it had the opposite effect. New and outrageous speculation flooded her head, images of Aimée being carried off by wild animals seemed an almost certain happening. Or maybe another group of survivors. No, those wicked criminals, evil men banished from United Africa. They had her and were doing who-knew-what to her.

"Yeah... not dead," Gift replied.

Urgent communication request, that's what the alert on her handheld meant. Plagued by hunger, the body had relieved the conscious mind of control and let the brain take over caring for it. Gift ate. The food masticating in her mouth tasted delightful, with a hint of spice. The alert was Raff, had to be. Gift had ignored several vidChat requests and watched, but didn't reply to, her last two messages. *Now Raff's using the urgent alert to get me to answer*, Gift assumed. After swallowing fully and wiping her mouth and fingers on a napkin, Gift accepted the urgent communication and Raff appeared in live vidChat.

"*Finally.* I've been so worried. *Ma*, that's not why I connected just now. We lost another one. Gift, we lost the other transport."

"*What*? How? What's happened?"

"So far, we know little. It was headed here from the R.F. and we lost contact, exactly like the other one, it up and disappeared. We're trying to isolate it the way we did the last time. We've got nothing so far."

"Is this crappy Russian Engineering?"

"*Hey.*"

Gift ignored Oksana's objection. Raff replied, "We've been over those ourselves. You've even gone over those systems. You said the design was excellent, and they're very well maintained."

"They are excellent Russian design." Oksana peppered her words with a dash of pride. She was Russian and now a junior engineer, but Gift couldn't see how she had any knowledge of those flying transports. Still, she was right.

Gift dialed it back. "Yeah, they're fine flyers. *Ma...* two crashed in what, two days?"

"Four, Gift. It's been four days."

It didn't add up on Gift's mental display. *Four days? No, not the point. What or who made the two flyers crash, or whatever happened to them?* "After all this time? Both crashed? This makes no sense. Oh mamma. Could this be more sabotage? Are they doing—are *we* doing this again?"

"There's no one left of those—"

Hands cupping ears ineffectively muffled the sound. Oksana's face withdrew and her eyes disappeared into a hard-pinched squint. The klaxon hit a pitch that caused physical pain in the ear canal. Gift hadn't been involved in setting up the colony's internal security systems, monitors, or alerts. She had no idea what this meant, but Raff was gone—not cut off in words for the blaring alarm, the connection terminated.

"What's happening?" Gift shouted, not sure to whom.

Oksana shrugged.

The two ran back to the Ops center to find Blessing with two members of her administrative staff, one hunched over a display. At least the klaxon ceased its deafening roar. Something terrible was happening, but they had no clue what. Blessing said, "The alert means something don *breach* our perimeter. We're scanning *even* now to see what—"

"Flyers," the man at the display said as dull as if he read the lunch menu, only with less emotive cadence.

"Flyers? Raff just told me we lost the other one. That's all we got. How... Wait, did you say... did you say *flyers*? As in more than one?"

"That's what I said. I'm seeing two... no... three flyers. These suckers are huge."

"How far out?" Blessing's tone smacked of anxiety.

"About twenty minutes. Could be sooner."

Blessing contacted Bright to tell him to get Rebecca and Samuel safe, then to get all the children from the nursery. She then engaged the colony-wide announcement system and spoke calmly into it as her words bellowed through the domes and corridors, ordering everyone into security lockdown and every guard—Gift had gotten her to stop saying soldier—to their posts for intruder defense.

No idea came to Gift as to who was coming or why. The people they'd thus far met as outsiders, the Pioneers and Ubuntu, were not violent people and had nowhere near this level of technology or equipment. The flashing on her mental screen, an alert, an answer to an unasked query, implored her attention.

"New Republic of China."

Blessing wore a puzzled face as a mask. "What? They never don replied to a *single* message. We try well-well and they *never* answer. Why would they come here now?"

"Our transports. *They* shot'em down. Must have. I mean, look... we've united three colonies and two outside peoples. Maybe... I think, maybe they, they see us as getting stronger. And they're the only ones not included. Not with us, I mean. Could it be they see us as a threat? They broke our transports so we'd be sitting ducks?" While Gift understood the reference she didn't care for its consequences for the poor duck.

"You might be right-*Oh*. Who else could it be?"

Oksana looked at Blessing, then to Gift, and back to Blessing. "Don't rule out the Russian Federation. They've been cooperative, sure, but the colony is *not exactly* all in agreement. Some still cling to the old ways. They could see this as an opportunity to crush this union and assume a dominant position."

Pensive, Gift contemplated the statement, shocked by its implications and the source of the speculation. "So... they shot down their own flyers? And have a secret supply of bigger ones? How does *that* make any sense?"

The girl quickly snapped a reply, "I wouldn't be at all surprised if they had secret transports, weapons. It could be that they've had a coup, the military taking control of the government. If they saw my mom as that government, and those flyers working for the united colonies she supported, they'd shoot them down in a heartbeat."

Their whites took on a brighter intensity as Blessing's eyes widened. "Goodness. You really think that could be what it is? They are the strongest of us. My goodness."

"I may not have the most freedom of speech here... but let's not jump to any conclusions, okay? We don't know any—" Gift stopped her words and turned to the nameless man monitoring the incoming transports. "Hey, you. How far out now?"

41 | INTERNMENT: DAY ONE

"How far out now?" Gift realized the stupidity of taking time they should have devoted to a plan of action, to preparing for an invasion, and spending it speculating on what they couldn't know. They would soon find out who the visitors were and what they wanted, even if that would be their last thought before being exterminated. New Europa would have a difficult time defending an invasion. United Africa didn't stand a chance.

"About two minutes. But I'm guessing here."

"Oksana, you need to go. Get to the center dome, the guards will point you to a safe lockdown spot."

"*No*. I'm staying right here with you."

For the first time in her life—after unjust treatment, insults, home invasion—Gift had an instinct to reply with a smack to the face. It seemed the appropriate response, what Nadezhda would do. Of course, she'd do it as the girl's mother. No, as the leader of the R.F. If she was still the leader of the R.F. Gift let it go, realizing she had no control over the independent young woman's life—a life Gift helped to emancipate.

They felt its roar as much as heard it pass overhead, pausing over the dome as if greeting them in the center. The surrounding air took on added weight with items on the desk shifting as if it were being shaken. Without laying eyes on them or hearing the preliminary report, Gift could picture these transports as massive, much larger than the one borrowed from the R.F. and perhaps bigger than their heavy flyer.

"People of United Africa and distinguished guests from New Europa."

A voice boomed over the public address system, which Blessing hadn't activated. The accented English hit Gift's ears as something unfamiliar, assumed as clear evidence whoever spoke, spoke in a second language. At once her thoughts bounced back to the R.F. She had picked up several variations in the accents of the few who spoke English.

The articulate, masculine voice continued, "We wish no fight, no violence. No one needs to be hurt today."

Gift didn't appreciate the ambiguity. "No one needs to be hurt *today*. That doesn't speak to their overall intentions. What about tomorrow?"

"No one needs to be hurt, not today, not tomorrow, not ever." *That was super-creepy.* The mic wasn't on. "We have landed outside your colony and are coming inside to talk. If you do not fire or attack, you will not be fired upon. Look at our air transports, the weapons in our hands. We outmatch you greatly. If you make a defense, you are only taking needless lives. We are coming in to talk."

After checking the cameras to find what looked to be about three dozen men in front of each transport in what she called body armor, each holding intimidating weapons, Blessing gave the stand down order. U.A. guards would barely be an inconvenience to this force. Standing down was the right call, but Gift could see the conflict warring in the woman's eyes when she ordered it. Perhaps a part of her would have preferred to go down fighting. Oddly, Gift had the tug in her gut too—that was new and upsetting.

Nothing like Sergey's Rosgvardiya, even in the intimidating black armor, most appeared too small to be Russian guards. That they knew exactly where in the U.A. colony to go piled an added layer of trepidation as Gift's brain continued to race through possibilities of who they were and what they could want. A compliment of ten entered the office space just outside the tiny Ops Center, which was a closet of an equipment room crowded with Gift, Oksana, Blessing and her two people.

Leaving the men at their posts, the women exited the cramped space, abandoning its illusion of safety, to meet their conquerors in the adjacent office. Gift considered it the closest definition to put upon the unfolding scene and the sensations conjured up in her hyperactive mind. They were being conquered, politely.

When he removed his mask, the man at the head of the pack presented a face Gift recognized. Not that she knew the man himself, but where he came from and the people he represented. That it wasn't the Russians brought no comfort. At least she had familiarity with that enemy, who, as it turned out, wasn't the enemy after all. Could this be worse? Gift thought it a certainty. The other nine stood at attention, like Tom's *Tom the Guard* stance, with helmets on and weapons across their chests, fingers on the triggers. With a similar length to the rapid-fire guns she had seen, these were sleeker and thinner, yet looked more deadly, as if the others were... less lethal.

"Hello. Welcome to United Africa." Blessing stood tall and spoke in a steady voice, confident and strong.

"I am commander Chan of the New Republic of China. We are here regarding the air transports that have been forcibly shot down, unprovoked."

His pause made Gift think he expected a reply. Did he admit he and the N.R.C. took the credit for shooting down the flyers? *Did he shoot Aimée out of the sky?* Her instinct elevated far above a face-smack and took every bit of her strength, plus the presence of nine heavily armed soldiers in battle armor, to restrain herself. Was Blessing looking to Gift to end the silence?

"Hello Mister Chan. I'm Gift Ojo from the New Europa colony. We're here as guests of United Africa to assist in its revitalization. Your unannounced arrival has caught us unawares. Perhaps if you had replied to any of our—"

"*Enough.*" An authoritarian's command. "We are here about our flyers you shot down."

"Sorry, *what*?" Gift's melted brain could foster nothing else, given the outrages accusation *they* had attacked N.R.C. transports.

"In the last two weeks, three of our air transports were blown out of the sky. The damage was severe, loss of life. We will account for these atrocities and those responsible will be punished severely."

As her mind tried to keep up with her mouth, Gift let the words fly. "Excuse me, sir. First of all, we didn't shoot anything down. And second, there's this thing called the justice system. So you don't get to just walk in here and dictate terms and tell us people will be castigated. We are a new human species, elevated, and need to have a spirit of cooperation."

With his flat hair pressed onto his scalp from the helmet, Chan's face looked rounder than it may have been. From a stature far less intimidating than his tone, he replied, "That was a stirring speech. But there is a fact I will point out to you, as you seem to have missed the obvious. *I am* the justice system here. And *I do* get to walk in here and dictate terms because, if I didn't, there would be a crater where this pitiful colony used to be. So you see, Miss Gift Ojo of New Europa, the only cooperation here is you doing exactly as I say and telling me what I need to know."

"I see."

Oksana spoke up and at once Gift wished she hadn't. "Listen. You have no idea who you're dealing with. Gift is on the Board of Directors and one of its most powerful members. And my mother is the President of the Russian Federation. We are united. If you don't leave here now, you'll wish you had never come."

Oksana's *uhgh* was her only reply as her head turned briskly to the side. The crack from the back of Chan's hand on her face was sudden and sharp.

She held back her tears along with her words. The steam rose to forty-five degrees in Gift's head, reaching critical.

"So... you are the bratty young daughter of Nadezhda Anoykina. Thank you for sharing that useful information. And... we are fully aware of who Miss Gift Ojo is and her *powerful* role in your defenseless little colony. Look at you people, coming here like saviors. Telling me you're a new human species. Pathetic."

"You can't just—"

Gift's whack popped even louder and the sting on her cheek burned like fire on her skin.

Blessing lunged for the man and her fist connected with his face, making a cracking noise not unlike the splitting planks on the scary bridge. Gift imagined she had broken Chan's nose, a notion solidified as he straightened his torso and raised his head. A jagged protrusion pushed out of the middle toward his cheek as if his nose were an arm with a slightly bent elbow. Blood dripped from his nostril and a red line connected his eyes over the bridge of his nose.

Instantly, two guards subdued Blessing to the ground and Gift and Oksana each had their arms restrained at their backs. Chan flicked his hand and the guards raised Blessing to her feet. The pop of it assaulted her ears with greater intensity than any Gift had heard prior. Those had been distant echoes, this happened centimeters from her face and rang in her ears. The deafening sound came ahead of the realization of what had transpired, and Gift's brain didn't fully accept it until Blessing fell back with a thump on the concrete floor. Oksana's guttural scream was shrill.

Overcome by shock, Gift stared for an endless moment, searching for movement, even a flinch, but found none. Her gaze shifted to Oksana, and Gift hoped beyond all hope the girl would keep quiet. Her eyes met Chan's. He smiled as he wiped the blood from his nostril and upper lip with a small white cloth. Gift thought it too dainty for such a man.

Irises black as night pierced into Gift's soul as only her mother's ever did. And Fred's. But Chan's had a greater intensity. "So you see, Miss Gift Ojo, I very much do get to come here and dictate terms and decide exactly how people will be... *castigated*. Thank you for the new word. Are we in agreement on this point?" Gift nodded and dry-swallowed. "Answer me," Chan yelled.

"Yes," squeaked out. Gift fought hard to hold back the tears and bottle her anger, save it for when she might be able to do something with it other than get herself killed. Thankfully, Oksana did the same, though tears rolled over the lingering pink impression of the man's hand. The moisture in Gift's eyes was for Rebecca and Samuel, now orphaned.

"Good. Now, you and I will have a little chat. My men will escort the little Russian princess out and those two men who have been trying to signal the other colonies. All communications are jammed. Please, have a seat." He motioned with his hand to a chair beside Blessing's desk, only it wasn't hers any longer, her life had been extinguished before Gift's eyes.

"Where are you taking her?"

"No harm will come to her, I assure you. She is quite the prize. I am sure Nadezhda Anoykina will be most interested in learning her daughter is our guest and being well-treated. Now, please sit. And Miss Gift, this is the last time I ask."

Gift sat as the two nameless men that used to work for Blessing were escorted out, dragging the body with them. In the little office, Gift sat alone with the villain who had invaded the colony and taken control of it without a fight yet killed a brave woman. *How many ways can I kill you with my bare hands?* Gift thought. Something trained agents and assassins said in action vids. Only, Gift knew precisely zero ways to do so.

Chan's sinister smile declared victory. "That's better." His voice had a breezy whine. He brought his hands palm to palm and cupped his face. The crack sent shivers up Gift's spine and Chan groaned. His nose didn't look at all right, but the elbow was gone, and it ran closer to straight. "Now, let's talk about my flyers, shall we?"

"Do you have her?"

"Pardon?"

"On the transport from N.E. four days ago. She's missing. Do you have her?"

"You say words, but they have no meaning. But let us get something clear, just so we all understand the ground rules and can have a more pleasant conversation. I ask the questions... you answer the questions. Now Miss Gift, tell me why you shot down my three air transports."

That's not a question, was what Gift's mind formulated in reply. Fortunately, her mouth paused long enough not to get herself killed. "I think there's been a huge misunderstanding. Why would we shoot down your flyers? We've never even spoken to you."

"That sounded like *you* asking *me* a question. See how quickly things are deteriorating? Do you wish, perhaps, to ask yourself a question and then answer it? Alright then, tell me, why would you shoot down our transports?"

"We wouldn't. I mean... we have no reason. As I said, I, we, I mean, none of the colonies have heard from you. We've tried. Do you know that? I assume you know that. We did, we tried... so many times to contact you."

"And when we did not respond... your people decided to make us an enemy."

"An enemy? No. We don't have... I'm not... *Look*, we didn't shoot down any transports."

"We? I assume you mean your pitiful alliance. Can you be sure of that?"

"Yes, of course. We didn't do this."

"Right, because you are on the N.E. Board. Big shot over there. Then tell me, if you are so sure you and each of your allies did not do it, why did you think the R.F. attacked you today?"

"I don't follow."

"Perhaps you can follow your own conversation." Chan leaned his battered nose forward, closer to Gift's withdrawn face. "You thought it was us. Congratulations, by the way, on being right. But then you all talked about how the R.F. might be behind it. A secret Russian army, the little brat said, more air transports and weapons, a coup. Can you honestly say you are one hundred percent sure you, meaning all your colonies, did not do it?"

Gift paused. Her answer could mean life or death, for her and who knew how many others. "I guess not. But... if I could contact them? See that Nadezhda is still in charge, then yes, if she is, yes. A hundred percent." That wasn't true, and not just because Gift violated her new rule of nothing getting one hundred percent. She hadn't anywhere near that high a confidence level in Nadezhda. Although, staring the man in his broken-nosed face, she bumped Nadezhda up a bit higher.

"Contact her? I see why you are such a big shot—you have nerve. Tell me about the weapons in your possession. New Europa and the Russians. What do you have that can shoot down a flyer?"

"*Nothing*. You've disarmed the guards here, seen their weapons. We have stun-guns and such... for defense. How could we take down a flyer?"

"Are you asking me questions again?" His voice became even more stern and terrifying.

"No, sir. That was... rhetorical. Sorry."

"Lovely and smart. You learn quickly, my dear. Tell me about... the missiles. And do not give me any stories—that will upset me. You do not want to see me upset."

Gift swallowed audibly. "We found them... in an old Russian bunker. Turned out to be a, a, missile launch facility, and still had a few missiles in it. We're not sure they even work. We, we didn't use them, honest."

"Thank you for your... *honesty*. It seems you do learn quickly. That matches our data. Now think this through. All the colonies but the N.

R.C. are... *united*. Let us use that word without debating its merit. Three N.R.C. air transports have been shot down and you happen to have a missile launch facility. What conclusion do you suppose we should reach from this?"

"I... I don't know."

"Oh, but you do, Miss Gift. The answer is obvious. What is not yet obvious is whether you are complicit. If this sad little union of a so-called new human species of yours is working together against us. Or—*Or*. Yes, this is the paltry word that has you on the precipice, my dear, ready to fall. *Or*... Or is there a faction among your pathetic coalition working independently? You see, this *Or* is what keeps you breathing—and the little princess. Everyone in this filthy hole of a colony. Just two little letters, but do you feel the power in them? Do you see why I must remove it? Once there is no *Or*... there will be justice."

42 | DAY FOUR/FIVE

Gashes etched on a wall could count the days like some troglodyte's calendar before people learned to inscribe thoughts on dried animal skins. The idea of holding the hide of a dead creature wiggled Gift's shoulders for a moment. Did prehistoric humans care what day it was. Each day was a day to stay alive, find food, pee and poop—much as Gift's days had become. "Troglodyte calendars?" she said to her tiny cell. "Meet their prehistoric friends on Friday for tacos?" The thought made her chuckle, and the chuckle made her realize it was her first one in days.

Nothing in the claustrophobic box they kept her in could carve into the walls—metal and badly in need of a fresh coat of paint. In greater need of a good scrubbing with soap and water. Gift had no markings, no troglodyte calendar to track her days. *Was it five? No, not that long. It's been three... maybe three. Where'd five come from? That's how long it's been since I had a shower.* "That's right." *They kept me a day and a night in Ops.*

In the first thirty-some-odd hours of the N.R.C. occupation, Gift didn't sleep—dozing in a chair, head hanging down, hands tied behind her back, wasn't sleep. Then into a box, left alone for two sleeps Gift called nights, even though in her enclosure she had no idea of the time. *Maybe it was three sleeps. Four?*

Standing had been possible thanks to her not being overly blessed with height. Her head reached just below the ceiling. From corner to corner in the square closet of a cell, Gift could fully stretch her arms if she allowed a little flex in her middle fingers. On the metal floor the fetal position worked best if she tucked her feet beside the miniature toilet. That position may have been what left bruises on her knees, unless the guards gave her those.

A pipe below the small metal bowl on the ground took her waste somewhere, but not far enough to carry its stench away. She vomited into it a couple of times—meagerly fed, Gift had little to hurl up. Squatting to urinate or do her business on the basin that rose no more than thirty centimeters from the floor brought her knees to her chest. Standing on its rim allowed Gift's nose to get closer to the slim air vent—the musty staleness being the better choice over the toilet and body odors.

Yesterday, or maybe the day before, they had let her out of her cage. She slept at least once since then, could have been twice. Isolated, sitting in her paper-thin gown hugging her shins and rocking herself, she tried to understand why, not having been asked a single question in contrast with the barrage of questions in Ops. A few times in Ops, they roused Gift from sleep with a splash of cold water for more questioning. But that was Ops, the first day and a half, or two days. This last ordeal had been unlike any interrogation of her life. Humiliating, yes. Was that its sole aim? Were they slowly working to break her? Gift mentally reviewed the whole thing from the cell door opening.

Rewind, replay, pause, play at half-speed.

A clank had announced someone coming before the shrill of the metal hinges. The door swung open to Chan. The tiny cell became cramped when he stepped in wearing a black military uniform. He cocked his head under the low ceiling.

"I am alone and unarmed. This is your chance. Overpower me."

A turned back tempted her to strike. Not only because she recognized the obvious trap, her restrain also sprung from knowing she had neither the skills in combat nor the strength to use them. When he stepped out, Gift instinctively followed.

"Good. As I have said, you learn quickly."

The narrow, dimly lit corridor showcased the same soap- and paint-neglected walls. They passed three other cells with solid metal doors hiding their prisoners. Desperately Gift clung to hope of Oksana sitting behind one of those doors—better than the alternatives. The powerful little man oozed ruthlessness. He had shot Blessing in cold blood before Gift's eyes, and now he had a deliberate reason for coming to her alone.

Walking barefoot through the main dome Gift saw U.A. residents going about their daily work as if the N.R.C. hadn't been there. That struck her as odd. Of course, there were Chinese soldiers, but they were by a huge margin in the minority. Gift's mind shifted to military strategies she'd never learned, drafting a plan to take back the colony. Trying to turn herself into a giant and squashing all the soldiers had as likely a chance for success as any plan she concocted—no training, no contact, no idea of the situation in the colony.

Untied and walking behind the unarmed man, a human of flesh and bone, blood that bled as anyone, she just needed to take him down. No way to do it came to Gift, and he likely had more than a dozen methods to easily kill her shuffling through his mind at that moment. She followed him into... *Ops?*

Pause. That's wrong, not how it happened. We didn't go to Ops. Rewind. Replay.

Untied and walking behind the unarmed man, they exited the colony at the hatch beyond the Ops center. *Yes, that was it.* Maybe she could outrun him? "Oh, the part about him thinking of ways to kill me, that was probably right," Gift said to the box. The rocking intensified as Gift returned to the memory.

At the edge of the exterior farm, Chan said, "You see, my dear Gift, we are not the conquerors you think us to be. Behold. On the farm, U.A. cultivators and N.R.C. are working side by side."

Desperate eyes scanned the expansive area not finding Matteo, and Gift considered it a good thing—perhaps he got away. They saw instead the U.A. residents outnumbering the N.R.C. personnel by an order of magnitude, and *'working side by side'* meant U.A. cultivators being watched by N.R.C. guards. A colony with a history of violent uprisings to overthrow their own rulership did nothing. Why were they so submissive and beaten now?

"Hands behind your back," Chan commanded her.

"Why are we even out here?"

"Again, you forgot our lesson. Who asks the questions Miss Gift?"

The weight of defeat pulled her head down. "You."

"Very good. And tell me what lesson you learned from Miss Blessing about obeying me?"

Quickly her head leveled, and the black holes of his eyes pulled her in, stopping time. They showed so little white, like ominous doll's eyes set on a round face that almost resembled the one that creeped Gift out as a child. Masking it as a cough restrained a spontaneous chortle. Picturing that doll's face standing before her lessened her fear. *What was it he had asked?*

"Miss Gift, are you with me? What happened when Miss Blessing didn't obey me?" She shrugged a reply. "Use your words and tell me what happened. *Now.*"

The intensity of the last word brought the eyes of the cultivators to her. Chan's gaze shifted to notice them and came back to Gift over a crooked smile. He wanted those eyes there. Bending to reach his boot, he pulled a black-handled knife with a blade of about fifteen centimeters, smooth on one side, saw-toothed on the other. *So much for being unarmed.*

"Miss Gift, I will not ask again."

"You shot her in the head."

"Now, what did I ask you to do?" Slowly she released her interlocked hands and Chan grabbed her by the wrist. "*No.* I thought you knew how this works. Answer my question."

"You said to put my hands behind my back. That's what I—"

The enraged commander shoved her backwards into the support post for the monitor station, slamming her back against its hot metal. A zip tie dripping foamy spit dangled in Chan's mouth and he pulled Gift's wrists back and around the pole, its heat toasting her arms. He stepped back, leaving her facing the cultivators in her short thin gown. The tip of the knife found Gift's navel, and slowly snaked up her gown. The razor-sharp edge sliced tiny gashes in the thin paper fabric. She barely flinched when the point of the blade's tip nicked the skin at the collarbone. After tapping the side of the blade twice on her cheek he returned it to his boot.

"You see, I am not a monster." A wave summoned a soldier and, after speaking in Chinese, Chan said in English, "If she sits, shoot her. If she speaks, shoot her." Chan turned to Gift. "This will give you time to think. Review the lessons I have taught you, so next time you are ready for our conversation." To the soldier he said, "If anyone approaches her, shoot them," and walked away.

In full sunlight for the first hours of this new shame, her flesh roasted. The heat drenched her skin in salty dampness and drained what little energy she had. Having barely eaten and now severely dehydrated, her legs lost their will to support her. *'If she sits, shoot her.'* He must have known she wouldn't endure this. Was this his clever way of ordering an execution without ordering an execution? *I'll be dead soon.*

"Please," she said to the nameless soldier impersonating a statue. "I know I'm not to sit. I'm trying but I have no strength. I can't stay like this. I'm trying to obey. Please." In a panic Gift recalled her tormenter's words, *'If she speaks, shoot her.'*

He didn't move. Gift wondered if the man even spoke English. Her words brought eyes from the farm, but she couldn't see their faces for the setting sun silhouetting them. If she could make it until sunset, perhaps she'd have the stamina to stay on her feet, keeping her bullet in the soldier's gun.

Someone approached, calling to her mind Chan's last command, *'If anyone approaches her, shoot them.'* The soldier allowed the violation with a head nod. An African man, resident of U.A., looked Gift down and up, and stepped behind her. Relief washed over her when he cut her loose and she longed for the floor of her little cell. "*What?*" He twisted a strap around her wrists, lifted her arms, and fastened the strap to a spike on the pole above her head. Her weight pulled on her arms. "*Ow.*" The man walked away, leaving her on tiptoes to lengthen the gown barely keeping her covered.

At least the sun had set, taking its scorching heat. Gift's optimistic nature had a hard fight in this setting. That bullet started to look like the preferred option. *Wait. Chan said, 'so next time you are ready for our conversation.' He doesn't want me dead.* She considered dying just to spite him, and that lifted her spirits a little.

Startled by her gasp, Gift's face felt cold and wet. Where was she? When her eyes saw Chan in front of her, she realized she dozed off, hung from sore arms and aching shoulders as her weight pulled on the strap keeping her upright, keeping her alive. Her captor wore an elegant collarless black suit, accompanied by three men and three women, all in military formals. He had brought his dinner guests out to show off his captive as a trophy. They spoke in Chinese for several minutes before retreating. Before Chan walked off, he stepped up close to Gift, looked her down and up, and patted her cheek twice.

"Remember these valuable lessons."

Shivering uncontrollably, Gift knew she'd been in and out of consciousness. The intense darkness of the night had dropped the temperature dramatically over the drenched thin gown clinging to her skin. Its penetrating cold took her back to the freezing-water swim with Oksana and Aimée. Her bones trembled. As a mental excursion, Gift tried to keep herself in that memory, but the mind took another path. Tied to a pole and freezing to death, her thoughts moved to Aimée being lost, probably dead. With no knowledge beyond Oksana's internment, Gift could only guess the state of everyone else she loved. The weight of potential losses pulled on her with greater force than gravity's tug on her limp body.

If I die, will Oksana be his next plaything?

Gift woke in her tiny square prison with no memory of being taken from the pole or being moved. Perhaps she dreamed it, the nightmare ended. It took her a moment to realize where she was, still wearing the thin gown, the slits of Chan's blade confirming the reality of the memory. She struggled to call it to mind.

Rewind, replay.

Yes, she had collapsed when the soldier untied her from the pole, and she became the frizzy-haired girl tossed over his shoulder.

End replay.

That happened at least a day ago, or maybe two. *Three?* No visitors since, no other outings. A slot in the door opened once a day for a bowl of rice, not much more than a large spoonful, and a small cup of water. Such was the routine of each day. It must have been two days because Gift thought she had two meager meals. Unless they didn't feed her once a day. *Or was it three bowls?*

43

Now having full conversations with herself, at times Gift answered with counterarguments she'd later overturn. It took focus to keep from saying things she didn't want *them* to hear. Her arguments for and against building external habitats in New Europa got heated. Gift One insisted they were not ready yet, citing Sakura's medical reports to prove it. Gift Two argued from the other side of the cell that they could use recycled colony air in the habitat structures. But Gift One, clever woman, reasserted her position by saying it would be no different than sleeping in the colony, so why bother?

When not intensely debating herself, Gift would look up and scream to her captors. If not cameras, there must have been microphones, so she yelled for water often, one cup a day being grossly inadequate—if correct in measuring her days by scoops of rice and cups of water. "I thought you wanted to talk. What about our conversation? I'm ready. I've learned my lessons."

After a good whiff of her own body's odor made a gag nearly escalate to vomit, she grumbled, "I also really need a shower." That last one Gift would wish she could take back, the only one they answered. Hope and terror battled for dominance as the resonating clank signaled the door's opening, shrill and steady. The only person yet to speak to her grabbed Gift's thin gown by the shoulder and pulled her forcibly from the room. The flimsy fabric tore and flapped off her shoulder and her little toe throbbed with intense pain from slamming into the door jamb. Chan prodded Gift along the corridor to the last door she had wrongly assumed to be another cell.

Half the size of her Box back home, the room's walls, floor, and ceiling had white tiles with dingy gray film and black spotting along chipped grout lines. The corner of her eye found a drain of roughly a twenty-centimeter diameter in the center of the floor with a metal grating. Too small to escape out of, though she considered it before the warlord pushed her through the door with such force she fell to the ground, banging her knee. A second of cognitive clarity signaled her mind she was naked, her feeble gown in Chan's hand, ripped from her body and torn into ribbons like the flimsy paper it was.

The blank-faced man sealed the door behind him with her on the floor, knees pressed into her breasts, hugging her shins. Incredible pressure hit her from behind, icy-cold, pelting her spine and roving from neck to bottom, then repeating. A piercing second blast came in front, opening and recoiling her fetal positioning.

Face to his boots she traced his legs upward and saw the glistening round metal disk dripping water and Chan wearing a sinister smirk. As the blasts continued from all sides, hundreds of needles hit her skin, making it so raw from the abusive power and chill it burned. The assault lasted minutes that passed as hours, leaving her curled tight in a ball, folded legs pressed against her chest.

"What do you say?"

Her back to the evil creature, Gift shivered bare skinned on the tile floor. The flesh clinging to her bones resembled raw meat, showing bright red splotches dotted over the brutalized skin.

"Miss Gift, do you remember your lessons?"

"Yes," she whimpered.

"We kindly granted your request. What do you say?"

A full vocabulary of things she wanted to say passed her mental display before reason took over to keep her mute. As she considered what he would do if she said any of the things in her head, she saw only one option: give him what he wanted. Let him think he was winning, stay alive to win another day. With every fiber of her being wanting to insult the man, be rebellious, stand her ground, she had but one choice, which meant she had no choice.

"Thank you."

"Such fine progress we are making with you."

Pulling a hand from behind his back, Chan showed Gift another paper gown and in it she found an expression for her defiance, to fortify herself in a show of resolve. She propped herself slowly onto her knees then pulled herself up from the floor. With arms to her sides not covering her shame, she turned to face the monster and stood tall with shoulders back and let two breaths pass. Gift took a step toward him, retrieved the gown, stared at the man for two more breaths, then slipped it over her head. That simple act lessened his intimidation, empowering her to endure, even if only a mental notion.

They entered the Ops center, the office soaked in the memory of Blessing's murder. The nightmarish event lingered in a dried bloodstain on the floor. Chan motioned for Gift to take the chair she'd spent a day and a half in when he first arrived. It might have been two.

"You spoke honestly when I first asked you about the missiles. I truly appreciated that. It made me believe we could create a civilized relationship. And here we are, in pleasant conversation. However, my bold young friend, perhaps there is more to the story left untold. Do you remember the *Or* we spoke about?"

"Yes." Drops from her hair landed on the wet paper fabric clinging to her skin.

"Good. That *Or* still taunts me. We could not remove it. One little, how do you say it in English, with your expressions? One little... *hiccup*. No one we ask can remember where the missile launch complex is or that it even exists. Can you imagine that? You find a reserve of missiles that could take out a colony, let us say, as a *hypothetical*, a colony such as... the New Republic of China. Your people find these weapons and *oops*. You forget where they are. Now, Miss Gift, tell me if that seems believable to you."

Gift dry-swallowed and said, "No. But I—"

"Right. Right. Your 'no' will do, it is the correct answer. If you told me it sounded believable than you may as well tell me you are Nadezhda Anoykina. You are wise to answer honestly, my Gift. This is the basis of our relationship, as you see. There are so-called facts standing in opposition to each other. This *forgetting* is... not believable. We will call that fact one. Now, fact two is we have used various... let us use the word *techniques*, in efforts to help people remember. Fact three, no one can tell us where it is. You are an engineer; can you take these three facts and make one truth?"

"Well... not without knowing who you tried to... *help remember*. No."

"Such a smart woman. You may not ask me questions, so you phrase an answer in such a cunning way it *implies* I should give *you* information. Yes, very clever, my dear. While this upsets me—and remember, I warned you about that—you have not violated our agreement. To show you I am a reasonable man, not only will I not punish you for this, but I will also share some information. Come, my dear."

At the open door of the Ops communication room, Chan motioned with his hand for Gift to enter. His power-play there was to force her to walk over the blood-stained floor in her bare feet. Her power-play was to do it without looking like it bothered her. Chan was better at his. When they stepped in, his men left. Gift pondered over this oppressor's methods, keeping their engagements to him and her alone. He leaned in and pressed a button on the communication console. Gift loosened the fabric gallingly clung to her chest.

"United Africa, please reply." Raff on a vid message. "This is New Europa calling United Africa. Blessing, Gift, please reply. It's been three days since we lost contact. Both our transports are grounded, so we cannot reach you. Please reply with an update on your status. Gift, are you alright?"

Eyes wide, Gift said nothing.

"That was three days ago. Let me play you another one from this morning."

"United Africa, please reply. Are you in distress? Please rep—*Oh*. Oh my... Transports. Three heavy transports..."

A pause led to static. The evil man smiled.

"And finally, my dear sweet Gift, I am sure you will enjoy this next part."

"United Africa, Gift, *listen* to me... It's the N.R.C. *Oh Dio*. They've taken most of the colony. They took the admin building, captured most of the guards. *Oh Dio*. There's so many of them. We have *zero defenses*. Gift, we also lost contact with the R.F. I have no status on them. Please U.A., Gift, *respond*... if you can."

A hard click slapped Gift's ears when Chan slammed a fist on the button to stop the playback.

"Now you know their attempts to contact you have failed. We have taken your colony, as expected. But this is not where our *Or* lies, is it? No. It is between New Europa and the Russians. So did you catch the critical bit that helps me solve my *Or* dilemma?"

"New Europa's trying to reach the R.F. They lost contact."

"You do have a sharp mind. What does this teach me? If you were working with the Russians, you would try to reach them. If they were working with you, they would reply. So let me add this one thing that might make the difference. This may even help us solve our *Or* problem. Do you remember what I told you about the *Or* and your life? *Tell me*."

The power in the last words tightened her muscles. "I'm on a precipice and the *Or* is keeping me alive."

"I do hope not to kill you. Believe me, I do not wish this. One of the only good things about being here in this... *cesspool* of a colony, is these lovely interactions with you. If I lose that, I just don't know what I will do with myself. I guess I could see if the little princess would be as much fun... I apologize my dear Gift for straying off topic..."

Those black eyes stirred like Colony Lake during a storm.

"The one piece of information you must apply to this message from your risible colony is this: communication between New Europa and Africa was interrupted because we occupied the colony. We blocked all transmissions, as you saw when we arrived. Get ready to see where our *Or* fits in. Communication with the R.F. was lost *before* we took your colony. What does that do in your pretty little head? You tell me what this means."

"Well... I guess you're thinking the R.F. worked independently. That we, I mean, New Europa... I guess, also us here in United Africa, you can see we're not working together against you."

"There it is Gift, my lovely Gift. I am not ready to say for sure, but it looks as if we may soon take that *Or* out of the equation. And the good news is... The good news is we can go take that last colony. Of course, we were going to do that anyway. The good news *for you* then, is we do not need to take a more aggressive approach." Leaning his face in hers he continued, "You saw it, I know you did. Africa and the N.R.C. working together. You spoke so highly of the cooperation between your pitiful colonies. For you to imagine getting two pathetic, dying colonies that are not even real colonies to stop killing each other was such a wondrous accomplishment of a new *elevated* so-called *enlightened* human race—such shortsighted hubris... No. No. No. No. *No!*"

Chan paced frantically, his tone elevated, movements erratic. As if driving a nail with a hammer, he had raised and lowered his fist on each 'no,' then spun to face Gift.

"No, my beautiful Gift. *Oh*... Did I tell you the best part? This is the side of the *Or* that keeps you breathing. You and me Gift, we get to keep this wonderful relationship we cherish together. And now I know you want it too, having offered yourself to me. You are indeed my gift for being in this wretched place, and I get to keep you. But not here, no, this place is *disgusting*. Filthy. You will accompany me to the N.R.C. I can do so much more with you there."

Not that she hadn't seen it before, it became abundantly clear now Chan had lost his mind. A man holding her life in his hands and the fate of potentially all the colonies, was certifiably insane. The madman knelt on the floor before Gift and grabbed her wrists, laid his head on her lap for a moment then raised it to show the fierceness reignited in his eyes.

"I need those missiles for our new human society. It will be glorious, united under the New Republic of China—it is the only way. Throughout history nations divided, then realized independence made them weak, so they made unions, so-called alliances. Did you know their divisiveness had gotten so serious they created something called the United Nations? Such arrogance." Pausing, Chan stood. "No, it was stupidity. And arrogance too, we can throw that word in, it fits. They had member nations, supposedly united, at war with each other, each belonging to the thing ironically called the *United* Nations."

Cloudy on the details, Gift knew some of that history. It's what she desperately wished not to repeat. When a raging lunatic started making sense, Gift questioned her own sanity.

"You see now why your little pitiful coalition you suppose was so wonderful—it will not work. Cannot work. We need one strong colony. No, no, forget that—we are no longer colonies, are we? We have the entire planet now. We need one world government. It is the only way. Everyone needs to be ruled by a single authority, one set of laws, one judicial system."

The derogatory bit about her coalition aside, Gift saw his point.

"And who will rule? The N.R.C.? No. *Ha*. You thought that was it, you thought that was the answer. But no, the N.R.C. is weak. We have been hiding for over two hundred years. Once we were strong, feared. Now we need new rulership. I will build that... with you at my side."

Yep, he's nuts. But he said he suspected a secret faction in the R.F. Could there be? More of Yuri's people seemed a logical assumption. Gift remembered Oksana saying she suspected that. A metaphorical palm smacked Gift's forehead. *Wait, did he say he'd be ruling with* me *at his side? I offered myself to him? Oh mamma. In the shower. Now he wants us to be like some kinda king and queen? Does Stockholm Syndrome work in reverse? The raging madman doesn't even know the mistake he's made. He thinks he has everyone under his control.*

This war was far from over.

44

I nsanity existed in New Europa, but it scarcely escalated beyond claustrophobic madness—easily treatable. Gift knew serious mental disorders could cause irrational behavior, wide swings in mood or character, delusions of grandeur. Some mental illnesses gave the sufferer a highly inflated feeling of self-worth, an exaggerated importance, or a savior complex. Not that she dared diagnose the man mumbling indistinctly and pacing the floor in the tiny Ops communications room, she lacked qualifications for that. It didn't stop her from concluding he must be a hundred percent crazy, no need to cap it at ninety-nine.

I offered myself to him?

Among all the lunacies spewed, that stood out. After what Chan called a shower, Gift stood to defy him, to show that he hadn't broken her spirit. Had she imagined even a speck of a chance he'd take it in such a way, she'd have made a different choice. Yet, it may have worked in her favor. He had given her vital information and didn't even know it.

After their pitiful run with spy talk when under guard for suspicion of sabotage in their own colony, Gift devised a plan. With the reconnection to neighbors and the lack of a hundred percent certainty they had found all insurrectionists, she insisted on its need. Raff, Aimée, Tom, and others went along, perhaps to appease her. They developed simple codes to use in open and potentially monitored communications, and Raff had used them masterfully.

Returned to her cell, Gift mentally pieced it together, decoding the message within the message Chan allowed her to hear, *wanted* her to hear. 'Listen to me' meant instructions would follow. Raff had the brilliant idea to surround false statements with 'Oh Dio,' with everything sandwiched between being a misdirection. *What did she say between them?*

'Oh Dio. They've taken most of the colony. They took the admin building, captured most of the guards. Oh Dio.'

Soldiers from the N.R.C. had arrived as stated before the first 'Oh Dio,' but had *not* taken most of the colony, the admin building, or the guards. The part about there being many soldiers came after the second 'Oh Dio,' so it was true. The *how* of their victory hid in the line inspired by Tom's idea. He insisted on keeping their new advanced incapacitating defenses a secret, never spoken of over comms. If they were successful in warding off an attack and had neutralized the threat, they'd say they have 'zero defenses.'

Weapons she resisted making then headed two teams to create had worked as designed, zeroed out the threat and saved N.E. from a hostile takeover. The perimeter had been laced with sonic defenses and projectile stun guns, which the guards also carried. Sakura's chemical agent performed so well in tests they installed dispersal points at every entrance as well as in key places throughout the colony—including the admin building and its main comms office—the most likely targets of occupational forces. Hoped never to be needed, they had done their job. And Chan thought his army had taken the colony. With his own communications block employed, it could be days before he knew differently.

'*Listen to me,' Raff said*. It meant directions to follow. The final code Raff laced into her message was in the word '*respond.*' To ask for a reply message they were to say *reply*. Raff said 'respond,' a codeword for Gift to respond to whatever situation or threat she faced, not worrying about New Europa while not expecting help from them either. Raff told her to act. What could she do, isolated in her cell?

An air hose leak?

It sounded familiar, like a momentary burst of air escaping a coupler with a failing seal. The noise landed on Gift's ears hundreds of times. With no conceivable reason why an air hose or pressurized line would be anywhere near her cell, she dismissed it. Then it came again, only it sounded as if someone were mimicking the sound from a human voice.

"Psst."

Faint, but human. *Human.* Where? Who? The next cell over seemed a logical thought. *Oksana*? No, above her, the sound came from above. Lifting herself from the low, tiny toilet—she had finished peeing several minutes ago and hadn't bothered to get up—she stood on its rim to position her face near the thin slats of the air vent.

"*Hello*?" she whispered through cupped hands.

"Gift? Thank goodness."

"*Tina*. Tina, is that really you?"

"Yes, I'm here. Got Matteo and Bright."

"How... I... What do we do?"

"We get you and Oksana free."

"I'm in a metal box behind a locked door."

"We got it. But it will be a few hours, at least."

"Is Oksana okay? I haven't seen anyone."

"Bright says yes, they've left her be. Says they've only been interested in you. He suggested getting her first as no one is watching her or ever comes for her."

"No, good, yeah. Please get her safe. And if you need, leave me. Get her safe."

"We'll get you both. Just hang tight a little longer."

"Wait. The N.R.C. attacked N.E."

"We know. Been monitoring the Ops room. We saw the message Chan played you, why we're moving now. Raff said '*respond*.'"

"Right, good."

"Gotta go. Hang in there. We'll have you out soon."

Human contact. Trying to wrap her head around a new thought only brought a headache. After at least six days, she had her first chance for freedom. No, her own freedom lessened in importance. Save Oksana first. Gift hoped she said that to Tina, thought she did. Tina said freedom for her after Oksana, then they'd save everyone. The idea's raw energy invigorated Gift. "Don't be so self-righteous, Gift," she scolded herself. Laying down her life for her friends, her colony, was a given. But *not* dying and her friends and colony being safe made for a decent alternative to dying. A melody in her ears alerted her she was humming Vita a Venezia, Raff's song. Calmed by her own noises, she curled herself and waited.

When the door opened, Oksana appeared with Aimée. Assuming the rescue party had found her lost friend, Gift became overjoyed and leapt to her feet. The three shared a long-overdue embrace and Gift's eyes poured until her body could produce no more tears. When she pulled away Oksana said, "Oh my. You really stink."

"Yeah."

"I hear congratulations are in order." Aimée threw her a wide smile. "Come on, we need to get you over there. You know how he gets."

At her navel, Gift held a bouquet with two hands. That the flowers were white with a pleasant fragrance was all she knew about them. Walking through the field between the colony and the new exterior farm, she saw rows of chairs full of nameless people separated by a center aisle. In her thin paper gown, Gift walked for what felt like a kilometer before she saw Chan at the edge of the farm, waiting for her in a black collarless suit. It was to be their Union. With her tied to the pole and shivering, the vile man stood beside her.

Aimée said the usual words, blabbing on about being brought together by love or captivity, and how a Union is for life and for the good of the colony. From his boot, Chan pulled a knife and tapped the tip of its blade against Gift's cheek, flashed a sinister grin, and said, "You are *my* gift."

The clank of the door woke her from the nightmare.

Once again Chan came alone, but not in his military garb. He wore the same collarless black suit from when he put her on display however many days ago that might have been. With a crooked smile, he pulled a black dress from his back. Picturing him rummaging through the tote to find the dress, *her* black dress, sent shivers down her spine. The violation of the act transported her mind back to those guards, Beth and Albert, ransacking her things, tossing them on the floor. Now her black dress. *Hopper or sonic sink? Burn it.*

"You need to dress for dinner."

When she took it from his hand, he surprised her by turning his back. Now her mind flashed to changing to Tom's back a year ago. At the time, she considered it the most awkward and embarrassing thing she had ever done. This soared past worse, yet she felt a twinge of gratitude for his back and took the opportunity to change speedily. Perhaps she'd get her chance to exploit his unrequited love, get the upper hand. Knowing she had Tina, Matteo, Oksana, and Bright on the outside gave it a reasonable shot of success—though it came shy of ninety-nine.

In a room familiar to her, having had dinner there with Blessing a couple times, they sat head and foot at a rectangular table for six—Gift assumed herself the foot. A plate of food waited under a silver dome set before each diner. She had only seen such in old vids where well dressed people at extravagant dinner parties sat in anticipation as a waiter lifted the lid, exposing the most amazing meal. The two sat alone and she couldn't be sure she should lift hers until invited to do so by Chan as he lifted his.

Amazing wouldn't have been a fitting word to describe the uncovered plate under any normal circumstance, but the one she found herself in was far from normal. Having a diet of a handful of plain rice and a sip of water a day for a week, the modest serving of vegetables next to a protein Gift identified as a fish she didn't think to be tilapia became the most incredible thing in the world.

Hesitating until he took a bite, Gift fought animalistic urges to shove the food into her mouth by the fistful and lifted her fork to take her first bite. A warm pleasant feeling started in her mouth and traveled through her bones, relaxing her flesh for the first time in days. Her nostrils pushed out a satisfying exhale as she chewed. She chased the swallow by gulping half the tall glass of water in front of her.

"This is much better. Yes. Now you and I have a proper relationship. My dear Gift, you see it now, don't you? We shall bring order to this wretched place, your own beloved New Europa, the Russian Federation, and those miserable communities of barbarian surface dwellers, to restore the glory of the New Republic of China. It will be a splendid new world order and you, my beloved, will sit as a queen at my side."

Gift ate in silence as he monologued his grand plan for world domination between bites of food around less than acceptable eating etiquette. He did it again, and she didn't even have to use her feminine wiles or try to charm him into talking. When he expounded on his need to rally the support of key military leaders of the N.R.C. and boasted about holding the occupation of the United Africa colony with only a handful of soldiers, she learned his forces were much smaller than he presented. Most of those under his command had been sent to N.E. and Raff reported that they'd been subdued. Her call to respond gained further clarity—with most of Chan's soldiers gone, they had the upper-hand.

A chance presented itself, perhaps her only one. Tina, Matteo, and Bright were ready to act. If she and Oksana got freed, they could assemble the U.A. residents and take back the colony. The overwhelming need to get out of the room moved her to enact a plan, half-cocked as it was.

On her mental display—restored now by consumption of food and water—Gift pulled up a replay of Tom's self-defense training. Forcing a smile, she stood, sauntered leisurely to Chan, and said in the sultriest voice she could push out, "Like a queen... at your side." Donning a wide seductive grin, her finger drew a circle on the table—something she must have seen in a vid and thought to be a gesture of sensuality. When he smiled and reached for her hand, she gently laid it in his.

In her mind, he'd stand to face her. She'd drive one knee firmly into his crotch, doubling him over in agony. When he bent forward, the other knee would lift swiftly, breaking his nose again and knocking him out. *Just like Tom showed you*, she coached herself.

Wait, could Chan have been seeing the same?

He may have lost his mind, but the parts with military training still dominated his thoughts. In one motion, Chan twisted her around by the arm as he shot out of his chair. The bending of her limb behind her back dropped her head forward and before Gift knew what happened, she was on the floor. The sting on her cheek matched the ache his strike brought to her jaw.

"You may have failed my little test," he said in a wild, frenzied tone with fire in his eyes. "But it changes nothing. You offered yourself to me, and I will have you."

It didn't take a half-second for Gift to understand the threat in the words and what was about to happen. This was more than violence. She flailed and tried to kick but lacked the strength to overcome his physical dominance. Hoping someone might be close enough to hear it, she screamed as he smacked her face, stopping only when she could barely gasp enough oxygen to stay conscious after his knee crushed her abdomen, robbing her of air and energy. Fears escalated. The morbid dread that filled her came in the understanding of her powerlessness to stop what surely would happen. He was going to have her, to force himself on her.

With a knee in her gut and his hand pressed against her neck, choking the little air she was desperately trying to inhale, his eyes popped in a look of shock, and he froze. Chan leaned to the side and fell off her to the ground. The sight his fallen body unveiled behind it was Oksana standing over them with a rifle in her hands. With panting breaths, her chest and shoulders inflated and deflated in rapid succession, and her face showed hard and fierce. *Had she shot him?*

Tina ran in and gave the scene a wide round face with an open mouth. Darting in just behind her, Matteo dashed to Gift and helped her sit up on the floor. She was okay, mostly. A realization of what very nearly happened and how it didn't filled Gift with heated rage and gratitude that blended together in a haze of confusion.

"*Gift*, you okay? Did he hurt you?" *Matteo*? She found his face beside hers. It was magnificent. "Are you okay?"

"Yeah, I think... I think so. Oksana? Did you...? Is he...?"

Tina said, "She whacked him with the butt, knocked him out."

"He, he was about to..." Oksana's shoulders continued rising and dropping. "He was going to..." The seething young lady pointed the rifle at Chan as Tina sat him up to tie his hands and droopy consciousness began to enter him.

"*No*. Oksana no. Listen to me, sweetie. He didn't. I'm fine. Don't do this."

"He's a creep. A *monster*... He deserves to *die*."

Tears flooded the young woman's words in a jumbled mix of emotions Gift understood were not only for this moment. They had Yuri immersed in them, with pure rage, hostility, and hate—a need for vengeance springing from her own nightmarish experience. Oksana was Gift on the floor and the woman with the gun wasn't her. It was all the people who should have stopped him, should have saved her from her brother but didn't.

"Please," Gift pleaded as Mateo helped her to her feet. "Don't do this. This won't take away your pain. You won't be able to live with yourself. He's not worth it. You saved me. You stopped him. Oksana *please* put the rifle down."

The bang of its pop was deafening.

45

Deafened, ears ringing, horror flooded Gift's mind with wild thoughts of the new nightmare Oksana brought upon herself. The poor girl had suffered enough. Now this occupation, captivity, finding Chan on top of Gift, and taking his life in a desperate cry for vengeance. Her progress had been tremendous as she shaped herself into a grounded, stable, and joyous person. How might this devastation alter her character? What will she become?

Chan laughed.

A rifle shot. Gift was sure the gun fired, the hazy buzz lingering in her eardrum proof enough. Did the girl miss? Oksana dropped the rifle to the floor and covered her face with her palms and began sobbing so deeply and audibly it squeezed in Gift's already aching heart.

Grabbing the shattered young lady in a tight embrace Gift said, "Shh. Shh. It's alright sweetie. It's alright."

"I... I couldn't... do it." She whimpered through gasps for the air her weeping stole from her lungs.

"Because you're not a monster. It's him, not you."

A hint of calm softened Oksana's eyes. "Are you okay?"

"Yes. Thanks to you—you saved me. You're so strong and brave. I love you."

"*Weakness*. That is what you all show. And that is why the N.R.C. will—"

Silenced by the powerful fist of Tina slamming his face, Chan hunched over, slipping back into unconsciousness. Oksana chuckled, then Gift joined her.

"We need to move," Tina directed.

"Move where? What are we up against?"

Tina placed a reassuring palm on Gift's shoulder. "Bright, he's been awesome. Spying on them while pretending to cooperate. He believes many of his people are playing along, waiting for someone to lead them to take back the colony."

"Good. And I heard Chan talking, rambling on and on. He's more than a bit nuts, like truly insane. I think he sent most of his men to N.E. Pretty sure they have a small team here."

Matteo said, "Even as a small group, they're trained, well-armed soldiers, and have body armor."

"We need to get to Bright." Tina stepped into the doorway. "He'll organize his people for an offensive, says they're ready to fight for the colony."

Fight? Once again, the human being devolves to animal instincts. Gift had to hope they could do it without bloodshed as images of New Europa's insurrection flooded her mind's display while they sneaked down the corridor and into a small space just about as offensive to the nostrils as her cell had been.

"Gift, you know Bright."

"Happy we got you out. And you brought us the head of the snake. Well done." His eyes stayed for a minute on the unconscious body Tina had dragged in.

"I am sorry for your loss. Blessing was an extraordinary woman." His nod to Gift was somber. "How are Samuel and little Rebecca? Are the pikin safe?"

"Yes. All pikin. Blessing was our greatest loss."

"I'm so sorry." Gift fought to hold back tears. "Okay… what do we have for weapons? We do this with zero body count. Do we have any projectile tasers?"

As Board member and de facto leader of this bunch, Gift stepped up to plan the mission. Bright didn't share her perspective regarding her position.

"We will take care of this. We do not relish killing, but they've killed many of our people, shot Blessing and tossed her body outside like garbage. Our people gave her a proper burial. We will try to reclaim our colony with your zero-body count, but we will not hesitate to kill these vermin if needed-*Oh*." Pointing to Chan he said, "As much as I would like to shoot this one in the head and toss his lifeless corpse outside to rot, we are not the animals he is. This one will stand trial."

Happy with much, but not all, Bright said, Gift replied, "And we will help, at least with the trying not to kill anyone part. Do we know how many? Where they are?"

Matteo had that intel. "I've been watching them since they arrived. Most left for the raid on N.E. But the ones here are like some kinda magicians or something. I mean, they are few, but seem to be everywhere. They're mostly staying in the main dome, guarding its two exterior entrances, and a couple walking the perimeter, that's it."

"Agreed." Bright's voice, deep and powerful, instilled confidence in Gift. He was easily twice the bulk of Chan, and that little man overpowered Gift with little difficulty. Having Bright on her side bolstered her courage.

As Bright outlined his plan to gather people from the main dome work areas to rush and subdue the guards, Gift considered her black dress. "Not exactly dressed for a war." Having believed she didn't vocalize the thought, the words surprised her.

"Bright? Got anything Gift can wear?"

He sent Tina out to find her something while Matteo detailed his part of the plan. Night had fallen with little activity outside, and the farm workers slept in the outermost habitat. From there, Matteo would join them in taking out the few guards walking the perimeter and then rush those at the two colony entrances at the same time Bright would lead an interior ambush. When Tina returned with a coverall, it was a massive garment Gift figured could contain Bright's bulk. It wasn't ideal, but the black dress it would have to be.

"Okay, everyone knows their job and we have a go for midnight on the dot. Matteo, get those exterior guards before that. By midnight, you need to be at the entrances."

"Got it."

"Wait. What do *we* do?"

"Dear girl, you need to stay here." Bright's reply turned Oksana's face fiery red.

"He means we need to guard Chan. We can't let him escape or get rescued. It's job number one, the head of the snake." Gift's words calmed the young lady ready for a fight. Maybe too ready for it. She had barely tilted the rifle to land Chan's bullet a few centimeters over his head. So close to taking a life, Gift wanted her far from the fighting.

"Gift, I can stay with you... if you want." While she appreciated Tina's offer, Gift knew she'd rather go with Bright, and he needed all the help he could get.

"No, we're good. We'll keep the rifle and make sure this *kusok der'ma* doesn't move." Oksana's words came from a voice full of contempt.

"*Ma*, can we get to Ops, not to stay here? From there we can monitor the battle, maybe even call out to you if, I mean, if things don't go well. Also too, if Raff tries to reach us..."

"We risk moving him. Better for you to keep him here."

"No, she's right," Tina countered Bright. "If she can get eyes on them, she can warn us if something goes wrong."

The hulking man considered it. "We have no comms devices, so she'd have to use the public address."

"Right. But it's that or we get shot in the back."

With Matteo sneaked off to join the cultivators, Bright led the way from the odorous sewage flow-control room around the outer edge of the main dome. He held Chan—ankles and wrists tied and a gag quieting him—over his shoulder. Gift's mind remembered the frizzy-haired girl. They met once after Sakura treated her. Called Penny, she preferred *Pinch* even after the need for covert names had passed.

One guard stood post at the door to the Ops center. A series of hand signals floated between Tina and Bright, Gift clueless as to how the two understood them. While they ducked behind an adjacent building, Tina crept from view. Gift heard her greeting but couldn't make out the soldier's reply. A thump vibrated its way through the air and a loud whispered *Okay* called them forward.

After she dragged the soldier into the Ops center office, Tina made quick use of restraining and gagging her. Bright had propped Chan onto a chair and Gift pulled the zip ties tight. She had sat in the same chair for over a day and a half, maybe two, being interrogated. As she checked his hands, Gift pondered how justice often came with poetic irony. The role-reversal was empowering.

Oksana took her position in the communications booth off the main Operations office while Gift stood by the door, rifle in hand. Bright had told her, 'Be ready to shoot anyone that comes in that door.' She wasn't. How she wished for her sleek new taser projectile weapon. Standing near the stain of Blessing's dried blood, Gift contemplated if she'd have what it took to squeeze the trigger. No part of her she dug into for answers came up with a yes, so she hoped it wouldn't come to that.

Even after those long days that bled into each other, the fifteen minutes from 23:45 to midnight were the longest in Gift's life. Oksana called up limited visuals from security cameras, nowhere near as many or as good as what they had at New Europa. Dividing eight to a screen over two displays, she prioritized the feeds in areas where the team might be exposed. Gift approved and felt the tinge of pride for the youth's fortitude despite everything that transpired.

"I wish to be you when I grow up." Oksana smiled back at Gift's unexpected compliment. "One minute. Everyone in position?"

"Yeah, I think so. No idea about Matt's group. I hope he's okay."

"I'm sure he is."

Everything happened at once, as if time stopped to observe the battle. Gift ignored the grunts from Chan, only checking that his restraints looked sturdy, and his body couldn't separate itself from the chair. Her eyes stayed on Oksana, hers wide and bounding over the display screens. Nothing but silence fell upon their ears, besides their own heavy breathing. Just an eerie quiet.

Why did Chan stop his moaning?

Slammed from the side, Gift's feet came from under her as she fell hard to the floor, her upper torso crossing the threshold into the Ops closet. Chan and his chair were on top of her, his teeth clenched onto her left forearm like a rabid animal in a nature vid. Unsure if it was her blood or his, Gift looked at the red foaming around his mouth, dripping over her arm. Her mind told her she was lying in a pool of Blessing's warm blood, and she forced herself to dismiss the image. In the frenzy accompanied by Oksana's guttural screaming, Gift lost track of the rifle.

The raging lunatic got a hand loose and wrapped it around Gift's throat.

'*Go for the eyes,*' Tom's voice in her head instructed.

'*I can't reach,*' she shouted back to it.

An unmistakable auditory perception stiffened Gift's spine. Rifle fire. "*No*," Gift shouted as Chan fell off her, his body still connected to the chair, laying him on his side in a fetal position as the dark stain on his chest expanded.

Chasing away the realization of what poor Oksana had done, had to do, Gift felt the cool metal trigger under the curl of her index finger. She had taken the shot, taken a life. However vile and obscene, a life. Oksana gasped, but not at Gift and Chan, not for the gunshot. Her eyes found the trouble they'd been looking for and her finger smashed the public address button.

"*Tina*. Behind you."

Once Gift pulled herself to her feet, the pain of Chan's bite reached her brain, pulling her hand up to clutch her forearm. "What's happened? Is Tina...?"

"No. She heard me just in time. She's... she's fine. That *jerk*. He almost made me miss it."

"What am I looking at, which camera? Are they still fighting?"

"I think it's over. Look." Oksana pointed to one camera window, then another on the second screen. "See, they've captured all of them. It's over."

46 | Week Two

"What sense does it even make? I mean... could it be? Our insurrection to Yuri's faction in the R.F. to the coups and takeovers in U.A. and now this in the N.R.C.? Is this what we are?" Gift found it beyond difficult to accept Chan operated independently of the New Republic of China's government, even if it fit the pattern. *It's just too coincidental*, her logical brain kept saying. *Too convenient an excuse.*

"I know, Cara. I feel the same. *Ma*, what can we do?"

Raff and Gift had been catching each other up on the most recent of the unbelievable events of the last year. The people of N.E. had a much easier time of it, having warded off an invasion. Their lingering dread came from questions spurred by the loss of the air transports—the reason for which was still unknown but assumed to be Chan—and the comms blackouts. The ordeal in U.A. lasted just over eight days, with Raff in panic-mode for Gift and everyone else there with no idea what might have been happening.

Nadezhda Anoykina still ran the R.F. She called Oksana home on one of the commandeered heavy transports from the N.R.C. once they figured out how to pilot them. Oksana didn't want to go, and Gift preferred her to stay. Her kid sister had attached herself to Gift's side throughout the night—neither getting more than a few minutes of shuteye. Morning arrived and Gift, stretched well beyond her emotional limits, reached her physical ones. Caffeine was the only thing animating her, keeping her in conversation with Raff.

"You're saying N.R.C. is being cooperative? This is unbelievable."

"Allora, they're trying to save face. If this was a coup, it looks bad for them. For an entire week, they did nothing. If it wasn't a coup, they don't want to show their hand."

"At this point, it'd be nice if it were a coup. I mean, this Chan… he was a real bag of nuts. Truly crazy. Said he'd make me his queen when he took over the world."

"I'm so sorry for all you've been through."

"What do we do now? I mean, we're stuck here… that's fine. Well, not really, but they have a lot to clean up, and we can help. And the Ubuntu are already here. Mike came on the first transport with them early this morning. The Chinese never found them, left them be. Bright will be a good leader, think so anyway. He and his partner, wife he calls her, are caring for Blessing's children now."

"Those poor kids… I told the N.R.C. not to send anyone. They want to take the prisoners, but they also offered to help undo the damage their people caused."

"Can they undo the bullet in Blessing's head? Give her kids their mom back? What Chan did to—" Gift stopped there, unable to revisit her experience. Saying the words was torture, retelling the events felt too much like reliving them.

"What does Bright think? If he's taking over, it'll be his call."

"Guess so, yeah. He won't be quick to trust them after what's happened here. I'll let you know."

Familiarity came in assisting the people of United Africa with full co-operation of the Ubuntu people. They exuded such a comforting joy, even after all that happened. Of course, no one else had experienced the occupation as Gift had. Even Oksana had been left alone and treated humanely, kept in a room with two women high in Blessing's administration and getting more than a scoop of rice each day.

The caffeine held up its end of the bargain, keeping Gift going throughout the long day. She marveled at its power. Having been drained of physical energy and emotional fortitude for a week and awake for what she estimated to be over forty hours, the body had to stop. Gift learned only when she woke a few hours later on a makeshift cot that Bright had carried her from the Ops office where she'd leaned over the desk as her consciousness melted away.

Finally having peeled off the black dress, her body's odor embedded in its fibers, she showered. By sunrise, it had been thirty hours since they reclaimed the colony, and the rebuilding was underway, in full swing for its second day.

Sitting outside with Matteo to watch the light fall upon the farm, Gift took her first coffee. Mike and Tina joined and asked about Gift's arm. It wasn't as bad as she'd first imagined—the rabid psychopath's gag had prevented a deeper bite—it looked to be healing nicely. They shared a pleasant morning, made more so by the smell of freedom and the absence of Chan.

The world went dark.

The fright of Chan rushed over her—he had her again, covered her face, determined to make her his. *No, he's dead*, she was sure of it. The commotion of struggles fell upon her ears before everything closed in on her.

***

When she woke, a fleeting hope put her in *her* Box—she hadn't been home in so long it ached. On the cell's lower bunks, Gift found herself across from a still unconscious Tina. In the dim light she saw little else, so she stood—which proved more difficult than she imagined—then fell back onto the bunk. Head spinning, she had no idea where she was or how she had gotten there.

"Was I drugged? Knocked out?" she asked the room.

"We all were," the room replied, its voice familiar.

"*Mike?*"

His head leaned out from the bunk above Tina. "Yeah. What a headache. What the heck happened? Last I knew, we were having coffee. Where are we?"

As his questions descended on Gift, Tina and Matteo woke. Gift knew they'd been captured, tossed in a cell. That this was becoming familiar frightened her more than being in the new jail. At least she wasn't alone this time. Her eyes took the time to notice the green shorts and lighter green tank top they all wore. "Our prison clothes."

At once Tina sprung up and banged on the door. No panel, no handle to turn, no way out. Only the reverberation of her pounding fists came back in reply. They tossed ideas on who took them and where they were and settled on the N.R.C. as the only logical choice. *Guess their claims of having a rogue faction were a misdirection*, Gift concluded.

When the narrow panel halfway up the metal door opened, it contained four cups of water and four bowls of rice with mixed vegetables and tofu, each with a set of chopsticks. Unless a clever ploy, it solidified belief their captors were the N.R.C. The meager portion didn't satisfy Tina, but for Gift, it was meters above the measly plain rice scoops of her last prison. The panel remained open, and Tina and Mike examined it for a weakness, a way to reach an external door handle or release. An exercise in futility.

Conversation revolved around the speculations over why they had been taken, what the Chinese could want from them. No one came, and they agreed it must be late as they could barely keep their eyes open. The cell's already dim lighting hadn't dimmed further, but it did little to discourage sleep. Tina's snoring woke Gift to thoughts of how simple life was when they were one little colony on *Mars*. The world unfolding before them had an uncanny tendency to be harsh.

Awoken by the screech of metal hinges, they found four armed guards in body armor beyond the open door. One soldier pointed to Matteo and led him away first. The next took Tina, then one for Gift. She looked behind to see the last one escorting Mike into the corridor. When Gift and her soldier entered an interrogation room, a middle-aged woman in a gray military uniform gazed at her from a small metal table with an empty chair on the opposite side. The bangs of her shiny black hair cut her forehead in a horizontal line. Her hand sent an invitation to sit, so Gift did. The soldier of obvious rank scrolled on her tablet for a minute, looked at Gift, and placed it on the table.

"Miss Gift Ojo of New Europa."

"Yeah. And you are?" Only a cold stare in reply. "Why are we here? Where even are we?"

"You are guests of the New Republic of China."

"*Guests*?" She breathed out a *yeah right* sigh through closed lips. "I was a guest of your Commander Chan. So... I'm familiar with your hospitality."

"And Miss Gift, has your experience here thus far been the same?"

"Well... no. But we've only just gotten here."

"Indeed. Let me assure you we were not dishonest when we said Chan had pursued his own agenda. He was a respected leader in our military, highly decorated. Of course, it was the first field mission for him and his regiment. We regret he did not perform to our expectations. He did not always act under orders, nor do we condone some of his actions."

"So, you take responsibility for the occupation of the U.A. colony? And you tried to take New Europa as well?"

"We simply did what we must. And we would have taken the Russian Federation. A matter of self-defense, of self-preservation."

"I don't follow. I mean, it was you, you attacked us... unprovoked. We didn't do anything to you."

"This was the one goal with which we tasked Commander Chan, and he failed. We understand he had become a little out of his mind in the end, and you suffered for this. Again, we apologize for his actions. I understand you are the one who killed him."

To avoid the realism of a vocalized confirmation, Gift nodded.

"Do not worry, that is not why you are here. You will not be prosecuted for killing an officer of the N.R.C."

"*Prosecuted*? I didn't... You've *gotta* be kidding me."

"We do not kid here. Now, back to why we are here. You say you have not attacked us. Do you speak only for your colony, or for the R.F. and U.A. as well?"

"Officially? I can only speak for my colony. And... not even in an official capacity. I mean... on my own I have no actual... authority."

"Do you believe that neither New Europa, the Russian Federation, nor United Africa have participated in attacks against our transports?"

"Look lady, we've been trying to reach you for months and you never replied. We don't even know where your colony is. I mean... I have absolutely no idea where I *even am* right now. And we have nothing that could take down your transports."

"That is where the second part of Commander Chan's mission failed. We know about the missile complex you found and the cache of missiles in it. You see, Miss Gift, it seems your colony is the *only one* with the means to destroy our transports, correct?" When Gift didn't reply the intimidating woman continued, "We lost two small flyers and three heavy transports. The three heavies we sent to U.A. and N.E. are our last. We have grounded the last two small flyers for complete overhauls as we cannot rule out hacking and sabotage. I am telling you this in good faith, Miss Gift, because I do not blame you for the actions of your colony. Unless you, a member of your Board of Directors, were complicit."

"*Complicit*? In what? I don't even know what we're talking about."

"We will see about that, Miss Gift."

47

Before such a harrowing ordeal, Gift would not have assessed her courage and endurance anywhere near the levels she found in herself. Assuming her current captors had read through Chan's reports—perhaps not the crazier bits—they must have known what Gift had withstood. Might this result in them increasing the level of duress applied upon her even beyond Chan's malevolence? As she soon learned, that would have been preferable.

The last to return to the shared cell, Gift found the others battered and bruised. The flesh around Tina's left eye was a balloon inflated to its limit, on the verge of popping. Her bottom lip had been split, evidenced by dried blood on her chin. Various shades of purple splotched Matteo's abdomen. Blisters of intense heat littered Mike's back, so he sat shirtless on Gift's bunk. Remnants of tears were Gift's only scars from her day in the N.R.C. Guilt brought a fresh flow when those of sorrow had been expelled. No one had the strength to eat when the meals came, not even Tina.

"No questions? Really?" Gift couldn't believe they were only beaten and tortured with not a single question asked of them.

"Nothing." Tina paused. "It seems they think *only you* have whatever information they're after. Stay strong Gift. They'll use us to try to break you, but we can handle it. Don't tell them anything."

"What do they think you know?" Mike impatiently asked.

"Well... they're asking me, doing this to you, because... I do know about—"

"Careful Gift. No doubt they're listening to us." Unsure why she had forgotten, Gift appreciated Tina's reminder.

"That's just it. I do know something about what they're asking me, but they already know as much as me. I mean, I even told that... that... I told him. Back at U.A. I told him what I knew. It's not what they want, but... I really don't know more. I mean, not really. What happens to all of you when I can't tell them what they want?"

"We can handle it, like Tina said. Whatever they want, it's gotta be bad for us if they get it."

Matteo demonstrated unyielding support and showed such robust character. Gift hated that he was there and suffering because of her. She longed for the isolation of her tiny cell, even with that madman's visits.

To make her face him, Mike gently pushed on Gift's shoulder. "Not for nothing, we don't even know what we're talking about. I mean, just tell us what *they* already know so we know what the heck this is all about... Why they're doing this to us."

"What *they* know? Well... they know—Oh, if we get out of this you guys, you can't tell anyone what I'm about to tell you."

"More secrets, Gift. With you and Raff on the Board, I thought this crap was over. You promised us." Mike had a point, but in the moment, his being right annoyed Gift to no end.

"No, this is different. Hear me out and judge us later, okay? So, this whole thing is about the air transports, you know, the flyers, being shot down."

"Have they admitted crashing them?" Matteo asked.

"No, sweetie. Not ours, that's the point. *They've* lost a bunch, more than us... I mean the R.F. We don't actually have any. So, right... They lost two small and three of those heavy transports. Like the ones that came to

U.A. holding three dozen people in each. I mean, the woman told me that, anyway."

"And you believed her?" Mike hit an accusatory tone Gift didn't appreciate.

"Shut it Mikey. Let her talk."

"I don't know what to believe. All I know is Chan was on about the same thing. Only, he didn't tell me about the five, not the details, only that they think we shot down their flyers. The woman today, she said five. Anyway, they think *we* shot down five of theirs."

Mike raised his hands and let them fall onto his lap. "But this makes no sense. Do they have any idea what limited weapons we have? And we can't exactly take down flyers... *in China,* with puny stun guns now, can we?"

"*Mike.* What'd I say?"

Gift took Tina's hand. "No, he's right. But that's where the problem is. They, they think we *can* do it. And they're convinced we *did* do it."

"Again... *how?*"

"Missiles." Jaws dropped from the shocking one-word reply. "They think we used missiles to shoot them down. But if they crashed like ours, I mean the R.F.'s, that's a bit of an exaggeration."

"How the heck did they get that idea? I mean, I guess *they* don't even have anything like that, and they seem much more powerful than the R.F."

Mike flashed a look of confusion at Matteo. "Why do you say they don't have anything like that?"

"Well... they occupied then lost the weakest colony. Then they failed to take N.E. and stopped before even going after the R.F. If they had anything like missiles, and from what we've seen of them so far? I think they'd have wiped us out when they lost their first transport. Besides, every participant nation had to destroy all their weapons to join the colonization project, right?"

"Oh mamma. Matteo, you're right. That means they want these, not only to stop whoever's attacking them. Oh my... they, they... they want them to use *against us*."

"Or, to use to threaten us into submission." Gift could almost see the *lightbulb* over Tina's head. "Didn't that nut job Chan want all colonies, the whole world, ruled by the N.R.C.?"

"By *him*. But he was insane."

"Yes, but he was serious about being the king and having you at his side like a queen. *Ha*, I had you beside me on the bench for years, who knew I was in the presence of royalty." Gift pursed her lips at Mike's snickering.

Matteo leaned forward and moaned from his injuries. "We separate the real from the nuts by comparing what the woman here said. They lost transports and think we did it, that we have these missiles somewhere and we used them."

"*Exactly*. Where do they get the idea that we even have missiles? That's crazy," Mike said.

"Not... *exactly*." All eyes widened. "See... well, there, there *are* missiles and—"

"*What*? What the heck, Gift?" Tina spat.

"Settle down, let me explain. Okay, so those Pioneers, they lived in military bunkers for all those years since the colonies were sealed. That first one we went to, where they shot Miss Heller, is one of the smaller bunkers. Only... it had been a missile launch platform, and there are even a few missiles still there."

"My goodness." Matteo looked at her in disbelief.

Mike stood in the small space between the bunks and the toilet. "Are you kidding me with this? We found these missiles, and no one knows about this? Except somehow the Chinese, *they* know. Why the heck didn't we use them when they attacked U.A.? You mean we could have blown this colony off the face of the planet and ended this whole thing?"

"*That's* exactly why we didn't tell anyone. We can't use them. You of all people know the history of what we did with such weapons. World wars, so much death and destruction. We nearly killed all humans, more than once, with those... *mal'd* things."

"But that's not your call to make. Or the Board. This isn't something you get to decide."

Tina aimed a piercing stare at Mike. "Who then? Who should decide? *You*? Gift is exactly right. We can't have hot-heads ready to shoot missiles and destroy entire colonies."

Showing her palms, Gift hoped to calm the room. "Please, let's keep that part out of this. For now, I mean, the point is they know we have them. *Ciao*. We don't actually even have them. I mean, we don't even know if they work or have a clue how to use them, and never planned to even if we did."

"And these people just want you to tell them where they are?" A subtle hint underlined Matteo's tone to say, *maybe we just tell them*.

"I've told them, so many times, I don't know. I can't even point to it on a map. I can't give them what they want, and... they'll keep hurting you." Anguish drenched Gift's trailing words in sobbing no longer able to be restrained.

When Tina leaned forward, Gift lifted her arms, assuming the comforting embrace she desperately needed. Instead, Tina placed her nose against Gift's auricle and whispered, "Maybe you can use this. Tell them you can only find it by sight, get them to fly you over there."

Gift's eyes said no, her mind shouting she'd get caught. *They'd only hurt you and Mike and Matteo even more, maybe kill you all*. The fright in those thoughts tensed every one of Gift's muscles.

The door opened and the one guard commanded Gift to exit. Before Gift could rise, Tina launched from her bunk and landed on top of the soldier thrust to the ground. Tina's fists pounded repeatedly until her elbows locked and she shook violently before collapsing. When the soldier stood, he had a taser with uncoiled wires reaching Tina's chest.

"Pull her in," he said while retrieving the electrodes.

Matteo and Mike dragged the hefty body into the tiny cell. The soldier motioned Gift to step out and sealed the door behind her. Where they'd go and what might happen next, Gift couldn't guess. The empty corridors they traversed told her it must have been well past bedtime. They stopped in a communications room with the stoic nameless interrogator lady seated at a control console. She motioned for Gift to look at her screen.

"Raff."

48

Glimmers of hope flickered on occasion, shining moments in human history when people chose not to fight, standing up to disregard forgone conclusions. Gift strained her brain to recall an example her Nonna taught her. Several decades before the colonization project, it appeared her ancestral homeland would once again plunge itself into war and revolution. History often ran on a loop while staggering forward. The conflict in question, like many prior, lumbered on over resources and the financial gain they promised.

Gift thought it a vile thing—money, as they called it—a system of life based on economics with all its imbalances. It only seemed to cause problems ranging from crime and divorce—she learned of a high percentage of dissolved Unions—to full-scale warfare and global conflicts. But in that instance in Nigeria of long ago, they avoided escalation, prevented conflict. The key? Communication. Open and honest, its power dispelled rumors, halted accusations, and cleared up misunderstandings.

Perhaps the misunderstanding between their colonies could find similar clarification. Gift knew they hadn't used the missiles, didn't know how to use them, and they lost air transports too. *Could it be caused by something in the atmosphere? Or maybe Earth's magnetosphere?* If neither side had crashed the other's flyers, there had to be a rational explanation for it, some way to clear up the misunderstanding. Gift had to hope, attempt to get the chances to ninety-nine. Seeing they were trying to communicate was at least a start.

No comms repeaters to relay the signal—added between New Europa and the R.F. and later to the U.A. colony—real-time vidChat wasn't possible, so this was a delayed video recording. Still, it was communication, and that spark of optimism lifted Gift's heart, as did seeing Raff's image.

"Please, may I know your name?" Gift asked respectfully.

"I am General Xiang. Does that make me more human? Am I perhaps less intimidating to you now?"

"I just thought it would help us... to talk."

"Chan said you were smart and knew how to answer questions. I invited you here to show you how we are trying to resolve this petty matter of ours."

Invited? They used words like that, calling her a guest, but those were words devoid of meaning. Their actions spoke more truth, and Gift found the irony of them attempting to act hospitably or neighborly morbidly amusing.

"Yes, talking can clear up misconceptions. You'll see, we're not attacking each other. Together, we can learn what's happened to our flyers and how to stop it."

"A noble goal. Let us test your theory then, shall we?"

When Xiang played the recording, Raff's voice massaged a soothing balm on Gift's aching muscles. "...we also lost two air transports and suffered some loss of life. We are sorry for your losses. Please know we are not the aggressors here. We have not attacked your flyers and we accept your word in good faith you are not responsible for ours. We believe we can work together to solve—" Xiang cut it off there.

"*See*. It's what I said. We *can* work together. We, we both have the same problem. And it's not each other, it's something else, must be scientific. Like the magnetosphere or *something*? If our scientists, if they can work togeth—"

"Enough." The word had every bit of the authority of a high-ranking general. "Before you go on, you should see the next message after we asked about the missiles."

Raff's message resumed. "We have no access to launching missiles or anything that would present a threat to your colony. We repeat, we do not know where you are, even if we had such weapons we could use. And why would we? We have no quarrel with you, no reason to attack you or your flyers." The message stopped and Raff's face disappeared.

"The communication you speak of, Miss Gift... Is honesty not an important part of that? How should we react when it is obvious we are being lied to by your people?"

"*What*? Why... why do you say she's lying?"

"We learned your people found the missiles. Chan told you this, and you confirmed it. We know the Russians are aware of them. What we do not yet know, is which of you used them and why. Why attack us now?"

"We didn't, I promise."

"Promise? We are not children. The facts are obvious, do you not agree? It is clear we are not getting anywhere with talks, and your people cannot be trusted. So that brings us back full circle to one question you need to answer for us. This all stops when you answer just one simple question, Miss Gift. Where. Are. The missiles!"

Gift stiffened to the question shouted as a demand.

"At this point..." Gift dropped her shoulders, exhaled, and said, "I would tell you. Honest I would. But I truly don't know. Maybe? If I were... in a *flyer*? I might be able to recognize something."

"Put you on a flyer headed toward your New Europa? You do have nerve; Chan was correct about that too. No wonder he found you so enthralling... I believe you when you say you do not know where they are. I do. So, you will stay here and help me convince Miss Raffaella it is in your colony's best interests to tell us where they are."

"I can talk to Raff? Okay, I'll try. But I don't think anyone will tell you anything more. I mean, there isn't more to tell."

The general sat Gift in the seat before the display and stood behind her. "Now Miss Gift, you will read a message exactly as it is written. If you do not read it exactly as written, you may be most disappointed when you rejoin your friends."

Gift dry-swallowed and scanned her eyes hastily over the prepared statement. Her look to the powerful woman said, *are you kidding me*? but the words were careful not to escape her lips.

"Exactly as it is written."

The red light on the top of the screen blinked on and Gift saw herself in the camera image on the display. She had never seen such thick bags under her eyes and the dull green shirt did nothing for her complexion. After clearing her throat, Gift read the message as written—mostly.

"Raff. Oh *Dio*. Okay... 'I am a guest of the New Republic of China. I am being treated well and speaking of my own free will. I believe General Xiang and the people of the N.R.C. when they say they want peace. We all just want to find the cause of our transport failures. I believe we can work together toward this goal, and I encourage you to accept their offer. They know about our missiles, and they have logically concluded we must be the ones attacking them. I'm sure we would make the same assumption in their place.'"

Blinking hard at the next lines, Gift cleared her throat.

"'They are only asking permission to visit the missile launch facility to verify our statements that we have not used them. This is the best means to establish trust and cooperation between our peoples. We have done it with the R.F. and U.A. and I believe we can do the same with the N.R.C. Please accept their proposal. They have assured me I will be on the next transport and returned home, and I believe we can trust them. Chan operated outside his directives. I repeat, *I am* being treated well here. Please Raff, you must get the Board to cooperate.' Oh *Dio*, Raff, I hope to see you soon."

Gift slammed a palm on the desk. "There, I've done as you said. Now please stop hurting my friends."

"What you did here helps them. However, I need answers from you to… verify a hunch, as you call it. I agree with your friends that if you did indeed have access to these missiles and the ability to launch them, you would have at least used them as a threat, a deterrent when we occupied U.A. and came for N.E. But you did not. I keep wondering why. Tell me Miss Gift, why did your people not even threaten us with these weapons?"

Pensive, Gift hoped they'd drop it once they believed she didn't know where the missiles were. Only partly accurate, it was enough to be convincing as Gift spoke to the part that was true. She couldn't find the bunker on a map even though her life depended on it, but she didn't need to mention having been there. She couldn't direct anyone there—not *exactly*.

A look, the wrong word, her intonation, could give up Gift was lying. She was so awful at it, silence seemed the better option. Gift considered not answering would likely be taken as an admission of guilt or of holding back. What might that mean for Mike, Tina, her little Matteo? No, she needed to answer, and she needed to make it good.

"I really don't know much about what you're asking me. I don't want to seem uncooperative. It's just, just that I'm not who you must think I am. I mean, I don't know the things you seem to think I do."

"Then let us examine your truths. Like you, Miss Raffaella knows how to select truths and word them in such a way she conveys an idea that is a lie beyond the words that created it."

"I don't follow. We're being honest. You heard her. How can you say she's telling the truth *and* lying to you at the same time?"

"Let us do what they call reading between the lines. 'We have no access to launching missiles,' she said. Deliberately, she does not deny you have them. Her truth is that you cannot *launch* them."

Gift panicked more than a little and applied every gram of willpower to suppress any outward expression of her rising anxiety. Xiang was good, she figured that part out. The last Gift knew, they had not been able to gain control of the computer systems at the bunker and had no clue how to target or launch the missiles.

"Consider another example. She said, 'even if we had such weapons we *could use.*' Again, notice she does not deny having the weapons, even though this is what she is trying to make us hear. No, they have missiles, they just cannot use them. Is that not correct, Miss Gift?"

Gift hated that she gulped another dry swallow. She couldn't know what her body language gave away, betraying her where her tongue didn't. One thing Gift knew for certain; her efforts were failing. General Xiang surely saw it, saw right through Gift with no need for words. Now the only piece of missing information was the one she believed Gift didn't have. What would that mean for her and her friends?

The General directed Gift to the corner of the room to watch as she recorded her own message to follow Gift's, not waiting out the delay for a reply.

"Our friends of New Europa, by now I am sure you have been discussing the message we so graciously allowed Miss Gift Ojo to send to you. I urge you to ponder her plea so we may move forward unitedly. We propose sending a small delegation of inspectors, along with Miss Ojo, to your colony to retrieve representatives from your Board. From there, we will go together to the missile launch facility. In a show of our good faith, we consent to doing so in a way that does not reveal the coordinates to us. We wish only to verify your claim you did not fire upon us in hope of moving forward in peace. General Xiang out."

49

*O*nce *you eliminate the impossible, whatever remains, however improbable, must be the truth.* For the life of her, Gift couldn't recall who said it. On the walk back to her cell, one question rattled around in her head. Ideals of what she called a new human species, elevated above petty squabbles, greed, racism, disunity, and everything else that had diminished humankind to the few-hundred thousand or so remaining on Earth—Gift had no idea of the size of the N.R.C. population.

One side of the display her mind projected listed all the good they had accomplished since the airlock opened. It reunited their colony. Peaceful relations were established with the Russian Federation. They reached their elevated status by avoiding conflict with the Pioneers and repeated the same with the Ubuntu people. A new human species in action, working beautifully—until it didn't. The New Republic of China blamed them for atrocious attacks against them, and Gift couldn't argue the logic in the assumption.

The display's second column detailed how, when under attack from their own people, they were quick to suspect and blame the N.R.C. Why? Compared to theories about Martians awakened by terraforming, sure, it was the more reasonable assumption, a rational conclusion not based on bias or any previous narrow-minded ideologies. Gift could have thought that, but she didn't. Speculation brought her to an uncomfortable notion that wore like an itchy garment, tight in the wrong places. An improbable truth, the one remaining option.

Did we use the missiles?

All Gift could do she had done. Hopefully her *Oh Dio's* weren't edited out of her message. Of course, with words so obviously forced and unnatural, Raff was sure to spot the lies. As much as Gift would have preferred to believe her own words—not hers, the ones given her to speak—to be a reasonable course of action to a peaceful and nonviolent de-escalation, she didn't.

Pulling at Gift's conscience, nagging her with her own relentless optimism that had relented in the last weeks, the general's conclusions were reasonable. *We're no different. No Gift, we are better than that*, she tried to convince herself. The brain replayed Mike's words next, doing its best to keep the bits coming, desperate to reach a conclusion, hoping for the one she wished it to be. *As soon as he learned of the missiles, he wanted to use them.*

Rationalization came next, the logical process in Gift's mind. Mike had just been tortured and Gift knew all too well how that messed with the mind, leading to irrational thought and desperate actions. Claudia might have been a victim of manipulated Chemical Imbalance Disorder, Sakura's own silent confirmation over a dinner conversation all but confirmed it. Their own N.E. Board of Directors had been inept, hadn't treated Gift well as a suspect and person of interest. But could she balance that on a scale with the actions of the N.R.C.? Was placing a guard on her and not responding when she had to use the toilet, letting her pee herself, anywhere close to the measures applied on Gift over the last nine days?

Chan was insane. True, she was under the control of a genuine maniac, and could accept what General Xiang told her about him going beyond his directives. But there was no mentally ill commander behind the beatings and brutal torture of her friends. No way Xiang could disown those actions. *We are not the same*, Gift concluded as her guard escort reached to open the cell door.

Something slammed into her jaw and shoulder and Gift fell back, landing hard on the floor. The pain in her elbow was sharp. Dazed and confused, someone knelt on all fours beside her, and she tried to make out the words in the yelling. Not the screams of pain or tragedy, they were frantic, hurried, energetic. Then Gift understood it clearly. Perched atop the soldier, this time with Mike and Matteo pinning the guard's arms, Tina lifted the helmet and cracking thumps echoed off the man's face like a sledgehammer on concrete.

Gift cringed. "*Enough*. He's out. That's enough." They were out of their cell. "Now what? They must've seen this, *no*? They'll come for us. We might have made our situation much worse."

"Worse for *who*? You saw what they did to us." The pain behind Mike's words tormented Gift.

"Wait a minute..." Matteo looked down the corridor. "Why aren't they already here? I mean, we're right in the belly of the beast, so to speak. If this is the prison ward or whatever, wouldn't guards be here by now? Maybe they haven't seen us."

"No cameras?" Mike studied the ceiling. "That seems unlikely."

"No, he may be right. I mean... we know how camera-happy our Board had been, right? They were everywhere, watching everything, until we revised that policy. But when Boss, I mean Mister Bauer on the Board... When he went to see Claudia in... a jail cell, I guess it was... he said his visit never happened, wasn't recorded. I thought that odd at first, but then considered it could be we had no cameras where we didn't *want* anything to be seen. Maybe they did the same here."

Tina rubbed her hand over the top of her head. "Okay. We assume *that*, until we see differently. Matt's right, if they saw us they'd've been here as soon we took this turd down. Ha!" A deliberate chin scrunch mocked the unconscious man on the floor. "Didn't get that taser out fast enough this time, did ya buddy?"

Gently stroking her stinging jaw, Gift said, "We need a plan. I mean, what now? Belly of the beast and all."

"You're the only one who's been outside this corridor," Tina reasoned. "You need to get us to comms, or an office, somewhere we can try to contact N.E."

"Oh mamma. I was led around. I'm not sure if I can find anything. Also too, we're obviously prisoners. I don't think anyone else is walking around out there in these hideous green shorts and tank tops."

"Well..." Mike's eyes directed everyone's to the floor. "We've got a soldier uniform."

He and Tina began freeing the unconscious man of it.

"Oh, duh. It's crazy late too, there weren't many in the corridors, almost empty."

"That's good." Matteo wiggled into the uniform, the best fit of the four, as Tina and Mike dragged the underwear-clad soldier into the cell and locked him in.

Mike said, "Is it? Good, I mean. We'll be more conspicuous plodding along empty corridors in the middle of the night."

"No, I don't think so. There were only a couple guards we passed just now. And seeing me escorted by a guy in a soldier's uniform... they didn't flinch."

Holding their hands behind their backs—Tina thought it best to look like they were in restraints—a line of three walked in front of Matteo with him doing his best soldier impersonation. Grateful for the face-covering helmet, Gift hoped no one would question him as he didn't know a word of Chinese. Trepidation filled her as they reached the end of the corridor and opened the door.

They entered a large open space that Mike said looked like a mainte-nance workshop or engineering station. Tina pointed out huge parts that resembled the turbines of the heavy transports they had seen at U.A. At least the part about them also losing flyers seemed verified. Gift's mind drifted to Aimée, and she quickly yanked it back to the moment to wonder if temporal fluctuations in Earth's magnetosphere could have been severe enough over time to wreak havoc on two-hundred-plus-year-old electron-ics.

Flyers, airplanes they were called, were never bothered by such, but that was *before*. So much about the Earth had changed, she thought it could be possible. If not that, Gift had to believe something could be found to explain the transports crashing. No answer came, but searching for it took her mind off her lost, almost certainly dead, best friend. *Always have to keep going*. The other end of the maintenance space opened to a small dome.

"Which way, Gift?" Mike whispered.

Looking around, Gift pointed ahead to the left.

"Matt, you're out of soldier-mode. You need to look the part, bro." Tina was correct. Matteo had body armor, a helmet, and a long gun, but he carried himself like an escaped prisoner sneaking through enemy territory. "Man up. And the rest of us can't look like we're sneaking around. Play your part, walk in front of Matt like he's a soldier escorting us."

The first test of their charade came as they approached a guard, soldier, whatever they were. As they walked by, the corner of Gift's eye caught Mike's shoulder jerk forward. Her mind added what her eyes didn't see. Matteo must have pushed him with all the contempt a guard/soldier would have. *Well done, Matteo.*

Continuing through the small dome, they saw no one. Being the middle of the night, Gift assumed it was as expected. A moment's pondering took her mind to what time it would be in New Europa, assuming as when in the R.F. she must be in the future. When two corridors branched off, Gift faced a dilemma. For the life of her, she couldn't remember which one she passed through just a while back. On that escorted trip, Gift's mind occupied itself with other things.

"No, wait." She dug through subconscious memories. "When we came back, I remember, we came out of one corridor into this dome and there was a second corridor on my left—no, I mean on my *right*. It was on my right. So... facing this way, it's the one on the left. That means I came out of the one on our right."

Tina shook her head, looked dizzy. "You sure? We can't afford mistakes."

"Yeah, I'm mostly sure. No... I'm sure. This way."

The corridor widened into something like the housing block spokes in New Europa. The good thing was that it looked familiar to Gift, telling her she'd chosen the right corridor. Good, because she had slightly less certainty than she let on to the group. The only living soul they passed as they traversed the two-hundred-meter passageway was a cleaning person buffing the floor. Ambient sound provided by the buffer pad's circular pattern over the smooth surface of the concrete saturated the surrounding space. Focused on the task, the operator didn't so much as glance up from the machine as they passed.

The corridor opened to a larger dome approximately the size of any Citadome of New Europa, Gift surmised, if not a tad larger. She recognized the building they took her into, the one with the communications room they sought. How to enter became their next challenge, as no one's biometrics would do anything other than possibly signal an alarm. There was no guard at the door, but that didn't fill Gift with confidence. The locked door between them and their destination may as well have been a full troop of soldiers—just as impenetrable.

"There's gotta be a way in."

"Why Mike? Because we need one, there's gotta be one? I mean... so far, this was all pretty easy. Wasn't it? Easy, I mean. Also too, no cameras caught us this whole way. We just sneaked right through. Now we're here and we expect to find an easy way in?"

Pops from hands clapping encircled them.

"She is smart, I knew this." An unknown voice to the group, familiar to Gift, came from behind them. General Xiang stood not three meters to their backs with a dozen soldiers coming up behind her.

Emboldened by desperation, Gift took two steps toward the menacing figure.

"General, please. You must see that we need to work together and co-operate. We're not enemies. I mean, I get why you think that. Really, I do. When we had sabotage and terrorism in our colony, many were quick to blame you. Not you *personally*, I mean, the N.R.C. But we were wrong. The ones doing that to us...? *It was us.* I mean, people from our own colony."

"So, your proposal, Miss Gift, is we have some of our own people taking down our transports?"

"No. *Ciao.* What I mean is... we were wrong."

"If not our people, please, elaborate."

"Sometimes, often it seems, actually... our first jumped conclusions are not even close to correct. And when we act on those, we make matters worse. Please, can we just talk about this?"

As a soldier relieved Matteo of his gun and taser, the General waved her hand over the band of escapees. "You see, I said she was a smart one. And what your Miss Gift says is true, our first assumptions are often incorrect. They must be proven correct or incorrect only when facts present them-selves. Come now, all of you, to check those facts."

50 | Colony's Fall

In the communications room of the New Republic of China, General Xiang stood blank-faced with Gift, Tina, Mike, and Matteo—relieved of his body armor. With a dozen armed and armored soldiers in the next room behind a glass wall, she must have felt her guests weren't a threat. Opting to show them this information of hers rather than simply having them all beaten and tossed back into the pit from which they escaped was curious. If Gift had learned one thing about dealing with tunnel-visioned powerful leaders, they were not at all predictable. She couldn't guess Xiang's play.

"Miss Gift. Please tell your friends the peaceable offer I made to your people at New Europa."

"*Huh*? Me? Um... I heard you record a message, is all."

"I think we all agree this is not the time for your games. Now, please tell them what we proposed to your people."

Like a half-remembered dream, Gift requested a memory so distant she needed to jump-start her brain to recall it though it happened mere hours earlier.

"Okay. Well... first, it was Raff, I mean N.E., that offered to work together. We keep trying to convince you that we weren't doing any of this." Xiang grimaced and flashed a face equally cold as stone and fiery hot to Gift. "And you, you told Raff, I mean New Europa, not just Raff. You said you knew about the missile facility and wanted to send a small delegation to inspect it… make sure we hadn't launched any."

"Considering we were attacked, and you have weapons, Miss Gift, does our position seem reasonable to you?"

"I guess, yeah."

"Of course. This is logical. Now, please tell your friends, and remind yourself, did we threaten retaliation? Did we ask for control of the missile complex or even to know its location?"

"No."

"No, we did no such thing. We only—"

"But you *did* retaliate. I mean… you occupied United Africa, killed people, shot their leader right in front of me. And you tried to do the same to New Europa… but we stopped you. You have been the aggressor, not us."

"Much of what happened at U.A. was unfortunate, and again, not under our orders. But overall, that occupation was most peaceful. We intended the same for N.E. And let me correct you on your comment about aggression. It is clear we were attacked, lost several transports. Again I remind you, you have the weapons to do this. We needed to defend ourselves and learn what happened and how to stop it. We acted in self-defense. Aggression was your people using the missiles against our flyers."

"*No,*" Mike said with bravado. "We wouldn't do that. We lost flyers too and I'm pretty sure we didn't shoot down our own."

Dazed, Gift looked for a moment into Mike's eyes before turning to the general who could have ordered them all shot on the spot. "We've told you; I told Chan and you. *We* lost transports. We have a common problem, and it may not be an enemy. There may not be anyone to retaliate against or to hate for this. It must be something scientific, something messing with our systems. We've had these… glitches in our comms, equipment going haywire. All we're doing is trying to cooperate, work together, to solve—"

A sharp pop stifled Gift's words and jerked her head, the intensity of the backside of Xiang's hand stinging her cheek. Instinctively, Gift's palm raised a stop signal to Tina, who had leaned in to pummel the general so tiny compared to the riled woman's bulk, lowering the gun of the soldier behind her friend who nearly died just then in her defense.

It was loyal friendship.

It was beyond stupid.

"You see, Miss Gift is the wise woman I knew her to be." Looking at Tina, Xiang said, "She just saved your life. 'Solve this together,' she said. And this is what we offered in our latest message. And how was our very reasonable offer received? This is what I brought you in here to see. To show you the situation as it is, not as your one-sided minds imagine it to be."

The general pushed the button on the console calling up a new recording. Once again, Raff spoke for New Europa. "...too wish to establish peaceful cooperation. What we propose is, you send your delegation here, along with Miss Ojo and the others of N.E. in a show of good faith. We can begin deliberations with assurances we can settle this matter, working together on our common issues."

General Xiang stopped the playback, freezing Raff's face on the screen. "So, you see, it is *your* people not willing to talk openly. It is *your* people hiding truths we already know. They are unwilling to cooperate."

Inner courage Gift was still learning to identify pulled her shoulders back. "*What*? Did you *not* hear what we just heard? I promise you they'll listen to your delegation. They want peace. New Europa is not a military colony, has guards and weapons for defense only. Our goal is to establish peace with all colonies, yours included, like we did with Russia, Africa, and the two groups of outsiders. We can do the same with you, I'm sure of it."

"You really should not promise things over which you have no control. You are a clever one, using words ascribing your people as peacemakers. But history teaches us what Commander Chan forgot in his twisted ambitions to make peace by conquest. When peace and so-called unity come by threat of force, fear of extermination by the stronger power, it is no basis for peace, no unity. It leads to unending conflict, insurgencies, insurrection, civil wars. Our history is littered with examples of this."

"That's not what we're doing. You heard her." Mike pointed emphatically at Raff's still image and Gift wished with all her might he'd shut up. "We're offering peace through talks, negotiations, not by force or threat."

"Miss Gift, I ask you to keep your dogs on their leash. Your bulldog was almost shot for her aggression and this one needs a muzzle."

Unsure what type of dog a bulldog might be or what a muzzle would do, Gift understood the woman clearly. She raised two palms to her friends in reply to her new orders, which she grasped to be a stern warning.

"We need to stay level-headed and find the way forward. If we don't escalate this into more fighting, more violence, we all win. By working together, we can stop this here and now."

"Words are all your people offer. We will go nowhere from here while you continue to hide the facts. Your people still do not admit having control of the weapons to destroy us, yet they propose peace. They wish us to release the four of you, leaving us no leverage to hold. They wish us at their mercy. This is not a way for peace. This is—"

Blaring sirens filled the space, adding weight to the air swirling around Gift's head. Nothing like any klaxon or alert she'd heard at N.E. or U.A., she immediately recognized it as most ominous. A clear call to the sleeping colony to rise and prepare for the worst. Calling up her mental display Gift searched all plausible scenarios to apply to this new critical situation and found only one. *Could Chan have been working with others? Did he have a section of supporters in the military still acting on his mentally unstable orders?*

"Wǒmen bèi gōngjíle."

"Wǒmen bèi gōngjíle."

Words without meaning to Gift were shouted at the General, who looked amazingly calm and collected. Roused to a posture adding to her domineering countenance, she grabbed a fistful of green tank top and pulled Gift close. From a stern face just millimeters from Gift's, she said, "Why are you attacking us?"

"*What*? This can't, can't be us. Whatever this is... it's, it's not us."

Gift's words appeared to fall unheard on the General's ears as she looked over her display, reading characters Gift knew meant words but understood none of them. That such drawings made sense to Xiang was fascinating but not in the moment. The moment filled itself with anxious fear. Their lives were in danger, but from whom?

"It seems your people have learned how to launch their missiles."

Xiang's words swirled like a windstorm in Gift's head. What alternative could her mental display offer? *Is it us?* she wondered in fear of the answer. *Even if we figured out how, would we?* She couldn't think that, but everything surrounding the moment consuming her made it difficult not to.

"It can't be us. We wouldn't... It can't be."

Xiang barked something unintelligible. Gift heard the sounds escape the general's lips and struggled to find their meaning. Who was she talking to? Soldiers seized Tina, Mike, and Matteo, and dragged them out. Each shouted or mumbled something, Gift couldn't be sure what. Their words were nothing more than noise filling the space between the klaxon's crescendos. Gift stood alone in the small ops room with the latest of her daunting captors.

Stinging slaps popped against Gift's cheeks, inflicting one then the next with numbing pain.

The enraged woman demanded, "Why are your people doing this? What code did you hide in your message?"

"*Nothing*. I... I... I have no idea what's happening."

"They are willing to attack us even with you here. You think us the enemy, the aggressors, the evil monsters, and they attack us, *unprovoked*. Tell me who are the aggressors here? Who are the monsters?"

The weight of the words shook Gift in the knees and the uneasiness spread through her bones, unsteadying her. No, it wasn't that. The whole room shook, not just her. What could cause the entire colony to quake? Morbid fear piled atop her fright became strong enough to dominate her mental cognition, taking control of the body.

As if watching someone else, Gift saw herself squeezing Xiang. Thoughtlessly, her back pressed into the wall, her arms wrapped around the general's chest. Her captor-now-captive faced her soldiers, all with guns fixed on Gift—the life of their commander between them being the only thing keeping Gift alive.

"And what exactly is your plan here, Miss Gift?" The general's voice exuded calm.

Gift had no plan. The body had moved absent of mind, not the conscious part of it. With her back against the hard surface of the wall's illusion of protection, her captor subdued in her arms, and several bullets with her head as their destination, Gift forced the body to obey.

Once Xiang was released, the guns pointed themselves to the floor. For reasons Gift couldn't fathom, they hadn't killed her as she imagined they would. With her value as a hostage negated by an attack with her inside the New Republic of China, Gift wondered, *How am I still alive?*

General Xiang resumed reading her display as rumbles sent vibrations through Gift's body, gently shaking the desk, rattling the walls and door of the small room she was going to die in along with Xiang. *Why are the blasts so distant and about every two minutes?* Gift considered the method of attack. The dome hadn't been hit, and nothing was crumbling around her. By comparison, the explosions of the N.E. insurrection were far worse, much more damaging.

Of course. If they learned how to fire the missiles, N.E. would only use them as a warning, Gift concluded. "A warning."

"What do you mean, a warning?"

It took Gift a moment to decode the puzzled woman's question. She didn't speak to her screen, not in Chinese. In English, she asked Gift about a warning. *Why?* A logical assumption told Gift her thought must have escaped as words, as they often did.

"I mean, it must be. If... I mean... if New Europa has learned how to use the missiles, target, and fire them? They'd only use them as a warning. They don't want to hurt anyone. We—"

"Peace by threat, as I told you."

"No. That's not us. It's not who—"

The room went dark. Everything turned red. Lights cast a crimson glow, saturating the space. Xiang's display was flashing, had been since before the colored lights changed the mood of the room. The general hadn't noticed it when she turned to question Gift. A message from New Europa.

Appearing distraught, Raff's pale face filled the screen, wearing the unfamiliar look as a mask. "Why are you attacking us? We told you we wish to talk..." The next rumbling was heard but not felt. Jostled, Raff continued, "We are defenseless. Please withdraw... We surrender. *We surrender.*"

Gift's heart sank into her stomach, the acid consuming it. Her colony became the focus of her dread, the N.R.C. threatening the lives of all her people. Who else would attack? The next rumble boomed with more intense sound waves striking her eardrums and more violent quaking, knocking her to the floor on her backside. The general grasped the console to keep her balance.

"Why are you doing this?" she demanded again.

Rising to her feet, Gift steadied herself. "You saw Raff's message. They're being attacked. Is this some sorta trick? You kept us alive so you could say *we* attacked *you*, giving you justification to conquer us."

"*Trick*?" Xiang went blank-faced.

In everything happening around them, the attack, the sirens, the quaking, it took Gift's words to break her stern, calm countenance. In that moment, Gift shed her belief that this was a hoax, a ploy to appear the innocent party, acting in self-preservation while being the aggressor. This was something else. Whatever this was, it was happening to both their colonies and neither knew the *who* or the *why*.

Without Xiang touching it, her screen displayed another face.

Aimée! *How*? *What*? "She's alive!"

"Who is alive? What trickery is this?"

What is she doing on the general's screen? And why is her face puffy and her hair so weird, almost like she's... under water?

Aimée spoke with none of her personality.

"People of the colonies of Earth, I am addressing you on behalf of the United Republic of Mars. I am assured they have come in peace, and I am speaking of my own free will. What you have just experienced was a message only, they wish us no harm. The U.R.M. has ships over the colonies of the Russian Federation, New Europa, the New Republic of China, and United Africa. As you can see, no major damage has been inflicted and they wish for there to be none.

"I am assured this is to be a peaceful reintroduction of the U.R.M. to the colonies of Earth. They have come to foster unity among us all, an end to the conflict they have been monitoring between the N.R.C. and the coalition of other colonies. They will soon convene a joint convention of leadership to discuss the peaceful transition to U.R.M. occupation and to build one world government to move us forward as a reunited human race.

"You are advised to stand down and surrender, ending all hostilities, and to gather all weapons at your transport landing pads for confiscation. Please comply to ensure there is no needless harm or loss of life. This is to be a peaceful transition, the start of a new era for humanity.

"Welcome to the United Republic of Earth."

| Epilogue |

Ten weeks had passed since the unexpected arrival of the United Republic of Mars, and Melody became antsy. She ached to do something, but what? While allowed to continue monitoring and maintenance tasks in her work assignment, she had significantly limited access since the U.R.M. data operators gained control of Ops and reset all the command codes.

Despite Raff's adoration for her proficiency and being promoted to Senior Data Operator, Melody didn't believe she could override the lockouts. Plan B was good, and she was proud of herself for it, even if she couldn't be sure how useful it would be and didn't know who to try first.

In many ways, life hadn't changed. Guard uniforms of N.E. black became U.R.M. blue, and people mostly carried on as normal. Coffee breaks with Frank Bauer were her lifeline to what was going on in New Europa, and she was hopeful her plan would give them some idea of the state of the other colonies.

Waiting for Frank at the coffee bar, Melody considered for a moment how they both had automatically slipped back into using their codenames now that they were once again sharing in a covert operation.

"Good morning, Boss," Melody said.

"Morning, Red."

"I finally found her. Same cell they had Claudia in."

"That's excellent. Then I can get to her. And what about Miss Heller?"

"Not in level minus one with Raff, but that's all I know. My access is really limited."

"Finding Raff is huge. I can get her out."

"And do what?"

"We need to get her to the missile complex. It's our only defense against these Martians."

Red said, "But I thought she hadn't cracked the code yet, can't target or launch them."

"She was close, that's why they have her in holding. They desperately want to find it before we could use them."

"How do they even know about them? I mean, I had no idea until you told me a few weeks back."

"Those imbeciles at the N.R.C. forced Gift to mention it on comms."

"Poor Gift. She's a remarkable woman... I was hoping to chat with her first, but if she's in China, maybe I'll try Mike at U.A."

"Wait, Red? You really think you can reach the other colonies unnoticed?"

"I think so. It uses only basic level data stream access, and only Raff was ever clever enough to spot it. With a few modifications, I can get my chat to work over the uplinks to U.A. and R.F."

"I need you to try the Russians first."

"Why? We don't have anyone there, do we?"

"Not that I know of. We need to have Sergey meet us at the launch bunker."

"Why do we need Sergey?"

"They're Russian missiles. The system and its manuals are in Russian. Besides, they call themselves guards, but Sergey is a soldier with military training from before. And if we're at war, we'll need men like him."

"My goodness." Red settled herself with two breaths. "I guess I never really thought of this as a war."

"It is what it is, Red. It is what it is. Try to reach Sergey, tell him we should be there in a week."

"Okay Boss."

To Melody's delight, she reached Nailya Usanova with little difficulty. When Melody installed the app she had written for the rover data, she noted her terminal ID. Nailya said the occupying forces permitted no one outside their wall, yet she was convinced Sergey could get out.

- RF: Is good plan.

- NE: If Sergey's team can reach the complex.

- RF: Da, he will. I get message to Sergey in evening.

- NE: Good. Hopefully he can take off soon.

- RF: We have no flyer to take off. He will use ground transport he calls Zil.

- NE: Right.

- RF: Dear, he has not knowledge to fire missiles.

- NE: We know. If all goes well, Raff will meet him there.

- RF: Let us hope all goes well.

***

'May fortune favor the foolish.' Melody recalled the words but not where she read or heard the quote. To finalize the details, Boss met Red for an afternoon coffee neither wanted.

"Boss, they've got Raff in custody, under guard. If you free her, they'll doubtless respond, comb the place for her, lock us down."

Boss raised an eyebrow. "Of course."

"What about Claudia? You think she could do it?"

"I considered that. Since we converted that small cultivator's habitat block to a sort of prison, no one cares who's there. We could get her out with no one noticing."

"So, you agree that's the better play, send Claudia?"

"No." His reply squinted Red's eyes. "Raff is months ahead of her on those systems, the only one that can do this. Hans worked with her and has been confined to their Box. We'll take them both to the complex. But we may be able to use her just the same."

"Claudia? How?"

"Here. If you work with her here, maybe you take back control of our data systems."

"Can we trust her? She's a saboteur. Look what she did to us when she was on our data stream."

"True. But as I said months ago, question her methods; the goal was to stop the secrets and, in her twisted way, to help the colony. And I think she actually did. Plus, *you* just suggested giving her control of tactical missiles."

"This is nuts. But okay. I have no idea how to get her out, or where to put her and not be discovered."

"With Commander Tucker in custody, Tom's planning an offensive. I'll ask him about Claudia. You know they have only a few dozen guards, right?" Red nodded though she hadn't known. "And the others in uni-form? They've been recruiting from *our* people. Our own people, working with them. And many will fight us—Tom is sure of it."

"Crazy. But I blame Aimée. She spews their propaganda, encouraging cooperation. I didn't believe it at first. I mean her, a traitor?"

"No dear, that's not what it is." Red's look said, *I'm not following, please continue.* "It took a few weeks, but she's managed to sneak a few hidden messages. We've gotten some great intel from her."

"Oh. That's great news."

"She coded a message about the secret recruitment of our people into the guard. Because of her, Tom and Sara were able to get some loyal to us to apply and fake their way through the indoctrination into their ranks. This will give us an upper hand when we move against them."

"It feels like the insurrection all over again, only we're on the other side. You realize we missed the anniversary."

Boss said, "I hadn't even thought of that."

"Who could think of much these days?" Red lost herself in a pause.

"Kid said he needs some time, but he can use the maintenance shaft behind her cell while I distract the guard from any noise. Her door is solid, so with any luck they'll not even know she's gone until we're well under way to the complex."

THANK YOU

I'm so excited you read my story and hope you enjoyed the new adventure with Gift and her friends. Follow them to the saga's epic conclusion in Colony's End.

As an indie author, it means a great deal to me that you enjoyed my work enough to read the second book. If you enjoyed Colony's Dawn and Colony's Fall, please tell a friend.

Stories by indie writers like me don't always find the audience that will enjoy them. It means so much to us, to me, to have reviews. Please consider taking just a couple of minutes to review this book.

Follow my writing and engage with me at: go.glassauthor.com/dawn

As a 'thank you' for subscribing you will receive a free copy of "All Lies", a New Europa novella exploring the beginning of Boss' misfit group of conspiracy theorists.

About the Author

Reading is a passion; writing is an obsession.

And *IT consulting is a job*. While N Joseph Glass enjoys the challenges of managing a virtual infrastructure, backups, email systems, and cloud environments, crafting stories is his cherished second job.

Born and raised in Brooklyn, NY, Glass lives and writes in Milan, Italy. A fan of science fiction and other genres, he loves to expound stories that are driven by relatable characters on meaningful journeys.

Drawing from personal experiences enriches the writing process and leaves readers feeling like they know the characters they spend time with in a story. That human connection between his characters, readers, and himself, fuels his drive as an author.

Optimistic views of the future through art always interest him, as Glass believes ours will be bright.

www.glassauthor.com

9 798986 659848